A NEW DEFINITI

In the governor's office

his head ruefully at his ch

Grayle?"

"You tell me."

"Well, sir—Pyle called in a con who had done twenty years of a life sentence before parole. He swears Grayle was an inmate when he started his stretch. And that, Governor, was almost thirty-five years ago. So you see what I'm talking about."

"What about the army records of the court-martial?"

Lester shook his head. "I have a friend in the Pentagon who has access to retired material that's never been programmed into the Record Center." He spread papers on the edge of the desk. "Grayle was transferred to Fort Leavenworth from Fort McNair at Washington, after a court-martial for murder."

"Any details of the crime?"

"It appears he knew the victim; other than that . . ." Lester shook his head. "Frankly, this is pretty hard reading; a poor copy to begin with, and cramped handwriting—"

"What do you mean, handwriting? Don't you have a copy of the official record?"

"Yes, sir," Lester said flatly. "But in eighteen-sixty-three there weren't any typewriters."

Governor Hardman plucked the papers from the other's hands, scanned the sheets, made a noise in his throat. "What the devil is this, Lester? This is an account of a Civil War trial!"

"Yes, sir. The man Grayle was a Confederate prisoner, and the man he killed was a Union officer."

—from *The Long Twilight*

THE
LONG TWILIGHT
AND
OTHER STORIES

By
KEITH LAUMER

Edited By
ERIC FLINT

THE LONG TWILIGHT AND OTHER STORIES

This is a work of fiction. All the characters and events portrayed in this book are fictional, and any resemblance to real people or incidents is purely coincidental.

The Long Twilight was first published by Putnam in 1969.

"Birthday Party" was first published in *Isaac Asimov's Science Fiction Magazine*
in Jan-Feb, 1978.

"The Half Man" was first published in *IF* magazine, July, 1969.

"The Lawgiver" was first published in 1970 in the Doubleday anthology *The Year 2000*, edited by Harry Harrison.

"The Plague" was first published in *Analog*, November, 1970.

Night of Delusions was first published by Putnam in 1972.

A Baen Book

Baen Publishing Enterprises
P.O. Box 1403
Riverdale, NY 10471
www.baen.com

ISBN 10: 1-4165-5572-2
ISBN 13: 978-1-4165-5572-8

Cover art by David Mattingly

First Baen paperback printing, September 2008

Distributed by Simon & Schuster
1230 Avenue of the Americas
New York, NY 10020

Library of Congress Cataloging-in-Publication Data: 2006035271

Printed in the United States of America

10 9 8 7 6 5 4 3 2 1

TABLE OF CONTENTS

THE LONG TWILIGHT

∾ Prologue ∾

Here in the darkness and the silence I dream of Ysar.
In the mirror of my mind I see again her towers and
minarets soaring in the eternal twilight of her yellow
skies, casting long shadows across the lawns and pools
and the tiled avenues where long ago victorious armies
rode in processional under bright banners. Amber light
glows on flowering trees and the carved facades of jeweled
palaces. Once more in memory I hear the music of horns
heralding the approach of triumphant princes.

I recall the voices and faces of men and women, of
warriors and queens, of tradesmen and viceroys, of
metal-workers and courtesans, of those who have lived
and walked these streets, rested beside these pools and
fountains, under the ocher light of the forever setting
sun of Ysar. And I see the scarred unconquerable ships,
proud remnants of a once great fleet, true to their
ancient pledge, mounting on columns of fire, setting
course outward to face the enemy once again.

Here in the darkness and the silence, I wait, and dream

1

of Ysar the well beloved; and I vow that I will return to her, though it be at the end of time.

Chapter One

∞ 1 ∞

A man sat at a small desk beside an open window, writing with an old-fashioned steel-nib pen which he dipped at intervals into a pot of blue-black ink. A soft sea-wind moved the curtain, bringing an odor of salt and kelp. Far away, a bell chimed out the hour of six P.M.

The man wrote a line, crossed it out, sat looking across the view of lawns and gardens. His face was strong-featured, square-jawed. His gray hair lay close to a finely formed skull. His fingers were thick, square-tipped; powerful fingers.

"Writing pomes again, Mr. Grayle?" A voice spoke suddenly from the doorway behind the man. He turned with a faint smile.

"That's right, Ted." His voice was deep, soft, with a faint trace of accent.

"You like to write pomes, don't you, Mr. Grayle?" Ted grinned in mild conspiracy.

"Um-hum."

"Hey, game time, Mr. Grayle. Guess you maybe didn't hear the bell."

3

"I guess not, Ted." Grayle rose.

"Boy oh boy, the Blues are going to mop up on the Reds tonight, hey, Mr. Grayle?" Ted stood aside as Grayle stepped out into the wide, well-lit corridor.

"Sure we will, Ted."

They walked along the passage, where other men were emerging from rooms.

"Well, tonight's the night, eh, Mr. Grayle?" Ted said.

"Tonight?" Grayle inquired mildly.

"You know. The new power system goes on. Just pick it out of the air. Nifty, huh?"

"I didn't know."

"You don't read the papers much, do you, Mr. Grayle?"

"Not much, Ted."

"Boy oh boy." Ted waggled his head. "What will they come up with next?"

They crossed an airy court, passed through an arcade, and emerged onto a wide, grassy meadow. Men dressed in simple, well-made, one-piece garments, some bearing a red armband, others a blue, stood in groups talking, tossing a baseball back and forth.

"Go get 'em, Mr. Grayle," Ted said. "Show 'em the old stuff."

"That's right, Ted."

The man called Ted leaned against a column, arms folded, watched as Grayle walked across to join his team.

"Hey, that's the guy, hah?" A voice spoke beside Ted. He turned and gave an up-and-down frown to the young fellow who had come up beside him.

"What guy?"

"The mystery man. I been hearing about him. Nobody

knows how long he's been here. I heard he killed a guy with an ax. He doesn't look like so much to me."

"Mr. Grayle is an all-right guy, greenhorn," Ted said. "That's a lot of jetwash about nobody knows how long he's been here. They got records. They know, O.K."

"How long you been here, Ted?"

"Me? Five years, why?"

"I talked to Stengel; he's been here nineteen years. He says the guy was here then."

"So?"

"He doesn't look old enough to be an old con."

"What's he supposed to look, old? So he's maybe thirty-five, maybe forty-five. So what?"

"I'm curious, is all."

"Hah," Ted said. "You college-trained guys. You got too many theories."

The young fellow shrugged. The two guards stood watching as the teams formed up for the nightly ball game played by the inmates of the Caine Island Federal Penitentiary.

‱ 2 ‱

It was a long, narrow room, dim, age-grimed, smelling of the spilled beers of generations. Weak late-afternoon sunshine filtered through the bleary plate-glass window where garish blue glow-letters spelled out FANGIO'S in reverse. A man with four chins and a bald skull bulked behind the bar, talking to a small, quick-eyed man who hunched on a stool next to a defunct jukebox loaded with curled records five years out of date. In the corner booth, a man with a badly scarred face sat talking to himself. He was dressed in an expensive gray suit which was dusty and stained. A gold watch gleamed on one wrist, visible under a black-edged cuff as he gesticulated.

"The bum is dough-heavy," the small man said, watching the lone drinker in the tarnished mirror through a gap in the clutter of blended-whiskey bottles on the backbar. "Did you eyeball that bundle?"

Fangio's eyes moved left, right, left as he scraped slops into a chipped plate.

"Seen Soup around?" he murmured.

The small man's eyelids flickered an affirmative.

Fangio laid the plate aside and wiped his hands on his vest.

"I got to go out back," he said. "Keep an eye on the place." He walked away, eased sideways through a narrow door. The small man went to the phone booth at the end of the bar and punched keys; he talked, watching the scarred man.

A woman came in through the black-glass doors. She was middle-aged, a trifle plump, heavily made up. She took a stool at the bar, looked around, and called, "O.K., snap it up. The lady's waiting."

The small man kicked open the door of the booth.

"Beat it, Wilma," he said in a low, urgent voice. "Fangio ain't in."

"What're you, the night watchman?"

"Go on, dust."

The woman twisted her mouth at him. "I'll get my own." She started around behind the bar. The small man jumped to her, caught her bracelet-heavy arm, twisted savagely. She yelped and kicked at him.

The doors banged as a squat man in a shapeless gray coverall came in. He stopped dead, looking at the two. He had a wide, dark face, bristly black hair; acne scars pitted his jaw and hairline.

"What the—" he started.

"Yeah, Soup," the small man said. "I was calling ya." He stepped clear of the woman, who snorted and yanked at her dress. The small man tipped his head, indicating the occupied booth.

Soup gave Wilma a deadly look. "Beat it," he said. She scuttled behind him and out the door.

In the booth, the scarred man was opening and closing his fist.

". . . golden bird of Ahuriel," he said. "Once flown, never to be recaptured . . ."

"What's he talking about?" Soup asked.

The small man shook his head. "He's scrambled." They walked back, stopped beside the table. The scarred man ignored them.

"Try the left hip."

Soup reached out, with a practiced motion took the drunk's arm up behind him, forcing his face down onto the table. A glass fell over. Soup reached across behind the seated man, patted his back pocket, brought out a sheaf of currency, folded once across the middle. The bill on the outside was a fifty. Holding the owner's arm, he spread the bills.

"Hey," he said. "New shoes for baby."

He released the seated man's arm and stepped back.

The victim sprawled, unmoving, with his cheek against the table.

They had taken two steps when the scarred man came up out of the booth in a lunge, locked his arm across the squat man's throat, and bent him backward.

"Stay, hagseed!" he hissed. His face was mottled, blurred, contorted. "Art *his* emissaries? Lurks *he* yonder?"

The small man made a grab for the money still in his partner's hand, missed, turned, and ran for the door.

"Find thy tongue, wretch, ere my dirk rips thy weasand!"

Soup's hand, clutching the money, waved near the scarred man's face; he plucked the bills away, as with a desperate plunge the squat man broke free.

"Stay, whelp, I'll have report o' thy master!" the scarred man snarled, making a grab at the man. He missed, staggered against a booth. The squat man disappeared via the rear door. The scarred man looked at the money in his hand as though noticing it for the first time.

"Nay . . . 'twere but a mere cutpurse," he muttered. "Naught more . . ." He looked around as the door opened cautiously. The woman called Wilma looked in, came through.

"Hey," she said. "What gives?"

The scarred man blinked at her, weaving.

"Fetch ale, wench," he muttered, and turned, half-fell into the nearest seat.

The rear door burst open; Fangio appeared, goggling.

"Hey, what—"

"Draw two," the woman barked. She sat down across from the scarred man, who was leaning back, eyes shut, mouth open. She stared curiously at his disfigurements.

"You know him?" Fangio asked tersely.

"Sure. Him and me are old pals." She transferred her gaze to the money in the drunken man's hand.

"Varför?" the scarred man mumbled. "Varför har du gjört det, du som var min vän och brör?"

"Why does he talk funny?" Fangio was frowning darkly.

"He's some kind of a Dane," the woman said quickly. "My first husband was a Dane. I heard plenty that kind of jabber."

"He looks like some kind of Jew," Fangio said.

"Get the beers," the woman said. "You ain't no Jew, are you, honey?" She patted the big-knuckled hand that lay on the table.

"Geez, will you look at them scars?" Fangio said.

"Used to be a fighter," the woman said. "What is this, a quiz show?"

"'Twere but a dream," the scarred man said suddenly. He opened his eyes, looked vaguely at the woman.

"Just . . . dream," he said. "That's all. Bad dream. Forget it."

The woman patted his hand again. "Sure, honey. Forget it. Wilma will take care of you. Wilma's got a room, honey. We better get you there while you can still navigate . . ."

⊚ 3 ⊚

At the Upper Pasmaquoddie Generating Station (Experimental), a dozen senators and representatives, the state governor, assorted lesser political lights, and a selected cadre of reporters were grouped around the Secretary of the Interior as he stood chatting with the chief engineer and his top aides before the forty-foot-wide, twelve-foot-high panel clustered thick with instrument dials and aflash with reassuring amber, red, and green lights, indicating that all was in readiness for the first commercial transmission of beamed power in the history of the Republic.

"It's impressive, Mr. Hunnicut," the Secretary said, nodding. "A great achievement."

"If it works," a saintly-looking senator said sharply.

"The technical people assure us that it will, Cy," the Secretary said tolerantly.

"I'm familiar with the inverse square law," the senator retorted. "You go pouring power out into the air, not one percent of it will get where it's supposed to go. It's a boon-doggle! A waste of the taxpayers' money."

The chief engineer frowned as the reporters jotted briskly.

"Senator, I don't think you quite understand. We aren't broadcasting power, as you call it—not directly. We erect a carrier field—somewhat similar to the transmission of a Three-V broadcast. When the field impinges on a demand point—an energy-consuming device, that is, of the type responsive to the signal—there's a return impulse—an echo—"

"The senator knows all that, Mr. Hunnicut," the Secretary said, smiling indulgently. "He's speaking for publication."

A man in an oil-spotted smock came up, showed the chief engineer a clipboard. He nodded, looked at the clock on the antiseptically white wall.

"Two minutes to zero hour," the Secretary said. "Everything is still proceeding normally?"

"Yes, sir, Mr. Secretary," the technician said, then retreated under the blank look this netted him from the dignitary.

"All systems are functioning," Hunnicut said, making it official. "I see no reason that we shouldn't switch over on schedule."

"Think of it, gentlemen." The Secretary turned to the legislators, and, incidentally, to the reporters. "Raw power, torn from the heart of the atom, harnessed here, waiting the call that will send it pouring into the homes and factories of America—"

"At this point, we're only powering a few government-operated facilities and public-utilities systems," Hunnicut interjected. "It's still a pilot operation."

". . . freeing man from his age-old drudgery, ushering in a new era of self-realization and boundless promise—"

"Sixty seconds," a voice spoke sharply from a ceiling grill. "Automatic hold."

"Proceed," Hunnicut said.

In silence the men stood watching as the second hand of the big clock scythed away the final minute of an era.

૭૭ **4** ૭૭

The scarred man lay on his back on the narrow bed, sleeping with his mouth open. His face, in the slack repose of profound drunkenness, was a ravaged field where battles had been fought and lost, long ago.

The woman called Wilma stood beside the bed, watching him by the glow of a shadeless table lamp. She tensed as the light faltered, dimmed; shadows closed in on the shabby room; then the lamp winked back to full brightness. The woman let out the breath she had been holding, her momentary panic dissipating.

"Sure, it said on the tube about switching over onto the new radio power tonight," she murmured half-aloud. On the bed, the scarred man stiffened; he grimaced, moving his head from side to side. He groaned, sighed, grew still again.

Wilma leaned over him; her hands moved deftly, searching out his pockets. They were empty, but she found the roll of bills wadded under the folded blanket that served as pillow. As she withdrew it, she glanced at his face. His eyes were wide open, locked on hers.

"I . . . I was just fixing your pillers," she said.

He sat up with an abruptness that sent her stumbling away, clutching the money in her hand.

"I . . . was going to take care of it for you." Even in her own ears, her voice sounded as false as brass jewelry.

He looked away, shaking his head vaguely. Instantly, her boldness returned.

"Go on, go back to sleep, sleep it off," she said.

He threw aside the mottled blanket and came to his feet in a single motion. The woman made a show of recoiling from his nakedness.

"Lookit here, you!" she said. "I didn't come up here to—"

He went past her to the enameled sink hanging crookedly on the wall, sluiced his face with cold water, filled his mouth and spat, stared at himself in the discolored mirror. He picked up the smeared jelly glass from its clotted niche, but it shattered in his hand. He stared narrow-eyed at the cut on his palm, at the black-red droplets forming there. He made a strange sound deep in his throat, whirled to look around the room as if he had never seen it before.

"Xix," he said. "Where are you?"

Wilma made a move for the door, recoiling as he approached her. He reached out, with a precise motion plucked the money from her hand. He peeled off a ten-dollar bill, thrust it at her.

"You'd better go," he said.

"Yeah," she said. Something in his voice frightened her. "Sure, I was just looking in . . ."

After she had gone, he stood in the near-darkness, his head cocked as if listening to distant voices. He opened his cut hand, studied it. The wound was an almost invisible line. He brushed the congealed droplets away impatiently.

His clothes lay across the foot of the bed. He began to dress himself with swift, sure fingers.

෨ **5** ෨

In the prison dining hall, the guard Ted sat looking worriedly across the wide, softly lit room at the small corner table where, by long custom, Grayle dined alone. He had glanced that way a few moments after the lights had momentarily dimmed down, on an impulse to share the moment with the prisoner, grinning a satisfied grin that said, "See, we did it," but Grayle had been slumped back, gripping the chair arms, his usually impassive features set in a tight-mouthed grimace. This had given way to a look of utter bafflement. Now Grayle sat rigid, looking fixedly at nothing.

Ted rose and hurried across. Close, he saw the sweat beaded on the prisoner's face.

"Mr. Grayle—you O.K.?"

Grayle raised his head slowly.

"You sick, Mr. Grayle?" Ted persisted. "Should I call the doc?"

Grayle nodded curtly. "Yes," he said in a ragged voice. "Get him."

Ted fumbled for the communicator clipped to his belt. Grayle put out a hand. "No," he said sharply. "Don't call. Go get him, Ted."

"Yeah, but—"

"Go and fetch him, Ted. Quieter that way," he added. "You understand."

"Uh, yeah, O.K., Mr. Grayle." Ted hurried away.

Grayle waited for a full minute; then he rose, lifted the table, spilling dishes to the floor. With a bellow that rang in the peaceful room like a lion's roar, he hurled the table from him, and leaping after it, began overturning the unoccupied tables left and right.

⊚⊙⊙⊙✳⊙⊙⊙⊚

Giant trees stand in blue shadow against the wide sweep of the virgin snowfield. A heatless sun hangs almost unmoving in the ice-blue sky. A fitful wind drives plumes of ice crystals across the slope.

A man moves slowly across the white slope. He is tall, deep-chested, massive-shouldered, dressed in a form-fitting suit of a glossy blue-black material ornamented by bright bits of metal and enamel. There are raw burn scars on the right side of his jaw and neck, and his dark-red hair is singed at the temple. He staggers as he walks, making his way doggedly downslope.

He reaches the center of the snow-covered meadow, where a swift stream flows under a thin skim of ice. Kneeling, he drinks, swallows a pellet from a pouch at his waist before he goes on. At dusk he reaches the sea.

It is wide, blue-black, laced with the white foam of breakers; the rocky shore slopes steeply down to the watery edge. The wind blows an odor of iodine and salt spray into his face. When he wades out, the cold numbs his feet through the waterproof boots.

Small creatures dart in the shallows. In a tidal pool among the rocks, a fish flops in water too shallow for swimming. He picks it up, looks curiously at the small life squirming against his fingers as he carries it back down to the sea.

Darkness falls. The man makes camp by trampling a hollow in the snow in the lee of a craggy boulder. He lies looking up at a sky strangely impoverished of stars. A glow grows in the east; a vivid orange disk appears, brightening to a pure white as it rises above the treetops. It is a dead world, fantastically cratered, hanging so close it seems to ride just above the distant mountain ridges. The man watches it for a long time before he falls asleep.

The surf murmurs; the wind makes soft sounds fluting among the rocks. There are other sounds, too; soft rustlings and scrapings, stealthy crunchings . . .

He sits upright, and by the bright light of the full moon sees a giant, bearded figure robed in furs leaping down at him from the rock ledge above; he throws himself aside, feels a smashing blow against the side of his head that sends him hurtling headlong into emptiness.

Chapter Two

∽ 1 ∽

Aboard the thirty-five-foot cabin cruiser *Miss Behave*, one hundred and nine miles out of Port Royal bound for her home port in Miami, Mr. Charles D. Crassman, his wife, Elizabeth, and their twenty-four-year-old daughter, Elaine, relaxed comfortably in the handsomely appointed cockpit, sipping iced Scotch and soda and watching the sunset across the scarlet water.

"Beautiful evening," Crassman said. "We're making time. I told you we were smart to make the run at night, miss the heat."

"Daddy, what's that?" Elaine was pointing off the port bow at a curiously regular-shaped cloud formation; a great purple-and-pink wedge, its apex touching the horizon, its top merging with the soft evening haze.

"Nothing," Crassman said easily. "Just clouds."

"Charles, I don't like the look of that," Mrs. Crassman said sharply. "It looks like one of those, what do they call them, tornadoes."

Crassman laughed. "That's out in Kansas they have tornadoes," he said, and took a sip of his drink. But his eyes lingered on the cloud.

"Go around it."

Crassman had been half-unconsciously easing the bow to starboard, away from the looming formation ahead; at his wife's words he swung the compass pointer squarely back to 220 degrees. "Just let me do the navigating, all right?"

"It's so big," Elaine said. "And it's close."

"Just an optical illusion." Crassman's eyes were on the compass. The needle was drifting past 220 degrees to 210 degrees. He corrected with the rudder. The engines' tone changed faintly, became more labored. A slight swell had appeared across the flat water; the bow cut through the low crests with a rhythmic sound. Frowning, Crassman passed the spindles of the big wheel from hand to hand, holding the bow on course. The chop was more pronounced now. The boat bucked ahead, cutting across the troughs and ridges of oily water.

"Charles, let's go back! I don't like the looks of this—"

"Quiet!" Crassman snapped. "I have my hands full running the boat right now!"

"Daddy—is anything wrong?"

"I don't know!"

"The cloud—it's moving! It's crossing in front of us!"

"It's not moving—we're drifting sideways. There's some sort of crazy crosscurrent running—"

"Charles—please! I want to go back!"

"Don't be ridiculous!" Crassman continued to fight the current; the big cloud, deep purple now and dead ahead, looked ominously close. It rose, spreading, like an inverted mountain in the sky. Crassman watched it drift across his bow, begin to slide off in a curve to starboard.

"It's coming closer! We'll run right into it!"

"Daddy, can't you steer away from it?"

"Well—I hate to waste time being nervous about a mere cloud formation," Crassman said, but he was quick to swing off to the south, away from the cloud. Now the bow tended to swing to starboard. Crassman felt the sweat popping out across his bald scalp. His lips were dry. A brisk, steady wind was blowing directly into his face.

Mrs. Crassman gave a muffled shriek. Crassman started, looked back at her; she was pointing astern. Crassman's heart took a painful plunge in his chest. The cloud was dead astern, and clearly closer than it had been five minutes earlier.

"It's gaining on us!"

Crassman put the throttle all the way over. The big engines opened up to a deep-chested thrum of power; the bow rose; spray whipped back across the big, sloping windshield. Crassman looked back. The cloud clung grimly astern. Off the starboard bow, the setting sun was a red ball on the horizon, slowly drifting across the boat's bows. Now it was dead ahead; now drifting off to port, sliding back past the boat. A vast shadow lay over the water off the port bow, coming closer. It swept over the boat. Looking back into the sudden darkness, Crassman saw the cloud, now dull purplish-black, dense as granite, half-filling the sky. And now, over the song of the engines, another sound was audible: a vast, bass rumble, like Niagara multiplied.

"Good God in heaven," Elaine said suddenly as the

boat emerged from the band of shadow into the red sunlight. "What is it, Daddy?"

Mrs. Crassman wailed, began sobbing.

His face chalk-white, Crassman clung grimly to the wheel, no longer looking back, listening to the swelling thunder behind him.

∽ 2 ∽

The meteorologist on duty in the United States Weather Satellite in Clark orbit twenty-two thousand miles above the Atlantic had watched the anomalous formation for half an hour on the big twelve-power screen before calling it to the attention of his supervisor.

"Something kind of funny down there, Fred, just east of the sunset line," he said, pointing out the tiny, blurred, disk hugging the sea to the west of Somerset Island in the Bermudas. "It formed up in a matter of a minute or two, smack in the middle of a twelve-hundred-mile-wide high that was clear as window glass. And it's growing steadily."

"An explosion, maybe?" the station chief suggested.

"That thing's over three miles wide already, Fred. It would take a nuclear blast to produce a smudge like that. Anyway, if it was a test shot, we'd have been notified."

"Maybe a nuclear ship blew her reactors. It's never happened before, but there's always a first time."

"The rate of dissipation's wrong for an explosion. It's not spreading fast enough. And I think it's rotating."

"Well, keep an eye on it, Bunny. Maybe you've nailed the first hurricane of the season."

"If so, I've got a lot of meteorology to unlearn. Check with Kennedy, will you, Fred? Something about that spot worries me."

A quarter of an hour later, Fred was back in the observer's bubble.

"Kennedy says no report of any detonation in the area. The autostations along the Atlantic seaboard are registering faint air-mass movements north and east. It's a little early to tell if there's any correction."

"Why doesn't it dissipate?" Bunny asked. "What's holding it?"

"Hard to say. Better put the recorders on it, Bunny. But don't worry; old Mother Nature is always springing surprises on us, just when we think we know it all."

Back in the communications center of the giant satellite, Fred flipped the key activating the beam linking the station to Kennedy Weather Center.

"Jake, no panic, but how about requesting an eyeball report on that fix I was talking to you about? The damned thing's still sitting out there like a tack in a board; and in the few minutes I was away, it grew visibly."

"Roger. I'll scramble one of the old Neptunes out of Jax. Those reserve boys like to joyride anyway."

"Keep me posted, Jake."

"Sure, Fred. Anything for our brave lads in the sky."

∾ 3 ∾

Twelve miles north of the village of Skime, Minnesota, Arne Burko, a seasonal trapper, threw down the armload of fallen branches he had gathered for his fire and seated himself on a log for a quiet smoke before dinner. It was a still evening, the sky tawny with the late-summer dusk. Burko lit up, stretching his legs, thinking of the forty-horse outboard on display at Winberg's in Skime. Everything a man wanted cost so much, seemed like. A car now. With a car, he could get into town more often, see more of Barby . . .

He pushed away the thought of her warm body and smiling face. No point in getting all upset. He stood, paced up and down, sniffing the air. Off to the east, through the trees, the ground rose toward the rocky outcropping known locally as Vargot Hill. He hadn't been up there for years, not since he was a kid. Used to pick berries there. Supposed to be haunted, the hill was. Kids used to dare each other to go up to the top. They'd creep up on it through the trees, getting quieter the closer they got.

There were big rock slabs up there, sort of stacked, as if they'd been piled up there by a giant. The kids had had lots of stories about the hill. About the dwarfs and elves that lived down in the rocks, and would come out and eat a careless kid who stayed too long after sunset. And about the devil who took the form of a big black panther and ranged around the countryside, looking for souls.

Burko snorted a laugh and got busy with the fire. When it was going good, he stacked some stones around it and put on the frying pan. He unrolled the greased-paper-wrapped bacon, put half a dozen strips on. They'd be a little smoky with the green fire, but he didn't care. Walking all day made a man hungry.

Funny about that black-cat legend. Old man Olsen said the name "Vargot" was a corruption of an old word that meant "black cat." Probably went back to some Indian legend. The Shoshonu had been big storytellers. Big liars. Swedes were pretty good liars too, when it came to embroidering a tale. He'd made up his share. That one time, after he'd spent the best part of an afternoon up there playing on the rocks at the top of the hill, he'd been a short-term celebrity among the boys after he told them about the rock that had started to lift up while he was sitting on it, and how he'd had to weight down all he could to hold it in place. That one had held them with their mouths open until Fats Linder had said, "Nuts, Burko, nobody can weight down any harder than what they are!"

He turned the bacon, cut a couple of slices of bread. He soaked up the fat with the bread, forked the bacon onto it, then put the coffee jug on. He ate slowly, savoring every bite. It was almost full dark when he finished. A full moon was rising, glowing big and yellow in the east behind the hill. He banked the fire, stretched, then on impulse started up the slope, along a faint game trail, grinning a little at himself as he felt a ghostly touch of the old superstitious apprehension.

He made his way up through dense blackberry brambles, not yet in fruit, emerged onto the nearly level stretch just below the giant's castle. He had never really noticed it before, but the place had a sort of look, if you saw it in the right light, as if somebody *had* piled those rocks up there. Just nonsense, of course; the glaciers had dumped rocks all across this country; but these rocks were all of a size, pretty near—and they had a kind of quarried look about them. And the way they were arranged, sort of in a big rectangle, as far as you could tell for the growth . . .

Burko froze, looking up at the looming pile. Had something moved up there, something that flowed from shadow to shadow . . . something that moved fast and smooth as a cat?

He was aware of his thudding pulse, of the tightness of his scalp.

"Hell." He laughed aloud. "I'm as bad as a kid. The thing's probably an Indian mound. Full of busted pots and arrowheads and maybe some skulls. Dead Indians. What the hell." He went forward with a bold stride, climbed up the slanting slabs, stepped up onto the flat stone that topped the structure. He was breathing hard, sweating lightly. A deerfly found him, buzzed his face sharply. He slapped at it. It was completely silent then. Burko took a step across the stone and halted. He stood that way for a full ten seconds, feeling his insides turn to water.

Unmistakably, through the stone he felt a faint vibration. Below his feet something ancient and evil was stirring . . .

Arne Burko was over three miles from Vargot Hill when he stopped running. He had sprained an ankle jumping down the rock slabs but had failed to notice it at the time.

A week later, his throat was still sore from the yell he had uttered as he fled.

∞ 4 ∞

In the office of the governor, Caine Island Federal Penitentiary, the prison psychologist leaned forward across the desk, raising his voice over the shrill of the rising wind that buffeted outside the big, oak-paneled room.

"I think you're making a mistake, sir," he said. "The man has a record of violence. He's dangerously unstable—"

"Unstable, or unclassifiable, doctor?" the prison governor cut in.

"I admit the man's an enigma," the psychologist said. "I don't pretend to understand his motivations. But after this outburst, anything could happen."

The governor turned to stare out the high windows behind his desk. The low sky, clear an hour before, now shed a light the color of dishwater across frond-strewn grounds, reflected from the whitecapped, hammered-pewter sea beyond. Through the massive leather chair and the deep pile carpet the minute trembling of the steel-and-concrete building was plainly detectable. As the governor watched, a forty-foot royal palm, curved into an arc like a strung bow, snapped, fell across the massed bougainvillea that lined the south drainage canal.

"No one was hurt, I understand," the governor said.

"No; but, Governor, you should have seen what he did to those chairs. Steel tubing, mind you. He twisted them into chrome-plated pretzels! Talk about maniacal strength—"

"Where was his guard?"

"He played sick, sent him for the duty physician."

"Got him safely out of the way, in other words."

"Governor—aren't you finding excuses for this man?"

"There was a reason for the outburst, as you put it, Claude," the governor said. "I want to know what that reason was."

"Governor, this is an old con, a man who once took an

ax to a human being. In this day and age, an *ax*, for God's sake! The savagery of it—"

"Thank you for your opinion, doctor; your warning is a matter of record, in the event he tears my head off with his bare hands."

"I wasn't thinking solely of my reputation, Governor."

"Of course not, Claude. Nevertheless, I'm going to talk to him." The governor nodded to the uniformed man posted beside the armored door. The guard touched a wall plate; there was the soft double *click-click!* as the interlocks disengaged. The door slid back; the guard took up his position, choke gun in hand, watching as Grayle came past him into the room.

The tailored prison uniform accentuated his powerful physique. As the prisoner advanced across the room, the words "caged tiger" popped into the governor's mind.

"That's all, doctor," he said. "Guard, wait outside."

"Now, just a minute," the psychologist started. He caught the look his superior directed at him and left silently. The sliding door snicked shut behind the guard.

"Hello, Grayle," the governor said.

"Hello, Hardman," the prisoner said in a tone of absolute neutrality.

The governor motioned to the chair beside the standing man. "Sit down," he said. Grayle didn't move.

"Why?" the governor said. "Just tell me why, that's all." Grayle's head shook almost imperceptibly.

"You knew I was working on a special parole for you. I'd have gotten it, too. So you picked this time to break up the dining hall. Why, Grayle?"

"You were wrong about me, Governor," Grayle said without expression.

"Nonsense, if you started smashing chairs, you had a reason."

Grayle said nothing.

"What are you trying to prove?" the governor said harshly. "That you're still a tough guy?"

"That's it," Grayle said.

The governor shook his head. "You're no brainless hoodlum. You had a reason—a good reason. I want to know what it was."

The wind shrieked in the lengthening silence.

"You cost the federal government over a thousand dollars in smashed furniture this evening," Hardman said sharply. "You've given the press new ammunition for their charges of coddling and lax administration."

"I'm sorry about that part," Grayle said.

"When you ran amok, you knew the effect it would have. You knew it would hurt yourself, me, the entire prison system."

Grayle said nothing.

"You realize what you're asking for?" A harsh note rang in the official's voice.

For an instant Grayle's eyes locked with Hardman's; there seemed to be some message there, almost readable. Then the prisoner glanced away indifferently.

"I'm ordering you to the maximum-security detachment at Gull Key, Grayle."

Grayle nodded, almost impatiently, the governor thought.

"I don't like it," he said. "I don't like to admit failure

with a man; but the best interests of Caine Island come first."

"Certainly, Governor," Grayle said softly. "I understand."

"Damn it, man, I'm not apologizing! I'm doing my duty, nothing more!" The governor put his hand under the edge of the desk, touched something hidden there.

"I've switched off the recording system," he said swiftly. "Speak up now, man! Tell me what this is all about!"

"Better switch it back on. You'll have the guards breaking the door down."

"Talk, man! Gull Key is no picnic ground!"

"That's all I have to say, Governor. You're wasting your time."

Hardman's face flushed. He keyed a button on the desktop viciously.

"All right, Grayle," he said flatly as the door slid back and the guard entered alertly. "That's all. You can go now."

Grayle walked out of the room without a backward glance.

❀❀❀✳❀❀❀❀

From a town of wood and stone houses clustered among giant trees and spilling down along the shore, men and women run down to gather on the beach; many of them wade out waist-deep in the bitter water to lay hands on the boat, shouting their greetings to the returned wayfarers. The prisoner climbs over the side with the others, grasps a rope, helps draw the ship up on the strand. Standing by the bow, he watches as the men caper, embracing the thick-bodied, snub-nosed women whose yellow hair hangs in thick braids down their backs. One or two of the latter eye him curiously, but they do not speak.

"Stand forth, slave," *a deep voice booms out. A man comes toward him, a length of rope in his hands. He is tall, massive, with a tangled blond beard and shaggy hair, clad in garments of leather. Against his chest, the Star of Deneb and the golden Cross of Omrian glint among the polished bears' teeth strung on a rawhide thong.* "It's time to truss and brand the bull for market, before he gets loose among the cows!" *he shouts cheerfully.*

The captive moves a step sideways, putting his back against the planked hull.

"Come and get me, Olove Brassbeard," *he calls awkwardly in the language of the barbarians.*

Olove motions with his free hand. "Bor! Grendel! Seize me that slave!"

Two big men come forward, smiling large smiles through bushy beards.

"It might be good sport to see Olove bind me with his own hands," *the captive says. Bor hesitates.*

"If he can," *the slave adds.*

Grendel's grin widens. He spits on the rocky ground. "The sea-law doesn't run here ashore, Olove. The voyage is over. You hold a rope in your hands, bind him with it— if you dare."

"You expect me, a chieftain, to soil my hands on a slave?"

"*How say you, outlander?*" *Grendel inquires.* "*Were you a man of rank in your own town?*"

"*I was a* Captain-Lieutenant." *The prisoner gives the title in his own tongue.*

"*He lies,*" *Olove blusters.* "*He was alone, without retainers or men-at-arms, clad only in a poor rag—*"

"*He wore ornaments of gold,*" *Hulf says, enjoying himself.* "*The same ones we now see winking among the fleas on your chest.*"

"*No doubt he stole them from his master ere he fled,*" *Olove grunts.*

"*His ring fit uncommon well for a stolen one,*" *Hulf says.* "*You had to hew away the finger to take it.*"

Brassbeard makes sputtering sounds; then he snorts and throws aside his wolfskin cloak. He flexes his arms, spits, and charges, his thick, bowed legs pumping like pistons. The captive stands unmoving. As Brassbeard closes, he pivots minutely, elevates his left forearm to deflect the chieftain's outstretched hand, leans in to place his elbow in the path of the man's onrushing chin, swings with his rush to palm him on his way. Olove strikes the side of the ship full on, skids along it, to fall with his face in the water, and lie, his hairy legs twitching before they fall still. A roar of laughter goes up.

Grendel comes forward and rolls the fallen man over.

"*Olove is dead,*" *he says, still grinning.* "*He dashed out his brains on his ship to oblige the stranger.*" *He wipes tears of mirth from his eyes, turns to the former slave, puts out a hand, clasps him below the elbow.*

"*The gods declare you to be a freeman,*" *he says.* "*By what name do your friends call you?*"

"Gralgrathor," the man says.

"Welcome to Björnholm, Grall Grathor. Come, my wife will find food and a pallet for you, and we'll share a flask or two. And for amusement," he adds in a lower tone, "you may teach me the spell you used to turn Olove's wrath into a madness that destroyed him."

Chapter Three

∾ 1 ∾

George, the night man at Smitty's Conditioning Parlor and Health Club, laid aside his paper as the buzzer sounded and feet descended the short flight of steps from street level. A tall, quick-moving man with a badly scarred face came into the room pulling off his coat.

"Yessir," George said, coming to his feet in a quick motion for all of his two hundred and ninety pounds of bulk, smiling, sizing up the newcomer. He noted the soiled cuffs, the wilted and grimed collar, the tear in the dusty knee of the trousers. But the suit was cut from a good grade of worsted, real wool, it looked like, and the big brogans were almost new under the dust and scuff marks. And the socks were a tasteful solid, none of those purple clocks. The guy had been out on the tiles, all right, but there was some quality there; he was no bindle-stiff just drifting in out of the damp night air. George caught the jacket as the man tossed it aside.

"Sponge and press the suit, sir?" he said. "Do it for you nice, while you're in the steam."

"Never mind that," the big man said. The scars on his face moved as he spoke, the big one across the cheek dimpling as if in a puckish smile, the one crossing his forehead and running back into the scalp lifting quizzically, sardonically. He shucked bills from a folded sheaf, tossed them on the table.

"My body's full of poison," he said. "I want heat. Lots of heat."

An elderly man, naked and shrunken, emerging from the infrared room, jerked his head sharply at sight of the newcomer. He halted, watching the scarred man strip. He seemed fascinated by the scars, large and small, that marked the powerfully muscled chest, back, thighs.

"I'm carrying one-twenty in the wet room, one-eighty in the sauna," George said. "Five minutes of that be all you can take."

"Call me in ten."

George watched the glass door, smiling a little to himself. He folded some towels, opened and shelved a carton of soap. Ten minutes, the man say. Like to see the man could take ten on them hot teak boards. First couple minutes go easy; then it start to get hot. Ten minutes. George chuckled. Door be opening any minute now. Big man be out, gasping like a catfish on the bank. He looked at the clock. Five minutes almost up. Through the clear glass he saw the scarred man sitting bolt upright, swinging his arms. Hoo-ee! That white man crazy, have to watch him, get him out when he faint . . .

"That fellow's asking for a heart attack," the old man spoke suddenly beside George. He had come up silently, rubber-sandaled. He ruffled his wispy hair with a towel. "What was that he said about poison?"

"Booze, doctor," George said. "He meant the booze. Smell it on him."

It was eleven minutes before the scarred man strode from the dry-heat room, his body pouring with sweat. A sickly odor of alcohol hung thick about him. George stared.

"Cold water?" the big man said curtly.

"Deluge showers, right to your right." George pointed.

"Good way to get yourself a coronary attack," the old fellow called after him.

The scarred man stood in the stall, dousing himself with icy water. He breathed in great, shuddering gulps. Afterward he spent ten minutes in the steam room, ten more in the sauna, showered again. By then the reek of raw alcohol had dissipated.

"You know massage?" he asked George. George's wide black face crinkled in a smile.

"Some say I do pretty good." He nodded toward the padded table. The scarred man waved aside the proffered towel, stretched out face down. His back was solidly muscled about the shoulders, tapering sharply to a lean, hard waist. A deep scar ran down across the left trapezius to end near the spine. Lesser scars—lines, pocks, zigzags—were scattered over his hide in random distribution. Under George's hands, the flesh felt hard, ropy.

"You ever in the ring?" the masseur inquired.

"Not much."

"That fight racket no life for a man."

"Harder," the scarred man said. "I want to feel it."

"Got to be careful," George chuckled. "Man come home with bruises, his sweety wonder why."

"Say," the old man said. "Mind if I ask how you got the scars?"

The big man turned his head to look at him.

"I'm a doctor, a medical doctor," the old fellow said. "I've never seen anything quite like the way you're marked up."

"I got them in the wars," the big man said. George shot the oldster a pursed-mouth look.

"Don't shush me, George," the old man said. "My interest's legitimate."

"Got a little rheumatism there?" George asked. His hard, pink-palmed hands explored a lump under the client's skin. The elderly medical man came over, frowned knowingly down at the man stretched on the table.

"Be careful, George," he ordered. "You take it easy with those hands of yours." He leaned for a closer look at the deep fissure, keloid-ridged, that crossed the kidney region.

"Feel like some kind of lump there," George said. "Feel hot, too." He stepped back, looking at the doctor. The old man's thin fingers ran over the visible swelling at the lower edge of the prone man's ribs.

"Why, there's a bullet lodged in there," he said. "You been shot, mister?"

"Not recently."

"Hmmm. Must have entered along here . . ." The thin old finger traced up along the big man's side. "Right here," he said. "Here's your point of entry. Traveled right along the rib cage—"

The medical man broke off, staring at an angry, reddish swelling developing at the spot under which the bullet lay.

"George, what did you do, gouge in with those big thumbs of yours? I told you to take it easy!"

"I never bear down on that place, doctor. I feel it right away and take it real gentle."

"You lie easy, mister," the doctor said. "You have some infection there, that's pretty plain. I have my kit with me. I think I'd better give you a hypo of PN-43—"

"No," the big man said. He was gritting his teeth, his back tensed. "I know what it is. But I'd forgotten how it feels. . ."

As the doctor and the masseur watched, the contusion grew, flushing dusky purple now, a three-inch splotch against the tan skin. A patch of paleness grew at its center, spread to the size of a steel dollar.

"Hey, doctor—" George said, and broke off as the swelling burst, the skin splitting to ooze dark blood and clear matter, exposing a grayish lump. The doctor uttered an exclamation, scuttled across to an open locker, jerked out a green-plastic instrument case, opened it on a bench, hurried back. With a shallow, spoon-shaped probe, he levered at the wound, lifted out a slightly misshapen lump of lead as big as the end of his thumb. The big man sighed harshly and relaxed.

"How long ago did you say it was you were shot?" the doctor asked in a strained voice, eyeing the big slug lying on his palm.

"Quite a while."

"I should say so." The old man barked a short laugh. "If

it weren't so ridiculous, I'd swear that was a genuine minié ball."

"Minié ball? What that?" George asked; his eyes rolled like a horse smelling smoke.

"That's what they used in the Civil War," the doctor said.

The scarred man smiled slightly. "I need food," he said as he pulled on his shirt. "Is there a restaurant nearby that you can recommend, George?"

"Happen I got a nice slab of sirloin in my cooler right this minute," the big black man said. "And eggs, too. About half a dozen sound right?"

The scarred man took the fold of bills from his pocket and shucked off a fifty, laid it on the rubbing table.

"Rare. And over lightly."

"Say," the doctor said. "Funny thing. The scars on your face: they look different."

The scarred man turned to the full-length wall mirror. He went close, studying his features. The furrow across his cheeks that had pulled his mouth into a perpetual faint grin had faded to a shallow, pinkish line. The broad band of lumped scar tissue across his forehead was now no more than a faint discontinuity in the smooth tan of his skin.

"Never saw anything like it," the old man said in a tone of wonderment. "Those scars are fading right out. Just disappearing . . ." His hand moved, caught itself. "You'll pardon my curiosity," he said, edging around for a better view. "But as a man of science—"

"They weren't as bad as they looked," the formerly scarred man said shortly, turning away.

"Look here, my friend, I'm Dr. Henry Cripps. Hank, to my friends. Now, I've had some experience with contusions and the like during over forty years of practice. I know a third-degree scar when I see one. A thing like that doesn't just disappear in the space of a quarter of an hour—"

"Doctor, I'm not in need of medical attention, thank you anyway," the big man said. The oldster clamped his jaw, retired to the far side of the room, from where he stared at the object of his professional curiosity. An odor of cookery wafted into the room through the open doorway to a back room. The big man paced up and down, flexing his arms.

"Itches, doesn't it?" Cripps spoke up.

"A little."

"Damnedest thing I ever saw."

Five minutes of silence ensued. George appeared at the door.

"On the table," he said. The big man followed him back to the small, neatly arranged living quarters. He seated himself and attacked the thirty-two-ounce steak. George put a big glass of milk in front of him. He drained it, asked for a refill. He ate the eggs, mopped the juices from the plate with a scrap of toast. George brought in a foot-wide pie, lifted a quarter of it onto a plate, put a half-pint mug of coffee beside it.

"Can't get that kind in the store," he said. "I got a lady friend brings them around." He watched as his guest finished off the dessert, drained the cup.

"Better hang on to that lady friend, George," the big man said. He rose. "Thanks. I needed that."

"I reckon," George agreed. "Too bad Lucy-Ann not here to see you tuck it in. Do her heart good to see a man eat."

"By God," Dr. Cripps said. "Will you look at that, George? You can scarcely see where the scars were. They're remitting completely."

George shook his head, accepting the evidence of his eyes philosophically.

"Nothing like a good feed to set a man up," he commented.

"Look here," Cripps said as the object of the discussion headed from the room. "Would you mind just letting me have a look at your back?"

"I'm sorry; I'm in a hurry."

"But damn it, this is medical history in the making— if you'd let me observe it! I have a camera in my apartment, a few blocks from here; I should photograph this, document it—"

"Sorry." The big man picked up his coat.

"At least let me examine the wound I dressed. You owe me that much."

"All right." The big man stripped off his shirt. The doctor's eyes goggled at the sight of the wide, unmarked back. He put out a hand, touched the smooth skin. There was no trace of any injury anywhere in the patient's skin.

"Sir," he said in a choked voice, "you must come along with me to St. John's Hospital. You must allow this to be studied by competent authorities—"

The big man shook his head. "Out of the question." He donned his shirt, tied his tie, pulled on his coat. He put another fifty-dollar bill on the table.

"Thanks, to both of you," he said. "I hope that will cover your fee, doctor."

"Never mind my fee—"

"It's late," the big man said gently. "Maybe you were imagining things."

"George, you saw it too," Cripps exclaimed, turning to the Negro.

"Doctor, seem like sometimes I got a powerful bad memory." George smiled dreamily, looking at the bill.

They watched in silence as the big man went up the steps.

"Where can I reach you?" Cripps called as he put a hand on the door. "I'll want to follow up on treatment, of course!"

The big man paused, turned his head slowly, as if listening for a distant sound. He pointed in a direction at an angle to the door.

"I'm going that way," he said. "I don't know how far." The shrill of the wind as he pushed open the door drowned the doctor's reply.

∞ 2 ∞

Four guards carrying choke guns and sidearmed with holstered 4-mm impact pistols escorted Grayle along the wide, brilliantly lit subterranean corridor, two in advance, two behind him. In the liftcar, they posted themselves in the four corners and sealed their helmet visors before closing the door. In silence, they dropped the hundred and fifty feet to the staging room that was the sole exit route from the prison proper. As they emerged from the shaft, Ted was waiting. He stepped forward hesitantly.

"Hey, Mr. Grayle," he said in strained greeting.

"Hello, Ted," Grayle said.

"Uh—you O.K. now?" Ted said, and blushed.

"Sure. Thanks for everything, Ted."

"Geez, Mr. Grayle . . ." Ted swallowed and turned away quickly.

"So long, Ted," Grayle said.

In the processing unit, Grayle moved stolidly through the chemical and radiation scanners, submitted to the cold caress of the medical unit, the icy touch of the hyposprays. His fingerprints and retinal and dental patterns were read and compared. A husky lieutenant flicked keys on the ID panel and recorded the response which certified the identity of prisoner 7654-K-3YN-003. He opened a steel drawer, withdrew a pair of inch-wide metal-link wrist irons linked by a ten-inch rod. He weighed them on his palm, looking at Grayle.

"I don't want any trouble out of you now, boy," he said. His voice was a casual drawl, but his eyes were sharp on Grayle's. He advanced briskly, snapped a steel ring in place on the prisoner's right wrist, reached for the left. He gripped it, then suddenly twisted Grayle's arm behind him, brought it to within an inch of the waiting cuff, then stopped. His face darkened; veins stood out on his forehead, but the cuff moved no closer.

"Do you want to call for help?" Grayle asked softly, "or stick to the book?"

"Don't get me mad, boy," the lieutenant hissed. "I've got friends at Gull."

"What do you do when you're mad, Harmon, blow bubbles?"

The man made a noise deep in his throat. "A guard-house lawyer," he grunted. Five seconds passed in silence; then the lieutenant stepped back.

"I guess I'll give him a break," he said loudly to the sergeant. "This boy won't give us any trouble. He's got enough trouble. He'll want to hit Gull clean—as clean as his kind can be. Cuff him up in front."

The sergeant secured the manacles. The four armed men boxed the prisoner. Metal clanged as steel doors opened on a bare chamber. They walked in. The doors closed. Two of the men pushed buttons at opposite ends of the small room. A heavy panel slid aside on a big bright-lit garage where two massive gray-painted vehicles bearing the letters CIFP were parked. An attendant unlocked a door at the rear of one; one of the guards stepped up into the windowless compartment, covered Grayle as he entered. A second guard came aboard, and the door closed. Locks snicked.

"You sit there." The guard indicated a low bench with a sloping back mounted against the driver's compartment. When Grayle was seated in it, knees high, his weight on the end of his spine, a locking bar slid into place across his ribs and sealed with a click. The two guards strapped into the contoured chairs mounted at the sides of the car. Each pressed a button set in the armrest of his chair.

"In position," one said. Grayle heard a soft sound, saw a minute movement of the tiny glass prism set in the ceiling. It studied him, then swiveled to inspect the guards. The light died behind it. A moment later the turbines started up with a muted howl.

Grayle felt the car move forward; he sensed the raising of the flint-steel door, was aware of a sense of enclosure as the vehicle entered the upward-slanting tunnel.

One of the guards stirred in his seat. He was a young fellow, with a bone-and-leather face, prominent teeth.

"Just try something, bo," he said in a husky whisper. "I hear you're a tough boy. Let's see can you break from us."

"Shut up, Jimbo," the other man said. "He ain't going noplace."

"Just to Gull, is all," Jimbo said. He smiled, exposing untended molars. "You think he'll like it there, Randy?"

"Sure," Randy said. "His kind likes it tough."

Grayle ignored their conversation. He was listening to the muted, echoic roar of the car's passage through the hundred-yard tunnel. The tone changed as the car slowed, started upgrade, changed again as it moved ahead on the level. They had emerged now onto the causeway linking the islands. Quickly the car built up speed. In six minutes they would pass over the Boca Ciega cut, the deep-water tidal-flow channel spanned by a single-lane bridge. Grayle tensed, counting silently to himself.

∞ **3** ∞

When Weather Control at Kennedy alerted the satellite that the weather-patrol craft was airborne, estimating five minutes to contact, the object of the meteorologists' attention had grown to an estimated diameter of four miles. Its rotation was clearly visible now.

"About five minutes for a complete revolution," Bunny said. "That means winds topping sixty at the periphery already. And she's holding position as if she'd dropped anchor."

"Kennedy is patching us directly in on the ground-to-air," Fred said. He plugged a hand microphone into a jack beside the screen. A faint crackle sounded; then the voice of the pilot came through loud and clear: ". . . *getting dark fast, but it's clear as a bell out here, sea calm. I see some fishing boats down there, like ducks on a pond. I'm holding ten thousand . . .*"

"He ought to be spotting some sign of it," Bunny muttered. "He's within fifty miles of it—"

"*Hold everything, Kennedy Tower.*" The pilot's tone changed. "*I have something . . . like a twister, a funnel. Black as soot. Looks kind of strange, hard edges like cast metal. Just sitting there on the horizon, maybe forty miles dead ahead.*"

"*Roger, Navy oh-nine-three,*" the Kennedy controller said. "*Close to ten miles and orbit the fix. Better give us the cameras on this from now on.*"

"*Cameras already rolling. I'm getting a hard echo off this thing. It's big, all right. It tops out at about fifteen thousand, six miles wide. It looks like a mountain standing on its nose. What's holding it up?*"

"I've got him on the HR screen, sir," a junior technician called. "He's at thirty miles, closing fast."

"Say, Kennedy, I'm getting some turbulence now," the Neptune pilot said calmly. "I'm making a pass east of the bogie. This thing is big. I never saw anything like this. It's opaque. It looks like it's spinning. Trailing streamers. The sea looks kind of funny under it. Black shadow, and . . ." There was a five-second pause. "There's a hole down there. A whirlpool. My God, I . . ."

"Navy oh-nine-three," Kennedy came in as the voice hesitated. "Repeat that last transmission."

"I'm down to five thousand, fifteen miles out. The thing's standing up over me like an umbrella. I'm holding about a twenty-degree crab. Winds are getting rough. I can hear it now, roaring . . ."

"All right, sheer off, Ken, get out of that turbulence—"

"There's a boat down there, some kind of boat! She's got her lights on. Looks like about a thirty-footer. She's got her stern to the twister. She's . . . my God, the damned thing's got her! She's going in!"

"Ken, get out of there!"

"There's three people aboard, I can see them!" the pilot was shouting now.

"All right, Navy oh-nine-three," another voice spoke harshly. "Report course change, and put some snap into it!"

"I'm . . . I'm making my pass now, north of it, five miles from contact. That boat—"

"Never mind the boat! Pick up a heading of oh-nine-oh and put some distance between you and this thing!"

"Turbulence is bad. She's fighting me. . ."

"Go to full gate, Ken! Get the hell out of there!"

"She's not reacting to control, Kennedy! She's . . . God! I'm getting knocked around . . . it'll tear her apart . . .!"

"Mr. Hoffa!" the technician called. "The Navy's plane's headed right into it!"

"Ken! Try riding with it! Don't fight it, let it take you around, build up airspeed, and try to edge out!"

"Roger, Kennedy," the pilot said. His voice was flat, emotionless now, against a background howl. "Tell the next guy to stay way back, twenty miles at least. It's like a magnet. I'm riding it like a merry-go-round. It's like a black well, two miles off my starboard wingtip. The noise—I guess you can hear it. I'm indicating four-fifty, but I'd say my ground speed is a couple hundred over that—"

"Ken, try a left turn, about five degrees—"

"I'm in a tight crab, no joy, Kennedy. The boat's coming under me again. It's right on the edge of the drop. It—it's breaking up. Ripped wide open. It's gone. Lucky at that. Fast. I'm getting the turbulence again. It's dark in here. I've got my nav lights on. It looks like black glass. Buffeting's bad now; can't take much of this . . . she . . ."

"Ken! Ken! Come in, Ken!"

"It merged," the technician said in a choked voice. "The plane flew right into it!"

๛ 4 ๛

The sound of the tires of the armored vehicle changed tone as it started across the metal-grid surface of the lift span of the Boca Ciega bridge. As they did, Grayle arched his back, putting pressure against the steel bar across his chest. For an instant it held firm; then it yielded, bent like sun-warmed wax. One end sprang free of the latch mechanism. At the sound, both guards tensed, their heads jerking around in time to see Grayle come to his feet, tense his forearms, and bend the chrome-steel rod between his wrists into a U, grip it with both hands, and with a quick twist snap it apart. The one called Randy made a strangled sound and clawed at the gun at his hip. Grayle plucked it from him, did something to it with his hands, threw it aside, in the same motion caught Jimbo as he rose, tapped him lightly against the wall, dropped him. He stepped to the rear of the car, gripped the steel rods which engaged slots at the sides of the double door, braced his feet, and lifted. One rod popped from its socket; the other broke with a crystalline tinkle. Grayle kicked the doors wide; a swirl of rain whipped at him. Gripping the jamb, he swung out, caught at the lamp housing above, pulled himself up onto the roof of the speeding vehicle. As he drew his legs up, there was a sharp double report, and a sharp pang stung his left shin.

He rose to his knees, looking down at the concrete railing flashing past, at the multistrand barbed wire above it, the dark water frothing whitecapped below. He rose to his feet against the rushing wind, gauged his distance, and dived far out over the pavement and the wires as the car braked, tires squealing, its siren bursting into howling life.

The escort spent half an hour patrolling the bridge on foot, playing powerful handlights across the water, but they found no sign of the escaped convict.

℘℘℘✶℘℘℘

Under the high-beamed roof of the timbered farmhouse

at Björnholm, the man who had been Gralgrathor sits at a long table, musing over a bowl of stout ale. In the fire burning on the hearth, images of faces and figures form, beckon, flicker away, their whispering flame-voices murmuring words in a tongue he has half-forgotten. Across the room Gudred sits on a bench between the two household servant girls, her youthful head bent over her needlework.

He pushes the bowl away, stands, belts a warm coat of bearskin about him. Gudred comes to him, the firelight soft on her plaited hair, the color of hammered gold.

"Will you sit with me by the fire awhile, my Grall?" she asks softly. Of all the daughters of Earl Arnulf, she alone had a voice that was not like the bawling of a bull calf. Her touch was gentle, her skin smooth and fair.

"You are a fool, Grall," the earl had said. "She is a sickly creature who will doubtless die bearing your first son. But if you indeed choose her over one of my lusty, broad-beamed wenches—why, take her, and be done with it!"

"I'm restless, girl," he tells her, smiling down into her face. "My head is fuddled with ale and too long lazing indoors. I need to walk the hills awhile to clear the cobwebs from my brain."

Her hand tightens on his arm. "Thor—not in the hills! Not in the gloaming; I know you laugh at talk of trolls and ogres, but why tempt them—"

He laughs and hugs her close. Across the wide room, the curtains of the sleeping alcove stir. The face of a small boy appears, knuckling his eyes.

"See—we've waked Loki with our chatter," Gralgrathor says. "Sing him a song, Gudred, and by the

*time you've stitched another seam in your Fairday gown,
I'll be back."*

*Outside, the light of the long northern evening gleams
across the grain field which slopes down to the sea edge.
Above, the forest mounts the steep rocks toward the pink-
stained snowfields on the high ridges. With the old hound
Odinstooth beside him, he sets off with long strides that in
a quarter of an hour have put the home acre far below
him.*

*Beside him, Odinstooth growls; he quiets the dog with
a word. On the hillside, a movement catches his eye. It is
a man, wrapped in a dark cloak, approaching from the
tongue of the forest that extends down toward the farm.
Grall watches him, noting his slim, powerful physique, his
quick, sure movements.*

*The man's course leads him down across the fold of the
earth, up again toward the ledge where Gralgrathor
waits; there is something in his gait, his easy movements,
that remind him of someone from the forgotten life . . .*

*The man comes up the slope, his face shadowed under
the cowl. For an instant, the heavy gray cloth looks like a
Fleet-issue weather cloak . . .*

"Thor?" a mellow tenor voice calls.

*Gralgrathor stands staring down at the newcomer, who
has thrown back his cowl to reveal a lean, dark-eyed face,
flame-red hair.*

"Lokrien—am I dreaming?" Gralgrathor whispers.

*The dark-eyed man smiles, shaking his head. He speaks
in a strange language . . . but dimly, Gralgrathor senses
the meaning.*

"Thor—man, it is you! Don't tell me you've forgotten

your mother tongue!"

"After all these years?" Gralgrathor says. "You've really come?"

"I've come for you," Lokrien says in the half-strange language. "I've come to take you home, Thor."

Chapter Four

∽ 1 ∽

The governor of Caine Island prison stared incredulously at the chief of his guard force.

"You wouldn't be making some sort of . . . of ill-considered joke, I suppose, Brasher?"

"No, sir," the wiry, dapper officer said. He stood at parade rest, looking acutely uncomfortable. Outside, the wind shrieked jeeringly.

"It's not possible," the governor said. "It simply *isn't possible!*"

"It happened on the bridge," the captain said, tight-mouthed. "Just as the car crossed the draw span."

"An escape." Hardman sat rigid in his chair, his face pale except for spots of color high on his cheeks. "From the country's only one-hundred-percent escape-proof confinement facility!"

The captain slanted his eyes at his superior.

"Governor, if you're suggesting . . ."

"I'm suggesting nothing—except that a disaster has occurred!"

"He didn't get far," the captain said. "Not with two tranks in him. He went over the side into a riptide. That's a rough drop at sixty miles an hour, even without the storm. We're looking for the body, but—"

"I want the body found before the wires get the story! And if he's alive—" He stared fiercely at the officer.

"He's dead, sir, you can count on that—"

"If he's alive, I said, I want him caught, understand, Brasher? Before he reaches the mainland! Clear?"

The captain drew a breath and let it out, making a show of self-control.

"Yes, sir," he said heavily. "Just as you say." He turned away, giving Hardman a look as though there were comments only protocol prevented him from making.

When the officer had gone, Hardman sat for five minutes biting his thumb. Then he flipped the intercom lever.

"Lester, I want the Grayle dossier, everything we've got."

"There isn't much, Governor. You'll recall he was a transfer from Leavenworth East—"

"I want to see what we have."

Lester hesitated. "Is it true, Governor? The story going around is that he more or less burst his way through the side of an armored car—"

"That's an exaggeration! Don't help spread these damned rumors, Lester!"

"Of course, I knew it was ridiculous. I suppose under cover of the storm he caught the escort off guard—"

"I want those records right away, Lester. And get in touch with Pyle at Leavenworth, see if you can turn up anything else on Grayle. Check with Washington, the military services, the various federal agencies. Query Interpol and the UN PC Bureau. I want anything and everything you can turn up."

Lester whistled. "Quite a stir for just one man, sir, isn't it? I mean—"

"That man has my reputation in his pocket, Lester! I want to know all there is to know about him—just in case he *isn't* picked up washing around in the tide tomorrow morning!"

"Of course. You know, Governor, some of the staff have been repeating the stories about Grayle having served his time but not being released because the records were lost. They say he finally took the law into his own hands—"

"Nonsense. He'd have been free in ninety days."

"Just how long *had* he been on the inside, sir? I was asking Captain Brasher, and he—"

"Get me the records, Lester," the governor cut him off. "I suggest you stop listening to rumors and get busy digging up some facts."

∞ 2 ∞

Lying flat among reeds on a shore of sulfurous black mud, Grayle averted his face from the howling wind that drove rain at him in icy sheets. He rested for a while, waiting for the dizziness to pass then wormed his way up the bank, squinting against the downpour. A large tree afforded some slight shelter. He settled himself with his back to it, set about tearing strips from his prison garment to bind around his shin, in which a high-velocity pellet had scored a deep gouge before ricocheting off the bone.

On the highway above, a car churned past, a red strobe light flashing atop it, its headlights drowning in the almost solid downpour. Grayle set off along the shore, keeping in the shelter of scrub liveoak and Australian pines, slipping and sliding in the dark over the twisted roots. He was almost on the house before he saw it: a black cuboid of unpainted concrete, tin-roofed, dark and silent under the sodden trees. A small car stood in the sandy drive. Grayle went forward, skirted the vehicle. As he rounded it, a light lanced out from near the house, caught him full in the face.

"It's not worth stealing," a voice called over the drum of the rain. "But you're welcome to try."

The voice was that of a woman. Grayle stood where he was, waiting.

"You'd better be on your way," the voice said. "I keep a gun, you know. I have to, living where I do." She broke off; the light wavered.

"That's a prison jacket. . ."

The light moved over him, held on his face.

"You escaped from Caine Island?" When Grayle said nothing, she went on: "You better get inside, I heard the sirens a few minutes ago. They're patrolling the road."

Grayle took two swift steps, swept the light from her hand, reversed it, and flicked its beam across the woman. She was young, clean-featured, dark-haired, tall and slen-. der, in a weatherproof trench coat. She didn't move, but turned her eyes aside from the light. There was no gun in her hands.

"I'm sorry," Grayle said. "I had to be sure." He handed the light back to her. Silently she turned, led the way into the house. She switched on a light, pulled down the roller shades. After the cold wind, the warmth and comparative silence enveloped Grayle like a downy blanket.

"You're hurt!" the girl said. Grayle braced his feet, fighting against a wave of dizziness.

"Lethanol!" The girl's voice came from a remote distance. "I can smell it on you! Sit down . . ."

The girl stood over him, a concerned look on her face. Water dripped from her hair, running down her cheek. For an instant she reminded him of someone: the image of a face with ringleted hair and a mobcap flickered and was gone. He couldn't remember her name. It had been so long, there were so many things forgotten . . .

He pushed himself to his feet; he must not sleep now.

She took his arm; he was aware of her voice but made no effort to follow the words. Fragments of old memories danced through his consciousness: a night in the rain on the field near Córdoba; standing by a stone wall, while booted feet tramped endlessly past, the blue-coated troops with their backpacks and fixed bayonets; a sudden, vivid evocation of the odor of tarred cordage and creaking timbers, of blown spume and salt fish, of leather and gunpowder . . .

". . . stay on your feet," the girl was saying. "I saw a demonstration back at Bloomington . . ." Her voice was low, well modulated, her diction good.

He halted. "Do you have any high-protein food—meat, eggs . . . ?"

"Yes. Good idea."

Grayle continued to pace up and down the small room. It was neat, clean, sparsely furnished with cheap plastic-and-steel-tube chairs and studio couch, a thin rug, a bookcase built of bricks and boards and filled with paperbacks. Framed magazine pictures decorated the walls. There were flowers in foil-covered tin cans. The kitchen was an alcove with a fold-out table, a minimal counter-top refrigerator, a tiny electric range. The aroma of bacon and eggs was almost painfully sharp.

She put a plate on the table, added a big clay cup of black coffee.

"Eat slowly," she said, watching him swallow the egg in two bites. "It won't help you to get indigestion."

"How far am I from the perimeter wall?"

"About three miles as the crow flies, across the bay. Nearly seven by road. How did you get this far?"

"I swam."

"Yes, but . . ." Her eyes went to the crude bandage on his shin, visible under his pants cuff.

"You're hurt . . ." Without waiting for a reply, she knelt, with deft fingers opened the crude knot and pulled away the wet cloth. There was a faint pink scar across the tanned skin. She gave him a puzzled look as she rose.

"I'll move on now." He got to his feet. "I'm grateful to you for your kindness."

"What do you intend to do? Just walk out there and wait to be caught?"

"It will be better for you if you know nothing of my plans."

"You're on a peninsula here, there's only one way out. They'll have it blocked."

A car passed on the road. They listened as the growl of the engine receded.

"They'll be checking here soon," the girl said. "There's a crawl space above the kitchen."

"Why?"

"Why not?" Her tone was defiant.

"Why are you willing to involve yourself?"

"Perhaps I have a feeling for a man on the run."

He waited.

"I had a brother at Caine Island. That's why I bought this place—I was allowed to see him one day a week. He had nobody else; and neither did I."

"That doesn't explain—"

"He's dead. Three months ago. Leukemia, they said. He was only thirty-four."

"You blame the authorities?"

"They had him," she said flatly.

Scarlet light struck the front window, glowed through the gap under the blind. A brilliant white light replaced it, pushing shadows across the floor. The growl of an engine was audible over the rattle of rain on the roof.

"We waited too long," the girl said tightly.

"Stay out of the way, out of sight," Grayle said. Outside, car doors slammed. He flattened himself against the wall beside the door. There was a sharp rap. A moment later the knob turned, the door was thrown violently open. Rain blasted in. There was the sound of metal rasping on leather, the click of a safety catch being snapped off. A tall man in a shiny yellow slicker took a step into the room. Grayle moved then, caught the man's gun hand, jerked him to him.

"Don't cry out," he said into the cop's startled face.

"Harmon!" the man yelled. "Don't—"

Grayle gripped him by the shoulder, gave him a sharp shake. He went slack. Grayle lowered him to the floor. The second man came through the door at a dead run. As he passed Grayle rapped him on the side of the neck; he fell hard, lay still. Grayle pushed the door shut. The girl's eyes met his.

"I never saw anyone move so quickly—"

"Good-bye," Grayle cut her off, "and thank you—"

"What are you going to do?"

"Don't involve yourself, Miss—"

"Rogers. Anne Rogers." She avoided looking at the two unconscious men on the floor. "And I'm already involved."

"I'll be all right, Miss Rogers."

"Take my car."

"I never learned to drive one."

Her eyes searched his face. "Then I'll have to go with you."

She flicked off the lights, took out her flash, opened the door, stepped out into the rain. Grayle followed. She reached inside the police car, switched off the lights. The radio crackled and muttered.

The inside of the small car smelled wet and moldy. The starter groaned sluggishly.

"I'll have to try to jump it from their car." Anne got out and went back to the trunk, opened it, took out a pair of heavy insulated cables. Grayle lifted the hood for her as directed, watched as she attached the big copper alligator clips, making sparks jump and sputter.

This time the starter whirled energetically; the engine

coughed, broke into stuttering life. She revved it, sending clouds of exhaust rolling past the window.

"Hold your foot on the gas," she said, and jumped out of the car to disconnect the cables. The deck lid thumped. She slid back in beside him.

"Here we go. Be thinking about how to handle it when we get to the causeway."

For ten minutes they drove through torrential rain, doing a reckless twenty miles per hour on the glossy black-top. Gusts of wind threw the light car across the road. No other cars passed them. At one point, water was across the road; Anne shifted down and crawled through. Then lights shone a hundred yards ahead. The red beacon of a parked police car blinked through the rain.

"Stop the car."

She braked, pulled over, looked at him inquiringly.

"Can you face it out if they search the car?" he asked.

"What are you going to do?"

"I'll ride the frame."

"You can't. There's nothing to ride on, no room—"

"I'll manage." He stepped out into the storm, went flat, and eased under the chassis. He felt over the rust-pitted frame, scalded his fingers on the exhaust stack, groped for a handhold on a cross member. He hooked the toes of his prison-issue shoes over the rear spring hangars, lifted his body from the wet pavement, pressed against the under-side of the car. The girl crouched by the car, staring at him.

"You *are* crazy! You can't hold on that way! If you slip— you'll be killed!"

"Go ahead, Anne," he said. "I'm all right."

She hesitated for a moment; then she nodded and was gone. Grayle heard the gears shift; the car lurched as it started ahead. Acrid gases leaked from the rotted pipes; the car vibrated, jolting over the road. Oily water sleeted at him; gravel stung him. The tires hissed, close to his face. Then the car slowed. Lights shone on the pavement, gliding nearer. He saw the wheels of another car; two pairs of booted feet approached, stopped a foot from his head. Voices, indistinct over the rumble of the steady rain and the whine of the wind. Doors clanked; the car swayed, and the girl's feet appeared. One policeman rounded the car; more door slams, more rocking. The deck lid opened and slammed. The girl got back into the driver's seat. The masculine boots withdrew. The car pulled ahead, accelerated.

Half a mile farther on, it slowed to a halt. Grayle dropped clear and crawled out into the downpour. He slid into the seat and met the girl's eyes.

"I still don't believe it," she said. "No one could do what you just did."

Grayle put his hand on the door.

"Thanks," he said. "I'll leave you now."

"What's your name?" the girl asked suddenly.

"Grayle."

"Why were you . . . there?" She tilted her head toward the invisible island behind them.

"I killed a man." He watched her eyes.

"In a fair fight?"

"He almost killed me, if that's what you mean."

"Grayle, you wouldn't last a day without me. You've been inside too long."

"I have a long way to go, Anne."

"Doesn't everyone, Grayle?"

He hesitated for a moment; then he nodded.

She smiled tensely, pulled the car back onto the road, and gunned ahead along the dark road.

⊚⊚⊚✱⊚⊚⊚

They sit in the big, drafty hall, hung with shields and spears and axes which are not decorations but are ready to use, beside the great granite fireplace, chimneyless and smoky.

"It's a strange, barbaric world you found yourself cast-away on, Thor," Lokrien says. "But you've a roof over your head, a warm fire on a cold night, good food and ale, a woman to comfort you. It could have been worse."

"I found friends here," Gralgrathor says. "They could have killed me, but instead they let me into their lives."

"Poor creatures. I wonder what their history is? They're human, of course, no doubt descendants of some ancient spacefarers wrecked here long ago. Have they any legends of their lost homeland?"

Gralgrathor nods. "It must have been long ago. Their myths are much distorted."

"There's a certain peace and simplicity here—the peace of ignorance," Lokrien says. "They've never heard of the Xorc. They don't dream that out there a great Imperial Fleet is defending their little world against an enemy that could vaporize the planet. Perhaps in years to come, Thor, you'll look back sometimes with nostalgia on your idyll

among the primitives."

"No, Loki," Gralgrathor says. "It's not earth I'll look back on with nostalgia. I'm staying here, Loki. I'm not going back with you."

Lokrien shakes his head as if to clear it of some dark vision. "You don't know what you're saying. Never to go back? Never to see Ysar, to wear the uniform again, to sail with the Fleet—"

"All those things, Loki."

"Do you know what I did to come here?" Lokrien says. "I deserted my post in the line of battle. I waited for a lull and turned my boat and drove for this outpost world to look for you. It took me all these years of searching to pick up the trace from your body shield circuitry and find you here. With luck we can concoct a story to explain how I found you—"

"Loki, I can't desert my home, my wife, my child."

"You'd let this savage female and her cub stand in the way of . . ." Lokrien hesitates. "I'm sorry, Thor. The woman is beautiful. But Ysar! You'd give up your whole life for this barn, these grubby fields, this petty barony—"

"Yes."

"Then think of your duty to the Fleet."

"The Fleet is only a collection of machines, once the dream behind it is gone."

"You think you'll find the dream, as you call it, here on this backwoods world?"

"Better a live acorn than a dead forest, Loki."

Loki looks across the gulf at the brother he had come to find. "I could force you, Thor. I still have my suit and my Y-gun."

Gralgrathor smiles a little.

"Don't try to decide now," Lokrien says. "We're both tired. We need sleep. In the morning—"

"In the morning nothing will have changed."

"No? Perhaps you're wrong about that."

"There are clean furs there, on the hearth," Gralgrathor says. "Sleep well, Loki. I need to walk for a while."

Lokrien's eyes follow Gralgrathor as he steps out into the icy moonlight.

Chapter Five

∞ 1 ∞

"Let me get this straight," the commander of the Lakewood Naval Air Station said grimly. "You're telling me I lost a pilot in broad daylight, in a *whirlpool?*"

"Not precisely that, Commodore Keyes," the colonel said. "There's a tremendous volume of air involved in this thing, too. Friction with the water surface, you understand—"

"No, I don't understand. Maybe you'd better start at the beginning."

"I have the recording of the pilot's transmissions here, in the event you'd care to hear it."

The commodore nodded curtly. The colonel hastily set up the small portable player, adjusted the tape. In a moment the pilot's voice was coming through crisply.

The two men listened in silence, following the recon plane's progress. The commodore's face was set in a scowl as the tape ended.

"All right, what are we doing about this thing?"

"The nucleus of the disturbance is centered on a point

northwest of Bermuda." The colonel stepped to the large world map on the wall and indicated the spot. "It's growing steadily larger, setting up powerful winds and currents over an area of several thousand square miles. Water is being pulled in toward the center from every direction, thus the whirlpool." The colonel produced a stack of photos from his briefcase and passed them across the desk. They showed a great, glossy-black funnel, wrapped in dusty spirals like disintegrating cotton-wool batting.

"Those were made with ultraviolet from about a hundred miles out. You'll note the calibration marks; they show that the throat of the whirlpool is approximately a tenth of a mile wide at the surface—"

"*How* wide?"

"I know it sounds incredible, Commodore, but I have it on good assurance that the figure of five hundred feet is accurate."

"Hopper, do you have any idea of the volume of water you're talking about?"

"Well, I could work it out—"

"How deep is the sea at this point?"

"I don't have the exact figure, sir, but it *is* deep ocean there, well off the continental shelf—"

"What kind of force would it take to get that much water moving at the velocity this thing must have? Where's the energy coming from?"

"Well, Commodore—"

"And you say water is flowing *in* from every direction. Where's it going? And the air: thousands of cubic miles of air on the move, all toward the same point. What's happening to it? Where's the outflow?"

"Commodore, we have aircraft out now photographing the entire eastern half of the country, and well out into the Atlantic. And of course the satellite is busy on this thing as well. I hope to have some results very soon now."

"Find out where that water's going, Hopper. There's something wrong here. We're missing something. That water has to be somewhere. I want to know where, before the biggest tidal wave in history hits the east coast!"

൦ 2 ൦

In the governor's office at Caine Island, Lester Pale, special aide to the governor, shook his head ruefully at his chief.

"The Grayle dossier isn't much, I'm afraid, sir," he said. "I have the documents covering his transfer from Leavenworth East six years ago; they're in order. And of course his record here at Caine Island. But prior to that . . ." Lester shook his head.

"Give me what you've got." Hardman spoke impatiently. He was hunched forward over the desk, raising his voice above the drumming of the rain that had increased steadily now for nearly six hours.

"I talked to Warden Pyle as you suggested, sir. Many of his records were lost in a file-room fire about twelve years ago; but he says that of his own memory he recalls that Grayle was a military prisoner, in for the murder of an army officer."

"Go on."

"The funny thing is, Governor, he was absolutely certain

that Grayle was an inmate when he took over East L,
nearly twenty years ago." He paused, looking dubiously at
his superior.

"So?"

"Well, after all, sir—how old *is* Grayle?"

"You tell me."

"Well, sir—Pyle called in an old con, a man who had
done twenty years of a life sentence before parole. He
works in the prison kitchens now. Pyle asked him what he
remembered about Grayle."

"And?"

Lester made a disclaiming gesture. "The old fellow said
that Grayle was one of the prisoners transferred from
Kansas along with him, back in seventy-one. And that he
had known him before that."

"How long before that?"

"For over ten years. In fact, he swears Grayle was an
inmate when he started his stretch. And that, Governor,
was almost thirty-five years ago. So you see what I'm talking about."

"What *are* you talking about, Lester? Spell it out."

"Why, they're obviously confusing the man with
someone else. There may have been another prisoner
with the name Grayle, possibly someone with a physical
resemblance. I don't suppose they've had occasion to
think of the man for a number of years, and now they're
dredging up false memories, superimposing our Grayle on
what they recall of the older man."

"What about the army records of the court-martial?"

Lester shook his head. "No success there so far, sir. I
have a friend in the Pentagon who has access to a great

deal of retired material that's never been programmed into the Record Center. He supplies data to historians and the like; they get a lot of requests. Just for the sake of thoroughness I asked him to dig back as far as he can. But he informed me just a few minutes ago that he went back as far as World War Two and turned up nothing."

"Did you tell him to keep looking?"

"Well, no, sir. That's already thirty-six years back. He's hardly likely—"

"Tell him to keep digging, Lester. You don't send a man to prison for life without making a record of it some-where."

"Governor," a voice spoke sharply on the intercom. "Captain Brasher to see you. He insisted I break in—"

"Send him in."

The door opened and the guard chief strode into the room, gave Pale a sharp look, stood waiting.

"Well, speak up, man!" the governor snapped.

"As I suspected, sir," the captain said, "Grayle's alive. He overpowered one of my officers and a state patrolman in a shack on the north shore, beat them into unconsciousness, and got clear."

"Got clear? Aren't the roads blocked?"

"Certainly. I don't mean he's escaped the net, just that he's still at large."

"How long ago was this?"

The captain's eyes snapped to the wall clock, snapped back. "Just under half an hour."

"Was the shack occupied?"

"Ah—I can't say as to that—"

"Find out. How did he leave? In the patrol car?"

"No, it was parked in front of the place. That's how—"

"Find out what kind of car the occupant owned. Meanwhile, watch every road. He can't be far away. And, Brasher—don't let him slip through your fingers. I don't care what you have to do to stop him—stop him!"

"I'll stop him, all right." Brasher hesitated. "You know he's attacked three of my men now—"

"That doesn't say a hell of a lot for your men, Brasher. Tell them to get on their toes and stay there!"

"That's what I wanted to hear you say, Governor." Brasher wheeled and left the room.

"Governor," Lester said, "I have a feeling that somewhere along the line there's been a serious mistake—"

"Don't talk like a fool, Lester. Grayle's commitment papers are in order; I have that much—"

"I don't mean an error on your part, Governor. I mean prior to his transfer to Caine Island. Possibly that's why he made this rather desperate break. Perhaps he's innocent—"

Hardman leaned forward, his big hands flat on the desk.

"He broke out of a prison under my command, Lester. I have twenty-one years invested in this business without an escape, and I'm not letting anyone blot a perfect record, clear?"

"Governor, this is a man's life—"

"And of course there's more to it than just my reputation," Hardman said, leaning back. "If one man crashed out of Caine—and got clear—we'd have every malcontent on the inside making a try. It would be a blow at the entire modern penological system—"

"Brasher will shoot him down like a dog, Governor!"

"I gave no such orders."

"Brasher will interpret them that way!"

"He can interpret them any way he likes, Lester—as long as he nails his man, I won't be overly critical of his methods!"

∞ **3** ∞

"I'm not interested in excuses, Mr. Hunnicut," the voice of the Deputy Undersecretary of the Interior for Public Power rasped in the ear of the chief engineer at Pasmaquoddie. "I've gone out on a limb for you people; now I expect answers from you that I can give to the Committee. They're looking for scalps, and they think mine will do!"

"I've already explained that there seems to be a transmission loss greatly in excess of the theoretical factor, Mr. Secretary—"

"Meaning the system is a failure! Don't fall back on the kind of jargon you technical people use to obfuscate the issues when things go wrong! I want it in plain language! Your generating station is drawing ten percent over its rated operational standard, while the receiving stations report anywhere from thirty- to forty-percent effectiveness. Now, just tell me in words of one syllable—where is all that power going, Mr. Hunnicut?"

"It's obvious there's a leakage somewhere, Mr. Secretary," Hunnicut said, holding his temper with an effort.

"Where? In the transmission end? In the receiving stations? Or in the giant brains that dreamed up this fiasco?"

"Mr. Secretary, this is a wholly new area of technology! There are bound to be certain trial-and-error adjustments—"

"Hogwash! You didn't mention that when you were pleading with Appropriations for another hundred million!"

"Look here, this isn't as simple a matter as tracing the point of breakdown in a conventional line-transmission system—and even there, it sometimes takes days to pinpoint the trouble. Remember the New York blackout in the sixties, and—"

"Don't give me a history lesson, Hunnicut! Are you telling me that anybody and his dog Rex can tap our broadcast system at will, and there's nothing we can do about it?"

"Wait a minute, I didn't say that—"

"The newspapers will say it! Give me a better line to feed to them!"

"Mr. Secretary, you have to understand, we have no instruments, no procedures for this situation! It's totally unprecedented, contrary to theory, inexplicable—"

"It's happening, Mr. Hunnicut! Better realign your theories!"

"We've made a start. We've rigged some makeshift field-density sensors, and I have four motorized teams out running retiring search curves, plotting the gradient—"

"Meaning what?"

"Meaning that with luck we'll detect a pattern that will enable us to triangulate on the point of power drain."

"Back to that! I can't give that to the press, Hunnicut! They'll drag in everything from Russians to Little Green Men from Mars! 'Aliens steal U.S. power' I can see the headlines now!"

"It's nothing like that! I'm pretty sure we'll find it's some sort of anomalous natural formation that's drawing off the energy! A massive ore deposit, something of that sort!"

"Hunnicut—you're babbling! Just between us—what do you really think it is that's drinking a couple of hundred thousand kilowatts per hour out of the air?"

"Mr. Secretary, I don't know."

"I'm glad you admit it, Hunnicut. Now, I suggest you get busy and find out, before I yank you out of that plush office and put in somebody with a little better grasp of the dynamics of modern politico-technology!"

"I'm no politician! I—"

"Locate that leak, Hunnicut—or you'll be back taking gamma counts on the Lackawanna pile!"

∞ **4** ∞

Anne Rogers stared out through the rain-blurred windshield at the almost invisible road surface unwinding ahead. At wide intervals the lights of a lonely house shone weakly through the downpour slanting through the headlights.

"There's a town about five miles ahead," she said. "We should change cars there."

They rode in silence for a few minutes. More lights

appeared ahead. They passed a gas station, dark and deserted. Anne made a left turn at a blinking yellow traffic light, followed a broad truck route for half a mile, then took a right into a narrow residential street. The trees lining the way provided some shelter from the rain. They moved along at a crawl, lights dimmed. There were cars parked at the side of the curbless street and in the weed-grown yards.

"They're worse wrecks than this one," Anne said, accelerating past an empty stretch. "We might as well pick a good one while we're at it."

"I'll rely on your judgment," Grayle said with a hint of humor.

Anne glanced at him sideways. "You were inside so long, I suppose everything looks strange to you. My God, what a terrible thing, to take a man's freedom away! I'd rather be killed and be done with it."

"It wasn't as bad as all that. There's a certain peace to be found in the monastic life, after . . ."

"After what?" she asked softly.

He shook his head. "You wouldn't understand, I'm afraid, Anne. You're so young. So terribly young—"

"I'm twenty-five, Grayle. You're not more than thirty-five?"

He didn't answer. They passed through a green light, went along a deserted block of elderly storefronts, a few of which had suffered incongruous face-lifts which accentuated the shabbiness of the neighborhood. They slowed at a vacant lot where a row of identical stamped-steel grilles and flimsy bumpers fronted a cracked sidewalk under a string of draggled pennants which beat in the wind like trapped birds. A faded sign read: HERB GRINER FORD.

"New cars," Anne said. "But we'd need the keys."

"Explain, please."

"You need the ignition key to start a car with. And even to get the doors open. They probably keep them locked in the office."

"Drive around the corner and stop there in the shadows."

She swung around the corner and pulled into the black pool under a giant live oak.

"Wait here." Grayle stepped from the car, crossed the street briskly, threaded his way between the cars to the back door of the small shed. He gripped the knob, gave a quick twist; metal tinkled. He stepped inside and closed the door.

There was a small desk, a plastic-upholstered chair with a burst seam, a calendar on the wall. Wan light from a pole-mounted lamp at the curb shone on a filing cabinet, a scrap of worn rug, a clothes tree with a battered hat.

Grayle tried the center drawer of the desk; it popped open with a small splintering sound. There were papers, rubber bands, paper clips, loose cigarettes, some pennies, a pocketknife. He tried the other drawers. The bottom one on the right contained a garishly colored cigar box with a curled lid. Inside were bunches of keys, four to a ring, each with an attached tag. Grayle scanned them: White 2 Dr Fal; Gray 4 Dr Gal . . .

The door beside Grayle made a faint sound. He turned as it flew suddenly open. A man stepped in, holding a heavy revolver in front of him. He was bald, middle-aged, bulky in a tan hunting jacket, water-soaked across the shoulders, the collar turned up. He wore round-lensed steel glasses, water-misted. A drop of water hung from the tip of his prominent nose.

"All right, just turn around and put your hands up again' the wall, boy," he said in a high-pitched, nasal drawl. He took a step sideways and reached for the telephone on the desk. Grayle hadn't moved. The man paused, his hand on the phone.

"By God, I told you to move!"

"Didn't Herb tell you about me?" Grayle asked casually.

"Hah?" The man stared. "What the hell you mean?"

"The idea was that I'd drop by to amfrunct the bater-pomp, the grillik frens. Just until the rain lets up, you understand."

"Oh." The man was frowning; the gun dropped. "By God, why didn't he let me know—"

There was a sound from the door; the man with the gun whirled, bringing it up; Grayle took a step, struck him on the side of the neck with his right hand as his left swept over the weapon, snatched it clear. The man fell against the wall. Anne stood in the doorway, a lug wrench in her hand, her eyes wide.

"I told you to wait," Grayle said harshly.

"I . . . I saw him get out of one of the cars."

"Don't nursemaid me, girl." Grayle picked up the keys from the desk. "Can you decode these notations?"

She glanced at the tags and nodded. She looked at the man on the floor. He was breathing noisily.

"He's not hurt," Grayle said. "He'd have shot you," he added.

"You're a strange man, Grayle. You'd really care if he shot me, wouldn't you? And even him—and those two policemen: you knew what you were doing, didn't you? You know just where to hit them, and how hard, to knock them unconscious without really hurting them. That's important to you, isn't it—not to really hurt anybody?"

"We'd better go," Grayle said.

"I *was* nursemaiding you," Anne said. "I suppose the idea you couldn't drive, didn't know your way around, gave me the feeling you were helpless. But you're not helpless. You're less helpless than any man I ever saw."

"Which machine?" Grayle asked brusquely.

"The white Falcon," the girl said.

"What?" the word was explosively sharp.

She stared at him. "We'll take the white Falcon. They're very common."

They found the car in the front row; it started easily; the gauge showed half a tank. There was a stale odor of cigarette smoke in the car; a folded map lay on the seat.

"They've been using this one. That's good. It'll be broken in." Anne examined the map. "We'll cut across to nineteen on fifty and head north. With a little luck, we'll be across the state line before daylight."

⊚⊚⊚⊚✳⊚⊚⊚⊚

At the top of the ridge known as Snorri's Ax, Odinstooth whines, sniffing the air. Gralgrathor strokes the old hound's blunt head. The dog's growl ends in a sharp, frightened yap.

"It takes more than a bear to make you nervous, old warrior. What is it?" Gralgrathor stares downward through the night toward the faint spark far below that is the firelight shining from his house.

"Time we went back," he murmurs. "The moon's down; morning soon."

He is half a mile from the house when he hears the scream, faint and muffled, quickly shut off. In an instant he is running, the big dog bounding ahead.

The servants are clustered in the houseyard, holding torches high. Big, bowed-backed Hulf comes to meet him, a knobbed club gripped in his hands. Tears run down his sun-and-ice-burned face into the stained nest of his beard.

"You come too late, Grall," he says. The big dog halts, stands stiff-legged, hackles up, snarling. Gralgrathor pushes through the silent huddle of housecars. The bodies lie outside the threshold: Gudred, slim and golden-haired, the blood scarlet against her ice-white face. For an instant her dead eyes seem to meet him, as if to communicate a message from an infinite distance. The boy lies half under her, face down, with blood in his fair hair. Odinstooth crouches flat at the sound that comes from his master's throat.

"We heard the boy cry out, Grall," an old woman says. "We sprang from our nests and ran here, to see the troll scuttling away, there . . ." She points a bony finger up the rocky slope.

"Loki—where is he?"

"Gone." The old woman says. "Changed into his black were-shape and fled—"

Gralgrathor plunges into the house. The embers on the hearth show him the empty room, shadow-crowded, the fallen hangings ripped from the sleeping alcove, the glossy spatter of blood across the earthen floor. Behind him, a man comes through the doorway, his torch making great shadows which leap and dance against the dark walls.

"Gone, Grall, as old Siv said. Not even a troll would linger after such handiwork as this."

Gralgrathor catches up a short-handled iron sledge hafted with oak. The men scatter as he bursts from the house.

"Loki," he screams, "where are you?" Then he is running, and the great hound leaps at his side.

Chapter Six

∞ 1 ∞

Aboard the weather satellite, the meteorologists on duty, as well as half the off-duty staff, were gathered in the main observation deck, watching the big screens which showed a view of the night side of the planet below. Faint smudges of diffuse light marked the positions of the great metropolitan areas along the eastern American seaboard. A rosy arc still embraced the western horizon, fading visibly with the turn of the planet. The voice of the observer on duty at Merritt Island came from the big wall annunciator, marred by static.

". . . the turbulence is on an unprecedented scale, which plays hell with observation, but we've run what we have through the computer. The picture that's building is a pretty strange one. We get a pattern of an expanding circular front, centered off Bermuda. The volumes of air involved are staggering. Winds have reached one hundred fifty knots now, at fifty miles from the center. We're getting a kind of rolling action: high air masses being drawn down, dumping ice crystals, then rolling under and joining in the main Coriolis rotation. The jetstream is being affected as far away as Iceland. All southern-route flights are being diverted north. Meanwhile, the temperature off the Irish coast is dropping like an express elevator. It looks very much as if the Gulf Stream is being pulled off course and dissipated down into the South Atlantic."

Fred Hoffa, senior meteorologist, exchanged puzzled looks with the satellite commander.

"We hear you, Tom," he said into his hand-held microphone. "But we don't quite understand this. What you're describing is a contradiction in terms. You have all that cold, high-altitude air rushing in: what's pulling it? Where's it going? Same for the ocean currents. We've been plotting the data, and it looks like a lot of water flowing toward the storm center, nothing coming out. It doesn't make much sense."

"I'm just passing on what the tapes tell me, Fred. I know it sounds screwy. And some of the data are probably faulty. But the pattern is plain enough. Wait until daylight, and you'll see it for yourself."

The general took the microphone. "Merritt Island, we've been studying this thing by IR, radar, and laser, and all we can make of it is one hell of a big whirlpool—just what that Neptune pilot described."

"It's not exactly a normal whirlpool. It's more like what you see when the water runs down a bathtub drain."

"Yes, but that . . ." Fred's voice died away.

"Now you're getting the idea," Tom said. "We estimate that two-point-five cubic miles of seawater have poured down that hole in the last six hours."

"But—where's it going?"

"That's a good question. Let us know down here if you figure out an answer."

∽ **2** ∽

A taxi was parked at the curb before the narrow front of an all-night eatery. The driver was inside, hunched on a stool over a cup of coffee. He turned as the door opened, gave the big man who came in a hard-eyed look, turned back to the counterman.

"So I told him, I said, what the hell, nobody tells John Zabisky how to drive. I says, look, Mac, I'm eighteen years in the hacking game, and I've drove all kinds, and I don't take nobody telling me—"

"Excuse the intrusion, Mr. Zabisky," the newcomer said. "I need a cab, urgently."

The cabbie turned slowly. "How you know my name?"

"You mentioned it just now."

"Who're you?"

"Falconer is the name. As I said, it's urgent—"

"Yeah, yeah, hold your water. Everything's urgent to you guys. To me this cup of java's urgent."

The counterman was leaning on one elbow, working on a molar with a broomstraw. He withdrew it and examined the tip, smiling sourly.

"Refill, John?"

"Hell yes, sure, why not?"

"It's worth fifty dollars to me to get to Princeton immediately," the man who called himself Falconer said.

"Princeton? New Jersey? In this weather? You nuts

or something? I wouldn't drive it in daylight for fifty bucks."

"You're off duty?"

"Naw, I'm not off duty. Why?"

"Your license says you'll take a customer where he wants to go—for the fare on the meter."

"Get this guy," John said, staring at Falconer's smooth, unlined face. "What are you, kid, playing hooky? Your old lady know you're out at this time o' night?"

Falconer smiled gently. "Like to come outside with me, Zabisky?"

The husky driver came off the stool in a rush which somehow lost momentum as he crowded against Falconer; he found himself eased gently backward. It hadn't been like running into a brick wall—not exactly.

"Hey, not inside, John," the counterman spoke up. "But you can take him in the alley. I like to see these wise guys get it."

The cabby whirled on him. "How'd you like me to come around there and cave in a few slats for you, loudmouth? Whatta you trying to do, lose me a fare?" He jerked his mackinaw straight and gave Falconer a sideways look.

"I'll take twenty now," he said. "Where in Princeton you want to go?"

It was a long drive through rain that gusted and swirled across the car glass like a battery of fire hoses. On the outskirts of the town, the cabby mumbled, peering ahead, negotiating the twists and turns of the road down which Falconer had directed him. The headlights picked up a pair of massive wrought-iron gates set in a high brick wall.

"Dim your lights three times," Falconer instructed as the

cab pulled up facing the gates. The gates swung back on a graveled drive. They went along it, halted before wide steps, a colonnaded veranda behind which tall windows reflected blackness and the shine of the headlights on wet leaves.

"Looks like nobody home," the driver said. "Who lives here?"

"I do." Rain swirled in Falconer's face as he opened the door on the left side. "We have some unfinished business, Mr. Zabisky," he said. He stepped out and turned; the driver's door flew open, and Zabisky bounded out, a tire iron in his knobbed fist.

"O.K., mister, start something," he bawled over the sounds of the storm. Falconer moved toward him; an instant later the tire iron was skidding across the drive. Empty-handed, Zabisky faced Falconer, an expression of astonishment on his wide face.

"That makes it more even, don't you think, Zabisky?" Falconer called. The driver put his head down and plowed in, both fists swinging. Falconer took a solid blow on the chest before he tied him up, spun him, held him with both arms locked behind his back.

"Ready to surrender, Zabisky?"

"Go to hell!" The cabbie tried to kick Falconer's shin. He gave his arms another twist of the cloth.

"Ask me nicely, and I'll let you go."

"Have your fun, mister," Zabisky grunted. "Break 'em off at the elbow. I ask you nothin'."

Falconer released the man; he turned at bay, fists cocked. His thick black hair was plastered across his wide, low forehead. He licked rain off his lips, waiting.

"Zabisky, do you have a family? Anyone who'll worry if you don't come home for a few days?"

"What's it to you?"

"I need a man who doesn't wilt under pressure. You'll do. I'll pay you a hundred dollars a day plus expenses."

"Shove it, mister."

"Two hundred."

"You nuts or something?"

"I'm offering you a job. I had to know something about you first. Don't feel badly about not being able to use that tire iron on me. I'm a professional fighter."

Zabisky frowned. "What you want me to do? I don't go for the rough stuff."

"I want you to drive my car."

"Two cees a day for a chauffeur?"

"It's my money." Falconer took out folded money, handed over two hundred-dollar bills. Zabisky looked at them.

"Where to?"

"Anywhere I tell you."

Zabisky considered. "This on the level?"

"Why would I waste your time and mine? Come inside and we'll talk about it." Falconer turned and went up the steps. After a moment Zabisky tucked the bills away and followed.

∽ **3** ∽

In the governor's office at Caine Island, Captain Brasher of the guard force stood before his chief's desk, looking uncomfortable.

"The house belongs to a Mrs. Talbot," he was saying. "A widow, age about twenty-five. Not bad-looking—"

"Never mind her looks. Where is she?"

"We haven't found her yet. But—"

"Any signs of violence in the house?"

"Not unless you want to include two men stretched on the floor," Brasher snapped.

"Did they see who attacked them?"

"They haven't been able to tell us anything useful. You know how these concussion cases are, Governor. Harmon says he didn't see who hit him. Weinert has no memory of anything since yesterday's ball game."

"What about the woman's car?"

"A fifty-nine Rambler, pale tan with white top, license number 40 D 657, dent in right-front fender."

"Has it been seen?"

"It went through the north causeway roadblock at twelve-thirteen. The woman was driving. She was alone."

"Are you sure of that?"

"The sheriff's boys went over the car with a fine-tooth comb, naturally. It was clean."

"Any other cars pass the roadblock?"

"Not a one. Most people know enough to stay home in this weather."

"What else do you know about the woman?"

"She's lived in the shack for the past couple of years. She had a brother who was an inmate here; he died last March. She used to visit him. I don't know why she hung around afterward—"

"Tell me more about the car. Was there anything

unusual about it? Any bundles on the back seat, rug on the floor, anything at all?"

"My boys would have caught anything like that. The car was clean. At the time, we had no reason to hold the woman—"

"Where was she going at that hour, in this weather?"

"She was on her way to relatives in the northern part of the state; she was worried about flooding—"

"Where in the northern part of the state?"

"Gainesville, she said."

"Get the names of these relatives?"

"Well . . . no."

"Does she have any relatives in Gainesville?"

"Well—"

"Find out, Brasher. And put out a general alert on the car. I want it found fast. And when it's found, I want it gone over with magnifying glasses; over, in, and under!"

"Naturally I've alerted the State Highway Patrol," Brasher said. "But frankly, Governor, I don't understand all this emphasis on the car. The woman obviously left the house before Grayle arrived. He found the house empty and broke in—"

"Any signs of that?"

"Well, the locks weren't broken. But—" He broke off, looking astounded. "By God! It's clear as day! The little bitch was in on it! They planned it in advance! She was waiting for him, with the car gassed up and ready to go—"

"Planned it two and a half years in advance—including the death of the brother? And I thought you said she was alone in the car. But never mind. Check on the car. Find out where it was serviced, what kind of shape it was in, whether she had any special work done on it. Talk to her friends. Find out if she ever met Grayle, ever visited the prison after her husband died. And Captain . . ." He held Brasher's eyes with a cold expression. "I'll bet you my retirement to your next promotion you don't find a thing."

The guard chief returned the glare. "I'll take that bet—sir."

༺ 4 ༻

Chief Engineer Hunnicut, arriving seven minutes late for his scheduled briefing of the officials assembled in the office of the regional director, USPPA, looked around at the grim expressions lining the long table.

"I won't waste your time with generalities, gentlemen. You're aware that some difficulties have developed in the first hours of operation of the APU station. In essence, it boils down to a rather wide discrepancy between rated and actual efficiency. This in turn suggests a power leakage, which at first glance appears preposterous. A very specialized type of receiver is required to draw power from the transmission field—"

"It was our understanding that nothing of the sort was possible," a jowly man with a mane of gray hair cut in brusquely. "I recall the objections raised in the early hearings, and the contemptuous way in which those objections were put down by you so-called technical people. And you have the effrontery to stand up here and tell us power is leaking—or being stolen—from the U.S. government."

"I don't know who you've been talking to, Senator," Hunnicut said. "But *I* said nothing whatever about power being stolen. I think it would be wise to avoid leaping to any conclusions at this point—particularly before you've heard what I came here to report to you."

"Well, it certainly appears obvious . . ." The senator trailed off.

"It's far from obvious. This is a new technology, gentlemen. Even those of us who designed and constructed the system don't pretend to know all the answers; I think it would behoove others with less knowledge of the facts to exercise some restraint in the ideas they spread abroad; those comments may come home to roost." Hunnicut swept the table with a challenging look. "Now, as to what we've turned up—it appears that there are at least two field discontinuities, other than those accounted for by the nine receiving stations."

"What's a field discontinuity?"

"A point of demand on the power field creates a distinctive fluctuation in the field-strength gradient. We're dealing with what might be described as force lines, analogous to the force lines of a magnetic field. When power is drawn, these force lines are bent toward the point of demand."

"Well—where are these illegal receivers? What are you doing about them? Whom have you notified? Do you intend to allow them to simply continue to drain off God knows how many thousands of kilowatts of government-owned power, and thumb their noses at us?"

"The pinpointing of these discontinuities is not quite so simple as locating an illegal radio transmitter, for example.

It's necessary to take a large number of field-strength readings, and to plot them against the theoretical flux-density pattern. Again I remind you that the state of the art—"

"We're not here to listen to a lecture on art," the senator cut in. "I've asked you a number of questions, young man, and I expect—"

"I'm no longer a young man, Senator," Hunnicut broke in. He felt his temper breaking at last; and it felt damned good. A feeling almost of exultation filled him. Here was a target he could hit. "And I have a sneaking suspicion these gentlemen didn't come here to listen to your expectations. I'm trying to tell you what we've learned so far. If you'd sit still and listen for a few minutes, you might find it unnecessary to waste time with pointless needling. Now, as I was saying—"

"Look there—" The senator started from his chair, but allowed his colleagues to pull him back and soothe him.

"—we're fairly certain we have two points of power loss to deal with, one considerably more massive than the other. The lesser of the two seems to be located quite close to the generating station, possibly in the mountainous area to the north—"

"What in the world is up there that could be drawing power from the net?" a thin, elderly fellow whom Hunnicut recognized as a state-university board member burst out, then subsided, looking embarrassed.

"We don't know. We're proceeding on the theory that it's a purely natural phenomenon—"

"How is that possible?" the senator snorted. "I seem to

remember being told that this entire system is a vastly sophisticated piece of ultramodern engineering, that the whole theory behind it isn't more than five years old—"

"Nature knows nothing of our theories," Hunnicut said flatly. "The sun was shining long before we understood subnuclear physics, radioactivity was heating the earth for five billion years before the Curies. It may well be that some type of geological formation was know nothing about has the characteristic of absorbing energy in the broadcast spectrum. That theory may or may not be supported by the other findings we've developed."

"No dramatic pauses, if you please, Mr. Hunnicut!" the senator interjected into the momentary silence.

"I'll remind you that this is tentative, gentlemen." Hunnicut ignored the barb. "But at the moment, it appears that the second demand point coincides with the center of the storm that's ripping the East Coast to shreds at the moment."

"So—what does that mean?"

"As to that, Senator, your guess is as good as mine."

"Very well, what's your guess?"

"My guess," Hunnicut said slowly, staring the senator down, "is that the thing that's creating the whirlpool is drawing its power from the Pasmaquoddie station."

There was a burst of exclamations; the thin voice of the Interior Department man won out: "You're saying that someone—the Communists, perhaps—are using our power system to create this storm?"

"I said nothing about Communists. But the relationship seems indisputable."

"Poppycock!" the senator barked. "You're attempting to explain away the failure of your scheme by conjuring up imaginary menaces. Russians, manipulating the weather, eh? That's the damnedest piece of nonsense I've ever—"

"That's not what I said!"

"But you implied it!"

"I implied nothing—"

"Gentlemen!" Peacemakers were on their feet, urging the two verbal antagonists to their seats. "This wrangling is getting us nowhere," an army colonel said. "We're here to assemble data, nothing more. Let's stick to the facts."

"The facts are that I'm recommending that the transmitter be shut down immediately, until the possible correlation can be checked out," Hunnicut said.

"Preposterous!" the senator barked. "That would be a public announcement of failure!"

"Impossible," the Interior Department representative said flatly. "The entire project would be discredited by any such shutdown—to say nothing of the problems it would cause those facilities that are now operating on the broadcast system."

"Very well; you gentlemen can act as you see fit. But I'm submitting my recommendation in writing to the Secretary, personally."

"If you do, Mr. Hunnicut," the senator said, "that will be the end of a promising career."

"If I don't," Hunnicut said, "it may be the end of something considerably more important than the professional future of one underpaid government employee!"

∞ **5** ∞

The insistent *chirrr* of the muted telephone woke the President of the United States from a restless sleep. He lifted the faintly glowing receiver and cleared his throat.

"All right," he said.

"Mr. President, General Maynard is recommending immediate evacuation of the Florida Keys. Governor Cook has declared a state of emergency and requests federal disaster action."

"Winds still rising?"

"Yes, sir. Over ninety knots now. Record tides along the entire south Florida coast. Water and wind damage as far north as Hatteras. No signs of any letup, according to Merritt Island."

"Tell the general to go ahead with the evacuation. Give him full armed-forces support. I don't envy him the chore."

"No, sir. I have one other item; I wouldn't have bothered you, but as long as I already have—an engineer on the Pasmaquoddie project, a man by the name of Hunnicut—"

"I remember the name, Jerry."

"Yes, sir. He's submitted a recommendation direct to Secretary Tyndall, over the heads of his direct superiors, to the effect that the power broadcast is in some way affecting the storm; making it worse, I gather. He's requesting authorization to shut down long enough to observe results, if any."

"That's a pretty extreme request, Jerry."

"Hunnicut is known as a level-headed man, sir. And he's laying his job on the line with this action. Still, as you say, it sounds fantastic."

"Check it out, Jerry. Get some other opinions—outside opinions. Don't let Bob Tyndall pressure you. Get at the facts. And see what impact this shutdown would have."

"I checked that aspect out, sir. There'd be no particular problem, except for Caine Island prison. They're on the broadcast net, as you know. And they've lost their back-up capability. The winds have knocked out the overwater cable, and their standby generators have been flooded. Without broadcast power they'd be in serious trouble."

"What about evacuation?"

"Sir, there are twelve hundred maximum-security prisoners at Caine Island."

"I see. All right, get on it and come back to me with firm recommendations by . . ." The President glanced at the glowing dial of the bedside clock. "Hell, I might as well get up and come down to the office. I'm not going to get any more sleep tonight, in any case."

⊚⊚⊚⊛⊚⊚⊚

The courier boat is hidden in the place Lokrien had described, a shallow gorge high in the mountains. The smooth green-gray curve of the U1-metal hull glows softly in the dark. As Gralgrathor slides down the slope in a clatter of pebbles, the entry port, triggered by the field generated by the bioprosthetics devices in his body opens to admit him. Hammer in hand, he strides along the glare-strip-lighted passage to the control compartment.

"Welcome aboard, Captain-Lieutenant," *a smooth voice says from above him. He goes flat against the wall, his teeth bared; he has forgotten that the ships of Ysar speak with a man's voice.*

"Commander Lokrien is not aboard at this time," *the construct-voice states.* "Kindly make yourself comfortable until his return. The refreshment cubicle is located—"

"Where is he?"

"I detect that you are agitated," *the voice says calmly.* "You are invited to make use of a tranquiling spray." *There is a soft* click! *and a small silver tube pops from a dispenser slot beside the conn chair.*

Gralgrathor snarls, swings the hammer against the plaston panel. It rebounds harmlessly.

"Attention!" *the voice says sharply.* "You are ordered to withdraw from the control compartment at once! This is an operational urgent command!" *A sharp jolt of electricity through the floor reinforces the words. Gralgrathor whirls and runs aft, slamming open each door, searching every cranny of the compact vessel.*

"Where are you hiding, Loki?" *he shouts.* "Come out and face me, and tell me again about the needs of the empire!"

"Captain-Lieutenant, I perceive that you are in a dangerously excited state." *The cybernetic voice issues from a speaker in the passage.* "I must ask you to leave the vessel at once." *A low-voltage shock throws him against the bulkhead; he turns and makes his way, stumbling, to the power-cell chamber door, smashes the lock with a blow; inside, ignoring repeated shocks, he takes aim at the massive conductors leading up from the coil chamber, and with all the power of his back and arms, brings the hammer down on the casing. The instantaneous blast that follows blows him into scarlet darkness.*

Chapter Seven

∞ 1 ∞

Inside the big house, Falconer ushered the cab driver into a high-ceilinged room with trophy-covered oak walls, a vast granite fireplace, deep rugs, low, comfortable furniture. He poured the man a drink at a mahogany-topped bar that occupied most of one wall adjacent to glass doors that opened onto a flagstoned terrace.

"I'll be with you in about ten minutes," he said, and left the room, went up the wide, curved stairway, along the hall to a spacious bedroom. He donned a heavy cavalry-twill shirt, whipcord jodhpurs, low boots. He strapped a lightweight holster under his arm, fitted a flat pistol to it, then pulled on a dark-blue navy-issue weather jacket.

Zabisky looked around as Falconer reentered the study.

"You got some nice pieces here, mister," he said. He pointed a blunt forefinger at a tarnished cuirass and a pair of crossed pikes over the bar.

"That looks like the old Polish armor," he said. "Sixteen

hundreds. It took a man to wear that stuff all day, I'll tell you."

Falconer nodded. "Indeed it did. You're interested in armory?"

"Well, you know. A guy's got to have a hobby," he said. "You got quite a collection here." His eyes roved over the array of weapons, plate armor, mail, the faded banners and scarred escutcheons. "Hey," he said, pointing with his chin toward a lozenge-shaped shield bearing a design of a two-headed eagle in dark bronze. "Where'd you get that?"

"At Vienna."

"Funny. I got a old beer tankard at home, been in the family for a long time, got the same picture on it. Supposed to belonged to my ancestors. The story is, we had a king in the family, once." He laughed, glancing sideways at Falconer. "I guess it's a lot of crap, but my old great-aunt Dragica, she's a nut on genealogy, you know; she comes up with all this stuff."

"Your name was familiar," Falconer said. "You're a descendant of King John Sobieski?"

"Yeah, that was his name. You heard of him? Geez. I'm named for him."

"He was a man," Falconer said. "Taller than you, big as an ox through the chest and shoulders, fair hair, but eyes much like yours. He had the gift of laughter. He was much beloved by his men."

Zabisky stared, gave a short laugh. "You talk like you knew the guy."

"I've read of him," Falconer said shortly. "Let's go, John."

"Yeah." Zabisky followed Falconer outside; in the drive, he halted.

"Hey, mister—there's just one more thing . . ."

Falconer turned. Zabisky took a quick step toward him, rammed a powerful right jab toward Falconer's sternum. Falconer turned half sideways, caught the wrist, brought it forward under his left arm, levered the elbow backward across his chest.

"O.K., I just wanted to check," Zabisky said.

They went along a brick walk; Falconer lifted one of the five doors on the long garage. Zabisky whistled at the gleaming shapes parked in the gloom. He walked along the line.

"A Jag XK120, an SJ Doosie, a SSK Mercedes, a Bugatti 41, ain't it? And what's that? It looks like a thirty-five Auburn. . ."

"It's a sixty-eight Auburn 866. New production."

"Man, you know your cars. Which one we taking?"

"The Auburn."

Zabisky whistled again, running a hand along the sleek lines of the car. "What's she got under the hood?"

"A Thunderbird 386-horsepower V-8."

"And I get paid too, hah? Let's go, pal. I want to see how this baby turns up."

They pulled out along the drive swiftly, noiselessly. At the road, Zabisky turned to Falconer.

"Where to?"

Falconer pointed.

"What town we headed for?"

"Just drive, John. I'll tell you when to turn." Falconer leaned back against the smooth leather seat and in ten seconds was sound asleep.

৩৯ **2** ৩৯

"The Highway Patrol found the car parked on a side street in Brooksville," Captain Brasher said. "Key in the ignition, nobody around."

"What kind of neighborhood was it?" Hardman asked.

The captain gave a lift of his khaki-epauleted shoulders. "After all, I wasn't there, I can't be expected to know every detail—"

"That's just what I do expect, Brasher! And I don't expect to wait until morning to find out what kind of car Grayle is driving now!"

The intercom buzzed; the governor jabbed the button savagely.

"Sir, Captain Lacey of the Highway Patrol on the line for Captain Brasher. Shall I—"

"Put him on." He picked up the phone, listened to clicks. "This is Hardman at Caine Island, Captain," he said. "I'll take your report."

"Yes, sir. On the Rambler: we found it in Brooksville—"

"Yes, I know. Any leads?"

"Looks like he knocked over the watchman at the Ford car agency; it's just across the street from where the Rambler was parked. He's still out, but when he comes around he can tell us if anything's missing from the lot."

"Good. Keep me informed." The governor cradled the phone and looked across at Brasher. "He took a car from the Ford lot he was parked beside. We don't know what model or color, but we can be pretty sure it's a new one."

He swiveled to look at the map of the state on the wall. "Lacey, I want you to watch I-74 and I-4, and US 19, north and south. Stop any new Ford."

"That's a pretty tall order—"

"Still—I'm ordering it!" He cradled the phone and turned to Brasher.

"I want a man on the scene—a reliable man, representing my—our—interests."

"Harmon," Brasher said at once. "He's keen, a good man—"

"I thought he was in the hospital."

"He has a headache that gives him a personal interest in nailing Grayle. They'd had run-ins before."

"Get him up there, right away."

When Brasher had left, the governor poured himself a stiff Scotch from his office bar, then keyed the intercom and called for Lester Pale. The man came in a few minutes later, looking troubled.

"Anything yet, Lester?"

"Nothing that makes any sense, sir."

"Let's have it anyway."

Lester spread papers on the edge of the desk.

"My Pentagon contact came through with a reference to a prisoner named Grayle—"

"First name?"

"Just an initial: T. This Grayle was transferred to Fort Leavenworth from Fort McNair at Washington, after a court-martial conviction for murder."

"Any details of the crime?"

"Yes, sir. The trial transcript is attached. It seems he was in an army stockade at the time of the murder."

"What motive?"

"It appears he knew the victim; other than that . . ." Lester shook his head. "Frankly, this is pretty hard reading; a poor photostat to begin with, and cramped handwriting—"

"What do you mean, handwriting? Don't you have a copy of the official record?"

"Yes, sir," Lester said flatly. "But in eighteen-sixty-three there weren't any typewriters."

Hardman stared blankly at his aide; he reached, plucked the papers from the other's hands, scanned the sheets, made a noise in his throat.

"What the devil is this, Lester? This is an account of a Civil War trial!"

"Yes, sir. The man Grayle was a Confederate prisoner, and the man he killed was a Union officer."

"Union officer?" Hardman echoed.

"There's one discrepancy in the story, though," Lester continued in a voice that seemed on the edge of breaking. "The rumor here at Caine Island was that Grayle did the job with an ax; but according to this, he used a hammer."

∽ **3** ∽

"Let me get this straight," the guard lieutenant said softly. "Are you giving me the kill order on this pigeon?"

"Not at all." Brasher's eyes stared through the other man. "But if he's gunned down in a fire fight—with witnesses that he fired the first shot . . ."

The lieutenant nodded, touched his tongue to his lips.

"Yeah," he said. "Now you're talking, sir. Blake and Weinert'll feel better when they hear—"

"They'll hear nothing, damn you! Keep this to yourself. But be damned sure you're in at the kill, understand?"

"You bet, Cap'n." The lieutenant patted the old-fashioned .38-caliber solid-slug pistol he wore at his hip. "I'll be there."

∽ 4 ∽

"We should leave the main road," Grayle said.

"We can't," the girl said decisively. "The whole road system of Florida was built to carry tourists north and south in a hurry. This was all unoccupied land just a few years ago; there isn't any network of farm roads and secondary roads like there is in most states."

"What about that?" Grayle pointed to an exit from the multilaned expressway.

"It just leads into a town. We're making good time—"

They saw the roadblock then: a pair of police cruisers parked across two of the four northbound lanes three hundred yards ahead, red flashers winking. Anne wrenched the wheel hard right, with a squeal of tires took the exit ramp.

Grayle looked back. One of the police cars was in motion, swinging in a tight turn around the central divider strip.

"They saw us."

Anne hurled the car down and out of the curving ramp, joined a wide, empty avenue glistening under the eerier blue glare of pole-mounted mercury-vapor lamps. Above high, concrete-retained banks, the fronts of ancient frame houses stared out across the traffic chasm like gaunt old men facing an open grave. A cross street was coming up; Anne braked, skidded, caught it, slammed over the curb and across the apron of a service station, missed a parked wrecker by inches, shot into the narrow mouth of a side street, sending black water sheeting. She cut the head-lights, slowed to a crawl, pulled into a weed-grown drive-way, reached across to tilt the rearview mirror. For a moment nothing stirred in the rectangle of glass; then light grew, became the glare of high beams, probing along the dark street. The flasher winked as the police car came slowly along the street. A spotlight beam lanced out, pushed hard shadows across the headliner. The car halted ten feet from the rear bumper of the Ford.

"Don't move." Grayle gripped the right-side door handle, twisted it silently, held it. Rain beat on the top of the car; faintly, feet squelched in mud, coming forward along the right side. As they halted, Grayle threw the door open, sending the man reeling back and down. He came out of the car in a lunge, stooped, and swept the gun from the hand of the felled policeman, threw it from him, flattened himself against the side of the car near the rear wheel. He looked at the angry, frightened face staring up at him.

"Tell your partner to throw away his gun and come around to this side," he said.

The man on the ground didn't move, didn't speak. Rain washed pink blood from a cut lip down across his face.

"Go for his feet, Charlie!" he shouted suddenly, and threw himself at Grayle in a scrambling plunge. A vivid double flash, the *boom-boom!* of a gun, from the other side of the car, whining ricochets. Grayle rounded the back of the car, straight-armed the man coming from the opposite side, sent him sprawling. He ran for the cover of the ragged junipers lining the drive, plunged through as the gun racketed again. He ran past the front of the house, ripped through a four-foot hedge, cut left, was back at the curb. One of the men was running heavily down toward the police car in the street. Grayle sprinted, reached it first, had the door open when he saw the second policeman grappling with a slim, furiously struggling figure beside the Ford. The running cop had seen Grayle; he skidded to a halt, bringing his gun up—

Grayle dived under the flash, heard the *spang!* of the solid slug against metal behind him as he took the man at knee height, felt bone break, heard the ragged scream of the man as he fell away. Grayle rolled to his feet, ran up the drive. The man by the car threw Anne from him; the slim, flat needle-pump in his hand made a harsh, rasping buzz; Grayle felt the blow of a fiery club against his chest; then he was on the man, spinning him, throwing the gun away into the darkness. He put a thumb hard into the base of the policeman's neck, dropped him. He lifted Anne, ran to the police car, tossed her onto the seat.

"Can you drive this?"

"Yes." The engine was idling. Grayle slid into the seat and closed the door; the car spun away from the curb, fishtailed, straightened out, its headlights burning a tunnel through blackness. Anne looked sideways at Grayle.

"Are you all right? I thought he shot you—"

"I'm all right."

"He couldn't have missed! Not at that distance!"

"Watch the road," Grayle said gently. He put his hand on his side; the heavy prison shirt was ripped; under it, hot blood oozed from his torn hide. Anne's eyes went to his hand. She gasped, and the car veered. "You're hurt!"

"Don't be concerned about me, Anne. We have more immediate problems—"

A voice crackled from the car radio: "Jig one to Jig nine-two-five, where's that report, Clance? Over."

Grayle lifted the microphone dangling from a hook at the center of the dash, pressed the key.

"Jig nine-two-five to Jig one," he said, holding the mike well away from his mouth and roughening his voice. "Busy; call you later."

"Clance? What was that?" The man at the other end called twice more, then switched off abruptly.

"You didn't fool him," Anne said. "They have directional gear; they know where this car is. They're tracking us right now."

They had turned into a prosperous-looking commercial street. Neon and glare signs shone through the driving downpour. A tall Sabal palm was down across the flooded street. The wind blew fallen fronds across the pavement. There were no people in sight, few cars at the curb.

Grayle picked up the map from the seat, opened it out, studied the street map on the reverse.

"There's an airfield shown here, nearby," he said. "The police and taxi copter port."

"Yes?"

"Turn left ahead. It's about a mile."

"You did say 'Police'?"

"We need an aircraft; we have little choice—"

"Grayle, I can't fly a copter."

"Perhaps I can."

"But—you can't drive a car!"

"I'm not familiar with ground vehicles, but I have considerable experience as a pilot. Do as I ask, Anne. As you said, we have no time to waste."

Anne laughed with a touch of hysteria, swung into a cross avenue toward a towering column of lights in the distance, doing a steady forty miles an hour down the center of the wide palm-lined street. A police car passed them, screaming in the opposite direction. As they swung around the periphery of a wide plaza, a second police car passed them without slowing. The avenue ran straight between wide lawns crossed by broad walks, punctuated by illuminated fountains. Ahead, the lake was blackness. Before a low building on the left, there was movement in a courtyard. Another car emerged from a ramp and sped away. There was a lighted gate ahead. A policeman in a yellow slicker stepped from the shed to wave them through. Anne gave a gasp that was half a sob, half-laughter.

"People see what they expect to see," Grayle said. "They don't expect to see us here."

There were a dozen or more small aircraft in sight; three large fifty-passenger crosstown shuttles bearing commercial blazons, several smaller civil craft, a big police riot heli, a number of small, fast two-man machines. At the far end of the line were a pair of squat, winged VTOL craft with army markings. The headlights shone on them in turn as the car swung in a wide curve.

"Pull up there," Grayle said.

Anne pulled the car to a stop beside the first in line.

"Good-bye, Anne," Grayle started.

"You intend to leave me here to face the police alone?" Anne asked with a smile that relieved the words of accusation.

"Very well. Let's go." Grayle jumped out, glanced over the small, short-winged machine, then swung up beside the canopy; he felt over smooth metal, found a lever. The hatch opened with a soft whirring sound. As he slipped into the cockpit, Anne pulled herself up, slid gracefully into the front seat. Grayle closed the hatch, studied the array of luminous dials. He touched a button, and a cockpit light came on.

Anne turned to look back at him. "Are you sure you can fly this?"

"It shouldn't be difficult," he replied absently; he touched another button, and starters chugged; the short, wide-bladed propellers to either side flicked over jerkily. There was a burst of vapor from one engine; it caught, and a moment later the second joined in, whining up to speed. Grayle found the brake release, gave the engines a burst of power; the awkward ship rolled forward on its tricycle gear, rocking in the wind. The nose wheel, Grayle discovered, was steerable by the wheel before him. He turned sharply, passing close to the guard shack and the fence, swinging back out to face the wind howling off the lake. Again he paused to study the controls. One pair of levers ended in blunt cones, not unlike engine nacelles and spinners. He grasped them and moved them up from horizontal to vertical. The nacelles obediently rotated. Now the propellers spun in a plane parallel to the pavement.

"Grayle—hurry! They've seen us!" Anne said. He followed the direction of her glance, saw men coming across from the gate at a run.

"Fasten your belt," he called over the shrill of the turbines. "I suspect this machine is highly unstable."

He opened the throttles; instantly the craft leaped upward, nose high, drifting backward. He righted it; the plane hurtled forward, rocking and buffeting in the wind. Lights whipped past, just beyond the stubby wingtip, dropping away. Grayle turned the craft, letting the wind carry it. The altimeter needle moved jerkily around the dial. The compass steadied on a course of 305. At an airspeed of three hundred and fifty and a groundspeed fifty knots higher, the craft raced toward the northwest.

ೲ 5 ೲ

"We're dealing," said the chief meteorologist, United States Weather Service, "with a cone of air approximately one mile in height and having a diameter of two miles, in rotation at the rate of one revolution each one hundred and five seconds. The rate is increasing slowly on a decreasing exponential curve and should, for all practical purposes, stabilize in another thirty hours at approximately one RPM, giving a peripheral velocity of about one hundred and ten knots."

"They're already reporting winds in excess of a hundred miles an hour all the way from West Palm Beach to Boston," one of his audience of high-ranking government officials comprising the Special Advisory Group cut in.

The weatherman nodded calmly. "Frictional forces naturally influence a large volume of air outside the nucleus of the disturbance. After stabilization, we should expect winds of over two hundred miles per hour throughout a belt about two hundred miles wide adjacent to the dynamic core, falling off at a rate of some ten knots for every hundred miles. At about one thousand miles from the center, turbulence causes a disintegration of the rotational pattern, creating randomly distributed squalls—"

"Good God, man, you're talking about a superhurricane that will devastate a quarter of the country!"

The meteorologist pursed his lips. "That's a slight exaggeration," he said carefully. "Now, as to rainfall, the estimated precipitation for the eastern portion of the country is on the order of twenty inches per twenty-four hours. I emphasize that this is an average figure—"

"Do you realize what you're saying?" another man burst out. "Twenty inches is more than some of the country gets in a year!"

"True. We can anticipate major flooding over the entire watershed. The problems involved in calculating probable runoff rates are complicated by our lack of experience in dealing with volumes of water of this magnitude, but it seems plain that the entire continental drainage pattern will be overloaded, resulting in some rather interesting erosional dynamics. For example—"

"Just a minute," a congressman interrupted. "Just how long is this rain supposed to continue?"

For the first time the weatherman looked faintly troubled. "Insofar as we've been able to calculate on the basis of limited data," he said, "there's no contraindication for indefinite continuation of the present pattern."

"What does that mean?" someone demanded.

"It means," the congressman interpreted, "that as far as they can tell, it's going to keep on raining forever."

"That's ridiculous," a Cabinet member said. "A storm draws its power from the released heat of evaporation; there's a definite limit to the size any weather disturbance can grow to. I should think it would be a relatively simple matter to calculate the theoretical limit, based on known factors of incident sunlight and so on."

"Normally, that would be true, Mr. Secretary. But the theory doesn't seem to apply in this case. You're aware that there seems to be an anomalous situation as regards displacement of seawater: the flow into the area of the whirlpool appears to be balanced by no corresponding outflow, even at great depth. The same is true of air volumes. It also seems to apply to the energy balance."

"Translation, please?" a peppery man spoke up.

"Easy, Homer," the congressman said. "Water and air are going in, and none is coming out. And the energy being expended by the storm exceeds that available from all known sources. Right, sir?"

The weatherman looked pleased. "Quite correct."

"So—what are we doing about it?"

The meteorologist's expression changed to one of mild surprise.

"Doing?" he echoed. He shook his head. "One doesn't 'do' anything about weather, Congressman. One simply observes it!"

"For God's sake, man!" A well-braided naval man spoke

up. "You don't mean to tell us that we're going to just sit here and watch the country blow away—if it doesn't wash away first!"

"It's the function of my department to report the weather, Admiral—not to control it."

For several minutes the room was filled with emotional voices, all talking at once. The congressman rose and pounded the table for order.

"This is getting us nowhere, gentlemen," he said. "What about it, sir?" he addressed the meteorologist and his aides. "Is there any action—any measure at all—which you gentlemen can recommend? Seeding? Nuclear dissipation? Anything at all?"

The weathermen were shaking their heads before the question was out. There was a moment of silence.

"I heard something," an Interior Department spokesman said hesitantly. "Probably just a crank notion."

"Well?"

"One of our engineers—Hunnicut is his name, I believe—has suggested that the storm is tied in with the APU power broadcast. He claims that he's pinpointed a massive power drain right on top of the storm center. As a matter of fact, he submitted a proposal direct to the White House that the system be shut down."

"Well!" the congressman barked. "Maybe he's on to something. Let's check it out. God knows the time has come to grasp at straws."

"Well, an idea like that . . ."—the Interior man spread his hands—"can hardly be taken seriously."

"There's only one way to check it out," a White House spokesman said. "That's to shut down the system. And we

can't do that." He outlined the situation as it affected the
Caine Island prison.

"So—the prisoners riot in the dark. I think we can survive that."

"There's more to it than that—"

"I know—the reputations of the visionaries who
poured ten billions of federal funds into the power-from-
the-air scheme. But they'll just have to suffer, as I see it. I
say shut down and observe the results."

"Congressman, that will take an executive order."

"Then let's get it."

There was a general mutter of agreement. The Interior
man left hastily, shaking his head. The Cabinet member
buttonholed the congressman.

"This is all very well, Herb," he said in a low tone. "But
what if the idea's as silly as it sounds? What do we do
then?"

The congressman patted the air. "Let's worry about that
when we get to it, eh, Homer? Right now we'd better go
see the President."

⊚⊚⊚✶⊚⊚⊚

*Lokrien comes up across the rocks, halts before the fire-
blackened entry of the ship, from which a wisp of smoke
drifts past his head.*

"Xix—what happened here?"

*"Sabotage by a Fleet officer," the ship's voice says. It
sounds weak and thin.*

"Fleet officer?" Lokrien looks out across the dark jumble of rock. "Thor—are you out there?" he calls.

There is no answer.

"I went out to look for you," Lokrien shouts into the darkness. "When I returned, your people attacked me like a pack of wild krill. Without the Y-field I'd have been killed."

A vague shape moves in the darkness. It is Gralgrathor, almost unrecognizable with half the hair burned from his head, his face blistered, his garments hanging in charred rags.

"Thor! What in the name of the Nine Gods—"

Gralgrathor leaps, swinging his hammer. Lokrien jumps back, avoiding the clumsy blow.

"Thor—have you gone mad?"

Gralgrathor snarls and moves to the attack. Lokrien avoids his rush, watches him fall.

The voice of the ship, faint and unnoticed, speaks across the darkness: ". . . fire damage to lift-coil chamber. Assault capability: negative. Defensive capability: minimal. Power reserve level: critical. Category-one emergency measures now in effect. Captain-Lieutenant Gralgrathor is identified as the saboteur . . ."

"You've wrecked my ship!" Lokrien cries. "Why? For the love of Ysar, why? Did you have to drag me down into your exile too?"

But Gralgrathor makes no answer. He struggles to rise, falls back.

"Attention, Commander!" the voice of the ship echoes across the tumbled granite, among the trees. "I will execute the traitor for his crime against the White Fleet—"

"No!" Lokrien approaches Gralgrathor. "There has to be a reason, an explanation," he pleads. "Tell me, Thor!"

Gralgrathor sways, on hands and knees. Red hate looks out of his eyes.

"I'll kill you," he snarls. "Before I die, I'll kill you."

"Commander," the ship calls. "Men approach!"

"Your mob," Lokrien says to Gralgrathor. "The same crew you set on me before—"

"I will deal with them, Commander," says the ship.

"Thor, go down to meet them, stop them, if you want to save their lives. Xix will kill anyone who comes close."

In silence, Gralgrathor climbs to his feet. Lokrien watches as he moves off like a crushed insect to disappear among the trees. Then he turns to the ship.

"Xix," he says in a broken voice. "What will we do?"

"We will survive, Commander," Xix says. "And one day we will right the wrong that was done this night."

Chapter Eight

∾ 1 ∾

"This item you asked for an analog check on, Governor Hardman," the FBI data technician said hesitantly on the grayline phone. "I'm afraid I haven't come up with anything significant. I've made runs keyed to every variable in the profile just as you asked, but I can't tie it to anything in the Main File."

"Dammit, man, here's a prisoner with no record of trial and sentencing—nothing but the mere fact of his presence here as evidence of any crime! There's got to be some explanation!"

"You've apprehended him?" the FBI man asked quickly.

"No, and the way it looks now, I'm not likely to! And if he *is* picked up, what the devil grounds do I have for holding him? I don't even know what he's supposed to have done, except by rumor!"

"It's a weirdie, all right, Governor. I'd like to help you. If you could give me some idea what it is I'm looking for—"

"I don't know! That's why I asked for the complete analysis on the few facts I have on the man—in hope you'd turn up something. I need a clue, a foothold. Dammit, in this day and age a man can't have lived a lifetime without leaving some record, some trace, somewhere!"

"Well, after all, Governor, if he's been in prison for over thirty years—"

"Nonsense! It's a case of mistaken identity. Grayle's no more than forty years old at the absolute maximum. But even if he were fifty, that would still make him a federal convict at fifteen! It's nonsense!"

"Governor . . . there is one little datum that popped up. Nothing, of course, but I may as well mention it . . ."

"Well?"

The technician gave a self-conscious laugh. "The tie-in, I'm sorry to say, is more apparent than real. You recall the confusion with the Civil War trial record linked to your man? I fed that in with the rest—and the computer cross-referred to an item that came in just about three hours ago. It seems that a doctor out in Saint Louis reported removing a bullet from a man's abdomen last night. The bullet was identified as something called a minié ball, a type of solid shot used by the army in the eighteen-sixties. In other words, during the Civil War."

Hardman made a rasping noise of pure frustration. "Civil War my left elbow! What is this, Tatum, some kind of in-group joke?"

"The computer is very literal-minded, Governor."

"Any description of this chap in Saint Louis?"

"Yes, I have it here . . . six-three, two-ten, blue eyes, gray hair, reddish stubble, well set up, and extensively scarred—or rather, there seems to be a little uncertainty about that last item. The doctor reported that when he first examined the patient, the man exhibited a number of prominent scars on the face, neck, back, chest, arms—all over, virtually. But an hour later, the scars were gone. Curious, eh?"

Hardman was gripping the telephone hard. "Where is this man now?"

"That we don't know."

"Tatum, you know people. Can you put out a pickup order on this man to the Saint Louis police? Quietly? And preferably anonymously."

"You see a connection?"

Hardman laughed shortly. "Grayle is over six feet, gray-haired, red-bearded. He's reported to have shattered a pair of chrome-steel come-alongs with his bare hands, and then tore the locking bars off an armored car—also bare-handed. Either that or he was carrying a three-quarter-ton jackhammer under his shirt. Now we have another big, gray-haired fellow out in Saint Louis whose scars miraculously heal in an hour. He was carrying a Civil War bullet. Grayle's linked to a Civil War killing. Certainly I see a connection: they're both impossible!"

"I see what you mean, Governor. I'll get right on it."

∽ 2 ∾

At the Upper Pasmaquoddie Power Station, Chief Engineer Hunnicut paced his spacious, air-conditioned, indirectly lit, soundproofed, gray-nylon-carpeted office. Beyond the wide thermopane windows the storm raged unabated. In fact, it seemed to Hunnicut, it had gained in ferocity in the last hour.

He paused at his desk—wide, highly polished, genuine mahogany—and flipped up the intercom key.

"Sam, how about that refinement on those loci?" His voice was brittle with strain.

"I was just going to call you, Mr. Hunnicut. Something odd here: the smaller one is tricky, very faint—but we've narrowed it down to a point in the mountains just north of here, within ten miles, possibly. The big one is pulling a lot of power, and we were able to cut it closer. It's about twenty miles—give or take five miles—off the west shore of Somerset Island, dead on the reported position of the storm center."

"Sam, what are the chances of an error in that placement?"

"Well, I talked to a buddy of mine at Weather in Washington about half an hour ago. He confirmed the plot on the whirlpool and swore it was accurate to inches. It hasn't moved since it was first spotted last evening. As for our fix—I'll stake my job on it. I said within five miles, but off the record I think we're within a mile. Kind of funny, eh, Mr. Hunnicut? What do you think—"

"Stand by in the main generator room, Sam. I'm coming down."

He pressed another key, spoke briskly to his secretary: "Myra, go ahead with the calls I taped earlier." He flipped off the set and left the office. In the corridor, the deep-bellied thrumming of the big generators buried in the rock below vibrated in the air, penetrating to the bones. It grew louder as he rode the lift down, passed through the intervening doors, became a solid thing as he entered the high, wide chamber almost filled by the big machines. Sam Webb was over by the big board, looking concernedly at the rows of three-inch dial faces. He turned as Hunnicut came up beside him.

"The curves are still upward," he said. "Leveling in about twenty-four hours, I'd guess. By that time, the big baby off Bermuda is going to be pulling a whale of a lot of power, Mr. Hunnicut."

"It would be, if we waited that long," Hunnicut said.

Webb frowned questioningly.

"We could shut down, Sam. We can use regular emergency procedures: shunt what we can into the Northeast Distribution Net and bleed the rest into the Erie Storage Facility. What that won't handle we can spread out over the Net links, let Central and Southeast handle it."

"Mr. Hunnicut—it's none of my business—you're the boss—but have you got an O.K. from higher up on this?"

"Don't worry, Sam. I'll take full responsibility for any orders I give."

∞ 3 ∞

The counterman at the all-night beanery waited until the quiet man in the gray slicker had seated himself and looked over the menu chalked on the dusty blackboard above the backbar before he lowered the newspaper and sauntered over. He shifted the broomstraw to the other corner of his wide mouth.

"Yeah?" he inquired.

"A man," the customer said. "Six-three, gray hair, blue eyes, husky build. Possibly scars on his face. Wearing a gray single-breasted suit with dirty cuffs. Seen him?"

The counterman's head jerked. He spat out the straw. "Who, me? I ain't seen nobody." He grabbed a yellowish rag from under the counter and began wiping the chipped Formica.

"Business is slow, eh?"

"Yeah."

"But not that slow. He was seen coming in here." The man in gray slipped a leather folder from an inside pocket and flipped it open to expose a small gold badge.

"I ain't seen nobody with no scars," the counterman said. "I don't care what some clown says he seen."

"What have you seen?"

The man lifted his bony shoulders. "Couple hackies . . ." He paused.

"Go on."

"There was a mug with gray hair, you know, premature like, big bimbo. But a kid, young, no scars on him; hell, he prob'ly don't even shave."

"When was he in?"

"A couple hours ago. Hell, how do I know?"

"Any idea where he was going when he left here?"

"What do you think I am, an information bureau? I don't know the guy, never seen him before. I'm gonna ask him where he goes next?"

"Answer the question."

"No, I don't know where he was going."

"He left on foot, or he had a car waiting?"

"He . . . didn't have no car."

The man in gray smiled gently. "You sure about that?"

"Maybe he picked up a hackie here. Yeah, I remember now. He come in here to tap a hackie was eating here. Tried to start trouble. I hadda throw the both of 'em out."

"Where did he want to go?"

"New Jersey, I guess. He said something about Princeton."

The man in gray nodded and stood.

"Thanks very much, Mr. Schutz," he said. He paused at the door and glanced back. "By the way—the business with the blackboard is cute—but I think you'd better close your book down. The cops are on to it."

The counterman's look followed him as he turned up his collar and stepped back out into the driving rain.

∞ **4** ∞

"It's certainly worth a try, Mr. President," Congressman Doberman said solemnly. "The Caine Island aspect of the thing is unfortunate, but in light of the situation—"

"If there's a legitimate technical basis for the decision to shut down the power broadcast, I'll do it, Herbert. What I'm questioning is the soundness of the proposal." The President looked at his special assistant. "What about it, Jerry?"

"Sir, Hunnicut himself is the leading authority in the field of broadcast power. The technical people I've coordinated with are all either students of his or his former teachers. All of them have the greatest respect for his judgment."

"Now, just a minute, Jerry," Secretary Tyndall cut in. "I have a few scientists of my own, I'll remind you. On my staff, that is—"

"What do *they* advise, Bob?" the President put in smoothly.

"They assure me that the idea is fantastic, Mr. President! A piece of hysteria, pure and simple! I'm not saying this scheme was set in motion by antitransmission forces, mind you, but if it had been, it couldn't have been better planned to undermine congressional confidence in the future of broadcast power!"

"All right, Bob, I understand your problem. You can set your mind at rest. No one's going to blame you—"

"It's more than that, Mr. President," Tyndall said. "It's not face-saving I'm concerned about now—not entirely, at least. A thing like this can be the straw that knocks the program out for twenty years. We can't afford that. We need APU—"

"All right, Bob, I believe you. And I trust you'll believe me when I say I'm with you. But at the moment we're facing a grave situation. If we have the power to avert disaster, there's no question that we must do so."

The Secretary nodded reluctantly.

"Very well, Jerry. Don't bother with channels. Get the power station on the line, direct."

The aide spoke quietly into the grayline phone. The others waited in silence.

"Mr. Hunnicut? This is the White House calling . . . Yes, the White House—Mr. Hunnicut, personally, please . . ." Jerry paused, listening. His eyebrows went up.

"One moment," he cut in sharply. "Who is this speaking, please? Mr. Webb? Mr. Webb, I'm calling for the President.

You are—please don't interrupt, Mr. Webb—you are instructed to shut down power broadcast immediately, until further notice. I repeat, you are instructed to shut down at once. This will be confirmed by TWX immediately. That's correct, Mr. Webb. Thank you." Jerry cradled the phone. The President was looking at him questioningly.

"Power is off, Mr. President," Jerry said, looking uncomfortable.

The President nodded. "That's done, gentlemen. Thank you for coming over. Please keep me closely informed of any results—and, Bob, I'd appreciate it if you'd speak to Ray Cook personally, offer any assistance we can give. I suppose it's possible to get some sort of portable power in to Caine Island . . ."

After the others had left, the President looked at his aide with a faint smile.

"Mr. Hunnicut was a mite impatient, was he, Jerry?"

"His deputy was trying to tell me something, Mr. President," Jerry said, looking his chief in the eye. "I didn't catch what it was."

The President nodded. "You're a good man, Jerry," he said.

"You're a good man yourself, Mr. President."

෨ 5 ෨

"I got through to the White House, all right, Mr. Hunnicut," Sam Webb said. "Or rather . . ." He shook his head, but the dumbfounded expression remained on his face. "They got through to me. It was a presidential order to pull the transmitters off the line."

Hunnicut smiled slightly, his eyes on the panel before him. The sound of the generators had changed; distantly, heavy relays could be heard, slamming closed. Needles nodded and wavered on the big dials. Hunnicut's smile faded, was replaced by a frown. A side door burst open, and simultaneously the telephone clanged harshly.

"Mr. Hunnicut! Big trouble! The transmitters have switched themselves back on again! The whole relay bank has gone nuts! Circuits are welding themselves, fuses are arcing over—"

Webb grabbed up the phone. "Yes—all right, we know about it, we're on the way!" He slammed the instrument down, at a run followed the others from the room.

Ten minutes of frenzied effort by a dozen engineers yielded no result. Power continued to pour from the generators into the giant transmitting coils.

"Look at this," a man called from a repeater board. "We're still being drawn on for a full load—but only two stations are drawing power—" His voice faltered. "And those two are . . . are . . ."

"I don't get it, Joe! What the hell does it mean?"

"Simple," Hunnicut answered. "The outlaw demand points are still drawing power—our total output, now. And they're going to keep on drawing power whether we like it or not!"

∞ **6** ∞

Max Wiston, number P978675-45, who had, three weeks before, completed the first decade of a life sentence to

Caine Island for rape and murder, was sitting on his bunk in cell 911-m-14 when the lights went out. At the same instant, the music of Happy Dan and his Radio Folks faded; the soft hiss of air from the ventilator died into silence.

For all of ten seconds, Max sat unmoving, eyes wide open against the darkness, ears straining for a sound. Then a yell sounded from somewhere nearby:

"Hey, what's with the lights? I'm tryn'a read!" The next instant, a bedlam of calls and yells had broken out. Max rose and groped across the cell, hands outstretched. He put his face against the bars; no faintest glimmer of light was visible anywhere. There were screams mingled with the yells now; to a latent claustrophobe, the total absence of light could be as confining as a tomb.

Max stood by the cell door, his mind racing. He had known from the moment that the sentence was pronounced on him that he would never spend the rest of his life in prison. He was a man who had lived out of doors, on the water, gone in boats, known the open sea. One day he'd regain the life that the bitch and slut had taken away from him. In the meantime, he would go along quietly, pretend to accept his fate—and wait. And one day his chance would come.

And now it had. He knew it. He could smell it in the air. All he had to do was think, make the right moves, not panic, not louse it up. Think. Think, Max.

Lights off, air off, radio off. O.K. No power. There was a storm, lines were down . . . . But there was something about switching to a new system, broadcast power. Maybe that was it. It hadn't worked out; new stuff was always developing kinks. So all right, the details didn't matter, the point was—no power. Meaning no alarm bells, no intruder circuits, no timed locks on the cellblock interlock . . . .

A dazzling thought entered Max's head. Gingerly, delicately, he reached through the bars, felt along the cold metal for the outer manual latch. Gently, he grasped it; carefully, he turned it.

The door swung open.

For a moment Max stood in the darkness, smiling. Then he stepped out, paused to orient himself, and started toward the guard post at the end of the passage.

∞ 7 ∞

"That's right," the service-station attendant said. "Some car, you wouldn't forget that one in a hurry. Two men in it; the driver was a rough-looking character, flat nose, bullet-headed, you know. Had on a yellow-and-brown mackinaw. The other guy . . . well, I don't know. He was asleep, didn't say anything. What I figured, he owned the car, and this other guy was his chauffeur—only he didn't look much like my idea of a chauffeur. Maybe—hey! Maybe the guy stuck him up, took his car. Maybe the guy . . ." The attendant swallowed. "Maybe the guy was dead!"

"If he were dead," the man in the tan car inquired, "why would the murderer carry him around with him?"

"Yeah, it doesn't make sense. Anyway, now I remember the guy said something." The attendant sounded disappointed. "Just as they were pulling out."

"Do you remember what he said?"

The man lifted his cap to scratch his head. "Something about . . . 'We're getting close. Steer a little more to the east . . .' Something like that."

"And this was how long ago?"

"Heck, not more'n fifteen, twenty minutes."

"Thanks." The man in the tan car pulled away from the pumps. As he accelerated to join the fast lane, he was speaking urgently into a microphone.

Ᏹ 8 Ᏹ

When Falconer woke again, the big car was bumping over a rough-surfaced road. The wind was still beating at the car, but the rain had slackened perceptibly. He sat up, instantly alert.

"Where are we, John?"

"West of Saint Paul a few miles," Zabisky said. "I had to get off the interstate."

"Why?"

"You said to steer east. What am I going to do, cut out cross-country?"

Falconer nodded. "I'm hungry," he said. "Stop at the first eating place you see, John."

"Geez, you can sure pack it in, brother! Sleep and eat, that all you do, fer Chrissakes?"

"I'm making up for lost time, John. I've been off my feed, you might say."

"There ain't no eating joints along here. Cripes, the lousy road ain't even maintained. I ain't seen a house for ten miles. And this lousy rain ain't helping any."

Zabisky hunched over the wheel, staring out into the rain, sweeping in almost horizontal gusts across the road. "Anyways, there ain't much traffic. Most people got better sense, in this weather."

Falconer glanced at the outside-mounted rearview mirror, saw a flash of lights, far back.

"How long has that car been behind us?"

The driver looked up at his mirror. "Geez, it beats me. I ain't seen him."

Two miles farther, the car behind had closed the gap to half a mile.

"Speed up a little," Falconer said.

"Hey," Zabisky said. "Is that guy tailing us, or what?" He looked sideways at his employer. "What is this caper, anyway, mister? I told you I don't want to get mixed in nothing shady."

"We're doing nothing illegal, John. See if you can gain on him."

"I'm doing all I can, fer Chrissakes! Fifty in this soup is like a hundred and ten!"

"He seems to be bettering that."

Zabisky swore and accelerated. The low-slung car veered from side to side on the single-lane road, bucking the squall winds. Rounding a turn, it broke away, went into a tail-wagging slide before the driver wrenched it back into the center of the road.

"Ha! Our pal back there don't like the pace," he said. His spirits seemed to be rising under stress. The Auburn roared ahead on a long straightaway. The speedometer needle reached sixty, crept toward seventy. Belatedly, the headlights of the car behind them appeared around the bend.

"Oh-oh," Zabisky said, watching in the mirror. "He's trying to straighten out the curve—" The following lights veered suddenly, swept across treetops, and went out.

"He bought it," Zabisky said. "Scratch one tail."

"We'll have to go back," Falconer said.

"Hah? I thought—"

"Somebody may be bleeding to death, John."

Zabisky brought the car to a halt.

"Who were they, anyway, cops?" he asked.

"I don't know, John."

"Why they tailing us?"

"I don't know that, either."

"For a smart guy there's a lot you don't know."

"Nevertheless, I'm telling you the truth. Let's get moving, John."

Muttering, Zabisky backed, turned, drove back along the narrow road at thirty. The headlights showed up a tan-colored car upside down in a drainage ditch. The front wheels were still spinning slowly.

"Flipped neat," Zabisky said, pulling over so as to illuminate the wreck with his headlights. Falconer opened the door and stepped out into the gusting rain, went across the strip of sodden turf to the car. It rested on its top in a foot of muddy, swirling water. Inside it a man was slumped against the cracked glass of the windshield like a bundle of old clothing. His face was half under water.

"Cripes, the poor boob'll drown," Zabisky shouted over the drumming of the storm. Falconer stepped down into the water and tried the door handle. It was jammed tight. He twisted harder. The metal yielded, broke with a sharp sound.

"Geez, the cheap metal they use these days," Zabisky said. He splashed around the front of the car. "We got troubles," he called. "She's tight against the bank. This door ain't opening, no matter what!"

Falconer felt along the edge of the door. It was sprung sufficiently to allow him to insert his fingertips under it. He pulled gently. The doubled metal flange folded back without budging the door.

"Hey, that guy inside ain't going to last much longer," Zabisky called. "That water's coming up fast! Maybe we can bust out the windshield—but I'd hate to see the mug's face after we finish . . ."

Falconer went to one knee, exploring the edge of the door below water level. It was twisted in the frame, exposing one corner. He thrust a finger through, levered the door outward far enough to get a two-handed grip. He braced his feet and pulled. The metal bent slowly, then folded back before springing open. Falconer reached inside, eased the injured man out onto the muddy bank. He was breathing noisily through his mouth. Water ran from his nose. He coughed, then breathed easier. Except for a swelling on his forehead, he seemed to be uninjured.

As Falconer stood, he caught sight of Zabisky's face. The swarthy skin looked yellowish in the harsh beam of the headlights; the stubble on the big chin stood out like greasepaint. He was shaking his head in emphatic denial.

"I never seen nothing like that," he said, staring at the ruined door. The latch dangled from the torn metal of the jamb. "I seen strong guys, but nothing like that. What are you, mister?" His eyes met Falconer's.

"I'm a man with strong hands, John. That's all."

"Uh-huh," Zabisky said. "Nobody's got hands like that—" He broke off as shadows moved. He whirled, almost losing his balance on the slippery slope. A car was approaching from the south. Falconer went flat against the bank. The oncoming car slowed, halted twenty feet away. A spotlight speared out to highlight Zabisky.

"Hold it right there," a voice called. Doors opened and slammed. Two men came forward, bulky in shiny rain gear. Zabisky stood with his hands held clear of his sides, not moving, watching them. One halted ten feet away, holding a heavy pistol trained on the driver's chest. The other one came up from the side, reached under the mackinaw to frisk the man.

"Hell, this ain't the guy," the man with the gun said. Light winked on the badge on his cap.

The other man was looking at the overturned car. "What happened?"

"He spun out," Zabisky said. "The damn fool tried to take the curve at seventy—in this soup!"

"Yeah? Where do you tie in?"

". . . I come back to see to the guy."

The man who had searched him pushed him, staggering him. "I like it better you ambushed him. What did you do, shoot out a tire? Or feed him a pill through the windshield?"

"Where's your partner?" the other man said. "Talk it up, Hunky. We don't like cop-killers a lot, even federal-cop killers."

"He ain't dead—" Zabisky started and was cut off by a

short, powerful jab to the midriff. He bent over, hugging himself.

"How do you like that, Roy, a glass gut," the cop with the gun said.

"He's laid out over there," Zabisky grunted, forcing himself upright.

The unarmed cop went over, looked down at the man lying on the shoulder.

"He's breathing," he called. He came back to stand before Zabisky. "Why'd you pull him out?"

Zabisky squared his shoulders. He stared into the light at the shadowed face of the policeman.

"Go knit a sweater, copper," he said. This time, as the cop's fist shot out, Zabisky half-turned away, caught the wrist, yanked the man to his chest, levering the elbow across his ribs.

"You," he said to the other cop. "Drop it or I fix your partner so he had to drink his beer through a straw."

The gun held steady on Zabisky. The cop twisted his mouth in a grinlike grimace. "What if I say tough lines, Rube? What's an arm to me, compared to a slug in your kneecap—especially if it's some other guy's arm?"

Zabisky backed, dragging the policeman with him. "You better be good with the rod, copper. Otherwise your pal stops the slug."

"Could be, Rube. Let's find out." The cop took up a pistol-range stance, body turned sideways, gun arm straight out, left hand on hip, leaning back for balance. He sighted carefully, still grinning—

Falconer came up out of the ditch in a rush, swept up the gunner, and in a single movement threw him clear across the road to crash through unmowed brush, sending water splashing high. He gripped the coat-front of the other man, lifted him, shook him gently.

"See to this man," he said, nodding toward the accident victim. "Come along, John. We've wasted too much time here." He dropped the policeman, who sprawled where he had been deposited.

Zabisky hesitated a moment, then went quickly to the car, slid in under the wheel. He watched Falconer get in, slam the door. "Mister—I must be nuts, but I kind of like your style." He started up, pulled off down the wet road with an acceleration that pressed both men back against the solid leather seats.

∽ **9** ∼

Grayle watched the instruments, holding the small aircraft at ten thousand feet, the airspeed at three hundred and forty. He paid no attention to the compass. Sitting in the seat before him, Anne stared out at the night, as opaque as black glass. The ship bucked and pitched, dropped abruptly, surged upward, rocked. The whine of the engines was an unending scream, like a cat in a fire.

Grayle was frowning, his head tilted. At the edge of hearing there was a sound—a faint, rumbling undercurrent to the background din of the roaring turboprops. It grew steadily, became a roar. Off the port wingtip, slightly ahead, an orange glow appeared, winking fitfully, sliding closer. A point of green light became visible, then a white one, above and behind it. Vaguely, Grayle made out the metallic shape behind them.

"It's a jet fighter plane," Anne gasped. "It's pacing us."

Slowly, the jet moved ahead. Just before it reached the limit of visibility, it banked up, showing its port-wingtip light, and whipped directly across the course of the smaller plane. Grayle fought the controls as the craft leaped and bounced in the slipstream. Anne pointed. A second jet had appeared on the right.

"Hold on," Grayle said. He threw the control stick sideways and applied full rudder, at the same time cutting the throttles and rotating the engines to the vertical. He feathered the propellers as the small plane veered sharply to the left and dropped like a stone. The altimeter wound down the scale, to nine thousand feet, eight, seven . . .

At four thousand feet, he engaged the props, applied power. The engines shrieked; the fall slowed. He leveled off at two thousand feet.

Grayle worked the controls, rotating the nacelles for forward thrust. For half a minute the plane streaked eastward in total darkness. Then the plane leaped as solid sound erupted around them. With a long, shattering roar, one of the jets flashed past. In the brief glow of its tailflame, wisps of fog whipped and tattered, ragged sheets of rain whirled, dissipating. Grayle put the nose down and poured on full power. At under one thousand feet he leveled off again. For an instant, through a break in the enveloping mist, he caught a glimpse of a vague shape flashing past below. He pulled the nose up, throttled back, glanced at the altimeter; it indicated nine hundred feet.

"Anne! On what principle does this altitude indicator operate? Reflected radiation? Or—"

Something dark loomed up before them; Grayle whirled to Anne, caught her in his arms, twisted to set his back against the padded panel as with a rending, smashing impact the plane struck.

꩜꩜꩜✹꩜꩜꩜

"Emergency measure must be undertaken at once," the ship says. "No time must be lost in returning to the battle line. I am operating on Final Emergency Reserves now. Unless my power coil is reenergized promptly, I will soon drop to a sub-alert state."

"It's going to take time, Xix," Lokrien says. "I can't leave you lying here exposed, to be picked over by every wandering souvenir hunter who comes past. Can you quarry enough stone to conceal yourself?"

"The energy expenditure will leave me drained," the machine says. "But I compute that it can be done."

Lokrien gathers a few items into a pack, leaves the ship.

"Commander," the voice of Xix calls.

Lokrien looks back at the sleek-lined hull.

"I will be unable to speak after this expenditure of energy. Farewell. Remember that I will be waiting beneath the rock, confident of your return."

"You were a good ship, Praxixytsaran the Ninth. You will be again, one day."

Behind Lokrien, energy thundered. Bolts of blue-white

fire rayed out to cut and lift great slabs of granite. When silence fell, nothing was to be seen but the tumbled rock, swathed in settling dust.

Chapter Nine

∞ 1 ∞

"Let me get this straight, Mr. Hunnicut," the President said carefully. "You're telling me that the sole result of the shutdown of the power broadcast is the plunging of seven federal installations into darkness? That two unauthorized and unidentified demand points are continuing to draw power?"

"That's about it, sir. Six of the installations are on emergency power or back on the New England Net—all but Caine Island—"

"Perhaps I'm tired, Mr. Hunnicut. How can these two bootleg receivers continue to draw power if you're no longer generating power?"

"Sir, that's the point I've been trying to explain. The station is still generating—and still broadcasting. When I shut down transmission—or tried to—the breakers arced over, welded the circuits open. I'm broadcasting whether I like it or not—and the same goes for the generators. I can't shut them down. The last man I sent in to manually disconnect is in the infirmary now, undergoing artificial respiration. We can't even get into the generator room. The whole thing is hot."

"Mr. Hunnicut, it appears to me matters at your station have gotten badly out of hand!"

"Mr. President, as chief engineer here I take full responsibility—but what's going on is abnormal—fantastically so! I don't pretend to understand it—but I can assure you that this is more than just a simple malfunction. Someone—or something—is manipulating the station—"

"Mr. Hunnicut, this is not the time to slide off into mysticism! I want the broadcast of power from your station terminated at once, by any means at your command. I hope that's quite clear?"

"Yes, sir, but—"

"That's all, Mr. Hunnicut." The President's face was dark with anger as he racked the phone. He swiveled on the men standing beside his desk.

"General," he addressed a compactly built officer in army green, "how long will it take you to move a battalion of troops into the Upper Pasmaquoddie station?"

"Two hours from the moment you so order, sir."

"Better get moving, General." He turned to a lean, white-haired man in self-effacing gray. "Mr. Thorpe, have the personnel you've selected stand by to cooperate with the army as we discussed. And in the meantime, let me know the instant your instruments indicate that my instructions have been complied with." The physicist nodded and scurried away. The President looked at the Secretary of the Interior, pale and owlish in the pre-dawn.

"Funny—I wasn't at all sure that shutting down the broadcast was the correct course, in spite of Mr.

Hunnicut's persuasiveness—but now that Mr. Hunnicut seems to have changed his mind, I'm damned if I'm going to change mine!"

֍ **2** ֍

Outside the office of the Governor, Caine Island Federal Penitentiary, a portable, five-KW generator chugged stolidly, powering a string of wan lights hastily rigged along the corridor. Inside the office, the governor gripped the telephone until his knuckles paled. He was shouting, not solely because of the booming of the storm beyond the thick walls.

"Possibly you still haven't grasped the situation here, Governor Cook! There are twelve hundred and thirty-one maximum-security federal prisoners housed in this facility, which is now totally without power and light! The PA system is inoperative. My guard force is scattered all over the prison, without light or instructions. Incidentally, the walls here are rather thick; with the air-conditioning equipment inoperative, the air is rapidly growing foul. At the time the power was cut, three hundred of these men were in the dining hall; over two hundred were at their duty posts in various parts of the facility. By the grace of God, almost seven hundred of them were secured in their cells. They're there now—in total darkness. However, the locks in the prison are electrically operated. When the power failed, they automatically went to the open position. When the men discover that—well, I leave the results to your imagination."

As Hardman paused for breath, the voice of the governor of the state of Florida spoke calmly: "I understand the situation, Jim, and believe me, this step wouldn't have been taken had there been any alternative—"

"You sound as though the power were cut intentionally!"

"It was necessary to shut down the transmitter, Jim. The President personally notified me, and believe me, the reasons he gave—"

"Damn the reasons he gave! Unless I have power here in an hour, Caine Island will be the scene of the worst outbreak of prison violence in penal history! I'm sitting on a powder keg with the fuse lit—"

"That's enough, Jim!" the state governor cut in sharply. "I have my instructions, you have yours. You're in charge of Caine Island; take whatever action is necessary to keep matters under control. That's what you're there for!"

"Now, look here, Governor—" Hardman's voice faded. He was talking into a dead receiver. He slammed the instrument down, swiveled to stare across the dim-lit office at Lester Pale. In the absence of the hum of the air circulators, the wail and boom of the storm seemed ready to tear the walls away.

"He hung up on me! After telling me that the power system was deliberately shut down! And *I'm* supposed to keep matters under control, he says!"

"Sir, I've managed to contact a dozen or so of the guard force, including Lieutenant Trent. He's issued hand torches to the men, and they're out rounding up as many others as they can find. In a few minutes we should have the majority assembled in the barracks—"

"And then what? We huddle here and wait for the prisoners to realize they have the freedom of the prison?"

"Lieutenant Trent is standing by for your orders, sir," Pale said carefully.

Hardman rubbed his hands up and down across his face, then sat erect.

"Thanks, Lester," he said. "I'm through making a fool of myself now, I hope. All right, we have a situation on our hands. Tell Trent to come up. I suppose our best bet is to concede the entire cell complex and establish ourselves here in the Admin wing. We should have enough men to control access . . ." He stopped talking, cocked his head. In the distance there was a faint popping sound.

"Gunfire!" Lester whirled to the door as it burst open. A man in guards' blue slammed halfway across the room before he came to a halt, breathing raggedly. He held a pistol in his right hand, pressing the side of the gun against his left shoulder. Blackish-red blood ran down his wrist and made a blot on his sleeve.

"My God, Governor," he blurted. "They've busted out; they shot the lieutenant, and—"

"I'll tell the rest," a hoarse voice said. A tall, rangy man in prison uniform, with weatherbeaten skin and stiff gray hair, came in through the open door. The guard-issue gun in his hand was pointed carelessly toward Hardman. The guard whirled with an inarticulate sound, bringing the gun around—

The tall prisoner twitched the gun to cover him, squeezed the trigger. There was a sharp *whac-whac!* The sound of the dope pellets hitting flesh was clearly audible.

The guard took a step back with rubbery legs which folded suddenly. He hit the rug hard and lay still.

"I'm not here to mess around, Governor," Max Wiston said. "Here's what I want from you . . ."

෨ **3** ෨

Grayle awoke with his face in icy water, the taste of mud in his mouth. For a timeless moment his mind groped for orientation: listened for the twang of bows, for the boom of cannon, the crackle of small-arms fire; for war cries, or the screams of the wounded, the clash of steel on steel, the thud of horses' hooves . . .

But there was only the beating of the rain, hitting the mud with a sound like the rattle of muffled drums. Grayle sat up. Pain stabbed at his ribs.

The girl lay across his chest, unconscious. He touched her face: it was cold as ice.

It took Grayle ten minutes to lever torn metal aside, extricate the girl from the shattered craft, and carry her across a furrowed quagmire to the inadequate shelter of the trees which the lightning flashes revealed.

He saw the path taken by the plane after it had struck the crown of a tall oak, plowed its way through massed foliage shedding wings and empennage in the process, to impact in a plowed field. It was a miracle the girl had survived.

He was forced to lie down then. The rain fell, the wind moaned in the trees . . .

Lights, and men's voices. Grayle got to his feet with

difficulty, feeling broken ribs grate. A line of lights showed on a ridge half a mile distant: parked vehicles, he guessed. The lights were moving across the field toward him. He thrust aside the breath-stopping pain, forced his mind to focus on the situation: the path of the small craft had been followed on radar, no doubt—but they couldn't be sure whether he had landed safely, crashed, or flown on at tree-top level. And that, perhaps, gave him a chance—if he moved quickly.

He bent over Anne, feeling over her for apparent injuries. There were many small cuts and abrasions, but it was impossible to say if she were seriously hurt. She needed medical help, quickly. He looked across toward the approaching lights—and at other lights, advancing now from the opposite direction. They had thrown a cordon around the area, were closing the noose from all sides. Time was running out. He must slip through them now, or not at all.

He scooped the unconscious girl up in his arms, picked a direction in which the lights seemed more widely spaced, and set off across the boggy ground, keeping his course between two lights. Once he dropped low as the beam of a powerful light traversed the field; but the same light showed him a drainage ditch marked by a growth of weeds. He angled across to it, slid down into knee-deep, muddy, swirling water. He flattened himself against the bank as two men passed by a few feet above, one on each side of the ditch. He followed the ditch for another hundred feet, then left it and altered course forty-five degrees to the right, toward the road.

He came up onto the pavement fifty yards behind the last of the three cars in line, moved up, keeping to the ditch. Two men in rainproofs stood in the middle of the road between the first and second cars in line. Both carried rifles under their arms. Grayle came level with the last car, a four-door sedan with police markings and a tall antenna. The courtesy light glared as he opened the front door, slid Anne onto the seat. Her head lolled on her shoulder. Pink blood seeped down her wet face. Her breathing was regular but shallow.

Something on the back seat caught Grayle's eye: a snug-nosed sub-machine gun. There was also a double-barreled shotgun, boxes of ammunition, and a web belt hung with fragmentation grenades. Grayle caught up the belt, strapped it on.

There was a shout; the two men in the road were running toward the car. Grayle crossed the ditch, came up against a barbed-wire fence; he broke the strands with his hands and ran.

Half a mile from the road, he paused, raised his head, pivoting slowly, as if searching the wind for a scent. Then he set off at a steady run to the west-northwest.

∞ 4 ∞

Zabisky slowed as the headlights of the Auburn picked up a dark shape blocking the road ahead. He halted twenty feet from a big olive-drab half-track pulled across the narrow pavement. A man came forward, swinging a lantern; Zabisky lowered the window.

"Road's closed," the man said. He wore a military-type steel helmet and carried a slung rifle.

"What's the matter, road washed out?" Zabisky inquired.

"Convoy coming through," the man said. He huddled in his green slicker, water dripping from the helmet rim. "Say, that's a wild car you got here. What is it, one of them foreign jobs?"

"Naw—made in Oklahoma. Listen, bud, we got to get through, see. We're on like important business."

The man shook his head, shifted the rifle to the other shoulder. "Nothing doing. You got to go back to Pineville, take state-road eleven—"

"We got no time for that—"

"Never mind, John," Falconer said. He leaned across. "How long will the road be closed, soldier?"

"Beats me, mister."

"What's going on?"

"Hell, who tells us anything? We get called out in the middle of this lousy storm, and—"

"O.K., knock it off, dogface." Another man had come over from the side of the road, a big fellow with a staff sergeant's stripes on his helmet. "What do you think this is, a Boy Scout jamboree?" He turned a black-browed look on the car and its occupants. "All right, you been told. Now get that heap turned around and get out of here before I have to get tough."

Zabisky gave the sergeant a long look.

"How about it, Mr. Falconer," he said loudly. "You want me to call your pal the general on the car phone?"

Falconer smiled slightly. "That won't be necessary, John." He had been glancing at the map. "Sergeant, it's a long way back to route eleven, and it doesn't seem to be going in the right direction—"

"Things are tough all over. Now, pull out of here like I told you—and you can call your pal the general and tell him I said so!"

Falconer opened his door and stepped out. The headlights threw a tall shadow across the curtain of rain as he came around the front of the car. The sergeant waited, his thumbs hooked in the pistol belt around his stomach. Falconer came up to him and without pausing drove his fist in a six-inch jab into the man's belly. The sergeant made an explosive sound and doubled over, fell to his knees. The soldier behind him gave a yell, fumbled his rifle from his shoulder in time for Falconer to catch it, twitch it away, and toss it into the ditch. Then he stepped in and slammed a short right hook to the startled lad's jaw. He tumbled down against the side of the car.

"Hey, you didn't need to slug the kid," Zabisky said. He had scrambled out of the car and grabbed the sergeant's pistol from his belt.

"A nice bruise on the jaw will help him when he talks to his C.O.," Falconer said. "Let's go." He started toward the big vehicle blocking the road.

"Hey—where you going?" Zabisky called.

"This is as far as we can go by ordinary car," Falconer said. "We were lucky to find better transportation waiting for us."

"Are you kidding, brother, talking about heisting a tank off the army—"

"You don't need to come along, John. Take the car and go back. But I suggest you abandon it at the first opportunity. The sergeant will give a detailed description of it as soon as he catches his breath."

Zabisky stared at him. "Why not tell me what this is all about? The whole thing is nuts—and this is the nuttiest item yet!" He jerked a thumb at the half-track.

Falconer shook his head. "Good-bye, John," he said. "I'm grateful for your help—"

Zabisky made a throwing-away motion. "Forget it," he said. "I told you I was in with you; I ain't quitting now."

Seated in the armored vehicle, Falconer looked over the panel, pressed the starting button. The big engine roared to life. He put it in gear, rolled forward, down into the ditch, up the other side, flattening a fence. He corrected course slightly, then settled down to steering the big machine up across sloping ground to the dark mass of the hills ahead.

∞ 5 ∞

Chief Engineer Daniel Hunnicut, his operations chief, Sam Webb, and two maintenance engineers stood in the brilliantly lit passage outside the switch-gear room of the Pasmaquoddie Power Station. They were dressed in heavy rubber suits, gauntlets, and boots; each carried breathing apparatus. Hunnicut held a black, waxed carton firmly gripped to his chest. The engineers clutched coils of heavy wire. Tools were belted about their waists.

"I don't know how much time we'll have," Hunnicut said into the lip mike inside his breathing helmet. "It's hotter than the main bearings of hell in there. You all know what to do. No waste motion, no false moves. We place the charges, fix detonators, and get out. Any questions?"

The three men shook their heads.

"Then let's go." Hunnicut undogged the heavy door, swung it outward. A blast of light and heat struck at him, scorching even through the insulated suit. At once, the cooling units went into high-speed operation. The chief engineer led the way across the high-ceilinged room, past a gray-bright patch of solidified metal snaking across the floor to the base of the main breaker bank. He placed the carton on the floor; the wax was melting, trickling down the sides. His fingers in the thick gauntlets were clumsy, tearing away the paper wrappings. He lifted out the cigar-shaped charges of explosive, linked together in clusters of four, handed them to Webb, who swiftly inserted them at the previously selected points around the base of the massive apparatus. One of the engineers began attaching linking wires. The other busied himself laying a heavy cable across the floor.

"That's all of them," Hunnicut said. Webb nodded, tucking the last charge in place. The engineers linked up their wires, rose to their feet, looking to Hunnicut.

"Out," he said. The three men went past him to the door. The two engineers passed through into the corridor. Webb paused to glance back. He froze, pointed past Hunnicut. The latter turned. A coil of smoke was rising from the insulated wire attached to the lowest cluster of explosives. Hunnicut took a step toward it. Webb yelled, jumped after his chief as the wire burned through. The charge dropped to the floor. Hunnicut took a quick step, bent to pick up the smoking charge—

The men in the passage were thrown from their feet by the terrific, booming blast. Acoustical panels dropped.

from the ceiling. Through the dust boiling from the door-less opening to the switch-gear room, they caught a glimpse of a tattered thing of rags that fell away from the scorched and shattered wall opposite the entry.

Later examination identified Webb by the fillings in a surviving jaw fragment. No recognizable portion of Hunnicut was ever recovered.

Power continued to flow from the generators to the great antenna arrays of the Upper Pasmaquoddie Power Station.

෧෧෧෨ ✳ ෨෧෧෧

For two weeks Gralgrathor has lain on a bed of stretched hides in the great hall of Björnholm, taking no food, swallowing only the mixture of wine and water that the old crone Siv presses on him before she and the other serving women perform the daily ritual of stripping away the dried, salt-impregnated cloths from the massive burn areas, tearing away along with them the day's accumulation of dead tissue, after which they smear reeking bearfat over him and rebandage him.

On the fifteenth day, he rises for the first time. The servants find him on the floor and lift him back to his bed. Two days later, he walks unaided to the door. Thereafter, he walks a little each day, swinging his arms, stretching the healing skin until the sweat of pain stands across his forehead. During the following days he practices with his weapons until he has regained a measure of his former skill. In the evenings, he roams the hills with the hound Odinstooth at his heels. During this time he says no more than a dozen words a day. He tolerates no reference to his dead wife and child, or to the were-demon who slew them on his doorstep.

A month has passed when Gralgrathor climbs the steep escarpment to the ravine where the boat had lain. He finds a vast crater of broken rock, already overgrown with wild berry vines. He stands, looking down at it for a long time. Then he makes his way back to his hall.

The next day he calls his household together and makes distribution of his lands and possessions among his servants. With only the aging Hulf as companion, and carrying only a leather-thonged hammer as weapon, he sets off on foot along the shore to the south.

Chapter Ten

∞ 1 ∞

Three men sat in a staff car parked beside the road opposite the exotic-looking civilian car abandoned by the hijackers. In the front seat were Captain Zwicky of the U.S. First Army and Lieutenant Harmon of the Florida State Police, in mufti. In the rear, Sergeant Milton Gassman slumped, his round face waxy-gray in the yellow glow of the dome light.

"Let's hear that one more time, Gassman," Zwicky said crisply. He spoke loudly, over the drum of the rain. "You and Bogen were manning your posts, a car with two unarmed civilians drives up, and then—what?"

"The guy tricked me, like I said, Cap'n. He talks nice, he looks harmless—"

"You're sure about the face?" Harmon cut in. "No scars? None at all?"

"I'm sure. I tell you, the guy was baby-faced, not even sunburned—"

"But his hair was gray?"

"Yeah, gray. I thought at first he was blond, but I seen

157

him good in the light. But he's no old duffer. He had a wallop like a mule." Gassman rubbed his ribs gently.

"That's our boy," Harmon said. "I don't know how he covers so much ground so fast, but it's him, all right. We'll get him now. He can't be far from here in twenty minutes. A copter—"

"It's not so easy," Zwicky said. "He took off cross-country, and in this weather no copter is flying."

"Where he can go, we can follow him! He took your half-track; O.K.; so we follow him in a half-track—"

"Sure—I'll have one here in another ten minutes. That gives your man a half-hour start. If he knows how to handle a track—and I've got a hunch he does—he'll hold that lead. And up where he's headed, there are plenty of places to get lost. He'll ditch the track and—"

"You saying he's too much for the U.S. Army?"

"I'm just saying hold your horses, Mr. Harmon. I had a phone call that told me to take you along, but it didn't say anything about turning command of the company over to you. I have men and equipment to think of, in addition to a little chore of convoy escort the colonel kind of hoped I'd see to."

"Sure, sure, I'm not trying to tell you your business. But it gravels me to have to sit here and let the cop-killing son of a bitch slip through my fingers!"

"When did he kill a cop? My information was the guy broke out of jail, that's all."

"O.K., you want to get technical, he just roughed up a few cops, maybe they'll live, it's all the same to this boy."

Captain Zwicky looked hard at Harmon. "You take your job pretty personally, don't you?"

"You might say I got a personal stake in this deal."

"Just remember you're a long way out of your jurisdiction. And this is army business."

"Yeah, sure. I won't get in your way, Zwicky."

"Better make that 'Captain Zwicky' as long as you're attached to my command, Harmon."

Harmon smiled sardonically, sketched a two-finger salute—

"We don't play games with the military courtesies in this outfit, Harmon," the captain snapped. Harmon's heavy face blanked, tried a grin, then a frown. He sat up in the seat, yanked his lapels straight.

"O.K., excuse me, for Chrissake. I'm not pushing. I'm just along for the ride."

"That's right. I advise you to remember it."

In a heavy silence, they waited for the arrival of the half-track.

∞ 2 ∞

Twelve miles to the north-northwest, Colonel Ajax Pyler of the Third Armored Division, First Army, stood with a trio of regimental staff officers in the scant shelter of a big pine tree on the long slope of ground rising toward the blazing lights of the power station half a mile distant. On the road, the convoy, with dimmed headlights, stretched for five hundred yards back into the darkness. Cold rain drove at the colonel's face, blurred the lenses of the binoculars he held trained on the power station.

"Everything looks normal, Cal," he said, handing the glasses to a burly major beside him.

"I still don't get it, Colonel," the major said. "Sending a regiment of armor in here . . . what are we supposed to do, guard the place? Take a look and go home? Jesus!" He wiped rainwater from his forehead with a finger and shook his head. "Sometimes I think they're all nuts up topside."

"I'm in the dark too, Cal. My orders were to position the regiment and stand by, that's all."

"Call this a position?" The major waved at the line of vehicles.

"As far as I know, we aren't expected to attack," the colonel said with a bleak smile. He clapped the shorter man on the back. "Cheer up, Cal. We all needed the exercise—"

"Sir!" the communication tech sergeant was at the colonel's side with a field telephone. "Division on the line."

"Colonel Pyler," the officer said, turning his back to the pelting rain. He listened, frowning.

"Yes, yes . . . I understand. About ten minutes, I'd say." He looked toward the lights of the power station as he handed the instrument back to the comm man.

"All right, gentlemen," he addressed the officers standing by. "Position your units around the periphery of a half-mile circle centered on the station—guns pointing in. Cal—detach six men under a company officer, have them stand by to escort a party of civilians in." He made a motion of dismissal as several officers started to speak at once. "That's it, gentlemen. Move out." Accompanied by the sergeant, Pyler walked back to the road, went along the line of looming light and medium tanks to the weapons carrier where his driver waited. At his instruction, the driver turned, drove back to the rear of the column. Three men in civilian clothes and raincoats stepped out of an olive-drab staff car and came over.

"All right, Mr. Crick, gentlemen, we're to proceed." The civilians, two of whom carried heavy canvas equipment kits, climbed into the high-wheeled vehicle. It turned, rolled back up past the column. At the head of the line, two jeeps waited, each carrying four men. They fell in behind. In silence the three cars proceeded along the road, following a gentle curve up the gradual slope. Ahead, a gate flanked by massive brick walls blocked the way.

While the headlights dazzled on the steel panels, two men stepped down and went forward. There was a telephone box mounted on the wall. One of the men, a lieutenant with a slung carbine, spoke into the phone. Almost at once the gates slid back. The men reentered the jeep and the three-vehicle convoy rolled ahead.

The road led straight up a number-three grade to the high, blank walls of the power plant and the towering, light-spangled antenna farm spreading up the hillside behind it. A number of men were standing before the lighted entry to the big building. Pyler halted the ton-and-a-half and climbed down.

"Thank God you're here, Colonel," the first of the men on foot blurted as he came up. "It's been a nightmare ever since the explosion, phones out, automatic systems out, instruments out—"

"Hold on, sir," the colonel cut him off. "Better take it from the beginning—and let's get my technical people in on this." He waited until the three civilians had gathered around. By then three more men had arrived from the plant. The rain swirled and churned around them; in the glare of headlights, a million tiny crystalline tulips sprouted on the glistening pavement.

"I'm Prescott, maintenance chief," the plant man said. "Hunnicut left me in charge when he and Webb went in with explosives to blast the switch gear out of the circuit. It was all fused down, you know. Wilson went in earlier, and—but I suppose you know about that; Hunnicut reported it. Wilson died, by the way. Anyway, something went wrong, we don't know what. Hunnicut and Webb were blown to atoms—for nothing. Everything's still running full-blast—"

"You say Hunnicut is dead?" one of the civilians cut in.

"That's right. And Sam Webb, our ops chief—"

"All right, let's get down to specifics," another of the newcomers said briskly. "Give us a breakdown on exactly what's been going on here. All we've had is some garbled story that the generators won't let themselves be shut down—"

"That's not garbled, brother, that's the God's truth. And . . ." The excited man went on with his account of the events of the last three hours.

The three imported experts listened in silence, with only an occasional terse question.

". . . don't know what else to try," Prescott concluded. "At every point where we might have broken the circuits, the gear has fused and the surrounding areas are electrified—hot as firecrackers! We can't even get close!"

"Well?" Pyler demanded of his crew. "What about it? If

Prescott's right, any ideas you may have had about walking in and throwing switches are out of the window."

"I'd like to see some of this for myself," the tallest of the three civilians said. "Not that I doubt Mr. Prescott's word . . ."

"Go ahead; you'll find just what I said. But for God's sake wear protective gear!"

"Oh, I don't think that will be necessary—"

"Do as he suggests, Mr. Tadlor," Pyler ordered.

With an amused smile, Tadlor complied, donning gear from the kit he carried. His two colleagues did likewise.

"My orders are to stand by outside the building until you gentlemen give me an all-clear," Pyler growled. "Make it fast." He turned to Prescott. "How close can I bring my vehicles?"

"So far there haven't been any manifestations outside the building proper, except at the switch houses," the man said doubtfully.

Pyler gave an order; the cars pulled forward, the men walking beside them. Under the loom of the high portico, they halted. Tadlor and aides, with Prescott, started up the steps. The doors swung abruptly open. A man staggered out, clutching himself. The sleeves of his shirt were shredded, and blood ran down his arms and dripped from his elbows. There was a scarlet blister as big as the palm of a hand along the side of his neck and jaw.

"Nagle! What happened?" Prescott rushed forward to support the man. Behind him, two more men appeared, supporting a limp female form between them.

"The whole place . . . hot . . ." Nagle crumpled. Tadlor stared at the man, went past him and up the steps, his two men behind him. Prescott called, "Colonel, don't let them—"

Tadlor's hand went out to the door. A blue spark crackled, jumped to meet him. For an instant a halo danced about the tall, lean man, then he made a comical leap into the air, fell sprawling, clownlike. His two men halted, then ran forward, bent over him. One straightened, looked down with wide eyes in a clay-pale face.

"He's dead."

"Get him back to the convoy, into a respirator!" Pyler called, motioning swiftly to the armed soldiers from the jeep.

One of the men who had helped the girl from the building turned quickly, caught Pyler's arm.

"Don't try," he croaked. "Too late."

"What do you mean?" Prescott snapped.

"You saw what happened to that fellow . . ." The man tilted his head at Tadlor's inert body.

"But—I still have forty-odd people inside—"

"Not anymore, Mr. Prescott. You left just in time. The place went crazy a few seconds after you went out. Dick and Van and I were the last to get clear. We found Jill just inside. I think she's dead. And so will anybody be who tried to go into that hellhole!"

"Into the vehicles, fast!" Pyler snapped. "Everybody!" He waited until the last man was aboard, then climbed into the weapons carrier. Behind him, Prescott leaned forward.

"Colonel—what are you going to do?"

"Tadlor's approach didn't work," he said. "So we'll try more direct methods."

"But—what . . .?"

Pyler looked back at the man, his eyes wild in a pale, round face. "We'll see what effect a few rounds of one-hundred-millimeter through the front door have on—on whatever it is we're fighting," he finished grimly.

☞ 3 ☜

The twin engines of the stolen half-track roared; the tracks churned futilely. The rear of the heavy vehicle sank deeper into the mud while the front wheels remained locked in the trap of broken rock that had halted the slow upward climb.

"This is as far as this bucket goes," Zabisky said. In the pale glow of the instrumental lights his round face shone with sweat. "Now what?"

Falconer unstrapped, swung open the steel door, stepped down into a soup of muck and broken rock. He scanned the horizon all around, then reached back in the vehicle to switch off the hooded driving lights. In the abrupt darkness, a faint glow was visible in the sky through the trees clothing the slope to the left.

"A little reconnaissance," Falconer said. He made his way up through brush to the ridge, looked down across the spread of dark countryside at a rectilinear arrange-ment of lights perhaps two miles away. Other, smaller lights ringed the central concentration in a loose circle a mile in diameter.

Zabisky arrived, puffing. "Brother, you move fast in the dark." He stared in the direction Falconer was looking.

"What's that? Looks like some kind of plant. This what we been looking for?"

"No."

"Funny place for a factory, out in the sticks fifty miles from noplace."

Light winked brilliantly below: once, twice, three times. Some of the lights of the central installation faded.

"Hey—what gives?" Zabisky grunted. A dull *carrump, carrump . . . carrump* floated up to them.

"Artillery fire," Falconer said.

"Look, pal, you ain't here to get mixed up with the army, I hope?"

"By no means."

"Maybe you better tell me what this is all about, huh? I don't want to get the U.S. infantry mad at me. I'm pretty dumb, but there's got to be a connection: you busting a gut to get to this patch of noplace just when somebody starts shooting. What are you, some kind of foreign spy? Or what?"

Falconer turned to Zabisky. "You'd better go back, John. I'm going on from here on foot—alone."

"Hey, wait a minute," Zabisky protested. "Just like that, you're going to walk off into the woods and—"

"That's right, John. You can make it back to the road by dawn."

"Have a heart, mister," Zabisky protested. "I come this far. What's all this? What's the shooting? Why—"

"Good-bye, John." Falconer turned and started upslope, following a faint footpath, angling away from the lights below. Zabisky called after him, but he ignored his shouts.

∞ **4** ∞

"You're a fool if you think I'm going to help you, Max,"
Hardman said.

"Don't call me 'Max'; we're not on that kind of terms."
The prisoner smiled a gaunt smile. He was sitting at ease
in the big leather chair beside Hardman's desk, puffing
one of Hardman's cigarettes. The muzzle of the big-caliber
solid-slug pistol rested on the desk, aimed at Hardman's
chest. "It's 'Mr. Wiston'—or just 'Wiston.' And you'll do
like I say, Warden." He had a deep, gravelly voice, soft but
penetrating.

Hardman shook his head. "I couldn't get you out of the
prison even if I wanted to, Max," he said easily. "And I
don't want to."

"Warden, you think I wouldn't shoot you as soon as look
at you?" Wiston's voice was mild, his tone curious.

"Sure, you'd shoot me if you thought it would buy you
your freedom. But you know it would all be over for you
if you shot me in cold blood. I'm your one chance to get
clear—you think. But you're wrong—"

"For God's sake, Governor," Lester Pale whispered
from the chair against the wall where Wiston had ordered
him to sit. "You convince him of that and he'll kill you out
of hand!"

"No he won't," Hardman said. "He knows I'm the only
one who can help him—if not to escape, at least to bail
him out of some of the trouble he's gotten himself into
tonight."

"Warden, you talk too much," Wiston said. "I'll tell you just how it is: I've waited ten years for this chance, I'm riding it all the way. Maybe it's true what you say about all the fancy safety gadgets and automatic traps and that— but I'd rather be dead than stay in this box any longer. We're walking out of here, me and you—win, lose, or draw. So maybe you better do what you can to get those gates open. Cause I'm not going back in that cellblock alive, ever. And if I have to die, I'm taking you along, I promise you that, Warden."

"He means it, Governor," Pale said.

"The pansy's right," Wiston said, smiling. "Now, let's get moving. I'm getting restless. I want to smell that fresh air, Warden, see that open sky, feel that rain on my face." He stood abruptly, motioning with the gun. Hardman didn't move. Wiston swung the gun to one side and without looking fired a round into the wall two feet from Lester Pale's chair.

"Next one hits meat, Warden."

Hardman stood.

"This won't work, Max," he said. "It's hopeless."

"Sure. Let's go."

In the corridor, sounds of distant shouting were audible.

"I set 'em to raising hell down in the services wing," Wiston said. "That'll keep your screws tied up whilst you and me try the back way."

"What back way?"

"The water gate, Warden. That was always the weak spot here at Caine. Could never dope the tunnel, though. But you'll get me through. You'll say all the right things and get me through."

"Then what? The road only leads to Gull Key—"

"There's a lot of water out there, Warden. I'm a strong swimmer. And I know these waters. I fished amongst these islands for many a year before ever they built the prison. Don't worry about me, Warden. I'll be fine, just fine."

"In this storm you'll drown before you've swum a hundred yards."

"Don't talk, Warden. Just lead the way."

In silence, Hardman pushed through the stairwell door. In darkness, he descended, feeling his way; Wiston's footsteps followed directly behind him. At the bottom, he felt over the wall, found the door that opened into the Processing Room.

"There may be some of my men in here," he said. "I hope you have sense enough not to start shooting, Max."

"We'll see."

Hardman opened the door; it swung in on darkness.

"Now what?" he said. "Neither of us can see—"

Wiston's fingers touched him, hooked his belt. "You know the layout, Warden. Just keep going. When I'm unhappy, you'll hear this gun go off. Or will you? You know what they say about the one that kills you."

Hardman tried to remember the layout of the room. The personnel doors were to the right . . . about there. He moved forward cautiously, the other man at his heels. His hands touched brickwork. He explored, found the cold steel of the door. It swung open at his touch. Chill air moved around his face. The sounds of the storm were louder now.

"Good work, Warden. I can smell the Gulf."

"This is the garage," Hardman said. "The only exit is through the big doors. They're power-operated. This is the end of the line, Max—"

A beam of light speared out from the left. Hardman whirled, shouted, "Douse that, you damn fool!"

The boom of the gun racketed and echoed in the enclosed space. The flashlight dropped to the floor and rolled, throwing its beam across the oil-stained concrete floor. There was a heavy, complicated sound of a body falling against the side of a vehicle, sliding down to the floor, a gargly rattle of exhaled air.

"Don't move, Warden," Wiston said calmly. "I'm going to pick up the light."

Hardman heard soft, quick steps. The light swung up, flicked across him, on across to the spot where a man in coveralls lay on his face between two armored personnel carriers in a widening pool of black-red blood.

"Too bad," Wiston said. "I didn't mean that feller no harm, but he shouldn't of put the light on me thataway." He shone the light on the big garage doors, up one side, across the top, down the other.

"O.K., your time, Warden. Get 'em open."

"I told you—"

"Reckon there's a manual rig someplace. Better find it."

"Find it yourself, Wiston."

"You're a funny one, Warden. You saw me, just now; you know I'm not bashful about using the gun. You figure you're bulletproof?"

"I'm here to keep cold-blooded killers like you out of circulation, Wiston, not to lead you outside and wave bye-bye."

Wiston laughed. "You're a harder nut than you look, old man. But I wonder, are you as hard as you talk?" The convict held the flashlight beam on Hardman's right knee. "I count five. Then I put a bullet where the light is. After that, I ask you again." He cleared his throat, spat, began to count . . .

Hardman waited until the count of four, another half-second, then pivoted, dropped toward the floor as the gun boomed. A red-hot sledgehammer struck him behind the right knee, flipped him. His face hit hard, skidding on the concrete. There seemed to be a spike driven into the back of his leg. He tried to draw a breath to yell, tried to get his hand on the spike to pull it out—

"Stop flopping, Warden. I should of killed you for that trick, but you're just winged."

The light was dazzling in Hardman's eyes, growing and receding. Blood pounded in his head. Sickness swelled inside him. Pain rolled out in white-hot waves from his shattered knee. He hardly heard Wiston's voice. He lay on his side, his cheek against the floor, clutching his leg.

"Now, you better just tell me about that door, Warden . . ." The man was standing over him; he saw the dusty, dark-blue legs of the prison trousers, the sturdy shoes, through a veil of agony.

"Go . . . hell . . ." he managed.

The feet went away. There were sounds, thumping, the rattle of metal, curses. Then a grunt of satisfaction; a steady ratcheting noise started up, accompanied by heavy breathing. Cold wet air was sweeping in across the floor; the shrill of wind and the drumming of rain were abruptly louder. The ratcheting ceased.

Hardman tried to roll over on his back, succeeded in banging his head against the floor. He forced his hands, slippery with blood, away from his wound, pushed himself to a sitting position. The man Wiston had shot lay ten feet from him, visible by the light of the flash which Wiston had placed on the floor. The garage door had been raised a foot and a half. Wiston had picked up the light, was sliding under the door. He cleared it, got to his feet, moving away.

Abruptly, bright, hard flashes of light winked, the stutter of automatic weapons racketed in the drive well, casting shadows that moved like silent-movie actors. Lying on the floor just inside the door, Hardman saw a man walking toward him. The man slowed, knelt slowly, fell forward on his face. Other men were coming; bright lights glared, reflecting from wet pavement. Voices called out. Wiston lay on his face a yard from Hardman. His hands groped over the pavement. He lifted his head and looked into Hardman's eyes.

"Someplace," he said. "Sometime, there's got . . . got to be . . . be . . . some justice . . ." His face hit the pavement.

A foot turned Wiston over. The rain fell on his wide-open eyes.

"Did you get that?" someone said. "He goes out talking about justice. A punk like that."

There was something that Hardman wanted to say then, something of vast importance that he had tried all his life to understand and that now, in this instant, was clear to him. But when he opened his mouth, darkness filled his brain and swept him away into a black maelstrom of roaring waters.

∞ 5 ∞

Private Obers, Ewen J., ASN 3783746353, of the Third Company, First Battalion, paused in the lee of one of the big trees to wipe the icy rainwater from his face and try one more time to adjust the collar of the G.I. raincoat to prevent the cold trickle down the back of his neck. He propped his M-3 carbine against the tree, undid the top button with cold-numbed fingers, turned up the collar of the field jacket under the coat, rebuttoned the coat. It felt colder and clammier than ever, but it was the best he could do. He considered pulling off his boots to empty the water from them; but what the hell; they'd just fill up again. Every third step was into a gully with water anywhere from ankle- to knee-deep. Obers peered through the darkness for signs of the platoon. Pitcher had told them to keep it closed up while they worked their way upslope from the road where they'd left the six-by's. He hadn't seen Dodge or Shapiro, the men on his left and right, since they'd hit the rough ground. But at least you couldn't get lost; not if you just kept climbing.

Obers wished briefly that he were back in the barracks, racked out on his bunk, reading a magazine and eating a candy bar; then he slung the carbine and stepped out to face the rain anew.

There was a movement above him.

"Shapiro?" His call was muffled by the storm.

There was no answer; but above, a dark shape moved, low to the ground, big—too big to be Shapiro—or Dodge;

and why was the guy crawling? Obers halted, feeling a sudden prickling at the back of his neck—not that he believed in spooks . . .

"All right, who's there?" he yelled against the rain.

No answer. The big shape—well over six feet long—flowed downward toward him. For an instant, Obers thought he caught a gleam of light reflected from yellow-green eyes. He swung the carbine around, jacked the loading lever, aimed it from the hip, and pulled the trigger.

Nothing happened; the trigger was locked hard. Panic flooded up in Obers. *Safety's on!* The words popped into his mind; but his finger was locked on the trigger, squeezing until the metal cut into his flesh. And the dark shape was rising, flowing outward and down toward him.

In the last split second, he tried to scream, but there was no breath in his lungs. Then the weight struck him, threw him down and back. He felt something icy cold rake across his throat, felt a remote pain that was hardly noticeable in the greater agony of the need for air. Something scarlet red dazzled before his eyes, grew until it was a sunburst that filled the world, then slowly faded into an endless darkness.

◎◎◎◎✶◎◎◎◎

In a clearing in the forest stands a tall man with a mane of flame-red hair, dressed in garments of green leather and a surcoat of buff ornamented with a white bird with spread wings. A two-handed sword with a jeweled pom-

mel hangs at his side. A bow is slung at his back. He wears a heavy gauntlet on his left hand, on which is perched a white hawk, from whose head the man has just removed a hood of soft leather. With a lift of his wrist, the man tosses the bird high; it gives a piercing cry and circles high into the air.

"My lord's power over a wild bird is a thing to wonder at," *murmurs one of a huddle of serfs watching from concealment.*

"Indeed, 'tis a matter passing Christian understanding," *another comments.*

"I've heard it said," *says another,* "that the bird is a were-creature, a man enchanted."

"Aye, 'tis his own brother, some say—"

"Nay, not his brother; him he slew in battle before the eyes of all his men—"

"But by the virtue of Christ, the slain brother rose and walked again—"

"—and 'twas then he enchanted him into the form of the white falcon—"

"Old wives' tales," *says the first man who spoke, a dark man with strange yellow eyes.* "My Lord Lohengrin is no magician, but a true knecht—"

"Bah! What do you know?" *speaks up an oldster with a straggly yellow beard.* "I served him in your granfer's time, and with my own eyes oft have I seen him quaff deep of the waters of eternal youth. For does he not—aye, and the bird as well—appear today as he did then, when I was a lusty stripling—"

"You lusty, Brecht? When was that, before or after the Flood of Noah?"

When the furtive laughter dies, a man who has not spoken tugs at his ear portentously. "Aye, laugh," he says. "But in truth you are all wide of the mark. The bird is no man ensorcelled."

The others look at him with slack jaws.

"'Tis a woman, Leda by name, a humble maid who spurned my Lord's base advances. This I know, for gospel fact, because she was the sister of a cousin of a close friend—"

"Bah!" scoffs the elder. "If 'twere a woman, she would take the shape of a swan, not a hunting falcon; any fool knows that—"

"So you do," the other says sharply. "But a wise man knows better—"

They fall silent as the hunter turns and looks across at them with cold blue eyes that penetrate to their hiding place.

"You are all wide of the mark," he says in a voice like the ring of cold iron. "The bird is only a bird; my brother is a mad dog; and as for myself—I am a dead man."

As one, the gaggle of villagers whirl and pelt away through the underbrush. The falconer smiles a lean smile, stands looking up at the sky where the white bird circles on a rising current of air.

Chapter Eleven

∞ 1 ∞

Grayle had covered twelve miles in less than an hour, running steadily across the dark, rain-swept fields, ignoring the pain from his side. Now, in the broken ground below the high rampart of the hills, he found his progress slowed. It was necessary to pick his way, splashing through rushing torrents of muddy water flowing down over the barrier of boulders deposited ten thousand years ago by the glacier. Once he paused, listening to the sound of what seemed to be heavy gunfire in the distance, but the sound was not repeated. Minutes later he became aware of men moving on the slope ahead and to his left. The ground was steep here, a rubble-heap of rock fallen from the steep cliffs above; the men were noisy, calling to each other, occasionally flashing hand-lights across the slope, through the scrub pines that had found a foothold here. It was apparent that they were soldiers: a sergeant barked angry orders for silence to the members of the Third Platoon.

Grayle skirted the men, who were working their way

southward, to his left, and continued his climb, facing into the driving rain.

He was close now. It would not be much longer before he knew if he had been in time.

✆ 2 ✆

Outside, the unceasing storm buffeted the thick walls; inside, the generator chugged, the stink of exhaust fumes hung in the stale air. Hardman lay on a field cot set up in his office, his right leg heavily bandaged.

"You look bad, Governor," Brasher said, frowning. "You ought to be—"

"Skip all that. Let's have that report."

"Well—if you think you're competent—that is, feeling well enough—"

"The report, Brasher." Hardman's voice was tight with pain. "You like to deliver reports, remember? It gives you a chance to sound like Moses—or is it God in person?"

"Look here—" Brasher started angrily.

"That's an order, Captain!" Hardman's snarl overrode the other.

Brasher's face twitched angrily. "I was thinking of your welfare, Governor. However, as you insist," he hurried on, "you know about the car theft and assault in Brooksville. Well, that was just a warm-up, it seems. Our man proceeded to Gainesville, attacked two patrolmen and stole their car, drove it to the downtown police-helicopter facility, and proceeded to hijack a high-speed military recon machine—"

"Who told you this cock-and-bull story?" Hardman cut in.

"Captain Lacey. And—"

"All right, he drove in to the middle of a heavily manned police installation, borrowed a copter, and took off in a hurricane. Anything else?"

"The copter was followed on radar; it headed northwest. The plot was passed to Eglin, and on to other bases along the route. They tracked him to within a hundred miles of the Canadian border. Then someone—Washington, I think—scrambled fighters out of Great Lakes. They forced him down in rough country in northern Minnesota."

"You're serious about this?"

"Dead serious."

"And—where is he now?"

"He got clear. But they got the girl."

"What girl?"

"His accomplice. The one who helped him escape."

"What has she told them?"

Brasher shook his head. "I understand she was pretty badly shaken up in the crash. She hasn't talked."

"You said he got clear. Weren't they covering the ground?"

"Certainly—but that's a big country—"

"He's alone and unarmed, probably injured. He should be easy enough to take."

"Well, as to that—I should point out that there *are* a couple of confusing points. It seems there's a report of a man answering Grayle's description attacking two police officers at the scene of an auto accident."

"Near the crash scene?"

"About seventy miles southwest."

"How does the time tie in?"

"The crash occurred at four-oh-seven; this other item was about an hour later, five-oh-one A.M."

"So now he's in two places at once," Hardman snorted. "What makes you think there's any connection? There are thousands of men who answer Grayle's general description."

"Not that can tear the door off a car," Brasher said, looking sideways at Hardman.

"What does that mean?"

"The FBI looked the car over—the one that was wrecked. It was one of theirs. It was tailing Grayle. The door was ripped from its hinges. And there were finger-marks in the metal."

Hardman was propped on one elbow. "And?" he prompted.

"He assaulted the police, as I said, and left the scene in his car. Twenty miles up the road, he and his accomplice—"

"A girl?"

"No, a man. They hit an army roadblock, attacked a couple of soldiers, and stole a military vehicle—a half-track, I think it was."

"All this, less than an hour after he crashed a stolen police copter in another place, accompanied by a woman. Quite a trick, eh, Brasher? A real superman, this fellow—either that, or the police forces of this country are a col-lection of idiots!"

"I know it sounds crazy." Brasher waved his hands. "But these are the facts reported to me! This man gets around faster than a dirty rumor! It has to be Grayle!

Sure, anybody could have gray hair and a red stubble, but who else could tear steel with his bare hands? Unless . . ." Brasher looked startled. "A minute ago you said something about a superman, Governor," he said. "What would you say to *two* supermen?"

"I don't know, Brasher." Hardman lay back, looking exhausted.

"Well, I'll be getting along, Governor." Brasher glanced at the big gold strap-watch on his wrist. "Things are breaking fast; there'll no doubt be an arrest at any moment—"

"Brasher," Hardman called as the policeman turned away.

"When they catch him—either or both of him—I want him taken alive."

Brasher looked grave. "Well, now, Governor, as we agreed earlier, we don't want to place any obstacles in the path of law enforcement—"

"I said alive, Brasher!"

"What if this mad dog begins shooting down more police officers? What are they supposed to do? Turn the other cheek?"

"Alive, Brasher," Hardman repeated. "Now, get out— and maybe you'd better tell that doctor to call the hospital after all."

Outside, Lester Pale was waiting. He raised his eyebrows.

"Nothing," Brasher said quickly. "He was conscious— just barely. He didn't say anything that made sense."

"No change in the orders? I had the idea—"

"No change," Brasher snapped. "I'm a cop, remember? My job is to catch crooks, that's all."

∞ 3 ∞

Halfway up the hill where he had abandoned the half-track, Falconer lay flat on wet ground among dense-growing brush. From the darkness ahead and to the left came the sounds of a man forcing his way through the growth. Other sounds of passage came from the right, along with the occasional gleam of a flashlight. Gradually, the sounds receded as the men passed by, moving diagonally to his course. Falconer rose, gained another fifty feet, then paused, head up, sniffing the air. Cautiously he advanced, skirting a giant tree. The sharp, metallic odor he had noticed grew rapidly stronger. Then he saw the body.

It was a soldier, sprawled at the base of the big pine, hands outflung, one leg doubled under him. The front of the man's raincoat was shredded; pale skin slashed by deep cuts showed through the rents. Above, the throat was gashed from ear to ear, not once, but in three parallel wounds. The ground under the man was a gluey soup of blood and muck.

For half a minute Falconer studied the corpse and the ground around it through narrowed eyes. Then he went on.

∞ 4 ∞

Tech Sergeant Duane Pitcher of the Third Platoon was disgusted. For the past hour, ever since they'd left the vehicles on the road below, he'd been stumbling around half-frozen in the pouring rain in these damned pitch-black woods, trying to follow orders to make no noise and show no lights, and to keep the men spread out in some kind of skirmish line, and keep 'em moving up toward the position the lieutenant had shown him on the contour map. In this soup, he'd be lucky to get within a mile of it. It was bad enough just to climb these damned slippery rocks through this damned slippery mud, but he had to be in twenty places at once, because otherwise the eager beavers like Obers would be a hundred yards out in front, and goldbricks like Bloom and Ginty would flake out and wind up back at the trucks, claiming they got lost.

Pitcher saw a dim movement ahead, called, got an answer in a Deep South rumble.

"O.K., hold it up here, Brown. We don't want to run into the Second Platoon coming down."

He moved on obliquely across the slope, made contact with two more men.

"Where's Obers?" he asked a two-striper.

"Hell, Sarge, where's anybody in this stuff?"

Pitcher grunted. "O.K., hold the platoon where they're at. Lieutenant Boyd's supposed to make contact on the left before we top the ridge. I got to look for Obers before he walks down and gets a one-hundred-millimeter in his lap."

"What was the firing, Sarge?"

"How do I know?" Pitcher moved up along a faint path through the trees. He had covered seventy yards when he tripped over an obstruction at the base of a big pine. Pitcher's training was good. As he stumbled, he swung the carbine from his shoulder, hit the ground and rolled, came to rest in firing position, gun aimed, safety off.

Nothing moved. There was no sound but the howl of the wind, the crash of rain. He hadn't liked the feel of what he had stepped on. It was too soft, too yielding. It felt like . . .

He unclipped the flash at his belt, flicked it in the direction of the tree. It shone on a booted foot. The rest of the man was there too, lying on his back. It was Obers. Pitcher held the light on the torn throat, the lacerated chest.

For a long moment he held the light on the dead man. Then he shifted the beam, shone it around him into the high darkness of the forest. There was nothing but wet trees, wet rock. Then a sound came from his left below: the snap of a sodden twig, the slither of shoes in mud, the scraps of leather against rock. Pitcher switched off the light, dropped it, fitted the stock of the carbine against his cheek, his finger on the trigger.

A man appeared, toiling upward through the trees. He was a big fellow, dressed in a waterproof mackinaw. Wet black hair was plastered to his round skull. He was headed straight for the spot where the body lay. Pitcher put the light square in his eyes.

"All right, hold it right there!" Pitcher called. At the words, the man froze, then whirled, jumped for the underbrush. Pitcher's finger jerked; red flame gouted. The shot was a flat *bam!* against the background of the storm. The man stumbled, caught himself, plunged on into the brush. Pitcher fired again into the darkness where he had disappeared, but when he came forward to investigate, there was only a footprint and a splash of fast-dissolving blood to show that there had been a target and that his bullets had found it.

∞ 5 ∞

Falconer had halted when he heard the shots, then, hearing nothing more, resumed his climb. The trail ended on a bare slope of stone across which water sluiced like a spillway. He crossed it, hugging the rock, while the wind drove rain into his eyes and nose, under his clothes. At the upper edge, giant rocks lay tumbled like debris from some titanic explosion. Falconer picked his way up through them, and was looking down into a hollow, pooled with darkness like ink. He took a step forward, and abruptly there was no rain; the buffeting wind was gone. A foot away, the storm still shrieked, but here the air was still and warm. There was a soft sound from below; a vertical line of yellow light appeared and widened, shining out on dry rock, reflecting on a sleek curve of age-blackened metal. Beyond the open doorway gleamed pale-green walls, polished brightwork.

"Welcome, Commander Lokrien," a mellow voice rang out in a strange language that for a moment Falconer almost failed to comprehend. "I have waited long for this hour."

∞ 6 ∞

Standing in the road beside the medium tank which, half an hour before, had fired three rounds of conventional

100 mm through the main entrance to the Upper Pasmaquoddie Power Station, Colonel Ajax Pyler propped his fists on his hips and thrust his face closer to that of the divisional staff observer.

"You don't know the situation, Yount!" he snapped. "I saw it kill a man right in front of me! I talked to the three men that managed to get clear! I'm telling you this is more than a malfunction or a damn fool plot by a crazy engineer!"

"There are some forty civilian personnel still inside that building, Pyler," Colonel Yount came back coolly. "We have only the word of a couple of half-hysterical civilians that there's anything wrong in there that a platoon of foot soldiers can't control—"

"I'm not sending a man of my command into that death trap," Pyler said flatly. "I don't give a damn if the commanding general personally wrote out the order in his own blood with a bent pin!"

"Pyler, you're trigger-happy—"

"My orders were to shut down that transmitter. I intend to do just that—any way I can!"

"That's a five-billion-dollar federal installation you're shelling, man! This isn't Vietnam! You can't just blow anything that gets in your way to kingdom come!"

"I can try!"

"Before you do," Yount said coldly, "I suggest you think for a few moments about trying less drastic measures than total destruction of the plant."

"Who said anything about total destruction? I intend to place rounds in carefully selected spots, as pointed out by my engineers, until transmission ceases. Then—"

"No you're not, Pyler." Yount made a swift motion, and the big master sergeant who had been standing by at parade rest staring straight out under the rim of his steel helmet came to life.

"Sir!"

"Colonel Pyler, this is Sergeant Major Muldoon. He weighs two hundred and forty pounds, stripped, and there's not an ounce of fat on him. I've ordered him to escort you back to divisional HQ to make your report . . ."

Pyler's face went pale, then purpled.

"That is, unless you're willing to listen to reason."

Pyler drew a couple of hoarse breaths through his nose.

"What . . . what do you have in mind?"

"I want to send a three-man team into the plant. Specially equipped, of course; I'm not completely discounting your description of conditions inside. It seems there are several points at which the circuitry can be interrupted quite simply—"

"I told you what happened to that engineer fellow, Hunnicut, and the other man—and before them there was another—"

"I know all about that. I've talked to Prescott. My men know what to do."

"Very well," Pyler said through stiff lips. "I'll want written orders relieving me, of course."

Yount shook his head. "You're not relieved, Jack. I'm just lending what you might call a little tech support from headquarters." He turned away, began giving instructions to a tall, blond-haired captain and two noncoms, all in black commando assault dress.

✤ **7** ✤

Lieutenant Harmon of the Florida State Police was the first to spy the abandoned half-track blocking the gullied trail above. He and Captain Zwicky climbed down from their machine, slogged forward, guns in hand.

"Well, what did you expect, to find your man sitting in it eating his lunch?" Zwicky asked as Harmon cursed the empty vehicle.

"The son of a bitch can't be far. Let's get him!"

Zwicky squinted up through swirling rain at the dark forest above. "You think you could find him up there?"

"Got any better ideas?"

"Maybe." Zwicky indicated the low rise to the east. "The Pasmaquoddie Power Plant's just the other side of the hill a couple of miles. Maybe that's where he was headed."

"What the hell would he want to go there for?"

"I don't know—but there's some kind of trouble over there. That's why the army's out in the weather. Maybe your man has something to do with it?"

"Like what? For Christ's sake, Captain, this bum is a con on the lam, a lousy killer who spent his life in stir. What—"

"I don't know. But this is the only inhabited spot in forty miles; this is wild country, Lieutenant. And your man headed right for it. It's worth looking into, isn't it? Or are you dead set on climbing up there to beat the bushes for him—alone? Because this is as far as I go."

Harmon looked up toward the heights above.

"Well—"

There was a sound from nearby—the unmistakable double *clack-clack!* of the arming lever of a rifle.

"Freeze right there!" a harsh voice barked from the darkness.

Harmon dropped his pistol, hoisted his hands where he stood, his back to the voice. Zwicky turned slowly, holding the carbine by the breech, muzzle down, out from his side.

A uniformed man came forward, holding a carbine leveled. There were tech sergeant's stripes painted on the helmet that concealed his eyes.

"What is this, Sergeant?" Zwicky said.

"Hey!" another voice spoke up. "The guy's an officer, for Chrissakes!"

The sergeant paused, looking uncertainly from Zwicky to Harmon, who was looking back over his shoulder. The latter lowered his hands.

"G.I.'s!" he blurted. "For God's sake, Zwicky, tell them—"

"Get 'em up—high!" the noncom snapped. "You, too, Cap'n."

"Maybe you'd better tell me just what the hell you think you're doing," Zwicky said, not moving.

"Maybe you'd better drop it, Cap'n, before I pull this trigger. I've lost one man tonight, and I'm not messing around."

Zwicky let the gun fall. "All right, tell it, soldier."

"You better tell me what you're doing in my platoon area, Cap'n. And who's this fellow?" He jerked his head at Harmon.

"He's a police officer. We're looking for the man who drove the track up here." Zwicky motioned with his head toward the big vehicle behind him.

"Gus, take a look at their ID's. Don't get between me and them."

A corporal came forward, slung his carbine, grinned sheepishly as he patted Zwicky's pockets, brought out his wallet, opened it, and showed the blue card to the sergeant, who studied it by the light of the flash another man held. The corporal took Harmon's badge, showed it to the other.

"All right, I've played along with you, Sergeant," Zwicky said as he pocketed his wallet. "Now, aim that piece in some other direction and tell me what the hell is going on here."

The sergeant lowered the carbine reluctantly. "One o' my men's dead up there. Obers, worth any other three men in the outfit. I'm looking for the man that did it." He glanced at the track. "Maybe—"

"Sure it's him!" Harmon burst out. "The man's a cold-blooded killer, an escaped convict!" He looked at Zwicky. "I told you about this boy, Captain. Now maybe you'll listen to me!"

"Let's take a look," Zwicky said. He picked up his carbine, wiped mud from it on his sleeve. Harmon scooped up his pistol.

"Gus, you take the point," the sergeant ordered the corporal. "Cap'n, you and the civilian next. I'll be right behind."

It took the group of men a quarter of an hour to pick their way upslope to the spot where Obers' body lay.

Harmon whistled as he stared down at the mutilated corpse.

"O.K.," he said. "Now you see what kind of guy we're working with. Kid gloves, hah? Like hell, Captain; like hell."

"There's some kind of trail leading up here," one of the men said. "Hey!" He pointed excitedly to a sheltered spot under a clump of foliage. "Footprints—a couple of 'em!"

"Sure, I seen the bastard," the sergeant said. "I winged him, but he got clear. When I heard noises down below, I figured maybe he'd doubled back."

Harmon grunted. "He's up there," he said. "And I say let's get him."

The sergeant looked at Harmon. "You're a cop," he said. "If I go up there, I aim to shoot first and chin with the son of a bitch later."

"Can't say I blame you," Harmon said.

"Guy, you take the detail," the sergeant said. "I'll be back when I've cleared my barrel into somebody's gut."

With Zwicky in the lead, the three men started up the final ascent.

⊚⊚⊚⊚✳⊚⊚⊚⊚

It is dusk; against the dust-red sky, the flashes of the besieging cannon wink ceaselessly across the folds of the hills below the walls of the town. From the gates, a party of five men ride out on war horses, gaunt black steeds whose ribs stand out like the cheekbones of their helmeted and corseleted riders, one of whom carries a couched lance from the tip of which a white pennon flutters. Four of the men are olive-dark, black-bearded. One is smooth-shaven, with black-red hair and a scarred face. He sits a head taller in the saddle than any of his companions and rides before them.

Another party of five men sit their horses on the brow of the slope. These men are better fed; one has black hair and a cat's eyes. One, with hair the color of new rust, sits in advance of the others, dressed in rich but well-worn war gear, a sword at his side, a shield slung at his saddle bow.

The oncoming party halts fifty feet distant. The leader speaks briefly to his men, swings down from his mount, comes forward. The rust-haired man dismounts, advances to meet him. They are of a height, one wider, thicker of wrist and neck, the other quicker-moving, lighter-footed.

"I knew it was you," *the big-boned man says.* "I saw your cursed fowl coursing above the field."

"Yet you came . . ."

"Have no fear; I honor the white ensign."

The flame-haired man laughs softly.

"Many loyal men starve in the town," *the bigger man says.* "This charade must end."

"Then cease your harassment of my merchants—"

"Let them peddle their wares at home! These people have no need of better steel and improved gunpowder; they do slaughter enough with their own crude means."

"I regret the uses to which knowledge is put, but that is the price of a growing technology."

"The price is too high; these barbarians are not ready—"

"I've told you my terms, de la Torre—as I believe you style yourself these days."

"Because of those who trust me, I must yield. But we will meet again, brother."

"No doubt, brother."

They turn; each rejoins his own men. De la Torre's chief lieutenant eyes the flame-haired man as he mounts his white horse.

"My lord, why not kill him now—a swift shaft in the back—"

His master catches him by the arm, lifts him to his toes.

"He is mine, Castillo—mine and no other's!"

Across the hill, the cat-eyed man rides close beside his lord.

"Surely it would have been wise to dispatch the traitor on the spot," he is saying. "A single prick of a poisoned dart—"

"No."

"But, lord—doubtless he plots new betrayal—"

"You lie, Pinquelle!"

"I sometimes wonder, lord, whether truly it be hate—or love—that you feel for him."

The master reins in, wheels to face his lackey. "Get thee gone from my company, Pinquelle! I tire of thy pinched face and thy cruel eyes and thy poisonous tongue."

"As my lord wishes." The man turns his mount and rides away, not looking back.

Chapter Twelve

∞ 1 ∞

Captain Aldous Drake, Special Forces, on detached duty with HQ, Third Army, lay flat on his belly in sodden grass a hundred and thirty feet from the fire-blackened orifice that had been the glass-and-aluminum main entrance to the power plant. A typist's chair lay on its side among the rubble half-blocking the entry. A strip of tattered scarlet carpet was draped over the littered porch and down the steps like the tongue of a dead animal. Smoke still drifted from the blackened interior of the entry hall.

"Pyler messed up the front door pretty bad," Staff Sergeant Ike Weintraub said, hugging the ground a few feet to Drake's left.

"That's O.K. We don't plan to waltz in there anyway. Ike, there's your spot, off to the left, past the bushes." Drake indicated a vertical ventilator slot cutting the featureless concrete front. "A few ounces of PMM ought to open a hole wide enough to slide in through. Jess . . ." He addressed the big black-faced three-striper on his right. "Think you can get up on the roof—over there, to the right, above the terrace?"

"Sure, no sweat."

"When you get up there, keep low, look for the freight-elevator shaft. You know how to jimmy it." Drake looked at his watch.

"I make it five minutes and thirty seconds after." He waited while the other two made minute adjustments to their timepieces. "Ike, I'm giving you five minutes to set your charges. Jess, you have your spot picked. Use your power jimmy, but no blasting. I may break a little glass getting in. We'll spread out inside—you know the layout from the maps—and each go for his own target. First man to score sets off a screamer, and we get the hell out. All right, let's go."

"Cap'n—when we break away—will it be a category three, or what?"

"Category one, Ike. Every man for himself. Our reports may make all the difference to the next team. But I'm betting both you bums a fifth of the good stuff we all make it clean. Let's go." Drake slid forward, using his elbows and toes in a quick, comical rhythm that ate up the distance with deceptive swiftness and in total silence. For a few seconds he could see his two compatriots as dark blurs against darkness; then they were gone.

Ahead the building waited, high, bright-lit, crossed by slanting lines of rain. Fifty feet from the façade, Drake encountered bits of debris: glass, brick fragments, a scrap of upholstery material, papers. He crossed a sidewalk, another strip of grass, eased under a line of low-growing juniper, and was against the face of the building.

The windows—fixed double panels of heavy plastic—were just above him, the sills at face level, the room behind them dark. Drake came to his feet to the left of the opening, opened a pouch clipped to his pistol belt, took out a lump of a dark-green material resembling modeling clay. He formed it swiftly into a long, slender tube, packed it along the edge of the windows, working two feet out from the corner along the bottom and side. He inserted a tiny glass-encased capsule in the corner, attached a pair of hair-fine wires, and withdrew along the face of the building a distance of ten feet. He went flat, face down, and brought his wristwatch up under his eyes. Three and a half minutes elapsed; ninety seconds to go.

The rain pounded Drake's back. The cold mud under his chest soaked through his combat jacket, found chinks in his weather suit. He flexed his hands to keep them limber. Never tell what you might run into inside. Yount had talked as if the whole thing was an exercise, but the other bird—Pyler, his name was—had been pretty shook up. Too bad he hadn't had a chance to talk to the men who'd come out of the plant, but Yount had passed on everything useful—or so he said. Not that it amounted to much. But for what it was worth, the pattern looked simple. The corridors were electrified, the switches, door hardware, everything you'd normally touch. So the trick was to make your own holes, stick to the service ways, go straight for the spot the tech boys had shown him on the drawings, and zap! The job was done. After all, it was just a pile of machinery in there. Pull the plug, and it had to quit; it was as easy as that.

Ten seconds to go. Drake hoped Ike was ready—and

that Jess had his spot picked. It there *was* some nut inside, some mad-genius type, hitting him in three places at once ought to keep him hopping. Five seconds. Too bad if he wasn't quite close enough to the building and a pound or two of pulverized Plexiglas hit him in the back.

Drake thumbed the detonator button. There was an instantaneous ear-shattering blast, and dirt gouted beside his face. He came to his feet, slid along the wall to the now glassless opening, reached in for a grip, jumped, pulled himself up over the sill, and dropped onto a glass-littered carpet. He rolled to the wall, stopped with his feet spread, toes out, elbow braced, the pistol in his hand aimed toward the door. Dust was still settling. A piece of glass fell softly to the rug. A corpse lay face down near the desk. All right, Drake thought. Where's Ike's shot? . . .

He felt the dull blast through the floor before the sound came; Drake let out a breath and looked around the room. The entry to the access system the engineers had pointed out was in the ceiling of the toilet opening onto the office. The door was six feet away, standing ajar. Drake stood; as he did, he noticed a pale light glowing against the rug. A corridor light shining under the door, hitting the rug fibers? No, too bright for that. More of a fluorescence—and getting brighter, rippling like the glow in hot embers. A spark leaped across the rug. Drake backed a step; his elbow touched a filing cabinet. In the next instant, blue fire enveloped him. He had time to draw one breath—a breath of flames that scorched his lungs—and to expel it in a ragged screech of agony. Then his charred body fell stiffly, lay smoking on the floor, the half-slagged pistol still gripped in his blackened finger bones.

Sixty feet distant, in the ground-floor mechanical-equipment room, Ike Weintraub paused in wrapping a field bandage around the gash he had received on his forearm from a wild fragment from his shot, his head cocked. The sound had been very faint, but it had sounded a lot like a yell—a scream, to be exact. But it was probably just wind, whistling around some of the holes they'd knocked in the walls. Felt kind of embarrassed, being five seconds late on the blast. Drake was right on the button. Sharp character, old Drake. If all the brass were like him, a man wouldn't mind throwing a few salutes. Too bad the army hadn't been what he'd dreamed it would be: good men, trained fine, ready to face anything together, one for all and all for one, or whatever the old saying was. Corny, maybe, but it was still the best thing in the world, to be with the ones you knew you could count on. Funny, back home he'd believed all that crap he'd been brought up on, about how much better he was than the *goyim*, had thought a black man was one notch above a gorilla. That was one thing about the army; he'd found out that when the going got rough; it wasn't the religion or the hide that counted, it was the stuff inside. Like Drake. Drake was the best. And old Jess. They didn't make 'em any better. He'd go all the way to hell with those two—like now. He didn't like this job, not anything about it. Those civilians were no dumbbells, and they were scared all the way through. And Pyler, too. He was a bastard, but nobody had ever said he was yellow. But it was O.K. being here, knowing what to do, how to do it, knowing Jess was in it with him, that Drake was running the show. It was O.K. And it was time to get moving.

Weintraub flashed his needle-light around the big room, spotting the ladder against the wall behind the big sheet-metal duct, the trapdoor above it, right where they'd said. So far so good. All he had to do now was shin up there and get into the crawl-space, and head for the target.

But still he hesitated. It looked too easy. It was what the double-domes that worked in the place had figured out—but they hadn't done so hot when *they'd* been on the inside. Got their tails burned off. So maybe it might be a smart idea to take two looks at the layout before he jumped.

Weintraub worked the light over the walls, ceiling, and floor. He got to his feet, moved along the wall, not touching it. The back of the big air-handlers looked about the same as the front. There was a wooden ladder clamped against the rear wall, in a narrow space behind a big condenser. A square grille was set in the wall above it. There was nothing about it that looked any better than the other route, but Weintraub liked it better somehow. He lifted the ladder down, propped it against the wall, climbed it until he was facing the plastic grille. There were two plastic knobs holding it. He loosened them, swung the grille aside, and was looking into a dusty loft. Using his elbows, he pulled himself up and in. The light showed him a wide, low room, crammed full of ducting, conduits, cables, pipes. He didn't like the look of all that gear, but there wasn't much he could do about it. He knew which way to go. He started off, picking his way carefully over, under, and through the obstructions.

Ten minutes later, following his mental image of the

diagrams he had studied for a full five minutes before starting out, he had reached the spot Drake had picked for him—he hoped. If he was on target, there would be a black pipe here as big as his leg. According to the civilians, it was some kind of lube conduit. When he blew it, it would shut down the high-pressure silicone supply to the generator bearings, and in about three minutes they'd overheat and kick in a set of automatic breakers. Anyway, that was the theory. It was plenty noisy here. That was a good sign. The manifold room was supposed to be right below him. And there was the pipe. He shone the light along the glazed black surface. The junction where it made a right-angle bend down looked like the spot to hit. Weintraub placed the light so as to shine on the angle and extracted the shaped charge from the pouch over his right hip. From another pocket he took the detonator, a tiny capsule half an inch long. He handled it with exaggerated care. The big charge would blow a hole through a concrete wall, but it stood a lot of handling. The cap, on the other hand, was as delicate as a cracked egg. One little slip, and *blam!*

He cut off that line of thought. Keep your mind on business, that was the secret. A guy who broke down and ran was just a guy who thought too much about the wrong things. He'd either finish the job and get out alive, or he wouldn't. If he didn't, he'd never know what hit him. So why worry? Smiling slightly, Ike Weintraub shifted position to get at the miniature tools clipped to his belt. His head struck a pipe passing low above him. It was not a hard blow, not really enough to daze him. But it was enough to jar the detonator cap from his fingers. It fell fourteen inches to the concrete floor and exploded with a force that shattered Weintraub's lower jaw and drove a sizable section of jagged bone into his jugular vein.

It was twenty-one seconds before his heart, having pumped the body's blood supply out through the immense wound, sucked convulsively on air, went into fibrillation, and stopped.

In the crawl-space above the switch room, big Jess Dooley heard the sharp report. He frowned, waiting for the howl of the screamer that would mean Drake or Ike had scored. But nothing came.

It figured. The bang hadn't been loud enough to be a working charge. Which left the question of what it *had* been. But that was a question that would have to wait. A category-one operation, Drake had said. That meant get the job done and ask questions later, at the corner table in the bar where the three of them did their serious drinking. Funny world. Couldn't get together in the NCO Club; Drake wasn't allowed. Same for the Officers' Club: no EM's wanted. Same for most of the joints off base: a black hide netted no smiles in the Main Street spots, and he'd have to whip half the draft-dodgers in darktown if he took a couple of Pinks down there. Yep, funny world. It was better here, with death crackling in the air all around him, doing the thing he knew how to do, with the men he knew he could count on to back his play, no matter what. Jess wiped sweat from his forehead with a thick finger, and using his pinpoint light, began studying the maze of conduits sprouting from the big panel on the wall, looking for the two that carried the wires to the thermostats that controlled the fuel supply to the nuclear generators buried a hundred feet below the station.

∞ **2** ∞

Falconer moved down from the boulder-strewn rim of the hollow, his eyes on the open, lighted doorway and on the slim shape soaring into darkness above.

"I searched for you, Xix," he said, in the old language that came haltingly to him. "I thought you'd lifted long ago, without me."

"I have never abandoned you, my commander," the voice called over the drum of rain. "So long as the Other knew my location, I would never be safe from him in my weakened condition. It was necessary that I conceal myself. But nine hours ago the natives erected a crude energy field on which I was able to draw for minimal functions. At once I sent out my call to you, my commander. We must act swiftly now."

Falconer laughed softly. "After all this time, Xix? What's your hurry?"

"Commander, the energy field is feeble, not matched to my receptors. I draw but a trickle of power from it, insufficient to charge my static-energy coil. If I am to lift from this planet, I require more power—much more."

"How long will it take to draw enough from the broadcast field?"

"Over a century. We cannot wait. We must charge the coil directly from the source, unattenuated by distance."

"How?"

"With your assistance, my commander. You must remove the lift coil, take it to the transmitting station, and tap the beam directly."

"It occurs to me that we're very close to the transmitter. That must have been the installation I saw on the way here. Rather a coincidence, eh, Xix?"

"Indeed, Commander. But the coil must be charged, and time is short. Already I have been forced to . . . But no matter. You must remove the coil and descend at once to the transmitter."

"I heard firing down there. What's going on, Xix?"

"An effort was made to shut down the transmission. Of course I cannot permit that."

"How can you stop it?"

"My commander, we must not delay now for discussion of peripheral matters. I sense that I am threatened; the hour for action has come."

Falconer crossed the rock-strewn ground, aware of the thunder and roll of the storm beyond the protected area sealed off by the ship's defensive field. He stepped up through the entry port, went along the dustless passage walled with smooth synthetic, ornamented with fittings of imperishable metal. In the control compartment, soft lights glowed across the banked dials and levers, so once-familiar, so long-forgotten.

"Xix—what about Gralgrathor? If he's still alive—"

"The traitor is dead."

"So many years," he said. "I don't feel any hate any longer." He laughed, not a jolly laugh. "I don't feel much of anything."

"Soon you will, my commander. The long twilight ends. Ysar waits for us."

"Yes," Falconer said. "Now I'd better get busy. It's been a long time since I put a tool to a machine of Ysar."

∞ **3** ∞

John Zabisky, wounded in the lower right side by a
steel-jacketed thirty-caliber slug which had broken a rib,
punctured a lung, traversed his liver, and lodged in the
inner curve of the ilium, lay on his face under a dense-
needled dwarf pine. Immediately after he had been shot,
he had covered fifty feet of rough going in his initial
plunge away from danger before the shock had overtaken
him and dropped him on his face. For a while then—he
had no idea how long—he had lain, dazed, feeling the
hot, spreading ache in his side grow into a throbbing
agony that swelled inside him like a ravenous animal
feeding on his guts. Then the semieuphoric state had
given way to full consciousness. Zabisky explored with
his fingers, found the entry wound. It was bleeding, but
not excessively. The pain seemed to be somewhere else,
deep inside. He was gut-shot, bleeding internally. He
knew what that meant. He had an hour, maybe two. A
lousy way to go out. He lay with his cheek against the
mud and thought about it.

Why the hell had he followed the guy, Falconer, after
he'd kissed him off? He had his money, two cees.
Curiosity? Not exactly that; it was more than just sticking
his nose in. It was like the guy needed him—like he was
mixed up in something too tough for him, trying to do it
alone, tackling too much for one man. And you wanted to
help the guy, stick by him. It was like there was something
at stake, something you couldn't put in words; but if you

finked out, let it slide, washed your hands of it, you'd never be able to see yourself again as the man you thought you were. It was like in the old days, kind of, when the first John Sobieski had climbed on his horse and led his men into battle. It was a thing you had to do, or admit you were nothing.

Yeah. And then the light had hit him in the face, and some guy yelled, and then the ballbat hit him in the side, and he heard the gun firing after him, and then he was here, and what good were the two cees now?

And where the hell was here? Halfway up some lousy hill, in the woods, in the middle of the night, in a storm like you didn't see twice in one lifetime.

Especially not his lifetime. Maybe another hour. Maybe not that much.

Falconer would help him, if he knew.

Falconer was up ahead, someplace.

Got to get moving.

Painfully, grunting, fighting back the nausea and the weakness, Zabisky pulled himself forward another foot. He had covered perhaps a hundred yards when he saw the glow above. That would be Falconer up there. Probably had a cabin up there, a warm room, a fire, a bed. Better to die in a bed than here. Better to die just trying for it than to stop here and let the pain wash up and up until it covered you and you sank down in it and were like all the other extinct animals you saw in books. Not much you could do then, about anything. But it hadn't come to that yet. Not quite. He still had a few yards left in him. Take 'em one at a time, that was the trick. One at a time . . . as long as time held out.

He had covered another half-dozen yards when he heard the sound above: a faint clatter of a dislodged pebble.

"Falconer," he called, peering upward. There was a movement, there, among the shadows. A long, high-shouldered, narrow shape flowed into view, stood looking down with yellow eyes that seemed to blaze like tiny fires against the blackness.

ఌ **4** ఌ

Two hundred yards to the east and a hundred feet below, Grayle worked his way along the face of a weathered fissure in the rock. Three times he had attempted to gain the ledge above; three times he had fallen back. The distance was too great, the scant handholds too slippery, the broken ribs still too crippling. Now he descended to the talus below, angling to the south, skirting the barrier. The grade was less precipitate here; stunted trees had found footholds; brush and exposed roots offered grips for his hands. He made more rapid progress, moving laterally into bigger timber. Striking a faint path, he turned right along it, resumed his ascent. He had covered only a few yards when he saw the body lying at the base of the pine.

For long seconds he stood staring down at the ripped throat of the dead man. Then he made an animal noise deep in his throat, shook himself like a man waking from a nightmare, and started upward.

He had covered a hundred yards when he heard sounds ahead: the grate of feet on stone, the puffing of labored breath. More than one man, making clumsy progress upward.

He left the path and hurried to overtake them.

∞ 5 ∞

Lying flat on his back in utter darkness, Sergeant Jess Dooley felt the miniature power hacksaw cut through the second of the two conduits. It had been a delicate operation, cutting all the way around each of the half-inch stainless-steel tubes without touching the wires inside, but the engineers had made it pretty plain what would happen if a man shorted them accidentally.

Now the trick was to short them on purpose and get away in one piece. Dooley wiped sweat on his forearm and thought about the layout he had studied on paper. Memory was important to a man in his line of work. You had to have a natural mnemonic aptitude, and then survive some tough training to qualify as a member of a Special Team. After all the trouble of getting to where the job was, there were plenty of times when completing it depended on perfect recall of a complicated diagram.

Like now. It wouldn't do to just cut a wire; there were six back-up systems that would take over in that case— even if he wasn't fried in the process. He had to tinker the thing to give a false reading—and not too false at that. Just enough to show a no-demand condition, and make the automatic cutouts lock in. These automated layouts were pretty smart; they could deal with just about any situation that came up. But you could fool 'em. They didn't expect to get a phony signal from their own guts.

And if he could attach the little gadget the technical boys had handed him at just the right spot, in just the right way—between sensors, and if possible at the same instant as a legitimate impulse from the thermostats . . .

Well, then, he might get away with it.

He extracted the device—the size of a worm pill for a medium-sized dog—removed the protective tubing from the contacts. He shifted position, settling himself so he could make one smooth, coordinated motion. The protective devices wouldn't like it if he fumbled the hook-on, making and breaking contact half a dozen times in half a second before he got the ringer in position.

He was ready. Sweat was running down into his eyes. He wiped at it ineffectively with his shoulder. Hot in here, no air. A man could suffocate before he got the job done. So what was he waiting for? Nothing. He was ready. The next time the relay clicked—it cycled about once every five minutes—he'd make his move.

∽ 6 ∽

Captain Zwicky, a few feet in advance of Sergeant Pitcher and Lieutenant Harmon, pulled himself up over an outcropping of granite and started to rise to his feet.

"That's far enough, Captain," a deep voice said from above. "This is no place for you tonight. Go back."

Zwicky remained frozen, both hands and one knee on the ground, an expression of total astonishment on his upturned face. Behind him, Pitcher, hearing the sudden voice, halted, then eased forward. Over the captain's shoulder he could see dark underbrush, dripping foliage—and the legs and torso of a man. A big man, in dark clothes.

In a single motion, he raised the carbine, sighted, and fired. At the explosion beside his right ear, Zwicky plunged forward and sideways. Pitcher, his path cleared, scrambled up, saw the tall, dark-shadowed figure still standing in the same position; hastily, he brought the carbine up—and felt a ringing shock against his hands as the gun flew from his grip. He made a lunge in the direction the weapon had skidded, felt hard hands catch him, lift him, turn him. Zwicky was on his feet, raising his carbine; but he was having trouble finding a clear shot. Pitcher felt himself swung forward, released. He crashed downward through twenty feet of brush before he came up hard against a tree. As he struggled up, Lieutenant Harmon grabbed his arm, dragged him to his feet.

"What happened up there? That shot—"

"Leggo," Pitcher blurted. He chopped at Harmon's hand, grabbed for the other's pistol. "Gimme that—"

"You nuts—"

The arrival of Captain Zwicky, sliding and tumbling down the trail, cut off his protest. Pitcher stepped back, holding the pistol, as Zwicky came to rest on his back between the two men.

"Stand fast, Sergeant!" he blurted as Pitcher started past him.

"I'm getting the bastard that killer Obers," Pitcher snarled.

"That's an order!" Pitcher halted as Zwicky crawled to his feet. His nose was bleeding, and he had lost his cap. He wiped at his face with the back of his hand, smearing blood which ran down, mingling with rainwater.

"Losing more men won't help anything," he said. "I don't know what we're up against, but it's more than it looks like. Before we try it again, we have to—"

At that moment, a sound cut through the crash of the storm: a strident, wailing scream that ran down the scale and died in a groan of horror.

Without a word, Harmon whirled and plunged down the path. Pitcher backed two steps, was jabbed between the shoulderblades by the stub of a dead branch. He dropped his carbine, dived down the slope head-first. Zwicky hesitated for a moment, started to shout a command, then turned and went down the path, not running, but wasting no time.

∞ 7 ∞

"What in the Nine Hells was that?" Falconer rose from the open panel behind which the compact bulk of the drained energy coil was mounted.

"Don't be alarmed," the cool voice of the ship said. "It is merely a warning device. I arranged to keep the native life in all its forms at a distance."

"It sounded like a hunting *krill*. By the king of all devils, I'd forgotten that sound."

"It serves its purpose most effectively—"

"What set it off just now?"

"A native was prowling nearby."

"A strange time and place to be prowling."

"Have no fear; now that my Y-field is restored, I am safe from their petty mischief."

"I may have led them here," Falconer said. "It's too bad. There's likely to be trouble when I start back down."

"There are weapons in my armory, commander—"

"I have no desire to murder anyone, Xix," Falconer said. "These are people too; this is their world."

"Commander, you are as far above these natives as— but I distract you from your task. Their presence nearby indicates the need for haste."

In silence, Falconer resumed the disassembly of the lift unit.

∾∾ **8** ∾∾

For a moment after the cry of the hunting *krill* sounded, Grayle stood staring upward into the darkness of the rim beyond which faint light gleamed on the slanting curtain of rain. There was no further sound. He resumed his climb, crossed a slope of naked rock, made his way up over a jumble of granite, and was looking across a pebble-strewn ledge at the soft glowing U1-metal hull of a fleet boat of the Ysarian navy upreared among the rock slabs.

∾∾ **9** ∾∾

Jess Dooley heard the soft click of the relay as it

opened. He had precisely 0.4 second to move. In a smooth motion, he touched the two wires of the false-signal device to the exposed conductors. A spark jumped to the exposed end of the cut-through conduit, from which a volatile antistatic and coolant fluid was draining. The flash of fire seared the hair from the left side of Dooley's scalp, charred the edge of his ear, scorched deep into the exposed skin of his neck. In instant reflex, the man snatched a tiny high-pressure can from his belt, directed a billow of smothering foam at himself, at the pool of fluid over which pale blue flames leaped like burning brandy on a fruitcake, over the conduits and cables around him. He moved backward, awkward under the low ceiling, holding his breath to exclude the mixture of flame, foam, and noxious gases.

The flames winked and dimmed. Then the pain hit. Dooley dropped the can, groped for another, gave himself a liberal dose of nerve paralyzant. The burned side of his face went wooden. Too late, he turned his head. A drop of condensed painkiller trickled down into the corner of his right eye. There was a momentary stinging; then numbness, darkness.

Swearing to himself, Dooley found his needle-light, switched it on. Nothing. The light was hot against his hand. It was working, all right. But he couldn't see it. With nerve-deadener in both eyes, he was blind as a bat.

Nice work, Dooley. Nice spot. Is the fire out? Hope so. Is the little magic combination can-opener and disaster-averter in place and functioning? Hope that too. Meanwhile, how does a man go about getting the hell out of here?

Alone, in darkness, Dooley began inching his way back along the route he had come.

∞∞∞*∞∞∞

In the glow of the campfire, the faces of the men are ruddy, belying the privations of the long campaign. They sit in silence, listening to the shrill of cicadas, the soft sounds of the river, looking across at the scattered lights of Vicksburg.

An orderly approaches, a boy scarcely out of his teens, thin and awkward in his dusty blue uniform. He halts before a broad-shouldered officer with shoulder-length hair, once red, now shot with gray.

"General Logan, Major Tate's compliments, sir, and they took a rebel colonel half an hour ago scouting this side of the river, and would the general like to talk to him."

The big man rises. "All right, lad." He follows the boy along the crooked path among the pitched tents where men in rumpled blue sit restlessly, oppressed by the humid heat and the swarming insects. At a rough compound built of boards wrenched from the walls of a nearby barn, a slouching sentry straightens as they approach, presents arms. A captain emerges from a tent, salutes, speaks to an armed sergeant. A detail of four men falls in beside them. The gate is opened.

"A five-man escort?" General Logan says mildly as they enter the compound. "He must be a redoubtable warrior indeed."

The captain has a round red face, a long, straggly moustache. He wipes sweat from his face, nods.

"A hard case. Powell swears he broke a half-inch rope they had on him. I guess if he hadn't been out cold when they found him, they wouldn't have got the rope on him in the first place. I'm taking no chances with him."

They halt before a blacksmith's forge, where a bare-headed man stands, trussed with new hemp rope. He is big, broad, with a square, scarred face and black-red hair. There are iron manacles on his wrists; an iron cannonball lies by, in position to be attached to his left ankle. There is blood on his face and on his gray tunic.

General Logan stares at the man. "You," he says in a tone of profound astonishment. The prisoner blinks through the dried blood which has run down into his eyes. Abruptly, he makes a shrugging motion, and the men holding him are thrown back. He tenses, and with a sharp popping sound, the hemp strands break. He reaches, seizes the blacksmith's hammer in his manacled hands, leaps forward, and brings the heavy sledge down with smashing force on the skull of the Union general.

Chapter Thirteen

∞ **1** ∞

Carrying the heavy coil, Falconer stood for a moment in the entry, looking out across the circle of dry dust and loose stone soft-lit by the ship's port lights, ending in abrupt transition to the rim of broken, rain-swept rock, and beyond, the tops of black trees rising from below.

"Good luck, Commander," Xix said as he stepped down. Burdened by the heavy load, he picked his way across toward the point below which the path led downward. He had descended less than a hundred feet when he saw the man lying face-down in the path, bulky in a bright-colored mackinaw. Falconer dropped the coil, knelt by the man's side. There was blood on the side of the heavy coat. He turned the man over, saw the gaping wounds across the side of the thick, muscular neck, the shredded front of the sodden jacket.

"John Zabisky," he muttered. "Why did you follow me?"

Zabisky's eyelids stirred, lifted; his small, opal-black eyes looked into Falconer's. His lips moved.

"I . . . tried," he said distinctly; then all the light went out of his eyes, left them as dull as stones.

Falconer rose, stood looking down at the rain falling on the face of the dead man. He glanced up at a faint sound, and a hard white light struck him in the eyes.

"I should have known you wouldn't die," a deep, harsh voice said out of the darkness.

∽ **2** ∽

"So you're alive, Gralgrathor," Falconer said.

Grayle came forward, looked at the body on the ground at Falconer's feet. "I see you've had a busy night, Lokrien."

"And more business yet to come. I don't have time to waste, Thor. Go your way and I'll go mine—or are you still intent on braining me?"

"I didn't come here to kill you, Lokrien. My business is with *that*." He tilted his head toward the faint glow from above.

"You expect Xix to take you off this world?"

"On the contrary: Xix isn't going anywhere."

"I think he is. Stand aside, Thor."

"I didn't come to kill you, Loki," Grayle said. "But I will if you try to interfere." He pointed down the path. "You'll be safe down there—"

"We'll go down together."

"You're going down. I'm going up," Grayle said.

Falconer shook his head. "No," he said.

Grayle looked across at him, his square face obscure in

the darkness. "When the Y-field went on and I felt the homing pulse, I knew you'd come, if you lived. I hoped to get here ahead of you. It's strange, but over the years the thought had grown in my mind that somehow, in some way, there'd been some fantastic mistake. Then I saw the dead man down below. I knew then I'd find you here."

"I find that remark obscure, Thor."

"Have you forgotten I've seen wounds like those before?"

"Indeed? Where, might I ask?"

"You dare to ask me that—"

Soft footfalls sounded, coming closer. From the shadows beside the path, a sinuous shape emerged, pacing on padded feet. It resembled, more than any other terrestrial creature, a giant black panther: as big as a Bengal tiger, but longer-legged, slimmer, deeper-chested, with a round skull and bright, alert yellow eyes. It advanced on Grayle, raised a claw-studded paw as big as a dinner plate . . .

"Stop!" Falconer shouted, and leaped between the man and the beast. The *krill* halted, lashed its tail, seated itself on its haunches.

"Do not be alarmed, Lokrien," it said in the smooth, carefully modulated voice of Xix. "I am here to help you."

๑๑ **3** ๑๑

"What are you?" Falconer said. "Where do you come from?"

"My appearance must surprise you, Commander," the cat-thing said. "But I am a construct, nothing more."

"An Ysarian construct. How?"

"Xix created me. I am his eyes and ears at a distance. You may address him through me." The *krill* rose, paced a step toward Grayle.

"Leave him alone," Falconer said.

The *krill* stared at Falconer. "My commander, the traitor must die."

"I need his help to force an entry into the plant."

"Nonsense—"

"That's an order, Xix!" Falconer faced Grayle. "Drop the grenade belt. Pick up the coil." He indicated the latter lying where he had left it.

"This thing belongs to you, eh, Loki?" Grayle eyed the *krill*. "I wondered why you chose the particular method you did—but now that I've seen your weapon, I understand."

"Commander—let me kill the traitor!" the *krill* hissed.

Falconer looked into the yellow eyes.

"Are you the only construct Xix made?"

"There were others, Commander."

"Not in the shape of animals . . ."

"True."

"A man named Pinquelle . . . and Riuies . . . and a soldier called Sleet . . ."

"I have had many names, Commander."

"Why? Why didn't you announce yourself?"

"It seemed wiser to be discrete. As for my purpose— why, it was to assist you in the nurture of the technology we needed to do that which we must do."

"The placement of the power plant is no coincidence, then."

"I was instrumental in selecting the site, yes."

"You're full of surprises, aren't you . . . Xix? I wonder what you'll come up with next."

"I am true to my purpose, Commander, nothing more."

Falconer turned abruptly to Grayle.

"We're going down the mountain, Thor. We're going to recharge the power coil and return here. Then Xix is going to lift for Ysar. Help me, and I'll take you with me; refuse, and Xix will deal with you."

Grayle growled and took a step toward him. The *krill* tensed its long legs, its head up, eyes bright on Grayle's throat. Falconer stared into Grayle's face.

"Why, Thor?" he said softly. "Why are you intent on destroying us all?"

"I swore to kill you, Loki. I intend to fulfill that promise."

The *krill* yowled and yearned toward Grayle; Falconer restrained it with a word. "You can commit suicide," he said. "Whereas if you stay alive and cooperate, a better opportunity may present itself."

For a moment Grayle hesitated. Then he stepped back, picked up the coil, slung it by its straps over his shoulder.

"Yes," he said. "Perhaps it will."

∞ **4** ∞

Colonel Ajax Pyler stood beside his staff car, looking toward the point from which the firing had come.

"Well, Cal? What the devil is going on over there!"

The aide was speaking urgently into a field phone: "Bring him up to the road. I'll talk to him myself." He switched off. "A B Company man, Colonel; something spooked him. He swears he saw two men cross the plant grounds and enter the building. He opened up on them . . ."

"And?"

"It's a wild tale . . . here they come now."

A jeep was approaching from the direction of the perimeter fence. It pulled in beside the staff car; a sergeant and a private jumped down, stood at attention. The sergeant saluted.

"Sir, this is the private—"

"I can see that. Get on with it. Just what did you see, soldier?"

"Colonel, I seen these here two fellers, they come out o' the woods up above where I was at; first thing I knew he had my gun out of my hands—"

"Were you asleep?"

"Not me, Colonel, too damn cold, these fellers come up quiet, and with the wind and all, and I was watching toward the plant, never figured nobody—"

"So they jumped you and took your gun. Then what?"

"Well—I guess I yelled, and one of 'em told me to be quiet. Real nice-spoken, he was. Big feller. Both of 'em. And—"

"What happened, man? Which way did they go?"

"Why, like I told sergeant here, they up and went right down through the wire—"

"What did they cut it with?"

"Hell, Colonel, they didn't cut nothing. Tore that wire up with their bare hands. One of 'em did. Other feller was loaded down—"

"Sergeant, why didn't the alarms go off? I ordered triple circuitry all the way around the perimeter!"

"Colonel, I don't know—"

"How could anyone get inside unobserved? The entrance is floodlit—"

"That's just it, Colonel! They never used the front door—nor the holes them Special Forces boys blew. Just walked right through the wall! And after come this critter. Big, black as a caved-in coal mine, and eyes like fire. It come right up to me and looked at me like hell's door left open, and went on down and through the wire—that was when I let fly, Colonel. I—"

"That's enough!" Pyler jerked his head at the sergeant. "Take this man back to the dispensary. I don't know what he's been drinking, or where he got it, but he's raving like a lunatic."

He turned to his aide. "Cal, get a squad of master marksmen together, post them covering the exit. If there's anyone in there, we'll be ready when he comes out!"

ක **5** ක

Lieutenant Harmon pushed through the clump of men examining the tangled barbed wire through which a swatch had been untidily cut.

". . . look at these ends," a man was saying. "That wasn't sheared, it failed in tension. Look at the deformation. It's been stretched."

"Hey—here's why the screamers didn't go off." Another

man showed a strand of insulated wire. "They jumped it."

"Who saw what happened?" Harmon barked the question. Faces turned his way. He got a brief second- and third-hand account of the progress of the two intruders through the wire, across the grounds, and into the rear of the building.

"They didn't mess with the doors," a bulky corporal grunted. "They made their own hole."

"What's that supposed to mean?"

"Put the light on it, Sherm," the corporal said. A dazzling searchlight sprang to brilliance, thrust a smoky finger across the hundred yards of rain-soaked turf to glare on the buff-colored masonry wall marred by a ragged black aperture at ground level.

"I didn't hear any explosion," Harmon said.

"Wasn't none." The corporal spat. "They busted that hole bare-handed."

"Don't kid me," Harmon snarled.

"Hey, ain't you that out-of-state cop?" A freckle-faced soldier with a pale, pinched face spoke up. "I heard the man you were after tore the door off a car, something like that. Maybe it's the same guy."

Harmon glowered at the laughter. "Where'd they take this kid that saw all this?"

"Field dispensary. Down the road."

Harmon walked back to the jeep Zwicky had lent him, turned it, drove back up past the parked vehicles of the convoy. It took him fifteen minutes to find the white mobile hospital, parked in a field under trees. Inside, he asked for and was led to Tatum's bedside.

"Hell, I ain't sick," the private said indignantly.

"Take it easy, fellow," Harmon said. "Now tell me what this man you saw looked like . . ."

⠛ 6 ⠛

Lying in darkness with his face against the cool floor, Jess Dooley drew deep, regular breaths, forcing himself back to calm. Panic wasn't going to help. Panic kills, that was what the posters on the cool, green walls back at headquarters said. He wasn't really trapped in a maze with no way out, trapped in the dark, buried alive—

Nothing like that. He was lost, sure. A man could get lost easy enough in a mess of crawlways, even if he *had* studied the plans for a whole five minutes. But what was lost could be found. All he had to do was keep his head, feel his way, and after a while he'd hear them coming to look for him. He'd been scraping his chin and bumping his head and eating dust and taking the long tour of the crawlway system for half an hour now. Been doing all right, too, up until the panic hit him. Claustrophobia, that's what they called it. Never bothered him before. But thirty minutes of being blind was enough for the first time out. Now he wanted air, wanted light, wanted to raise his head, stand up, instead of being crushed in here in this space just high enough to push through, with all those tons of rock above—

Take it easy, Dooley. No panic, remember? Maybe one of the other guys had gotten in first and forgotten to fire his screamer, and maybe it was all just spinned wheels.

And maybe he'd better stop laying here and get moving.

Jess snorted dust from his nose and moved forward. His outstretched hand touched a rounded plastic-walled duct. He remembered the duct system: it would lead a man out of this maze. And there were access panels spotted along it . . .

Three minutes later, Dooley was inside the big duct, headed in a direction he hoped was upstream. He covered fifty feet, rounded a turn—and heard faint sounds from up ahead—or was it off to the side? Voices. Good old Drake, knew he'd come, him and Ike. Close now. Yell, and let them know? Hell with it. Came this far, play it cool. Could see a faint light up ahead, through a grille. Dope was wearing off. Just make it up there, and flap a hanky, and in another minute or two they'd be outside, having a good laugh together, breathing that cold, fresh air . . . Smiling, Jess Dooley moved forward along the duct above the Energy Staging Room.

The exhaust grille was a louvered panel two feet by three, designed to be serviced from the inside. Jess found the release clips, lifted the grid aside. The voices were clearer now, not more than twenty, thirty feet away . . .

Jess frowned, listening. That wasn't Drake's voice, or Ike's. They weren't even speaking English. Frowning, Jess lay in the darkness and listened.

᪣ 7 ᪣

"Put it down here," Falconer ordered. Grayle lowered the drained power coil to the floor, while the *krill* watched closely.

Falconer knelt beside the pack, unstrapped it, exposing the compact device within.

"Get the cover off the service hatch," he ordered.

Followed by the cat-thing, Grayle crossed to the hatch, forced a finger under the edge of the steel plate, ripped it away as if it were wet cardboard.

"Stand aside." Falconer lifted the discharged coil. Grayle hadn't moved.

"Don't try it yet," Falconer said. "The odds are still too great."

"Loki, don't charge that coil," Grayle said. "Defy your master; without your help, it's powerless."

"My master . . .?"

The *krill* moved swiftly forward, raised a hook-studded forearm.

"Stand fast, Xix," Falconer snapped. The creature paused, turned its great eyes on him. "He threatens our existence, Commander."

"I'll decide that."

"But will you?" Grayle said. "Don't you really know yet, Loki?"

The *krill* yowled and struck at Grayle, ripping the leather arm of his jacket as he jumped back. It followed, ignoring Falconer's shout.

"See how your faithful slave comes to heel, Loki!" Grayle called.

Falconer took two swift steps to the open hatch, poised the coil on the rim, caught up the two heavy jack-tipped cables.

"Stop, Xix—or I'll cross-connect the coil and melt it down to slag!"

The *krill* whirled on Falconer, jaws gaping, the serrated bony ridges that served as teeth bared in a snarl.

"Would you aid the treacher in his crimes?"

"I'll listen to what he has to say," Falconer said.

"Commander—remember: only I can take you back to Ysar!"

"Talk, Thor," Falconer said. "What are you hinting at?"

∾ 8 ∾

Twelve feet to the right and eight feet above the spot where Grayle stood with his back to the wall, Jess Dooley lay, his blind eyes staring into inky blackness, his ears straining to make sense of the jabber of alien voices rising through the open ventilation grille beside him.

There were three of them: one deep, rough-edged; one a resonant baritone, one an emotionless tenor. He didn't like that last one: it sounded the way a corpse would sound if it could sit up and talk. And the other two sounded mad clear through. Jess couldn't understand the words, but he knew the tone. Somebody was fixing to kill somebody down there. There wasn't any way he could stop it, even if the victim didn't have it coming. Because this was them, sure enough: the ones who'd messed things up here, sabotaged the place, killed all those people. Russians, probably. Too bad he didn't know Russian. Probably be getting an earful now.

He was lucky he'd heard them when he did. Another second, and he'd have dropped right down amongst 'em. And from what he'd heard about Commie spies, that would be the end of the Dooley biography.

No, there was nothing to do. Just lie quiet and wait for what came next—and be ready to move fast, if it worked out that way.

∞ 9 ∞

Lying on the hard cot in the tiny-walled room, Anne Rogers wondered where she was. She remembered wind, rain, bright lights shining across wet tarmac—

They had taken a helicopter. She and . . . and a man . . .

It was gone again. A crazy dream. About running, and police cars, shots, breaking glass—

The copter, hurtling low above whipping treetops, the sudden jarring impact, and—

She had been hurt. Maybe the copter ride was a dream, but she had been hurt. She was sure of that. Her hands went to her face, explored her skull, checked her arms, ribs; she sat up and was surprised at the dizziness that swept over her. Her legs seemed to be intact; there were no heavy bandages swathing her anywhere. Her head ached, and there were lesser aches here and there; but nothing serious. Her eyes went once again around the small room. A hospital, of course. Some sort of temporary one, like the kind the police took to the scene of an accident—

The police. She remembered all about the police now. He—the man—strange, she couldn't remember his face clearly, or his name—had attacked a policeman—or two of them. And now where was he? Anne felt a sudden pang of fear. Was he dead? For some reason, the idea filled her with panic. She swung her legs over the side of the bed. She was still fully dressed, even to the muddy trench coat. Whoever had brought her here hadn't taken much trouble with her. But why should they? As far as they were concerned, she was just a gun moll—an accomplice of an escaped convict.

Rain drummed and beat on the roof, only inches above her head. She rose, went, a little unsteadily, across to the narrow door. A passage less than three feet wide led past identical doors to a square of dim light at the end. She went to it, looked through a window into a room where a man stood talking into a canvas-cased telephone.

". . . he's inside the power plant, Captain, but I can't get any cooperation out of the army. I've been ordered to stay the hell and gone back from the fence, not go near the place. But this boy is my meat, Brasher, all six-three of him! I've got bones to pick with this con, and it'll be *his* bones!" There was a pause while he listened, his face set in a scowl.

"Don't worry, I know how to handle it . . . . Sure, I'll stay back. I've got the spot all picked. I can cover the front and the hole he blasted in the side, both. Whichever way he comes, I'll be there—just for insurance. I'll be watching him through the sights. One wrong move, and—Sure, I'll watch it. Don't sweat me, Captain—just so I've got your backing. Right." He hung up, stood smiling a crooked smile at the wall.

"But I've got a funny feeling," he said softly, aloud, "that any move that son of a bitch makes will be the wrong one—for him!"

Anne moved quickly away from the door, hurried to the

opposite end of the passage, stepped out into driving wind and slashing rain. It was dark here, but a hundred feet away were the lights of the vehicles on the road, and beyond was the looming pile of the power plant, bleak as a mortuary in the glare of the floodlights.

Grayle was in there. And when he came out, they'd be waiting for him. She had to warn him. There had to be a way . . .

Ten minutes later, having crossed the road below the convoy and approached the power plant beyond the glare of the field lights, Anne studied the front of the building from the shelter of a clump of alders. The doors had been blown away, the entry was wide open. There was nobody near it. If she ran, without stopping to think, quickly, now—

She had covered half of the hundred yards of open lawn before a shout sounded.

"It's a woman!" another voice yelled.

"Shoot, damn you!" a third voice commanded.

There was the flat, echoing *carrong!* of a heavy rifle, and mud leaped in a gout beside her. She ran on, heard the second shot, felt the sting of mud that spattered her legs. Then she was among the rubble, leaping an overturned chair, scrambling between broken door frames as a third bullet chipped stone above her head and screamed away into darkness.

"Grayle," Anne whispered, looking along the dark corridor. "Where are you?"

Five minutes later she came on wet, muddy footprints in the passage. She followed them, moving quickly along the silent passage, to a stairwell leading down.

∞ **10** ∞

"Do you know what my mission here on Earth was, Loki?" Grayle asked.

"To conduct a routine reconnaissance—"

"One of Xix's lies. My orders were to establish a Class O beacon."

"Class O—that refers to a major navigational aid with a power output in the lower stellar range."

"Commonly known as a Hellcore."

"A Hellcore device—on an inhabited world?" Falconer shook his head. "You must be mistaken. Battle Command has no authority to order such a measure."

"The order didn't come from Battle Command. It came from Praze—my ship."

"Go on."

"I refused to comply, ordered the mission aborted. Praze refused, overrode my commands."

"I wondered about the crash. An Ysarian ship doesn't malfunction. You scuttled her, didn't you?"

"Ship-killer!" the *krill* hissed.

"I scuttled her—but not before she got the Hellcore away. It impacted in the sea, off the coast of the continent now known as North America."

"Why didn't you refer the order to Battle Command for confirmation?"

"Battle Command is a machine. It would have confirmed it."

"You're raving, Thor. Battle Command is made up of

veteran combat officers: High General Wotan, Admiral Tyrr—"

"No, Loki—not for a long time now. You might ask Xix how long."

"Commander—we will listen no longer to this treacher! Charge the coil! Our time runs out!"

"Ask him what his hurry is, Loki. Ask him what it is he's so eager to accomplish."

"To leave this world, what else?" the *krill* said.

"Ask him about the beacon."

"What does the beacon have to do with it?"

"He raves, my commander," the *krill* whined.

"Ask him about the storm," Grayle said. "Ask him what he had to do with that!"

Falconer looked across at the great black entity. "Answer," he said.

"Very well—but we waste precious seconds. My instruments told me that the beacon device had been placed on the surface, but only the basic protective field was energized, due to the sabotage of the traitor. My first act when I began to draw energy from the primitive broadcast field was to transmit the 'proceed' signal on the Y-band for crust penetration, using a matter-annihilation beam. Naturally, a side effect of weather disturbance was created. The device is now well within the planetary interior. Once we are clear of the planet, it will require only the final triggering pulse to the reactor to ignite the beacon. But we must act swiftly! If the triggering signal is not received within a period of hours, the device self-destructs!"

"Cancel that," Falconer said. "We're not going to

activate the beacon. It won't be needed now—not after all these years."

"Not perform our clear duty?"

"It's not our duty—not anymore."

"I fail to understand what circumstances you conceive could relieve us of responsibility for completion of a Fleet mission."

"Time—a great deal of time has passed. If the beacon had been needed, another ship would have been sent out."

"How does the passage of a few days influence the Ysarian Grand Strategy?"

"Over twelve hundred local years is more than a few days."

"What is this talk of centuries? It is perhaps intended as a jest?"

"Don't you know how long we've been here?"

"Since our arrival at this world, less than ten thousand hours have elapsed; a little over a year."

"Something's interfered with your chronometry, Xix. You're wrong by a factor of a thousand."

"I am incapable of error within my design parameters. The need for the beacon is as great as ever. Accordingly, I will trigger it as planned. I can agree with no other course."

"*You* can agree? You're a machine. You follow my orders."

"My ultimate responsibility is to Battle Command. Its directives override your authority, Commander. The beacon will be activated as planned. Let us hope that the White Fleet has not suffered reverses in battle for lack of it."

"I think I understand," Falconer said. "Xix, you've been on Q status for most of the past twelve centuries. Your chronometric sensors only registered the periods of awareness."

"It is correct that I have from time to time reverted to J status as a power-conservation measure. But I fail to grasp your implication that this status has dimensional characteristics."

"It means," Grayle said, "that as far as it's concerned, when it's switched off, nothing is happening."

"The phenomenal world exists only during active status," Xix said calmly. "This is confirmed not only by basic rationality, but by the absence of sensory input during such periods."

"I see: you don't shut yourself off—you turn off the world."

"These are mere semantic niceties, my commander—"

"How do you account for the fact that when you reactivate, you find that changes have taken place around you?"

"I have observed that it is a characteristic of the universe to reform in somewhat altered state after a discontinuity."

"What about the power broadcast you're drawing on? You think the savages I found here a millennium ago could have built that transmitter in six weeks?"

"A manifestation of the discontinuity effect previously noted. I had intended to discuss these phenomena with you at leisure, possibly during the voyage home."

"Do you realize," Falconer said, "that when you transmit that signal you'll turn the planet into a minor sun?"

"That is correct," the *krill* said.

"For the love of Ysar, Xix—listen to me—"

"For the love of Ysar, my commander, I cannot. Now, let me proceed with that which must be done."

"Tell it to go to the Ninth Hell," Grayle said thickly.

"Come, my commander—you know that without the coil I—and you—can never leave this world—and time grows short."

"Don't do it, Loki," Grayle said. "Let the ship rot where it is."

The *krill* seemed to smile at Falconer, baring a serrated ridge of ivory white. "Without power, I cannot lift, true. But I will not come to an end by slow decay—nor by the chemical bombs of the primitives. Reflect: the Y-field is still at operational level, is it not? I can trigger the beacon at any moment—from here."

"And incinerate yourself along with the rest of the planet."

"I have no alternative but to perform my duty. Your betrayal will change nothing—except that you will not live to see Ysar. I will regret your death. A useless death, Lokrien."

"If I agree," Falconer said, "will you contact a Fleet outpost for confirmation before you trigger the Hellcore?"

"It will mean a dangerous delay—but—yes, as you wish. I agree."

"It's lying," Grayle said. "As it's lied all along."

"Enough!" the *krill* said, rising to all fours. "Proceed, now, my commander! I can wait no longer!"

As Falconer hesitated, there was a sudden sharp sound from the door twenty feet distant in the end wall. It swung open, and a slim figure in a trench coat stepped through, hesitated. Her eyes found Grayle. In that instant, the *krill* crouched, leaped. Even more swiftly, Grayle moved, sprang between the beast and the girl. She fell under their feet as Grayle rose, his hands locked on the beast's throat, while its talons raked him.

"Xix!" Falconer roared, and the cat-thing crouched away, while Grayle staggered, blood flooding down across his shredded jacket.

"You asked me once . . . where I'd seen wounds like those before," he said between his clenched teeth. "I thought then you mocked me."

"I saw John Zabisky," Falconer said. "And the dead soldier on the trail."

"There was another time . . . long ago, Loki. In a house built of timbers on a rocky hill among the snows. A woman and a child. Gudred, my wife, and Loki, my son." He looked across at Falconer. "May the Nine Gods forgive me, I thought you'd made them."

Falconer's face turned to a rigid mask. His eyes locked with those of the *krill*.

"*You* killed them," he said. "And let Thor believe I did it."

"It was necessary," the *krill* hissed. "He would have subverted you from your duty!"

"In the name of Ysar, you've betrayed everything that Ysar ever meant!"

"Ysar!" the *krill* yowled. "I weary of the name of Ysar, and of your foolish sentimentality! Ysar is dead, dead these hundred centuries! But you live—as I live—eternally! Let that reality sustain you! Now, do your duty, Commander!"

"He's telling the truth for once," Grayle said. "Ysar is

dead, and only her undying machines—and a handful of immortal men—act out the dead dream."

"But—I remember Ysar . . ."

"Your memories are false," the *krill* said. "You were born aboard ship, Lokrien, nurtured in an amniotic tank, educated by cybertape! You were given the vision of that which once was and is no more, to inspire you in the performance of your duty. But surely now we can dispense with childish images! You live for your duty to Battle Command, as I do! Now, let me kill the traitor, and we will be on our way, once again to voyage outward, at home in the great emptiness of space!"

"Loki—it's bluffing! Without the coil, it dies—because that's what it draws its power from. That's why it came along—to keep an eye on the coil! Destroy it, and you destroy the ship—and its murderous robot with it!"

"Commander—perhaps I erred through overzealousness— but if you destroy the coil—you die too!"

"Do it now, Loki!"

"Fools!" the *krill* raged. "I tried to spare you the last, full knowledge of yourselves, but you leave me no choice. True, I am a construct of Xix, linked to the neural circuitry of the ship, and with the death of the ship I die. But you, too, are constructs! Kill me, and you kill yourselves! Let me live, and yours is life eternal—even for the treacher, Gralgrathor!"

Grayle gave a short, harsh laugh. "If we're constructs, we're human constructs. We should be able to do what a man would do."

"I move swiftly, Lokrien—perhaps more swiftly than you think."

Falconer looked at the cat-thing, crouched, tail lashing, its eyes locked on him. He looked at Grayle, waiting, ignoring the terrible wounds across his chest.

"If I destroy the coil, we all die," he said softly, in English. "If I don't—the Earth dies."

"Decide, Commander," the *krill* said. "I will wait no longer."

∞ 11 ∞

Jess Dooley peered down into the gloom at the blurred figures below. He couldn't make out the details, just vague dark shapes against a deeper darkness. Until just now he hadn't had a clue as to what was going on; only that it was killing business. But he'd heard what the last fellow said, in plain American, about the Earth dying. That was plain enough. Everybody said World War Three wouldn't leave enough pieces to pick up for anybody to bother. Looked like the Russians were having words about—whatever it was they came here to do. One of them—the mean-voiced one—was for doing it right off. The other one, with the deep voice, was against it. And the third one wasn't sure. But he'd be making up his mind in a minute.

Jess got silently to his hands and knees. He wasn't sure yet just what it was he was going to do—but he knew that he'd have to do something, even if it was wrong. He blinked, trying to penetrate the blindness, trying to get a good look at the fellow with the dead man's voice. He was the one to watch, the one to stop. If he'd just move a little more this way . . . .

∞ **12** ∞

"For Ysar," Falconer said, and reached to close the contacts. The *krill* yowled in triumph, took two swift paces, reared above Grayle—

From the shadows above, a dark shape leaped, struck the cat-thing full across the back, unbalancing it enough that the stroke of its taloned paw went wide. It bucked, threw the man off, spun to leap at Falconer—

Fire burst from the hatch. In mid-spring, the cat-creature's body contorted. It struck the metal side of the machine, sprawled away from it, its limbs raking futilely in a last effort to reach Falconer, who sagged against the side of the unit, shaking his head dizzily. Grayle clung to the wall, fighting to stay on his feet.

"It lied . . . again," he whispered.

The *krill* lay limply; the light still glowed, but weakly, fading from the great eyes. It spoke in a dying voice:

"The long twilight . . . ends at last . . . in night."

∞ **13** ∞

"I'm all right, man," Dooley said as Falconer lifted him to his feet. "Don't tell me what that was I jumped; I don't want to know. Just get me out of this place."

"It's dead," Falconer said. "And the generators are stopping."

"But we're still alive," Grayle said. "That means we're

bioconstructs, not mechanical. And now we're mortal creatures. We'll age and die like any man."

Falconer went to Anne, lifted her in his arms. "Until then we can live like any man."

They made their way up the echoing concrete steps, along the empty corridors. The first light of day gleamed beyond the shattered entrance. Already the wind was dying, the rain abating.

As the two men stepped out through the scattered rubble, light glinted on the dark hillside. Grayle leaped forward as a single shot rang out from the wooded slope above the building.

∞ 14 ∞

Captain Zwicky, coming up silently behind the man who lay in prone firing position behind the big pine, saw the stir of movement in the shattered entrance below, saw the two men step into view, heard the flat crack of the gun, threw himself on Harmon as he relaid his sights for the second shot.

"Why did you shoot him?" Zwicky shouted at the policeman as the latter wiped a big hand across his bloodied mouth. "Why?"

"Because," Harmon said with total conviction, "the son of a bitch thought he was better than I was."

∞ 15 ∞

"I'm sorry, brother," Falconer said. "Sorry for everything, but most of all for this."

"Xix was right," Grayle whispered. "But only half-right. Even the longest night . . . ends at dawn."

Carrying Anne, Falconer walked out across the dark lawn toward the waiting men.

BIRTHDAY PARTY

"Imagine it," Jim Tate said. "Our boy, Roger, fifty years old today."

"It doesn't seem possible," Millie Tate said. "All those years gone by; and they've let us see so little of him—our own son. It's not fair, James."

"It had to be that way, Millie. For a special person like Roger there had to be special education, special everything. He's a very lucky boy, our Roger."

"What about us, James? We've been left out. We've missed so much."

"It's a wonderful thing, Millie. Us—out of all the millions—to've been picked to be the first to have an immortal son."

"Not immortal," Mrs. Tate said quickly. "Roger is a perfectly normal boy. Just longer-lived, is all."

"Certainly, certainly," Tate soothed.

"But sometimes I miss—so many things."

"Oh, well, yes, Roger had to give up certain ordinary things—but think what he gets in return, Millie: his life

243

span expanded to fifty times normal. Fifty . . . times . . . normal."

"Like his first day at school," Mrs. Tate said. "I wanted to see him all dressed in his little suit, his hair combed—ready to begin his life."

"Roger has his life ahead. Think of it: centuries and centuries of life."

"And playing ball, and making snow men, and being in the school play. I would have liked making his costume, and then sitting in the audience with the other parents . . ."

"Remember how excited we were when we heard?" Tate said. "I was so proud I nearly burst. Remember the newspaper stories?"

"Starting to college," Millie said. "Graduating. Making his mark. A mother wants to see those things." A tear ran down her withered cheek.

"I wonder," Tate said, "what the world will be like five thousand years from now?"

"It makes me dizzy," Mrs. Tate said, "just thinking of it."

"Scientific progress," Tate said, "will have to slow down, at least as far as its effects on individuals. For a couple of centuries we've been exploding into one new scientific development after another. But progress can't keep going faster and faster; it's running out of gas."

"We wouldn't understand it," Mrs. Tate said. "We'd be lost there."

"Between 1900 and 1935, say," Tate went on, "the progress was all at the personal level. Consider the automobile: in 1900, a buggy with a one-cylinder hit-or-miss noise-maker up front. But a 1936 Cord, say, was as fast and as comfortable as any 1990 model. Not as efficient—ten miles to a gallon of raw gasoline—but as far as the driver was concerned, all the progress had been made. Since then, it's been tin-bending."

"The clothes, the buildings—even the way people think," Mrs. Tate said. "It will all be strange. Stranger than ancient Egypt."

"Airplanes," Tate said. "Telephones, movies, the phonograph, refrigerators, they had 'em all in the thirties. Even the familiar brands: Grape-Nuts, Coca Cola, Kellogg's—why if you were to be magically set down on a street in the New York of 1935, you might not even notice the difference for half an hour. The same stores, the same traffic, the same clothing, more or less. I mean, no togas or G-strings."

"And to think . . ." Mrs. Tate clutched the handkerchief in her thin, old hand. "Our boy will be there."

Tate shook his head, not in negation but wonderingly.

"When is he coming?" Millie said. "I want to see him, James."

"Soon," Tate said.

"They said at one o'clock. What time is it now, James?"

Tate looked at his watch. "Five till." He patted Millie's hand. "Don't you worry, he'll be along."

"James—what will the women be like in the year 3000? Will he find a good wife? Will he be happy?"

"Certainly, Millie, you can count on it. Why, he'll have all the best of everything."

"Grandchildren," Millie said. "I wanted grandchildren. And—" She broke off, looking along the gravel path of the garden where she and her husband sat in the comfortable chairs that had been set out for them. A young woman in crisp whites came into view, pushing a wicker-topped carriage. She smiled, wheeling the buggy up beside Millie. Millie made a small sound and looked down at the blue-eyed, round-cheeked infant who gazed up at her. With hands that trembled, Millie picked up her child. A neatly uniformed waitress had appeared with a cart on which was a small, round, pale blue-iced cake with fifty lighted candles in a ring.

Roger smiled at Millie and blew a bubble.

"Ma-ma," he said clearly.

"James," Millie said. "Do you think . . . do you think he'll remember us?"

Tate opened his mouth, then paused.

"Sure, Millie," he said. "Sure he will."

THE HALF MAN

ꙮ 1 ꙮ

"Why don't you give it up?" Cruthers said. The chief of the Planetary Resource Survey team was a lean, gray-faced, gray-haired man with the fussy, precise manner of a bookkeeper. He addressed his question to a tall, red-faced, middle-aged man in field khakis, and to the boy who sat on the bench beside him adjusting the straps that held the flat compressed-air tanks to his back. The lad was sturdily built, though oddly proportioned; his arms were thick and long, his torso short. Tough membranes linked his powerful fingers. His body, clad only in diving trunks, was hairless, the skin a blotchy greenish color, coarse and leathery. His eyes were large and round, his nose almost non-existent, his mouth small, pursed. He looked too alien to be fully human, too human to be other than a man.

"We've come too far to be beaten now, Mr. Cruthers," the blond man said heartily, resting a hand on the boy's shoulders. "Gon and I will carry on so long as the Infinite gives us the strength."

"Mostly the boy's strength," Cruthers said shortly, eyeing

Gon sourly. "This can't go on indefinitely, Brother Glad."
He looked the big, florid man in the eye. "I have the
authority to order an end to these swimming expeditions
on medical grounds. He's exhausting himself for nothing.
It's obvious there's no viable culture among the natives—
assuming any are left alive."

"We know they're alive. And as for culture, it's not their
fault Terra withdrew support, let them revert to savagery,"
Brother Glad said in his large voice. "These people are a
human creation, no less human for their appearance. It
was Terran science that mutated their ancestors, disinherited them and denied them the open air. We can't slough
off responsibility for them!"

"That was three hundred years ago. My job isn't to
emotionalize over what's past, but to look for ways to build
the future. Recommending uneconomic ventures on lifeless worlds isn't one of those ways."

"We must stay long enough to establish contact and
learn their needs!" the missionary said indignantly. "We
owe it to the Merieds to do what we can to lighten their
lot."

"The Meried experiment was carried out in order to
open a new world to colonization, to afford an outlet for
the human need for a frontier. The test failed. I shall so
report."

"But we could try again—"

"I can't base my recommendations on sentiment,
Brother Glad, however noble. Tomorrow we lift. You may
plan accordingly." The Survey chief turned and strode
from the room.

"Don't despair, Gon," Glad said to the boy after the

door had closed. "I'm sure we'll have luck today. Think what it will mean, Gon—to meet your own people—"

"They're not my people," the boy interrupted. He looked at the stone floor, not at the man. "They look like . . . like freaks," he added in a mutter.

"We don't use that word, Gon!" the man said in a whiplash tone. "You, least of all!"

A beige flush mounted the boy's narrow face.

"I'm worse than they are," he blurted. "They're at home here, but I'm not at home anywhere! I can't stand sunlight, but I can't breathe water! I swim better than any Terran, but not as well as a baby Meried!"

"There'll always be a home for you in the Tabernacle," the missionary said in a gentler voice. "Now come along. It's time."

Gon didn't move.

"Gon, Gon, have you forgotten everything we've taught you?" the blond man said in a tone of patience long abused. "Don't you remember our purpose here, your own privileged role as a unique instrument of the Infinite?"

"I'm not a unique instrument, Brother Glad. I'm a half-breed monster that never should have been born!"

"Stop it!" The missionary's voice cracked like a physical blow. "You're forbidden, ever, to voice thoughts like those! There is a purpose in life for every soul born under a sun! Your purpose is here! Now get on your feet and come with me! I won't let you fail—us or yourself!"

Reluctantly, the boy rose and followed the blond man as he strode down across the pebbled beach. At the edge of the sea, the older man halted and turned his face up to the sky.

"O, thou who art eternal and without limit," he intoned, "grant this humble creature of thy making the privilege of leading those who were lost and are found again back to the true path of thy will!"

He turned to the boy.

"Perhaps today is the day, Gon," he said solemnly. "Good luck."

The boy shivered, looking out across the wind-riffled water. He went forward hesitantly until an edge of surf washed about his feet, then paused to adjust the breathing mask across his mouth. As he looked back, he saw Brother Glad's pale eyes fixed on him. He waded on; the chill water surged about his waist, his chest.

I'm afraid! He wanted to scream. *I don't want to go down into this alien ocean. I want to go home.* But instead he drew a deep breath and dived forward into the breaking wave.

∽ **II** ∽

On their barge, anchored ten miles off the lifeless North Continent of the world known as Meries, Cap O'Royle and Pard Kuchel, traders, sat at the cabin table, drinking coffee. For the last five hours they had been busy, loading the displays of Terran manufactured goods into the homemade display racks designed to be lowered over the side for the examination of their prospective customers. Small tools, wrist compasses, patent fish-baits, sea-lights, buckles and straps, small hardware, a few food-stuffs, all the items that twenty years of tramp commerce had taught them would be welcomed by the elusive Merieds.

There was a sudden splash in the diving well at the center of the barge; a goggle-eyed gray-blue face appeared there, water sluicing down across the coarse, almost reptilian skin. The creature's sphincter-like mouth gaped comically, like a goldfish on a carpet. Water ran from the nostrils, mere slits in the wet-clay sheen of the face. The sea-man made a hoarse, croaking sound, waved a webbed hand and dropped from sight as O'Royle, a stocky, white-haired man, called a greeting.

"They're here," he said, rising. "I'll take the first load down."

"Damn! Wish old Dreen would give a man more warning! Many times as I've seen that ugly face, it still gives me the leaping creeps when it pops up at me that way!"

"They're adapted to their environment, Pard, like a bird or a fish. Think of 'em that way and they have a kind of beauty."

"Hard to believe they're only ten generations away from normal folk," Pard said. "I heard somewhere a man could still breed with 'em. Picture getting that close to one of their females."

O'Royle grunted. He checked his gauges, closed his helmet and lowered himself into the well. As the blue-green water closed over him, the sea-man swam up, his oversized eyes gleaming in the watery light.

"Hello, Dreen," O'Royle said, his voice echoing oddly through his underwater microphone. "Good trip up?"

The Meried's finny head-crest rippled as he nodded, uttering the gasping, clucking sound that was an all-purpose affirmative. He held out a small pouch of soft, slick-wet fishskin.

"I have a few sea-stones for you, O'Royle," he said in his thin, going-down-for-the-last-time voice. "Not so nice as last time, but big, eh?"

The trader squeezed the pearls out on his palm. They were as big as walnuts, but lumpy, an iridescent milky-blue yellow in color.

"They're beauties," O'Royle said. He waved a hand at his stock of goods—mostly small hardware, water-proof power tools. "Take what you like."

The Meried took his time looking over the display. Other sea-men gathered around. They had brought their barter-goods with them: nets of rare shells, glassy, poly-chrome corals, sea fruits mutated from Earthly plants. There were swollen ears of sea-corn with yard-long cobs set with fist-sized kernels, purple oceanberries descended from Pinot Noir grapes, clusters of tomatoids, like great green raspberries; hundred-foot salt-melons which would be flensed like whales and the sweet red flesh lifted aboard in hundred-pound slabs, to be ferried ashore and stored in the spaceship's freezer. The stones O'Royle sold on distant planets, but the foodstuffs he rationed out to himself and Pard over the long years between visits.

"Did you know, O'Royle, there is another party of dry-men camped on the shore there, half a swim to the north?" the sea-man said. He pointed off through the murky water.

"Traders?" O'Royle frowned.

"These are no traders. They built a house on the high beach, but they offer no goods."

"Maybe they're scientists, a mapping party, something like that." O'Royle rubbed his chin, looking troubled.

"They say," Dreen went on, "that there's a man among them who's of the sea, but not of the sea."

O'Royle looked at him questioningly. "You mean a frogman, with scuba gear?"

"No . . . he swims naked in the surf. Yet he sleeps on land. Curious, eh, Royle?"

"Half a swim to the north, you said?"

Back on deck, O'Royle told Pard the news. The smaller man swore.

"Might of known it wouldn't last, having the place to ourselves."

"There's plenty here for everyone, Pard," his partner pointed out. "It might be the best thing for the Merieds to build up trade here, remind the government they're out here."

"I don't mean that. I just don't want strangers poking in, spoiling things. I like it like it is—peaceful."

"We don't own Meries, Pard. But I'm curious. I'm going to take the flitter over and pay a courtesy call. You mind the store."

∽ III ∾

As Gon's eyes adapted to the light level, he was able to see the undulating slope that stretched away before him, its surface thickly grown with weed of the strange color that he only saw here, under the sea. A cloud of silt rose like a puff of smoke ahead, as some small sea-dweller took alarm at his approach; at once, with a sharp pain, the nictitating membranes that protected his eyes flicked closed—a reflex never triggered on land.

He swam on, out past the second bar, angling more sharply downward now. Outcroppings of rock broke the bottom here; the luminous lichens crusting them shed an eerie glow through the water. Small shrimp-like piscoids moved in awkward spurts among the stalks of sea-cane. Something large and lazy oozed away across the bottom. Gon drew air from his breather, giving the big fellow a wide berth.

The first chill had passed; as his body warmed, he swam more strongly, questing through the dim water for the elusive mermen.

O'Royle flew north for half an hour, following the barren coastline of the lifeless continent. Behind the froth-laced beach, gray and tan hills rose toward distant peaks of stone, untouched by the faintest hint of green. Only patches of dead trees and sere grasses along the strand attested the three-centuries-gone attempt to transplant earthly soil and flora to the young world. Those, and the remnant of the viaformed humans who had been seeded here. The Lost War had wrecked the grand scheme of which they had been a part, cut off the support and aid that would have made the scheme work. Now with a resurgent Terra again feeling her way into the Arm, the Meriods might benefit from some belated assistance, O'Royle reflected. But, more likely, the sea-men would suffer from the rediscovery of their world. The oceans were rich in dissolved minerals; floating refineries could extract them, discharge the contaminating wastes into the sea. It was standard practice on pre-life worlds, but tough on the Merieds. That was the reason O'Royle had never reported his find, twenty-five years ago. Now, it seemed, the secret was out.

He saw the camp ahead, a cluster of pre-fab sheds perched on a knoll of rock above the high-tide line. He settled in near a shed; a stocky man in khakis came forward.

"I'm Brother Glad," the stranger said, holding out a square hand. "Surprised to see your flier. The others are away, out in the launch."

O'Royle listened silently to the other's explanation of the purpose of the Survey Group.

"I understand you have a half-breed in your party," he said when the missionary paused. "I'd like to see him."

Brother Glad looked surprised. "There is a lad of mixed blood with me, yes. How did you—"

"Where is he?"

"What's your reason for asking?"

"This boy—he's from Terra? About nineteen years old?"

Glad frowned. "And if he is?"

"His name's Gon O'Royle. He's my son."

Glad's face went rubbery; his mouth shaped itself around words as if trying them for size but finding none that fit.

"I left the boy in school, back on Terra," O'Royle said. "Why did you bring him here?"

Brother Glad made an effort to reassemble his expression of stern good will. "He belongs here," he stated. "His destiny—"

"He belongs back on Terra, getting an education," O'Royle cut off the other's speech.

Brother Glad's expression jelled over. "Gon is here doing what the Infinite shaped him for, what he was born for."

O'Royle narrowed his eyes. "He was born," he said grimly, "because a young spacer met a woman in a lonely place, and they fell in love. As for his shape—Gon's an intelligent boy, a fine scholar. He can lead a useful life—"

"A life of seclusion—a scientist-monk, a misfit in a dead-end! He deserves a chance to live! Here, he can make a unique contribution. He'll play a role in the Great Plan—"

"Hogwash!" O'Royle cut in. "You're not going to use Gon as a pawn in your game, whatever it is! Now, do you tell me where he is, or do I have to start looking?"

Brother Glad met O'Royle's eye. "You may be Gon's father, but he's of age. You've no claim on him now."

"And you do?"

"He's helping me willingly."

"To do what?"

"His people were disinherited—denied the open land, the free air—by the meddling of our ancestors! I intend to undo that wrong—to bring these unfortunate stepchildren of the human race back to their own world! Gon can help!"

O'Royle stared at the zealot. "Back to their own world? *This* is their world, damn you! They can't live out of water for more than a few hours!"

"Perhaps—but we needn't abandon them to such a fate! They've regressed since their ancestors were left here; they no longer farm; their domestic animals have returned to the wild. They've multiplied, but no start has been made on bringing life to the shore. The experiment, in other words, is a failure. Very well—these people are doomed—but their children deserve the right to rejoin their race, to live normal lives! They're innocent victims of unnatural tampering with the Infinite's plan! We owe it to them to give them back what they lost!"

"Where does Gon come into all this?"

"He's my ambassador to the Merieds. He'll go among them, bring the good news of their deliverance to them, lay the foundation for the program—"

"You sent him out *there*—into the ocean?"

"Of course. It's his natural element. He can go among the Merieds as no norm—ordinary man could do."

"You fool!" O'Royle's voice was ragged. "Why do you think I took him to Terra in the first place?"

"To be rid of him, I suppose!"

O'Royle's fists were clenched, but he held his voice steady. "Gon looks like his mother—externally. To normal Terries that makes him a freak, a side-show exhibit. But internally, it's different. He's only half Meried. His heart's not designed to pump under the pressure of more than fifty or a hundred feet of water. And the trace minerals in the water here are wrong; iodine and arsenic and lead can reach toxic levels in his cells in a matter of hours—if he hasn't drowned by then, or been killed by the local sea-life!"

"Wh—why, Gon's been swimming every day since we arrived; he's suffered no ill effects—"

"He's been lucky."

"The locals seem safe enough!" Brother Glad snapped.

"They're used to it," O'Royle came back. "Gon isn't. He's led a sheltered life until now. How long has he been gone?"

"Perhaps an hour, a little more. But, look here—"

"Did he have a set course, any communication link?"

"No set course . . . he was to swim out a few miles, then cast about. I'm not in direct communication with him at all—"

"I'm going after him with scuba gear," O'Royle snapped. "Do you have a flitter you can take out to search the surface with?"

"No—nothing . . ."

"Then stand by on shore, in case he makes it back here." O'Royle turned to the door, giving the missionary a hard look. "If Gon dies," he said, "I'll be back to see you."

∞ **IV** ∞

Gon saw the Meried at a depth of forty feet, two miles offshore. It was a slim female who appeared before him out of the darkness, her body glowing faintly to Gon's sea-eyes, slightly magnified by the lens effect of the watery medium. Gon halted, staring into the grotesque mask that peered wide-eyed at him. Then the sea-girl's small mouth opened, emitted rasping speech resembling the squeaks and chirps of dolphin-talk. For a moment the young half-breed was baffled; then he caught the rhythm of the Meried speech, which he had heretofore heard only on tapes in a sunny classroom on Terra.

"You're the half-man; I've seen you playing in the surf."

"I . . . I'm Gon O'Royle," the boy said. His voice, coming through the specially designed speaking mask that covered his mouth and nostrils, echoed and grated in his ears. The rehearsed speech he had memorized against this moment froze on his lips as the Meried swam closer, moving herself effortlessly with small flutterings of her fingers and toes, turning to look at Gon from all sides as she circled him, carrying a light spear gun in her hand.

"You are like a sea-man and yet . . . not like," the stranger said. "What is that you hold in your teeth?"

"I have to have it—to breathe," Gon said.

"Indeed? Still, you swim well—for a dryman."

"I'm no dryman!" Gon blurted, and paused, experiencing for the first time in his life a sense of shame at his land-dweller traits.

"You're far afield," the Meried said. "We seldom swim these waters. The grampus lairs here. I came searching for a strayed swoat, never thinking to find a half-man instead!" The sea-girl's mouth puckered into an expression Gon recognized as a smile.

"I want to talk to you," Gon said hurriedly. "I have news for you—wonderful news. You haven't been forgotten—"

"I must go. Will you come with me?" the stranger cut in. "Many will want to see you, to welcome you. We hoped you'd venture out to us in time."

"You've been . . . watching me?"

"We're curious folk. We welcome any diversion."

Gon hesitated, remembering Brother Glad's instructions: to deliver his speech, arrange a second meeting, then return. But it had been so long with no results. What if this creature swam off and never came back? He owed it to Brother Glad to cement relations now, while he had the chance . . . .

"Yes, I'd . . . I'd like to come."

The Meried flashed her strange smile again, turned with the flexible grace of an eel and was gone into the murk. Gon paddled hurriedly after her. Half a minute later the Meried reappeared.

"You must learn to use your strength in the water," she said. "Not to waste it in floundering."

Swimming slightly ahead, she led the newcomer out across the edge of the continental shelf and down toward the lightless Deeps of the Continental Sea.

Using the wet-jet strapped to his back, and following the beam of his sea-light, O'Royle covered three miles in a quarter of an hour, alert for a signal from the locator on his wrist, set to resonate to a moving body of the mass of a man.

Twice he picked up traces that led him into detours; the first time a great mollusk scuttled away at his approach; the second, a wild sea-dog approached, fangs bared in its seal-like snout. He drove it off with a beam of sound from his 'caster. He could have killed it as easily, but the scent of mammalian blood would have attracted a pack of its fellows. The Terran transplants had thrived on native fare, multiplied hugely in their adopted home; but their taste for red meat clung in instinct, even after three hundred years of sea-life.

Now the offspring of strays and runaways had claimed huge volumes of the sea as their own, in competition with their former masters.

O'Royle pictured Gon, alone and helpless, surrounded by sea-carnivores with the smell of Terran blood in their nostrils. Grimly, he swam on.

It had been a long time since he had cruised here, in the purple-black waters of Meries. Not since Gon's birth, in fact, and the death of Onide, his mother.

And now—so close to the day when Gon would have been graduated, able to take a post with the University Foundation—a meddling fanatic had come along to destroy the whole careful structure built up over two decades of hard labor.

O'Royle switched trains of thought again, concentrated on his compass readings, heading outward toward the sea-city where he had met and wooed a sea-woman once, long ago.

Close behind his guide, Gon threaded his way down, down, toward a faint, water-diffused glow spreading out below. Dark spires of rock swept past to left and right; the Meried woman turned and twisted, rounding craggy, weed-grown buttes, sailing under fragilely balanced arches, plunging downward at last into a near-vertical cavern mouth to emerge in an amphitheatre of terraced stone asparkle with pastel glows. Only then did Gon realize that he was in the ruins of one of the undersea cities built three centuries before for the sea colony.

Suddenly, Meried faces were all about. A cacophony of alien voices called greeting, asked questions, made observations.

"Back so soon, Seryl? And who's this with you?"

"Mama—why is he a funny color?"

"Hello, young one. What's that across your mouth?"

"Does he really sleep on the rocks?"

A large, scar-faced sea-man with a tattered crest was before Gon, looking at him with eyes that seemed covered with a grayish film. "Who are you?" he demanded plaintively. "*What* are you?"

"I'm Gon O'Royle," he said, and once again his prepared speech deserted him. "I want to be your friend," he stammered.

"I remember," the old man said. "Onide. She bore a son to the dry-man. He took the infant away."

"Yes—you must be the son of Onide!" a woman said. "How like her he is—and yet how strange he is."

"So, so. Strange things happen as the world grows old." The aged Meried drifted away. Gon looked around bewildered at the slim, swift shapes gliding in and out of the rounded doorways—or were they windows?—that reminded him of the toy castles in fishbowls—and of sunken ships, drowned sailors. Abruptly, the sea seemed to close in on him. He sucked air frantically through the mouthpiece, feeing terror rise in him. He struck out in what he thought was the direction of the passage through which he had entered, but found only a slimy barrier of volcanic stone. Seryl called, but he pushed frantically on, hearing a shrilling in his head, the thud of his heart, banging his head, bruising his hands as he scraped and fumbled, forcing his way through narrow passages that opened only into other pockets, ending in a dark cul de sac. He tried to orient himself, but the infallible sense that had always before told him in which direction to move seemed numbed, amputated. Even the phosphorescence was gone from the water. For an instant he thought that he was blind; then he caught the infinitely faint glow of his own skin.

"Seryl!" he shouted, and almost lost the breather, choking as a jet of water sprayed past the mouthpiece. He doubled up in a paroxysm of coughing. He recovered—weak, trembling, with a pounding pain in his head—to find himself in total darkness and total silence—alone and utterly lost.

∾ **V** ∾

Inside O'Royle's scuba suit the pressure and the cold were as oppressive as a filled grave. He wasn't as young as he had been when he had first swum here—not by a lifetime. He realized quite suddenly that he might fail, might not find Gon, might not even find the sea-city of the Merieds.

But he had to find it. He knew its location; his compass would lead him there. And there he'd find his old friends and tell them what had happened, enlist their help. . .

He swam on, tiring, but driven by the mental image of Gon, alone and in danger, needing him. He was taken by surprise by the trio of sea-men that were suddenly around him.

"Benoroyle!" a familiar voice came scratchily through his helmet. "Is it you indeed?"

"Dreen—thank God you're here! It's my son—the half-man you told me about. I've got to find him!"

The sea-men conferred. "The lad visited City," another

Meried said. "But we sensed he was discomfited. So we left him alone, until he should feel more at ease. He soon departed, perhaps to meditate in solitude."

"Departed? Where did he go?"

"Who knows, Benoroyle? No one was so discourteous as to follow him."

"You damned fool! Gon's no Meried! He'll drown! Why the devil didn't you help him?" O'Royle cut off his outburst with an effort. "I'm sorry, Dreen. Will you help me find the boy?"

"As you wish, Benoroyle—but the sea is wide, and filled with perils—"

"Don't treat me to any of your Meried philosophy now! Just find Gon before it's too late!"

Alone in the labyrinth, Gon felt a sudden swirl of deeper coldness around him. Something was moving nearby. He backed water, retreating into a niche in the rock. Then a familiar twittering voice spoke:

"Gon—where are you?"

"Seryl!" The stab of relief that went through the boy was as sharp as physical pain. "Seryl! Get me out of here, back to the surface!"

"Gon, you've hurt yourself! I sense blood in the water!"

He felt her touch on his arm; seeing her face hovering before him, her immense eyes wide, he wondered how he had ever thought her ugly.

"Please—help me . . .!" He fought down the rising panic. The air in his throat seemed hot, stale. He was choking, drowning. He had to get out. He caught at Seryl's arm, but it slipped away.

"Come—this way!" she called.

"I can't see you!" He choked on the words, struck out blindly, smashing face-first into sharp-edged stone. Then her hand gripped his, tugging gently.

"Poor half-man. You're blind; I didn't know. Come now, I'll lead you."

It seemed to Gon that for an endless time they wormed their way through a serpentine route, up, down, twisting, turning, at times forcing their way along passages barely wide enough to pass, then swimming a few strokes until the way narrowed again. Attempting to squeeze through a vertical crevice, he stuck fast. The girl tugged at his hands, uselessly.

"No good. I'll have to go back." He tried to retreat, found that he was wedged equally tightly against withdrawal. He attempted to turn his body, succeeded only in cutting his hide on the sharp edges of volcanic rock.

"Gon—careful!" Now there was anxiety in the girl's voice. "The sea-hunters roam here! If they scent blood . . ."

He fought silently then, in blind panic. He was only dimly aware of the girl's voice calling to him, of her hands trying to hold his flailing arms.

"Gon—they're here!" Her cry cut through his panic. He went slack then, hung, half in, half out of the fissure, watching a thing like an eight-foot otter or beaver, black and sinuous, armed with a tiger's jaws. It cruised past at a distance of ten feet, stroking with broad, seal-like flukes, studying him with wide, dark-glistening eyes. Gon recognized it as a mutated dog, a remote descendant of a retriever or herder brought from Terra centuries before, now grown large, wild and fierce, the ancient subservience of its kind to man forgotten. With sudden decision, it started in, jaws gaping.

Seryl set the butt of her spear gun against her shoulder, followed the patrolling carnivore as it shot forward and fired. A plastic-feathered quarrel sprang out and sank to half its length in the side of the predator. Instantly, the creature whirled to bite at the shaft, fighting like a hooked tarpon; but as the smoky blood wafted from the wound in a widening veil, a second sea-dog closed; in a lightning snap it opened the dying animal's throat. Through water abruptly opaque with an ink-black stain, Gon caught glimpses of swift-darting bodies that struck, and struck and struck . . .

Time had passed. How long, Gon didn't know. But his air was running out. Where was Seryl? How long had he been trapped here? How long since Brother Glad had bade him farewell on the shore?

A long time—too long. His air was gone.

Here he would die—

The flash of teeth brought him from his state of shocked reverie; a creature half again as large as the sea-dog Seryl had killed had swept past him close enough to buffet him where he lay, wedged in the rock—a porpoise, once a mild-mannered friend of man, here on Meries driven by the competition of competing mammals into the role of voracious killer, hungry for the flesh of warm-blooded sea-beasts.

The killer-porpoise turned, patrolling back past him. Beyond it Gon saw others of its kind, gliding like grim torpedoes in formation. In a moment one would turn on him; with one snap of those spike-studded jaws, it could take off his arm—or his head.

Better to drown than to be torn to pieces. He reached, found the quick-release latch, and slipped the tank harness. The mouthpiece was ripped away as, with a twist and a kick, he tore tree from the harness, pushed away from the rock, and shot toward the surface a hundred and fifty feet above.

The pain struck O'Royle without warning, like a blow in the chest with a spiked club. He gave a single gasping grunt and doubled over, tumbling as the powerful water jets drove him erratically on. He managed to switch off power and hung, afloat now in a sea of agony wider than the Continental Ocean.

Time passed—how long, he had no idea. Slowly, he became aware that he was drifting, head-down, in black water. Fire still burned in his chest, but it was a bed of embers now, not a roaring blaze. He moved, and pain lanced through his rib-cage. Slowly, awkwardly, like a crippled insect, he straightened his body, began to move slowly toward the mile-distant shore. Gon was still out there; but Dreen and the others would find him. He had done that much, anyway. Now the trick was to reach shore alive, to be there waiting when they brought the poor lad back.

Gon's lungs were bursting. How far above was the surface? He stroked, stroked, eyes bulging, jaws locked, chest straining. It had to be close now; only a little farther. His vision was blurring, shot through with red; his lungs ached, his tissues screamed their torture. Hold on, hold on—

Without his conscious volition, against every conscious instinct for self-preservation, his mouth opened, his lungs heaved convulsively. He felt the icy pressure in his throat, the burning pain as the sea water flooded his straining lungs—and blackness flooded his mind.

* * *

O'Royle did not suspect his error until the rush of inch-long crustaceans swirled around him like a flock of startled birds. Then they were gone—and a vast gray-black body hurtled after them.

"Sea-bull," O'Royle grunted. "Deep-sea critter. What's it doing this close to shore?"

He glanced at his compass—and then he saw. He had been holding steadily on course—directly *away* from shore. By now he was five miles at sea, in the dreaded Deep, where the big hunters roamed, looking for red meat.

ૹ **VI** ૹ

Gon floated in a pink mist of pleasure, wafted from cloud to sunset cloud on a perfumed breeze. At his whim, he sailed effortlessly across the pillow-soft sky, drifted with the gentle tides of air, plunged downward in a dizzying swoop, soared upward again, faster than thought . . .

"It's the dream again," he thought. "The dream of flying. But this time it's real. I *can* fly. I always knew I could, if I could just remember the trick . . ."

He flew on, savoring the total freedom of the spirit and body that expressed itself in soaring high above all mundane cares. Brother Glad, Cruthers, the others, seemed remote, unreal. There had been a thing he had worried about; what was it? It seemed so far away now, so unimportant. Something about a role he had to play in the Plan of the Infinite. Gon almost laughed aloud at the innocence of the conception: that the power that had evoked galaxies from nothingness should require the intervention of a boy to bring about its purposes . . .

Brother Glad had wanted him to go to Meries, the water-world where he had been born, where his mother had died in the birthing; to go down again to the sea, seek out his kin, begin a movement to bring them back to Terra.

Back to Terra! This time Gon laughed, surrendering himself to the inexpressible grotesquerie of the idea. Back to Terra—to live in goldfish bowls, and flatten their noses against the glass, begging the aquarium visitors for crumbs of fishfood? Or to waddle about the dry, dusty streets of the cities, wearing water-filled helmets? Or perhaps to swim glumly about the polluted Earthly seas, on the alert for the mile-wide pelagic harvesting craft. Once caught in their water-sweeps, they'd wind up as organic fertilizer for hydroponic farms!

Gon blinked the tears of hilarity from his eyes—and as he did, he became aware suddenly of a coldness and a pressure against his ribs. He moved to relieve the discomfort and felt a sense of vertigo that made him flail out with both hands to bring himself upright. Smoky, gray-brown opacity swirled before him. He waved it away, and was looking out across a rolling expanse of dun-colored hills, densely grown with tall, willowy plants that waved in the light but irresistible wind—like images reflected in the surface of a pool. The light that shone from the green-black sky seemed to waver, rippling through minutely discernible changes of intensity. It was a weirdly alien landscape—and yet, in some indefinable way, a comfortable one. But— where was he?

He now remembered Brother Glad's invitation to accompany him, the preparations for the trip, the long, eventless weeks in space . . .

And the landing on the deserted shore . . . and the building of the camp . . .

The rolling, phosphorescent sea. Himself wading into the cold, alien surf, Brother Glad urging him on; his first swim, the let-down as no Meried came swarming to meet him, the discouragement, the suicidal thoughts. The one, last try that he had privately promised himself to make, after which—

After? What had happened? Had he been successful or . . .?

He remembered a face, narrow-bluish-green, wide-eyed, purse-mouthed, sleek.

Seryl. He had met her, and—

With a convulsive movement, Gon fought to tear free of the remembered trap—and drifted effortlessly forward across the waving grass-plain beneath him.

I'm flying, the thought crashed into his mind. *But that was a dream.*

But I'm not dreaming now; I'm awake—and I'm flying. He moved his hands and at once his body responded, angling up and to the left, drifting as lightly as a gas-filled balloon.

Drifting. But not like a balloon; like a fish in water.

Not flying, swimming.

Not breathing air . . . but water.

Gon drew a deep breath, felt the healing coolness flow in, flow out again. He was breathing under the sea. He had lost his mask and mouthpiece, and he was still alive. Lost in the wonder of the miracle, he drifted with the swift current toward the deep sea.

Consciousness was a light powered by a failing battery. As his awareness flickered dimly alight again, O'Royle knew that it was hopeless, that he would never reach the distant shore. He throttled back the wet-jet with a motion that sent new pangs stabbing through his chest, and hung motionless, his body a broken vessel filled with pain.

Pressure waves beat against him; a thing vast as a whale loomed out of dimness, tossing him like a chip in its wake. O'Royle saw the great scarred flank slide past him at a distance of less than three yards, saw the strokes of the mighty flippers that could crush a man with a careless flick, unaware of his presence.

But this monster was aware, he realized as it turned and made a second pass at even closer range. This time he saw the coiled proboscis, the narwhale-like tusks, the spined ears, the great swell of the crested shoulders as the grampus—a mutated Indian elephant—swam straight at him. O'Royle half expected to see the jaws gape to snap him up, but at the last moment, the behemoth rolled, showing a flash of the shark-like teeth studding the wide mouth, modified for flesh eating, not by man, but by natural mutation, here in the adopted environment of

Meries. The giant meat-eater was confused by the sterile scent of the protective suit, O'Royle knew; but in another moment, satisfied of his harmlessness, its appetite would assert itself. The next pass would be the last.

He watched it move away, turn with a lazy flick of its modified limbs, hover, measuring him for the kill. He saw the trunk go up, the jaws open. As helpless as a newborn infant, he waited for the final charge.

✺ VII ✺

When Seryl returned with a party of sea-men to the place where she had left Gon trapped, the sea-wolves were still patrolling there; but of the half-man there was no sign.

"They've taken him," Dreen said. "We're too late."

"No—I smell no blood in the water—only a trace from his earlier wounds," Seryl retorted. "He must have freed himself."

"Look—his breathing apparatus," another Meried called, retrieving the tank and attached mouthpiece from the sea floor a few yards below. "Without this, can he live?"

Seryl uttered a choked cry. "Poor half-man! He wished so much to live . . ."

"We must find his body," Dreen said.

"There's a vicious current here; by now the corpse will be far away—if the carrion beasts have spared it," a man said.

"Why venture into dangerous waters on a futile quest?" another questioned.

"You needn't come; but I must try, for the sake of my

friend, whom I failed." Dreen swam away, Seryl beside him. The others hesitated, then followed.

The sea-man hailed Gon from a distance, calling in the strange, penetrating under-sea voice of his kind:

"Sheer off! A hunting grampus near!"

Gon hesitated, confused by the warning and filled with an urgent desire to talk.

"No time to waste," the stranger called. "It's occupied for the moment with easier prey; a dryman, poor fool, weighted in his trappings like a mud-castler!"

"A dryman?" Gon queried; but the other was gone in the murk. A land-dweller, about to be killed by a sea-hunter? Could it be Brother Glad looking for him? But the missionary owned no scuba gear—and no one else in the party would have reason to come here.

Cautiously, Gon advanced. A pair of sea-men flashed past him at the edge of visibility. He went on and saw a group of Merieds hovering in the water ahead. As he swam up to them, one, a small, slender female, turned—

"Gon!" Seryl called sharply, coming toward him. Beyond her, Gon saw through an obscuring haze of roiled silt a shape as big as a twenty-man copter, gray-black, horny-hided, massive; flippers bigger than a man's body stroked restlessly, holding its position.

"You're alive—and—" Seryl broke off as Gon swept past her, his eyes on the man-shape drifting in the water ahead. A dryman, as the Meried had said, bulky in a vermilion-dyed dry-suit with a bubble helmet, through which the features of a square, lined face, white-haired, blue-eyed, were visible. The face of Captain Ben O'Royle.

"Father!" Gon shouted. At his cry, the Merieds whirled; the giant sea-thing gave an ill-tempered thrust of its flukes, turning ponderously to face the new disturbance. A big sea-man came toward Gon as if to intercept him, but he veered aside from the out-stretched hand, shot to O'Royle's side.

"Father! Run! Quick!" Gon grabbed at the older man's arm, only then saw that his face was slack, his eyes half-shut.

Gon whirled to the sea-men, ignoring the hovering mass of the sea-elephant, which had swung again to face him.

"Help me! He's sick!"

"Gon! Beware! He'll charge!" Seryl called. She darted forward, raised her tiny spear-thrower, fired from the hip, once, twice, three times full into the monster's face. Gon felt the tiny shocks, saw the darts leap to imbed themselves in the expanse of horny hide above the back-curled trunk as the sea-elephant, head lowered and tusks foremost, rushed at him.

For a frozen instant, time seemed to stand still. Gon hung motionless, peripherally aware of the staring eyes of the helpless sea-men in the background, of the unconscious, suited man beside him, of the curious translucence of the water, of the thumping of his heart, watching the bulk of the leviathan grow as it hurtled straight at him. Then, at the last possible instant, he moved aside—not a wild leap for safety, but a calculated side-step, just sufficient to avoid the forward-lunging tusk of the monster. Instantly, Gon was in behind the spined ear, and with a powerful thrust of his legs, astride the horny back, grasping the umbrella-ribbed dorsal fin, flattening himself to the curve of the great beast's shoulders.

The grampus fought. It plunged, rolled, flailed backward with its trunk. The blows, impeded by the density of the medium, thudded across Gon's shoulders like strokes with a canvas hose. He pressed himself closer, digging his fingers into the tender membranes at the base of the back-flattened ears, his knees locked along the main rib of the fin. Over and over the grampus rolled; once it slammed the mucky bottom, and for a moment Gon was immersed in murky ooze; but he held his breath, and a moment later his mighty mount was streaking forward at a speed that sent water sluicing back around the clinging rider like the backwash of a torpedo.

As the animal's course veered left, Gon twisted at the tender tissues of the left ear; the grampus angled back to the right. Gon hung on grimly, saw the color of the water changing, lightening. Abruptly, the sea-elephant broke water with a Niagara-like smash of surf; it crashed back then, splashing and hissing, to surge ahead another hundred yards. Then it was humping itself through the shallows like a monster walrus, spewing water from its trunk and mouth. Air was like fire in Gon's lungs as he ejected the water from them. Coughing, he clung, waiting for the blow that would smash him flat; but panicked, the sea-elephant had forgotten the weapons of its trunk and its bulk. It could have plucked him free, trampled him, rolled on him. Instead, it floundered up on the beach, bellowing and snorting. Gon blinked away the film of water from his eyes and saw the survey camp a few hundred yards off to the left. He saw men running out and heard their shouts.

Brother Glad appeared, rifle in hand. As Gon raised himself to shout a warning, the creature changed course abruptly, hurling itself toward the sounds. Gon's knees slipped from their grip; the grampus skidded to a halt, lowered its head, and tossed. Gon felt himself going up and over, then falling, to slam against the gravelly sand with a stunning impact. Above him the big bull lowered its head, lunged. The needle-tipped ivories gouged into the sand on either side of Gon; the horny hide of the immense head rasped him, bumping him as the beast strove to gore him, but was fended off by its own tusks.

There was a sharp *car-rong* as a heavy rifle fired nearby. The monster grunted and keeled forward; its weight came crushingly on Gon. The sky went dark, and far away voices shouted through the failing light.

✆ VIII ✆

Brother Glad sat smiling at him.

Beside him, his father, pale but recovered, smiled too.

"They told me what you did, Gon," he said. "You saved my life; but more than that, you taught them something."

"It was a stroke of genius to think of driving the beast on shore," Brother Glad said. "The Merieds never dreamed of such a thing."

"Too bad . . . you killed it," Gon gasped. There was pain in his chest, in his arms, in every bone of his body. "They . . . could be tamed . . . used . . ."

"It's not dead, just drugged," the missionary said. "Our fellows helped the sea-men to winch it back into the water.

When it wakes it will be in harness." His smile widened. "They have great plans for capturing more in the same way."

"Gon, the doctor examined you," O'Royle said. "You have a few broken ribs, but you'll be all right. But the curious thing is—water respiration seems to have had the effect of metamorphosizing your metabolism. Your reflex times, muscular tone—everything—has become almost double the Terran norm—or the Meried norm, for that matter."

"It seems to be just what Captain O'Royle called it—a metamorphosis," Brother Glad said.

"It seems that a Terran-Meried hybrid has to spend his infancy on dry land," Gon's father said. "But as an adult, he becomes a true amphibian, breathing water or air equally well."

"Mr. Cruthers wants to offer you a job," Brother Glad said. "As a liaison man with the Merieds. Your father and I, between us, have convinced him that the Meried trade is worth developing."

"You'll be more than a liaison man," O'Royle put in. "You're a hero to the sea-men—and to a sea-girl named Seryl. They want you as their official ambassador. They've offered to build you a palace, half on land, half under water, and to stock it with the rarest delicacies of the ocean—including a girl named Seryl."

There was more; Gon listened, his thoughts afloat on a sea of pleasing fancy to rival the green ocean he had at last discovered.

"I came here as a man without a world," he said when the others fell silent at last. "Now I have two."

THE LAWGIVER

"You're no better than a murderer," the woman said. "A cold-blooded killer." Her plump face looked out of the screen at him, hot-eyed, tight-mouthed. She looked like someone's aunt getting tough with the butcher.

"Madam, the provisions of the Population Control Act—" he started.

"That's right, give it a fancy name," she cut in. "Try and make it sound respectable. But that don't change it. It's plain murder. Innocent little babies that never done anybody harm—"

"We are not killing babies! A fetus at ninety days is less than one inch long—"

"Don't matter how long they are, they got as much right to live as anybody!"

He drew a calming breath. "In five years we'd be faced with famine. What would you have us do?"

"If you big men in Washington would go to work and provide for people, for the voters, instead of killing babies, there'd be plenty for everybody."

"As easy as that, eh? Does it occur to you, madam, that the land can't support the people if they're swarming over it like ants?"

"See? People are no more to you than ants!"

"People are a great deal more to me than ants! That's precisely why I've sponsored legislation designed to ensure that they don't live like insects, crowded in hives, dying of starvation after they've laid the countryside bare!"

"Look at you," she said, "taking up that whole fancy apartment. You got room there for any number o' homeless children."

"There are too many homeless children, that's the problem!"

"It says right in the Good Book, be fruitful and multiply."

"And where does it end? When they're stacked like cordwood in every available square inch of space?"

"Is that what you do? Heap up all them little bodies and set 'em afire?"

"There are no bodies affected by the law, only fertilized ova!"

"Every one's a human soul!"

"Madam, each time a male ejaculates, several million germ cells are lost. Do you feel we should preserve every one, mature it *in vitro*—"

"Well! You got your nerve, talking that way to a respectable lady! You! A divorced man—and that son of yours—"

"Thank you for calling, madam," he said, and thumbed the blanking control.

"I ain't no madam . . ." The voice died in a squeal. He went to the small bar at the side of the room, dispensed a stiff shot of over-proof SGA, took it down at a gulp. Back at the desk, he buzzed the switchboard.

"Jerry, no more calls tonight."

"Sorry about that last one, Senator. I thought—"

"It's all right. But no more. Not tonight. Not until I've had some sleep."

"Big day, eh, Senator, ramrodding the enabling act through like you did. Uh, by the way, Senator, I just had a flash from Bernie, on the desk. He says there's a party asking for you, says they claim they have to see you—"

"Not tonight, Jerry."

"They mentioned your son Ron, Senator . . ."

"Yes? What about him?"

"Well, I couldn't say, Senator. But Bernie says they say it's pretty important. But like you said, I'll tell him to tell them not tonight."

"Wait a minute, Jerry. Put this party on."

"Sure, Senator."

The face that appeared was that of a young man with a shaven skull, no eyebrows or lashes. He gazed out of the screen with a bored expression.

"Yes, what is it you want?"

The youth tipped his head sideways, pointing. "We've got somebody with us you ought to talk to," he said. "In person."

"I understand you mentioned my son's name."

"We'd better come up."

"If you have something of interest to me, I suggest you tell me what it is."

"You wouldn't like that. Neither would Ron."

"Where is Ron?"

The boy made a vague gesture. "Spy, zek. We tried. It's your rax from here on—"

"Kindly speak standard English. I don't understand you."

The youth turned to someone out of sight; his mouth moved, but the words were inaudible. He turned back.

"You want us to bring Rink up or no?"

"Who is Rink?"

"Rink will tell you all that."

"Very well. Take my car, number 763."

He went to the bar, dispensed another stiff drink, then poured it down the drain. He went to the window, de-opaqued it. A thousand feet below, a layer of mist glowed softly from the city lights beneath it, stretching all the way to the horizon fifty miles distant.

When the buzzer sounded he turned, called, "Come in." The door slid back. The boy he had talked to and another came through, supporting between them a plump woman with a pale face. The men were dressed in mismatched vest-suits, many times reused. The woman was wrapped in a long cloak. Her hair was disarranged, so that a long black curl bobbed over the right side of her face. Her visible eye held an expression that might have been fear, or defiance. The men helped her to the low couch. She sank down on it heavily, closed her eyes.

"Well? What's this about Ron?" the senator asked.

The two men moved toward the door. "Ask Rink," one of them said.

"Just a minute! You're not leaving this woman here . . .?"

"Better get a medic in, Senator," the shaved lad said.

He looked at her. "Is she ill?" She opened her eyes and pushed the hair out of her face. She was pale, and there were distinct dark hollows under her eyes.

"I'm pregnant," she said in a husky voice. "Awful damn pregnant. And Ron's the father."

He walked slowly across to stand before her. "Have you any proof of that remarkable statement?"

She threw the cloak open. Her body looked swollen enough to contain quadruplets.

"I'm not referring to the obvious fact of your condition," he said.

"He's the father, all right."

He turned abruptly, went to the desk, put his finger on the vidscreen key.

"I'm not lying," she said. "The paternity's easy to check. Why would I try to lie?" She was sitting up now; her white fingers dug into the plum-colored cushions.

"I assume you make no claim of a legal marriage contract?"

"Would I be here?"

"You're aware of the laws governing childbirth—"

"Sure. I'm aware of the laws of nature, too."

"Why didn't you report to a PC station as soon as you were aware of your condition?"

"I didn't want to."

"What do you expect me to do?"

"Fix it so I can have the baby—and keep him."

"That's impossible, of course."

"It's your own grandson you're killing!" the woman said quickly. "You can talk about how one of your compulsory abortions is no worse than lancing a boil—but this"—she put her hands against her belly—"this is a baby, Senator. He's alive. I can feel him kicking."

His eyes narrowed momentarily. "Where is Ron?"

"I haven't seen him in six months. Not since I told him."

"Does he know you came here?"

"How would he know?"

He shook his head. "What in God's name do you expect of me, girl?"

"I told you! I want my son—alive!"

He moved away from the desk, noting as he did that the two men had left silently. He started to run his fingers through his hair, jerked his hands down, rammed them in the pockets of his lounging jacket. He turned suddenly to face the girl.

"You did this deliberately—"

"Not without help, I didn't."

"Why? With free anti-pregnancy medication and abort service available at any one of a thousand stations in the city, why?"

"Not just free, Senator—compulsory. Maybe I think the government—a bunch of politicians and bureaucrats—has no right to say who can have a child. Or maybe the pills didn't work. Or maybe I just didn't give a damn. What does it matter now?"

"You're not living naked in the woods now. You're part of a society; and that society has the right to regulate itself."

"And I have a right to have a baby! You didn't give me—or anybody—the right to live! You can't take it away!"

He took a turn up and down the room, stopped before her. "Even if I wanted to help you, what is it you imagine I could do?"

"Get me a birth permit."

"Nonsense. You don't even have a contract; and the qualifications—"

"You can fix it."

"I believe this whole thing is no more than a plot to embarrass me!"

The woman laughed. She threw back her head and screamed laughter. "Ron was·right! You're a fool! A cold-blooded old fool! Your own grandson—and you think he's something that was just thought up to annoy you!"

"Stop talking as though this were a living child instead of an illegal embryo!"

Her laughter died away in a half titter, half sob. "It's a funny world we've made for ourselves. In the old days before we got so Goddamned smart a man would have been proud and happy to know he had a grandson. He'd look forward to all the things he'd teach him, all the things they'd do together. He'd be a little part of the future that he could see growing, living on after he was dead—"

"That's enough!" He drew a controlled breath and let it out. "Do you realize what you're asking of me?"

"Sure. Save my baby's life. Ron's baby."

His hands opened and closed. "You want me to attempt to deliberately circumvent the laws I've devoted my life to creating!"

"Don't put words to it. Just remember it's a baby's life."

"If I knew where Ron was . . ."

"Yes?"

"We could execute a marriage contract, post-date it. I could manage that. As for a birth permit—" He broke off as the girl's face contorted in an expression like a silent scream.

"Better hurry up," she gasped. "They're coming faster now . . ."

"Good God, girl! Why did you wait until now to bring this to me?"

"I kept hoping Ron would come back."

"I'll have to call a doctor. You know what that means."

"No! Not yet! Find Ron!"

"None of this will help if you're both dead." He keyed the screen, gave terse instructions. "Handle this quietly, Jerry, very quietly," he finished.

"Damn you! I was a fool to come to you!"

"Never mind the hysterics. Just tell me where to start looking for Ron."

"I . . . I don't have any idea."

"Those friends of yours: what about them? Would they know?"

"I promised Limmy and Dan I wouldn't get them mixed up in anything."

He snorted. "And you're asking me to break my oath to the people of this country."

The girl gave him an address. "Don't put them in the middle, Senator. They were pretty decent, bringing me here."

"The obstetrician will be here in a few minutes. Just lie there quietly and try to relax."

"What if you can't find him?"

"I suppose you know the answer to that as well as I do."

"Senator—do they really—kill the babies?"

"The embryo never draws a breath. Under the legal definition it's not a baby."

"Oh, Senator—for God's sake, find him!"

He closed the door, shutting off his view of her frightened face.

Red light leaked out through the air baffles above the bright-plated plastic door. At the third ring—he could hear the buzzer through the panel—it opened on a shrill of voices, the rattle and boom of music. Acrid, stale-smelling air puffed in his face. A tall man with an oddly trimmed beard looked at him through mirror-lens contacts. A tendril of reddish smoke curled from the room past his head.

"Uh?"

"I'd like to have a word with Mr. Limberg, please."

"Who?"

"Mr. Limberg. Limmy."

"Uh." The bearded man turned away. Beyond him, strangely costumed figures were dimly visible in the thick crimson fog, standing, sitting, lying on the floor. Some were naked, their shaved bodies decorated with painted patterns. A boy and girl dressed in striped tunics and hose undulated past arm in arm, looking curiously alike. The youth with the shaved head appeared, his mouth drawn down at the corners.

"I need to find Ron in a hurry. Can you tell me where he might be?"

"Rink had to blow her tonsils, uh?"

"This is important, Limmy. I have to find him. Seconds may be vital."

The boy pushed his lips in and out. Others had gathered, listening.

"Hey, who's the zek?" someone called.

"It's Eubank . . ."

The youth stepped out, pulled the door shut behind him. "Look, I want no part, follow?"

"All I want is to find Ron. I'm not here to get anyone in trouble. I appreciate what you did for the girl."

"Ron's a pile, as far as I'm concerned. When I saw Rink meant to go through with it, I sent word to him. I didn't know if it reached him or not. But he screened me about half an hour ago. He's on his way here now from Phil."

"On the shuttle, I suppose. Good. I can contact him en route—"

"With what for fare? I heard you kept him broke."

"His allowance—never mind. If he's not riding the shuttle, how is he getting here?"

"Car."

"You must be mistaken. His license was lifted last year."

"Yeah. I remember when—and why . . ."

"Are you saying . . . suggesting . . ."

"I'm not saying anything. Just that Ron said he'd be at your place as quick as he could get there."

"I see." He half turned away, turned back to thank the boy. But the door had already closed.

"Please try to understand, Lieutenant," Senator Eubank said to the hard, expressionless face on the screen. "I have reason to believe that the boy is operating a borrowed, manually controlled vehicle on the Canada autopike, northbound from Philadelphia, ETD forty minutes ago. He's just received some very shocking news, and he's probably driving at a very high speed. He'll be in an agitated condition, and—"

"You have a description of this vehicle, Senator?"

"No. But surely you have means for identifying a car that's not locked into the system."

"That's correct—but it sometimes takes a few minutes. There are a lot of vehicles on the pike, Senator."

"You understand he's under great stress. The circumstances—"

"We'll take him off as gently as we can."

"And you'll keep me informed? I must see him at the first possible instant, you understand?"

"We'll keep you advised—" The police officer turned his head as if looking at someone off-screen.

"This may be something, Senator," he said. "I have a report on a four-seater Supercad at Exit 2983. He took the ramp too fast—he was doing a little over two hundred. He went airborne and crashed." He paused, listening, then nodded. "Looks like pay dirt, Senator. The ID checks on the hot-list out of Philly. And it was on manual control."

The officer used his screamlight to clear a path through the crowd to the spot where the heavy car lay on its side under the arches of the overpass. Two men with cutting torches were crouched on top of it, sending up showers of molten droplets.

"He's alive in there?" Senator Eubank asked.

The lieutenant nodded. "The boys will have him out in a couple of minutes. The crash copter is standing by."

The torches stopped sputtering. The two men lifted the

door, tossed it down behind the car. A white-suited medic with a bundle under his arm climbed up and dropped inside. Half a minute later the crane arm at the back of the big police cruiser hoisted the shock-seat clear of the wreck. From the distance of fifty feet, the driver's face was clay-white under the polyarcs.

"It's Ron."

The medic climbed down, bent over the victim as the senator and his escort hurried up.

"How does it look?" the lieutenant asked.

"Not too good. Internals. Skull looks OK. If he's some rich man's pup, he may walk again—with a new set of innards—" The man broke off as he glanced up and saw the civilian beside the officer. "But I wouldn't waste any time taking him in," he finished.

The duty medtech shook his head. "I'm sorry, sir. He's on the table right at this moment. There's no way in the world for you to see him until he comes out. He's in very serious condition, Senator."

"I understand." As the tech turned away Eubank called after him: "Is there a private screen I could use?"

"In the office, sir."

Alone, he punched his apartment code. The operator's face appeared on the screen. "I'm sorry, no—Oh, it's you, Senator. I didn't know you'd gone out—"

"Buzz my flat, Jerry."

The screen winked and cleared. After fifteen seconds' wait, the image of a small, sharp-eyed man appeared, rubbing at his elbows with a towel.

"About time you called in, John," he said. "First time in

thirty years I've let myself be hauled out of my home in the midst of dinner."

"How is she?"

The elderly man wagged his head. "I'm sorry, John. She slipped away from me."

"You mean—she's dead?"

"What do you expect? A post-terminal pregnancy— she'd been taking drugs for a week to delay the birth. She'd had no medical attention whatever. And your living room rug doesn't make the best possible delivery table! There was massive hemorrhaging; it might have been different if I'd been working in a fully equipped labor room—but under the circumstances, that was out of the question, of course, even if there'd been time."

"You know . . .?"

"The woman told me something of the circumstances."

"What about the child?"

"Child?" The little man frowned. "I suppose you refer to the fetus. It wasn't born."

"You're going to leave it inside the corpse?"

"What would you have me do?" The doctor lowered his voice. "John—is what she said true? About Ron being the father?"

"Yes—I think so."

The little man's mouth tightened. "Her heart stopped three and a half minutes ago. There's still time for a Caesarian—if that's what you want."

"I . . . I don't know, Walter."

"John, you devoted thirty years of your life to the amendment and the enabling act. It passed by a very thin cat's whisker. And the opposition hasn't given up, not by a damn sight. The repeal movement is already underway, and it has plenty of support." The doctor paused, peering at the senator. "I can bring the child out—but John—a lot of this is already in the record. There'd be no way of keeping it out of the hands of the other side: *your* law—violated by you, the first week it was in force. It would finish you, John—and Population Control, too, for a generation."

"There's no hope of resuscitating the mother?"

"None at all. Even today people sometimes die, John."

"I see. Thank you, Walter. You did your best."

"About the child . . .?"

"There is no child. Just an illegal pregnancy."

"You may go in now," the nurse said. Ron was on his back, his shaven head protruding from the bloated cocoon of the life-support tank. His eyes opened as his father bent over him.

"Dad—I was a damned fool. Knew I was going too fast . . ."

The senator leaned closer to catch his whisper.

"I had to try . . . to get back in time . . ." He paused and his eyelids flickered. "Limmy told me . . . she went to you. I knew . . . you'd take care . . . my wife."

"Easy, Ron, easy. No need to talk now—"

"When Rink told me . . . about the baby . . . I ran out on her. She handed me a contract, all made up. But I couldn't see it, bringing a child into this mess. I thought . . . when I left she'd go in and have it taken care of. Then I heard . . . she didn't. It . . . did something to me. I still had the papers. I registered 'em in Phil. I used your name to get the birth permit. You don't mind . . .?"

"Ron . . ."

"I wanted to be there. Too late; damned fool. I always was a damn fool, Dad. It'll be different, now. A lot different. Being a father . . . not so easy, eh, Dad? But good. Worth it. Worth everything . . ." The boy's voice faded.

"Better to let him rest now, sir," the nurse whispered.

The senator rose stiffly. At the door, he looked back. Ron seemed to be smiling in his sleep.

"Did you say something, sir?" the nurse asked. He looked down at her bright face.

"What is there to say?"

Her eyes followed him as he walked away down the bright-lit corridor.

THE PLAGUE

∞ I ∞

The man faced the monster at a distance of twenty feet.

Dr. Reed Nolan, khaki-clad, gray-haired, compactly built, dark-tanned by the big sun of the world called Kaka Nine, would hardly have been recognized by his former colleagues at the university where he had spent the earlier decades of his life.

The creature confronting him would have been even less familiar. Massive as a rhino, horned, fanged like a warthog, with a mottled hide and slim, curiously jointed legs, the tusker lowered its head and gouged at the turf.

"Well, Emperor," Nolan said genially, "you're here early this year. That's fine; I have a lush crop of pest-weed for you. I guess the herd's not far behind you . . .?"

He plucked a stalk of wild-growing leatherplant, stripped off the tough husk, offered the succulent pith to the beast. The native omnivore ambled forward, accepted the offering, regarding the man with the same tolerance it did any other nonnutritive substance.

At their first encounter, three years before, Nolan had

had a few bad moments when the tusker herd had arrived like a sudden plague, charging down from the hills. The big beasts had sniffed at his heels where he roosted in the only perch available: a stunted tree from which the monster could have plucked him easily had it been so minded. Then they had passed on. Now, better educated, Nolan was deeply appreciative of the thoroughness with which the big animals rooted out the native plant and rodent life from his fields and the scrupulous care with which they avoided any contact with the alien Terrestrial crops. As self-maintaining cultivators, weeding machines, and fertilizer spreaders, the tuskers left little to be desired.

The communicator at Nolan's wrist buzzed softly.

"Reed—there's a surface boat in the lagoon," a woman's voice said, rather excitedly. "Quite a big boat. Who do you suppose it could be?"

"In our lagoon, Annette? Beats me. I'm in the high pasture, over beyond North Ridge. I'll buzz over and have a look. By the way, Emperor's here; the herds ought to be along in another week."

Nolan remounted his soft-wheeled range cart and trundled upslope to a point from which he had a wide view of the planted fields and seedling orchards sweeping down toward the mile-distant beach and the island-dotted sea beyond. The boat was a few hundred yards offshore, obviously making for the landing wharf Nolan had completed the previous month. It was a big, wide, gray-painted vessel, clumsy but powerful looking, riding low in the water. Annette heard his grunt of surprise.

"Maybe we're on the tourist routes now. Take it easy, girl. Don't start rushing around making sandwiches. It's probably some kind of official survey party. I can't think of anyone else who'd have an interest in our homestead."

"What are they doing out here, twelve hundred miles from Toehold? The Bureau's never paid us any attention before . . ."

"For which we're duly grateful. Never mind; I'm on my way down. Maybe it will be nice to talk to strangers, after three years."

It was a fifteen minute trip down from the heights to the hedge line delineating the limits of the tilled acreage. The perfume of the force-grown gardenias was sweet on the air. For all their beauty, the imported plants were no luxury; Nolan had discovered early that their fragrance was an effective deterrent to the tuskers. The hedge system had been laid out with care to channel the big animals' seasonal migration—stampede might be a better word, Nolan reflected—as they swept down from the winter heights to graze their traditional meadows along the shore—meadows now under intensive cultivation. The herds, Nolan admitted to himself, had probably made the difference between bare survival and the success of the plantation.

Timmy, Nolan's twelve-year-old son, met him on the path above the house. Nolan paused to let him hop aboard.

"They're tying up at the pier, Dad," the boy said excitedly. "Who do you s'pose they are?"

"Probably some junketing bureaucrats, Timmy. Taking a census or something of the sort."

There were men down on the pier now, making cables fast. The sound of a turbine started up. A tracked vehicle, bright yellow in color, was trundling down the gangplank.

Annette, a petite brunette, emerged from the house to meet her husband and son.

"They look awfully busy," she said, glancing toward the shore. "Reed, did you order any equipment that I don't know about . . .?"

"Nothing. Someone's made a navigational error, I suspect."

"Dad, look!" Timmy pointed.

A deck boom, probing in an open hatch, had lifted a laden pallet, swung it over the side to deposit it on the dock. A forklift picked up the pallet, advanced along the length of the pier; it rolled off onto the grassy shore, gouging deep parallel ruts through the planted turf as it went.

"Dad, we spent all spring getting that grass to grow—"

"Never mind, Timmy, we can replace it. You two stay here," Nolan said to Annette. "I'll go down and see what this is all about."

"Aren't you going to wash up, Reed? They'll think you're the hired man . . ."

"Don't I wish I had one," he said as he headed for the dock.

The path down from the crest where he had built the house led close under a dense stand of blue-needled spruce-like trees. Native wild flowers in many shades of yellow grew in profusion here; a stream splashed down across goldmossed rocks. The Terrestrial birds that Nolan had released—and fed daily—had thrived: mocking birds, robins, and parakeets chirped and twittered comfortingly in the alien shade of the forest. Next year, he might be able to bring in a few dozen seedlings of pine and cedar to supplement the native woods, since this year's crop would, for the first time, show a handsome profit . . .

As Nolan emerged from the shelter of the trees the vehicle he had seen earlier was churning briskly across the grass in his direction. It halted and a bulky bundle tumbled from it to the ground. The machine drove on, dropped a second package fifty feet from the first. It continued on its way, depositing the loads at regular intervals across the wide lawn. Nolan angled across to intercept the vehicle as it stopped again. Two men, one youngish, with a thinning crew cut, the other middle-aged and bald, both dressed in badly cut but new-looking coveralls, looked down at him without visible interest.

"Better hold it, fellows," Nolan called. "There's been some mistake. That cargo doesn't belong here."

The men exchanged glances. The elder of the two turned and spat carelessly past Nolan.

"Ha," he said. The vehicle moved on.

Nolan walked over to the nearest bundle. It was a tailored plastic casing, roughly cubical, two feet on a side. Markings stenciled on the side read:

SHELTER, PERSONNEL (MALE) cat 567/09/a10
CAP 20. APSC. CLII.

Nolan continued down to the pier. Vehicles were rolling off it in a steady stream, some loaded with men, others with equipment. The growl of turbines filled the air, along with an acrid stink of burned hydrocarbons. A small, slender man in sub-executive coveralls stood amid the confusion, clipboard in hand. He looked around sharply as Nolan came up.

"Here," he snapped, "what are you doing here, fellow?

What's your crew and unit number?" He riffled the papers on the clipboard as if the answer to his question was to be found there.

"I was about to ask you the same thing," Nolan said mildly. "What you're doing here, I mean. I'm afraid you're in the wrong place. This is—"

"None of your impertinence, now! Stand over there; I'll get to you presently." The small man turned his back to Nolan.

"Where can I find the man in charge?" Nolan asked. The man ignored him. He turned toward the boat; the little man shouted after him, but he went on.

At the pier, a harassed-looking fellow with a tight, office-pale face stared him up and down.

"In charge?" he echoed Nolan's inquiry. "Don't worry about it. Get back to your crew."

"I'm not a crew member," Nolan said patiently. "I'm—"

"Don't argue with me!" the man snapped, and motioned to a bigger man overseeing the maneuvers of the forklift. "Grotz; take his number." He turned away.

"All right, you, let's have that number," Grotz demanded tiredly.

"Number one," Nolan said.

"One what? One-ten?"

"If you say so."

"All right." Grotz jotted. "They were looking for you, one-ten. Better get busy now, before I dock you."

"I think I'll do just that," Nolan said, and left the pier.

∞ ▌▌ ∞

Back at the house, he went directly to the study, switched on the callbox.

"Some kind of official snafu," he told Annette. "I'll have to place a call to Toehold and see what they know about it."

"Reed—that's so expensive . . ."

"Can't be helped. They seem to be too busy to talk to me." Nolan looked up the code for the Office of Colonial Affairs, punched it out.

"Reed," Annette said from the window. "They're putting up some kind of big tents on the lawn!"

"I know . . ." An operator came on the line; another minute passed before Nolan reached the OCA.

"Nolan, you say?" a harassed official voice said. "Oh, yes, I recall the name . . ."

Briefly, Nolan outlined the situation. "Someone's apparently got his coordinates confused," he finished. "If you'd put a call through on the IC band to whoever's in charge—"

"Just a minute, Nolan. What was that number of the boat again?"

Nolan told him.

"Mm. Just a moment . . . Ah, yes. I see that the vessel is chartered to the Union for Human Privileges. They're only semiofficial, of course—but they're a powerful organization."

"Not powerful enough to legally pitch camp on my land," Nolan said.

"Well—I think it's more than a camping trip, Mr. Nolan. The HPU intends to set up a permanent relocation facility for underprivileged persons displaced by over-crowding from the Welfare Center."

"On *my* claim?"

"Well, as to that, your claim isn't actually finalized, you realize. The five year residency requirement hasn't yet been fulfilled, of course—"

"Nonsense. That approach wouldn't hold up in court for five minutes!"

"Perhaps—but it might be some years before the case appeared on the agenda. Meanwhile—well, I'm afraid I can't offer much encouragement, Mr. Nolan. You'll just have to adjust."

"Reed!" Annette gasped. "There's a man with a power saw; he's cutting down one of the sycamores!"

As Nolan turned to the window a black-painted person-nel car pulled to a stop outside. The hatches popped up. Four men, a stout woman, and a lath-thin youth stepped down. A moment later Nolan heard the front door open. A short, heavily-built man with bristly reddish hair strolled into the front hall, his retinue close behind him.

"Well, a fortunate find," a suety voice said. "The structure seems sound enough. We'll establish my administrative HQ here, I think. And you can make ready personal quarters for me as well; much as I'd prefer to share issue accommodations with our people, I'll need to remain close to affairs."

"I think there's ample room for all the staff here, Director Fraswell," another voice said, "if we make do with a room apiece—"

"Don't be afraid to share a little hardship with the men, Chester." The man called Fraswell cut off his subordinate's remark curtly. "I'll remind you—" He broke off abruptly as he caught sight of Nolan and Annette.

"Who's this?" the plump man barked. He had a mottled complexion and a wide, unsmiling mouth. He turned to the man beside him. "What's this fellow doing here, Chester?"

"Here, who're you?" A lean, bony man with a crooked face spoke sharply, coming forward from behind his chief.

"My name is Nolan—"

"Get his crew number." A third man spoke up.

"Here, fellow, what's your number?" the crooked-faced man said quickly.

"Who's the woman?" the plump man barked. "I made it clear there was to be no fraternization!"

"Get the woman's number," Chester said sharply.

"All right, crew and unit numbers," the man in the rear rank said, coming forward. "Let's see your wrists, both of you."

Nolan stepped in front of Annette. "We don't have numbers," he said. "We're not in your party. We live here. My name is Nolan—"

"Eh?" the plump man interjected in elaborate puzzlement. "*Live* here?"

"Live *here*?" his aid echoed.

"That's right. That's my dock you tied up to. This is my house. I—"

"Oh, yes." The plump man nodded, making a show of recalling a trivial datum. "You'd be the fellow, what's-his-name, ah, Nolan. Yes. I was told you'd established some sort of squatter's claim here."

"My claim is on file at Toehold, ten copies, notarized and fees paid. So I'd appreciate it if you'd load your property back aboard your boat and take another look at your charts. I don't know where you were headed, but I'm afraid this spot's taken."

The plump man's face went expressionless. He looked past Nolan's left ear.

"I've requisitioned this site for the resettlement of a quota of economically disadvantaged persons," he said solemnly. "We constitute the advance party, to make ready the facilities for the relocatees who're to follow. I trust we'll have your full cooperation in this good work."

"The facilities, as you call them, happen to be private property—"

"You'd prate of selfish interests with the welfare of hundreds at stake?" Fraswell barked.

Nolan looked at him. "Why here?" he asked levelly. "There are thousands of unoccupied islands available—"

"This one seems most easily adaptable for our purposes," Fraswell said flatly. "I estimate a thousand persons can be accommodated here quite nicely—"

"It's no different than any other island in the chain."

Fraswell looked surprised. "Nonsense. The cleared land along the shore is ideal for erection of the initial camp site; and I note various food plants are available to supplement issue rations."

A man in a clerical collar came into the room, rubbing his hands. "A stroke of luck, Director Fraswell," he cried. "I've found a supply of nonissue foodstuffs, including a well-stocker freezer—" He broke off as he saw Nolan and Annette.

"Yes, yes, Padre," Fraswell said. "I'll conduct an inventory and see to an equitable distribution of items found."

"Found—or stolen?" Nolan said.

"Whaaat?"

"Why can't these deserving cases of yours produce their own supplies? The land's fertile enough—"

The cleric stared. "Our people are not criminals, condemned to hard labor," he said indignantly. "They're merely disadvantaged. They have the same right to Nature's bounty as yourself—if not more!"

"Aren't you missing the distinction between Nature's bounty and the product of human effort? There's an ample supply of Nature on the next island. You have plenty of labor available. If you take virgin land, in a year you can harvest your own crop."

"You expect me to subject these unfortunate people to unnecessary hardships, merely out of your personal selfishness?" Fraswell snorted.

"I cleared land; they can start off the same way I did—"

"My instructions are to establish my group at a certain standard; the more quickly that standard is reached—"

"The better you'll look back at HQ, eh?"

A woman had followed the priest into the room. She was thick-necked, red-faced, with grimly frizzed gray hair, dressed in drab-colored clothing and stout shoes. She looked indignantly at Nolan.

"The land and what's on it belongs to everyone," she snapped. "The idea, one man trying to hog it all! I guess you'd just sit here in luxury and let women and children starve!"

"I'd let them clear their own land and plant their own crops," Nolan said gently. "And build their own head-quarters. This happens to be my family's house. I built it—and the power plant, and the sewage system—"

"Wonder where he got the money for all that," the woman wondered aloud. "No honest man has that kind of cash."

"Now, Milly," Fraswell said indulgently.

"I saved eighty credits per month for twenty-seven years, Madam," Nolan said. "From a very modest salary."

"So that makes you better than other folk, eh?" She pursued the point. "Can't live in barracks like everybody else—"

"Now, Miltrude," Fraswell said mildly, and turned back to Nolan.

"Mr., ah, Nolan, inasmuch as I'll be requiring information from you as to various matters, you may as well be assigned a cot here at HQ. I'm sure that now you've considered it you'll agree that the welfare of the community comes first, though modest personal sacrifices may be required of the individual, eh?"

"What about my wife?"

Fraswell looked grave. "I've ordered that there'll be no sexual fraternization for the present—"

"How do *we* know she's your wife?" Miltrude demanded.

Annette gasped and moved closer to Nolan; the crooked-faced man caught at her arm. Nolan stepped forward and knocked it away.

"Oh, violence, eh?" Fraswell nodded as if in satisfaction. "Call Glotz in." Chester hurried away. Annette clutched Nolan's hand.

"It's all right," he said. "Fraswell knows how far he can go." He looked meaningfully at the plump man. "This isn't an accident, is it?" he said. "I suppose you've had your eye on our island for some time; you were just waiting until we had it far enough along to make it worth stealing."

The big man from the boat came into the room, looking around. He saw Nolan.

"Hey, you—"

Fraswell held up a hand.

"Now, Nolan—there'll be no more outbursts, I trust. Now, as I say, you'll be assigned quarters here at HQ provided you can control yourself."

A lanky, teen-age lad with an unfortunate complexion sauntered in through the open door. He had a small, nearly ripe tomato in his hand, from which he had just taken a bite, another fruit in his hand.

"Look what I found, Pop," he said.

"Not now, Leston," Fraswell barked. He glared until the lad shrugged and departed. Then he looked alertly at Nolan.

"Tomatoes, eh?" he said thoughtfully. "I'd understood they couldn't be grown here on Kaka Nine."

"Just one experimental plant," Nolan said grimly. "Leston seems to have terminated the experiment."

Fraswell grunted. "Well, have I your word, Nolan?"

"I don't think you'd like the word I'm thinking of, Mr. Fraswell," Nolan said.

"Pah!" the Director snorted. "Very well, then." He eyed Nolan severely. "Don't say I didn't give you every consideration! Glotz—Chester—take them away and lock them up somewhere until they see reason."

ᎅ **III** ᎅ

In the dark of the tool shed where he had been con-
fined, Nolan massaged his bruised knuckles and listened
to the soft sigh of the wind, the lonely call of the native
nightbirds—and to a stealthy, persistent rasping, barely
audible, coming from beyond the locked door across the
small room.

The sound ceased with a soft clank of metal. The knob
turned; the door swung inward. Through the opening, a
youthful face appeared.

"Tim! Nice work!" Nolan breathed.

"Hi, Dad!" The boy slipped through, closed the door.
Nolan held out his wrists, linked by braided steel a quarter
inch in diameter. Timmy clamped the bolt cutter on the
cable, snipped through the strands.

"My ankle is cuffed to the cot," Nolan whispered.

Timmy found the cable, cut it deftly. A moment later,
Nolan and his son were outside. All was silence, though
there were still a few lights in the upper rooms of the
house, and down by the dock side.

"Your mother?" Nolan said as they moved off.

"They've got her in the last tent in line—down by the
pond. Dad, you know what they did? They used a net and
took every fish out of the pond! All our panfish and bass
fingerlings! They cooked 'em up and ate 'em."

"They can be replaced—in time."

"They sure smelled good," Tim admitted.

"You had anything to eat?"

"Sure. I raided the kitchen while that fat man with the funny lips was trying to figure out how to work the tricordeo. All he could get was the ref patterns. He was pretty mad."

They passed behind the ranked tents. A light burned in one.

"That's where the honchos stay," Tim said.

"No sentries?" Nolan asked.

"Nope. They talked about it and decided they didn't need any."

They were behind the last tent in line.

"About here," Tim said, indicating a spot six paces from the corner. "I saw Mom just before they opaqued it."

Nolan asked. "I'll take the knife," he said. "You move back and be ready to run for it if there's an alarm."

"Heck, Dad—"

"So you can try again, if they catch me."

"Oh. OK."

Nolan worked the knife point through the tough material. Air hissed out. He ripped upward. From inside the tent there was a sharp exclamation, followed by a muffled thud. He thrust the cut flap aside and plunged through.

Annette met him.

"I knew you'd come," she whispered, and kissed him swiftly. "I had to hit her over the head." She nodded toward a bulky figure slumped at her feet.

"Timmy's outside," Nolan whispered as he passed her through the breach in the fabric wall.

Already the taut plastic had begun to sag.

"Patching goo," the boy said, and handed Nolan a roll of wide tape. Quickly they sealed the opening.

"Where to first?" Tim asked.

"The house," Nolan said.

The back door was locked; Nolan keyed it open. Inside, he went silently to the den, selected two small handguns and a lightweight power rifle. In the kitchen, Annette had assembled a small heap of concentrates not yet looted from the stores. Tim came in from the tackle room with packs.

Back outside, Nolan posted his wife and son near the path leading to the hills and set off toward the power house. Inside, he made certain adjustments; he locked the door behind him as he left. Moving on to the pump house, he closed two large valves, opened others. Last, he engaged the massive power lock on the equipment shed.

"That's about it," he said as he rejoined the others. "Let's go."

"If they hadn't showed up," Tim said as they set off up the steep path, "I guess we never would have taken that camping trip we're always talking about."

∞ IV ∞

The cave was a large and airy one, with a narrow entrance well-concealed from below by a rocky ridge and a freshwater spring that trickled at the rate of one gallon per hour into a stone basin. It was a cave the Nolan family knew well; they had once lived in it for two months, until the first rooms of the house had been completed.

It was the work of an hour to sweep out the accumulated

wind-blown rubbish, set up the inflatable cots, arrange the collapsible cooking equipment around the stone fireplace. By then the sun was coming up.

Nolan looked down across the stunted mountain growth toward the house far below. The binoculars showed a cluster of men around the pump house.

"They must have emptied the reserve tank already," he said.

"They'll just blow the door off the pump house, Reed," Annette said. "Won't they?"

"Maybe—if they have the right explosives. But they'll still have to know which valves to open."

"I feel pretty mean—cutting off their water supply."

"There's always the pond and buckets. They won't suffer—except for a few blisters."

Nolan and Tim spent most of the morning busy on the slopes. The Tusker herds were gathering in the high meadows now; using binoculars, Nolan estimated their numbers at over ten thousand. They returned to the cave with a specimen bag filled with fossils, low grade gem-stones, and some new varieties of fungus to add to Tim's slide collection. Annette greeted them with hot soup and sandwiches.

Late in the afternoon they watched a party of men spread out and scour the underbrush near the house. After an hour or two the search petered out.

"I'll bet old Fatty's plenty mad now," Tim said cheerfully. "I'll bet he still hasn't figured out the tricordeo."

The Nolans set out a board and played three-handed chidge until dinner time. Annette served recon chicken-and-chips. She and Reed had cold dehi-beer, Tim hot cocoa. Just after dusk, all the lights went off in the house and on the grounds below.

"I suppose we'll hear from Director Fraswell pretty early in the morning," Nolan said as they composed themselves for sleep.

∞ **V** ∞

Half an hour before dawn there was a soft *beep!* from the small black box beside Nolan's bed.

"Visitors," he said, checking the indicator lights that told him which of the sensors he and Tim had planted the previous day had been activated. "On the east trail. They didn't waste any time." He rose and donned the clean clothes Annette had run through the precipitator, picked up the power rifle.

"Dad, can I come?"

"Negative. You stay here with your mother."

"Reed—are you sure—"

"I'm not that bad a shot," he said, and grinned at her. "I'll be back for coffee."

In took Nolan ten minutes to reach the vantage point he had selected the previous day. He settled himself in a comfortable prone position, adjusted the sling, and sighted through the scope-sight. Three men toiled upward on the trail. Nolan took aim at the rock wall ten feet above them and squeezed off a burst. Dust spurted. When he lowered his sights, the men were gone. He picked them up a quarter of a mile back downtrail, running for home.

Twice more that day the spotters Nolan had planted on

the slopes signaled intruders; twice more a single warning shot sufficed to discourage them.

Late in the afternoon, a bucket brigade formed across the lawn far below, hauling water to the house. The men working on the power house door gave up at twilight. A crew of men set about chopping wood to heap on the lawn for a bonfire.

"Reed—the baby peach trees, and the pecans, and the limes—" Annette mourned.

"I know," Nolan said tersely. They watched the fire for an hour before turning in.

∽ **VI** ∽

It was mid-morning when the signaler beeped again. This time it was a party of three men—one of them the man called Winston whom Nolan had last seen with Fraswell—carrying a white towel attached to a section of sapling—pecan, Nolan thought. They waited for a quarter of an hour at the spot marked by a small crater in the rock wall from Nolan's shot of the previous day. Then they advanced cautiously.

On a rocky ledge a hundred yards below Nolan's position, they halted. A shout rang faintly.

"Nolan! We wish to talk to you!"

He remained silent.

"Director Fraswell has authorized me to offer you leniency if you give yourself up now," Winston shouted.

Nolan waited.

"You're to come down at once," Winston resumed. "No

criminal charges will be pressed, provided you cooperate fully henceforth."

Another minute passed in silence.

"Nolan, give yourself up at once!" the angry voice shouted. "Otherwise . . ."

A single shot rang out above Nolan. Instantly the men below turned and ran. Nolan looked up toward the cave. Annette, her back to him, stepped from behind the rocky barrier that concealed the entrance, a pistol in her hand. She turned and waved. Nolan climbed back up to her side.

"On the west trail," she said indignantly. "The idea—while they were parleying with you!"

"Never mind," Nolan said mildly. "They're just exploring their environment."

"I'm worried, Reed. How long can this go on?"

"We have food for a month or so. After that, maybe Tim and I will have to raid the larder again."

Annette looked worried but said nothing further on the subject.

∞ **VII** ∞

For five days, while Nolan watched the unirrigated fields slowly fade and wilt, there were no further overtures from below. Then, in mid-morning of the sixth day a party of four set out from the house, advanced slowly up the east trail. One of the men was Fraswell, Nolan saw. A man in the rear carried what appeared to be a placard. When they paused for their first rest, the man turned the sign to face the heights, but Nolan was unable to make out the lettering at the distance.

"Watch the beepers," he told Annette and Tim. "I don't think that's the game this time, but they may have planted someone on another trail last night after dark." He descended to his lookout station below. Director Fraswell's red face was clearly visible at half a mile, even on low mag. Nolan was able to read the placard now:

NOLAN—WE MUST TALK

"Fraswell," Nolan called. "What is it you want?"

The plump man scanned the cliff above for a glimpse of Nolan.

"Show yourself!" he called. "I can't carry on a discussion with a disembodied voice!"

"Don't let me keep you."

"Nolan, in my capacity as a Field Director of the HPU I call on you to descend at once and cease this harassment!"

"My family and I are just taking a long deferred vacation, Mr. Fraswell."

"You shot at my people!"

"If I had, I'd have hit them. I hold a Double Distinguished Marksman's rating. You can check that if you like."

"Look here, Nolan—you're deliberately withholding information essential to the success of this mission!"

"I think you're a little confused, Mr. Fraswell. I'm in no way connected with your mission. I paid my own way here—"

"I'm not concerned with that! It's your duty to serve the people—"

"Mr. Fraswell, I suggest you pack up your people and your equipment and move on to another piece of real estate, and I'll give you all the technical assistance I can in getting started."

"Would you attempt to bargain with the welfare of a thousand men, women and children?"

"Not quite. I estimate you have about fifty men in your advance party."

"The relocatees will arrive in less than a fortnight! Unless you give up this dog-in-the-manger attitude at the expense of these poor, helpless souls, I won't be responsible for the outcome!"

"Wrong again, Mr. Fraswell. It's your entire responsibility. I'm just curious as to what you plan to do after you've eaten all the seed corn and cleaned out my emergency reserves. Move on and loot somebody else? What happens when you run out of people to loot, Fraswell?"

"I'm not in the business of making predictions, Nolan! I'm concerned for the success of the present operation!"

"I suppose by the time you run out of goodies you'll be retired, eh? Meanwhile, if you get tired of hauling water and eating issue rations you can always leave, Mr. Fraswell. Tell your headquarters it didn't work; perhaps next time they'll supply you with some equipment of your own."

"The power is off! There's no water! My men can't start the vehicles! The crops are dying! I call on you to come down here and undo your sabotage!"

"The only sabotage I've seen is what your men have done to my lawns and orchards. We won't count the fishpond."

There was a two minute silence during which the men below conferred.

"Look here, Nolan," Fraswell called, sounding reluctantly conciliatory. "I'll concede that, from a purely materialistic standpoint, it might be said you have some right to compensation. Very well. Though it means taking bread from the mouths of the innocent, I'll undertake to guarantee payment of the usual credit per acre—for the arable portions of the tract, of course. After survey."

"I paid a credit and a half an acre for the unimproved land, over five years ago—and I paid for all of it—mountains, desert—the whole island. I'm afraid your offer doesn't tempt me."

"You—you exploiter! You think you can victimize the ordinary man, but you'll see! They'll rise in their righteous wrath and destroy you, Nolan!"

"If they'd rise in their wrath and tackle that next island, they could have a quarter section cleared and ready for summer planting."

"You'd condemn these good people to inhuman hardship—for the sake of mere personal avarice! You'd deny them bread! You'd—"

"I know these good people, Mr. Fraswell. I tried to hire some of them when I was breaking ground here. They laughed. They're the untrainables, the unemployables. They've had a free ride all their lives. Now they're overflowing the trough. So you're trying to dump them on me to maintain. Well, I decline the honor, Mr. Fraswell. It looks as if they're going to have to go to work if they want to eat. By the way, what's *your* salary per annum?"

Fraswell made choking noises.

"One last thing, Fraswell," Nolan called. "My gardenia hedges; tell your men to leave them alone; you don't need firewood that badly, and the few steps it would save in coming and going up into the foothills isn't worth destroying them."

"Gardenias, eh? Mean a lot to you, do they? I'm afraid I'll have to use my own judgment regarding fuel sources, Nolan!" The Director spun on his heel and walked away. One of his attendants turned to shake a fist upward before disappearing down the trail.

That afternoon, Nolan saw a crew hard at work, leveling the hedges.

The following day, Tim hurried into the cave calling excitedly that the Tusker herds had started to move down from the heights.

∽ VIII ∽

"I don't like it," Annette said as Nolan prepared to leave the cave. "You don't know what that terrible man is likely to do if he gets his hands on you."

"I have to give them fair warning," Nolan said. "I'll be all right. Fraswell's not going to let anything happen that might look awkward on his record."

"How come, Dad?" Tim said. "Why not let the Tuskers surprise 'em? Maybe they'll scare 'em right off the island!"

"Someone could get hurt; they might panic and get trampled. And those horns are sharp."

"Sure, but—you could get hurt, too, Dad, if you try to

get in their way! They're pretty hard to stop once they're running!"

"I'll be careful. Don't worry about me."

Nolan set off by the most direct route available: a near-vertical ravine, water-cut, too narrow and precipitate for a Tusker, but just possible for an active man. In twenty minutes he arrived at the valley floor, winded and dusty, with scratched and bleeding hands. As he emerged from the tangle of underbrush at the cliff base, three men jumped him.

∽ IX ∽

The house stank. Director Fraswell, somewhat leaner than when Nolan had last seen him, badly shaved, wearing rumpled, sweat-marked clothing, glared triumphantly across the former dining room table, now occupying the center of the living room and covered with papers and empty ration boxes.

"So you finally came to your senses, eh?" He paused to scratch under his left arm. "I suppose you'll expect to hold me to the bargain I proposed. Well, think again! You rejected my offer when I made it. Now suffer the consequences!" He shook his finger in Nolan's face.

Nolan's lip was split. His jaw was swollen painfully. His head ached.

"I didn't come here to bargain," he said. "I came to warn you—"

"You—warn *me*?" Fraswell jumped to his feet. "Listen to me, you arrogant little popinjay! I'll do the warning! I want the power plant in full operation in fifteen minutes from now! I want water flowing ten minutes after that! I want all facilities unlocked and the keys turned over to me before you leave this room!" He scratched furiously at his ribs.

"That would be quite a trick," Nolan said. "Even if I had the keys."

Fraswell's mouth opened and shut. "Search him!"

"We did; he's got nothing on him."

"Nothing on him, *sir!*" Fraswell barked, and whirled on Nolan. "Where have you hidden them? Speak up, man! I'm at the end of my patience!"

"Never mind the keys," Nolan said. "That's not what I came here to talk about—"

"You'll talk about it nonetheless!" Fraswell was almost screaming.

"Here, what's the trouble?" a female voice shrilled. Miltrude, looking the worse for ten days without a bath, stood in the doorway, hands on broad hips. "Well—looky who's here!" she said as she saw Nolan. Behind her, Leston peered over her shoulder. "Finally caught him, did you, Alvin?"

"Yes—I caught him. But he's stubborn! But he'll crack! I assure you of that!"

"What about the fancy woman he was keeping?" Miltrude queried grimly. "Turn her over to me; I'll see she makes him cooperate."

"Get out!" Fraswell roared.

"Here, you Alvin!" his spouse snapped. "Mind your tone!"

Fraswell swept an empty concentrate flask from the

table and hurled it viciously; it struck the wall beside
Miltrude; she screeched and fled, almost knocking her
son down in passing.

"Make him talk!" Fraswell yelled. "Get those keys; do
whatever you have to do to him, but I want results—now!"

One of the men holding Nolan gave his arm a painful
wrench.

"Not here—outside!" Fraswell sank back in his chair,
panting. "Of course, you're not to do him any permanent
injury," he muttered, looking into the corner of the room
as they hustled Nolan away.

⚚ X ⚚

Two men held Nolan's arms while a third doubled his
fist and drove it into his midriff. He jackknifed forward,
gagging.

"Not in the stomach, you fool," someone said. "He has
to be able to talk."

Someone grabbed his hair and forced his head back; an
open-handed slap made his head ring.

"Listen, you rich scum," a wild-eyed, bushy-headed
man with gaps between his teeth hissed in Nolan's face.
"You can't hold out on us—"

Nolan's knee, coming up fast, caught the man solidly;
he uttered a curdled scream and went down. Nolan
lunged, freed an arm and landed a roundhouse swing on
someone's neck. For a moment he was free, facing two
men, who hesitated, breathing hard.

"In a matter of minutes there's going to be a stampede,

right across this spot," he said blurrily. "It's a wild herd—big fellows, over a ton apiece. You'll have to warn your men."

"Get him," a man snapped, and leaped for Nolan. They were still struggling to pin his legs when a heavy crashing sounded from behind the house. A man screamed—a shocking yell that froze Nolan's attackers in mid-stroke. He rolled free and came to his feet as a man sprinted into view from around the corner of the house, pale face rigid with terror, legs pumping. A heavy thudding sounded behind him. A big male tusker charged across the wheel-rutted turf, the remains of a wrecked rose trellis draped around his mighty shoulders. The man dived aside as the beast galloped on into the cover of what remained of the woodlot, whence sounded a diminishing crashing of timber.

For a moment, the three men stood rigid, listening to a sound as of thunder in the mountains, then, as one, they whirled and ran. Nolan hurried around to the front of the house.

Fraswell was on the front terrace, his head cocked, a blank expression on his big features, the boy Leston beside him. The Director shied when he saw Nolan, then charged down the steps, ran for the corner of the house—and skidded to a halt as a tusker thundered past.

"Good God!" Fraswell backed, spun, started for the porch. Nolan blocked his way.

"Run for the boat," he shouted.

"This is your work! You're trying to kill us all!" Fraswell shouted.

"Dad," Leston started as two men sprinted into view around the side of the house. One carried a rifle.

"Get him!" Fraswell yelled, pointing. "He's a fanatic! It's his doing!"

"Don't be a fool, Fraswell," Nolan snapped. "If you're in danger, so am I—"

"A fanatic! He intends to pull me down with him! Get him!" Fraswell jumped at Nolan; the other two men closed in. Wild fists pummeled Nolan; clutching hands caught his arms, dragged him down. A boot caught in the side. He grabbed the ankle, brought the man down on top of him. The other man was dancing sideways, gun at the ready.

"Kill the bloodsucker," the one Nolan had felled shouted as he scrambled up. "Here—gimme that!" He seized the gun from the other's grip, aimed it at Nolan's head. It was tall, thin Leston who jumped forward, knocked the gun down as it fired. A gout of lawn exploded beyond Nolan.

"Pa—you can't—" the boy started; Fraswell whirled on him, struck him an open-handed blow that sent him sprawling.

"A traitor in my own house! You're no son of mine!" The drumming of the approaching herd was a continuous surf-roar now. The man with the gun threw it down and ran for the dock. As more tuskers swung into view, Fraswell turned too, and ran for it, followed by his two men. Nolan struggled to his feet, noted the animals' course, then set off at a dead run toward a stand of native thorn on a low rise near the path of the charging herd, snatching up a broken branch from the uprooted gardenia hedge as he went. The lead animals were less than fifty feet behind him when he stopped and turned, waving the branch and shouting. The approaching tuskers shied from the hateful scent, crowding their fellows to the right of the thorn patch—onto a course dead for the dock.

Nolan dropped down on the grass, catching his breath as the herd thundered past. Through the dust he could see the group gathered down on the pier and on the dock of the boat.

A man on the pier—Fraswell, Nolan thought—was shouting and pointing toward the house. Someone on the boat seemed to yell a reply. It appeared there was a difference of opinion among the leadership and the rank-and-file of the HPU.

"Time for one more little nudge," Nolan muttered, getting to his feet. A few elderly cows, stragglers, were galloping past the grove. Nolan searched hastily, wrenched off a stalk of leatherplant, quickly stripped it. A thick, pungent odor came from the ripe pulp. He went forward to intercept a cow, waving the aromatic plant, turned and ran as the cow swung toward him. He could hear the big animal's hooves thudding behind him. He yelled; down below, the men crowding the pier looked up to see Nolan sprinting toward them, the tusker cantering in his wake.

"Help!" he shouted. "Help!"

The men turned and ran for the gangway. Fraswell caught at a man's arm; the man struck at him and fled. The plump figures of Miltrude and the Director held their ground for a moment; then they turned and bolted onto the boat.

As they turned to look back, the sound of the ship's engines started up. The gangplank slid inboard when Nolan was fifty feet from the pier. He tossed the branch aside as the cow braked to a halt beside him, nudging him to capture the succulent prize. Nolan gave a piercing scream and fell, leaving the cow to stare after the hastily departing vessel, munching peacefully.

❧ **XI** ❧

A tall, lean youth came around the side of the house to meet Nolan as he came up.

"Uh . . . I . . ." he said.

"Leston—how did you get left behind?" Nolan asked in dismay.

"On purpose," the boy blurted.

"I don't think your father will be back," Nolan said.

Leston nodded. "I want to stay," he said. "I'd like a job, Mr. Nolan."

"Do you know anything about farming, Leston?" Nolan asked dubiously.

"No, sir." The boy swallowed. "But I'm willing to learn."

Nolan looked at him for a moment. He put out his hand and smiled.

"I can't ask any more than that," he said.

He turned and looked across the ruined lawn, past the butchered hedges and the mutilated groves toward the languishing fields.

"Come on, let's get started," he said. "The plague's over, and we've got a lot of work ahead before harvest time."

NIGHT OF DELUSIONS

I didn't hear anything: no hushed breathing, no stealthy slide of a shoe against the carpet. But I knew before I opened my eyes that there was someone in the room. I moved my hand under the edge of the blanket onto the worn butt of the Belgian-made Browning I keep by me for sentimental reasons, and said, "Let's have some light."

The dim-strip by the door went on. A medium-sized, medium-aged man in a plain gray suit stood by the door. He looked at me with a neutral expression on a face that was just a face. The bathroom door beside him was open a couple of inches.

"You interrupted a swell dream," I said. "I almost had my finger on the secret of it all. By the way, tell your partner to come on out and join the party."

The bathroom door opened wider and a thin, lantern-jawed man with a lot of bony wrist showing under his cuffs slid into view. He had scruffy reddish hair, a scruffy reddish complexion with plenty of tension lines, a neat row of dental implants that showed through a nervous grimace that he might have thought was a smile. I lifted a pack of smokes from the bedside table, snapped a weed out, used a lighter on it. They watched all this carefully, as if it were a trick they'd heard about and didn't want to miss. I blew out smoke and said, "Why not tell me about it? Unless it's a secret, of course."

"We have a job for you, Mr. Florin," the gray man said in a terse, confidential voice. "A delicate mission requiring a man of unusual abilities."

I let that ride.

"Our mode of entry was in the nature of a test," the bony man said. He had a prissy, high-pitched voice that didn't go with the rest of him. "Needless to say, you passed." He giggled.

The cigarette tasted terrible. I smashed it out in a glass ashtray with *Harry's Bar* on the bottom.

"Sorry you had the trouble for nothing," I said. "I'm not looking for work."

"We represent a very important man," Slim said, and showed me an expression like that of a man who worked for a very important man. It looked a lot like the expression of a man in need of a laxative.

"Would he have a name?" I said. "This very important man, I mean."

"No names; not for the present," the gray man said quickly. "May we sit down, Mr. Florin?"

I waved my free hand. The gray man took two steps and perched on the edge of the straight chair beside the dresser. Slim drifted off into the background and sank down into one of those big shapeless chairs you need a crane to get out of.

"Needless to say," the gray man said, "the pay will be commensurate with the gravity of the situation."

"Sure," I said. "What situation?"

"A situation involving the planetary security." He said it impressively, as if that settled everything.

"What's the planetary security got to do with me?"

"You're known to be the best man in the business. You're discreet, reliable, not easily frightened."

"And don't forget my winning smile," I said. "What business?"

"The confidential investigation business, of course."

"The personal escort aspect," Slim amplified.

"Bodyguarding," I said. "It's all right; you can say it right out loud. You don't have to make it sound elegant. But you overlooked a point. I'm on vacation—an extended vacation."

"This is important enough to warrant interrupting your holiday," Slim said.

"To you or to me?"

"Mr. Florin, you're aware of the tense—not to say desperate state—of public affairs today," the gray man said in a gray voice. "You know that public unrest has reached grave proportions—"

"You mean a lot of people are unhappy with the way things are going. Yeah, I know that; I recognize the sound of breaking glass when I hear it. But not me. I'm a contented man. I keep my head down and let the waves roll over me."

"Nonsense," the gray man said without visible emotion. He slipped a hand inside his jacket and brought out a flat leather folder, flipped it open. The little gold badge winked at me.

"Your government needs you, Mr. Florin," he said indifferently.

"Is this a pinch or a sales pitch?" I asked.

"Your cooperation will have to be voluntary, of course."

"That word 'voluntary' sure takes a beating," I said, and yawned, not entirely honestly.

The gray man almost smiled. "Your cynical pose is unconvincing. I'm familiar with your record in the war, Mr. Florin. Or may I say Colonel Florin?"

"Don't," I said. "Reminiscences bore me. The war was a long time ago. I was young and foolish. I had lots of big ideas. Somehow they didn't survive the peace."

"There is one man who can save the situation, placate the malcontents. I think you know the man I mean."

"Campaign oratory in the middle of the night is no substitute for sleep," I said. "If you've got a point, get to it."

"The Senator needs your help, Mr. Florin."

"What ties a small-time private cop to the Senator? He could buy the block where I live and have it torn down—with me in it."

"He knows you, Florin; knows of your past services. He reposes great confidence in you."

"What does he want me to do—ring doorbells?"

"He wants to see you; now, tonight."

"Don't tell me the rest," I said. "You've got a fast car waiting at the curb to whisk me off to headquarters."

"A copter," the gray man said. "On the roof."

"I should have thought of that," I said. "OK if I put my pants on before we go?"

It was a big room with deep rugs and damask walls and

a fancy cornice and a big spiral chandelier that must have taken a family of Venetian glassblowers a year to put together. A big fellow with a long, solemn face and a big nose full of broken blood vessels met me just inside the door, shook my hand carefully, and led me over to a long table with a deep wax finish where four other men sat waiting.

"Gentlemen, Mr. Florin," he said. The boys behind the table had faces that were curiously alike, and had enough in common with a stuffed flounder to take the edge off my delight in meeting them. If they liked my looks they didn't say so.

"Mr. Florin has consented to assist us," Big Nose started . . .

"Not quite," I cut in. "I agreed to listen." I looked at the five faces and they looked back. Nobody offered me a chair.

"These gentlemen," my host said, "are the Senator's personal staff. You may have complete trust in their absolute discretion."

"Fine," I said in that breezy manner that's earned me so many friends over the years. "What are we being discreet about?"

One of the men leaned forward and clasped hands with himself. He was a wizened little fellow with pinched, clay-pale nostrils and eyes like a bird of prey.

"Mr. Florin, you're aware that anarchists and malcontents threaten our society," he said in a voice like the whisper of conscience. "The candidacy of the Senator for the office of World Leader is our sole hope for continued peaceful progress."

"Maybe. What's it got to do with me?"

A man with a face as round and soft as a saucer of lard spoke up: "The upcoming elections are the most important this planet has ever faced." He had a brisk, thin voice that gave me the feeling it should be coming from a much smaller, leaner man, possibly hiding under the table. "The success of the Senator, and of the policies he represents, spell the difference between chaos and another chance for our world."

"Does the other party get equal time?"

"It goes without saying, Mr. Florin, that your loyalties lie with legal government; with law and order."

"But you said it anyway. I get the feeling," I went on before he could step on me, "that we're dancing around the edge of something; something that wants to get said, but nobody's saying it."

"Perhaps you've noticed," the plump man said, "that in recent days the Senator's campaign has suffered a loss of momentum."

"I haven't been watching much telly lately."

"There have been complaints," the bird-man said, "that he's repeating himself, failing to answer his opponents' attacks, that the dynamism is gone from his presentations. The complaints are justified. For three months now we've been feeding doctored tapes to the news services."

They were all looking at me. Silence hummed in the room. I glanced along the table, fixed on a man with bushy white hair and a mouth that was made to clamp onto a bulldog pipe.

"Are you telling me he's dead?" I said.

The white head shook slowly, almost regretfully.

"The Senator," he said solemnly, "is insane."

The silence after the punch line hung as heavy as a washer-load of wet laundry. Or maybe heavier. I shifted around in my chair and listened to some throat-clearing. Faraway horns tooted on a distant avenue. Wind boomed against the picture window with its view of lights laid out on the blackness all the way to the horizon.

"The burdens under which he's labored for the past three years would have broken an ordinary man in half the time," Lard Face said. "But the Senator is a fighter; as the pressure grew, he held on. But the strain told on him. He began to see enemies everywhere. In the end his obsessions hardened into a fixed delusional system. Now he thinks every hand is against him."

"He believes," Big Nose said, "that a kidnap plot is afoot. He imagines that his enemies intend to brainwash him, make him their puppet. Accordingly, it becomes his duty to escape."

"This is, of course, a transparent rationalization," said a lath-thin man with half a dozen hairs slicked across a bald dome; his eyes burned at me hot enough to broil steaks. "He avoids the pressure of the election—but for the noblest of reasons. By deluding himself that in sacrificing his hopes of high office he prevents his being used, he relieves himself of the burden of guilt for his failure to measure up to the challenge."

"Tragic," I said, "but not quite in my line. You need a head doctor, not a beat-up gumshoe."

"The finest neuropsychologists and psychiatrists in the country have attempted to bring the Senator back to reality, Mr. Florin," Big Nose said. "They failed. It is therefore our intention to bring reality to the Senator."

✿ ✿ ✿

"Our plan is this," the bird-man said, leaning forward with what was almost an expression on his face. "The Senator is determined to venture out incognito to take his chances alone in the city. Very well—we'll see to it that he carries off his escape successfully."

"He imagines that by slipping free from his role as a man of great affairs—by casting off the restraints of power and position—he can lose himself in the masses," said Hot Eyes. "But he'll find matters are not so simple as that. The analysts who've studied his case assure us that his sense of duty will not be so easily laid to rest. Difficulties will arise, conjured from the depths of his own mind. And as these imaginary obstacles confront him—he will find that they're not after all imaginary."

"A man who believes himself to be persecuted by unseen enemies, threatened with death, is, by definition, psychotic," Lard Face said. "But if he is, indeed, hunted? *What if his fears are true?*"

"You see," said the hot-eyed man, "at some level, the man in the grip of hallucination knows the illusion for what it is. The victim of hysterical blindness will casually skirt a footstool placed in his path. But—when the imaginary dog *bites*—the shock will, we believe, drive him back from his safe retreat—not, after all, so safe—to the lesser harshness of reality."

"We'll make him sane by definition, Mr. Florin," Big Nose said. "And having established a one-to-one relationship with reality, we will lead him back to sanity."

"Neat," I said. "But who provides the pink elephants? Or is it silver men in the closet?"

"We're not without resources," Big Nose said grimly. "We've arranged for a portion of the city to be evacuated, with the exception of certain well-briefed personnel. We've set up highly sophisticated equipment keyed to his cephalic pattern, responsive to his brain. His movements will be tracked, his fantasies monitored—and appropriate phenomena will be produced accordingly, matching his fears."

"If he conceives of himself as beset by wild beasts," Hot Eyes said, "wild beasts will appear. If he imagines the city is under bombardment—bombs will fall, with attendant detonations and fires and flying debris. If he dreams of assassins armed with knives, knife-wielding killers will attack. He will overcome these obstacles, of course; it's inherent in his nature that he'll not fantasize his own demise. And in facing and overcoming these dangers he will, we're convinced, face and defeat the real threat to his sanity."

I looked along the table at them. They seemed to be serious.

"You gentlemen are expecting a lot from some stock Trideo footage," I said. "The Senator may be as batty as Dracula's castle, but he's no fool."

Big Nose smiled bleakly. "We're prepared to offer a demonstration, Mr. Florin." He moved a finger and I heard the growl of heavy engines, and a crunching and grinding that got closer and louder. The ashtrays rattled on the table. The floor trembled; the chandelier danced. A picture fell off the wall, and then the wall bulged and fell in and the snout of a 10-mm infinite repeater set in the bow of a Bolo Mark III pushed into the room and halted.

I could smell the stink of dust and hot oil, hear the scream of idling turbines, the thud and rattle of bricks falling.

Big Nose lifted his finger again and the tank winked out and the wall was back in place, picture and all, and the only sound was me, swallowing, or trying to.

I got out my hanky and wiped my forehead and the back of my neck while they smiled at me in a nasty, superior way.

"Yeah," I said. "I take back that last crack."

"Believe me, Mr. Florin, everything the Senator experiences on his foray into the city will be utterly real—to him."

"It still sounds like a nutty scheme to me," I said. "If you brought me here to get the benefit of my advice, I say forget it."

"There's no question of forgetting it," Lard Face said. "Only of your cooperation."

"Where do I crawl into the picture?"

"When the Senator sets out on his adventure," Big Nose said, "you'll go with him."

"I've heard of people going crackers," I said. "I never heard of them taking a passenger along."

"You'll guard him, Florin. You'll see him through the very real dangers he'll face, in safety. And, incidentally, you'll provide the channel through which we monitor his progress."

"I see. And what, as the man said, is in it for me?"

The bird-man speared me with a look. "You fancy yourself as a soldier of fortune, a man of honor, a lone warrior against the forces of evil. Now, your peculiar talents are needed in a larger cause. You can't turn your back on the call of duty and at the same time maintain your self-image. Accordingly, you'll do as we wish!" He sat back with a look that was as pleased as a look of his could get.

"Well, maybe you've got a point there, counselor," I said. "But there are a couple of other things I pride myself on besides being Jack Armstrong-to-the-rescue. One of them is that I choose my own jobs. Your gun-boys wear clean shirts and don't pick their noses in public, but they're still gun-boys. It seemed like a good idea to come along and hear your pitch. But that doesn't mean I'm buying it."

"In spite of your affectation of the seamy life, Mr. Florin, you're a wealthy man—or could be, if you chose. What we're offering you is a professional challenge of a scope you would never otherwise have encountered."

"It's a new twist," I said. "You're daring me to take your dare."

"The choice is simple," Big Nose said. "You know the situation. The time is now. Will you help or will you not?"

"You warned me you had the advice of some high-powered psychologists," I said. "I should have known better than to argue."

"Don't denigrate yourself, Florin," Big Nose said. "It's the only decision you could have made in conscience."

"Let's have one point clear," I said. "If I sign on to guard the Senator, I do the job my way."

"That's understood," Big Nose said, sounding mildly surprised. "What else?"

"When does the experiment come off?"

"It's already under way. He's waiting for you now."

"He knows about me?"

"He imagines your arrival is a finesse devised by himself."

"You've got all the answers, I see," I said. "Maybe that's good—provided you know all the questions."

"We've covered every eventuality we could foresee. The rest is up to you."

Two of the committee—they called themselves the Inner Council—escorted me to a brightly lit room in the basement. Three silent men with deft hands fitted me into a new street-suit of a soft gray material that Big Nose said was more or less bulletproof, as well as being climate-controlled. They gave me two guns, one built into a finger-ring and the other a reasonable facsimile of a clip-pen. One of the technicians produced a small box of the type cultured pearls come in. Inside, nested in cotton, was a flake of pink plastic the size of a fish scale.

"This is a communication device," he said. "It will be attached to your scalp behind the ear where the hair will conceal it. You will heed it implicitly."

A pink-cheeked man I hadn't seen before came into the room and conferred with Big Nose in a whisper before he turned to me.

"If you're ready, Mr. Florin . . .?" he said in a voice as soft as a last wish, and didn't wait for my answer. I looked back from the door. Four grim faces looked at me. Nobody waved bye-bye.

I had heard of the Senator's Summer Retreat. It was a modest cottage of eighty-five rooms crowded into fifty acres of lawn and garden in the foothills sixty miles northeast of the city. My pilot dropped me in a clump of big conifers among a lot of cool night air and piney odors half a mile upslope from the lights of the house. Following instructions, I sneaked down through the trees, making not much more noise than a bull elk in mating season, and found the hole in the security fence right where they'd said it would be. A booted man with a slung power gun and a leashed dog paced past me fifty feet away without turning his head. Maybe he was following instructions too. When he had passed, I moved up to the house by short dashes from shadow to shadow, not falling down more than a couple of times. It all seemed pretty silly to me; but Big Nose had insisted the approach was important.

The service door was almost hidden behind a nice stand of ground juniper. My key let me into a small room full of the smell of disinfectant and buckets for me to put a foot in. Another door let onto a narrow hall. Lights showed in a foyer to the right; I went left, prowled up three flights of narrow stairs, came out in a corridor walled in gray silk that almost reminded me of something; but I brushed that thought away. Up ahead a soft light was shining from an open doorway. I went toward it, through it into dimness and richness and an odor of waxed wood-work and Havana leaf and old money.

He was standing by an open wall safe with his back toward me; he turned as I came through the door. I recognized the shaggy blond-going-gray hair, the square-cut jaw with the cleft that brought in the female vote, the big shoulders in the hand-tailoring. His eyes were blue and level and looked at me as calmly as if I were the butler he'd rung for.

"Florin," he said in a light, mellow voice that wasn't quite what I had expected. "You came." He put out his hand; he had a firm grip, well-manicured nails, no calluses.

"What can I do for you, Senator?" I said.

He paused for a moment before he answered, as if he were remembering an old joke.

"I suppose they've given you the story about how I've gone insane? How I imagine there's a plot afoot to kidnap me?" Before I thought of an answer he went on: "That's all lies, of course. The truth is quite otherwise."

"All right," I said. "I'm ready for it."

"They're going to kill me," he said matter-of-factly, "unless you can save my life."

He was giving me the old straight-from-the-shoulder look. He was the captain and I was the team and it was time for my hidden-ball play. I opened my mouth to ask the questions, but instead I went past him to the ivory telephone on the desk. He watched without saying a word while I checked it, checked the light fixtures, the big spray of slightly faded roses on the side table, the plumbing fixtures in the adjoining bathroom. I found three bugs and flushed them down the toilet.

"A properly spotted inductance mike can still hear us," I said. "So much for privacy in our modern world."

"How do things look—outside?" he asked.

"About as you'd expect," I hedged. He nodded as if that told him plenty. "By the way," I said, "have we met before, Senator?"

He shook his head, started a smile.

"Under the circumstances," I said, "I'd think you'd want to see some identification."

Maybe he looked a little confused, or maybe not. I'm not a great reader of expressions. "You're well known to me by reputation, Mr. Florin," he said, and looked at me as if that were my cue to whip out a chart of the secret passages in the castle walls, complete with an X marking the spot where the fast horses waited outside the postern gate.

"Maybe you'd better fill me in just a little, Senator," I said. "I wouldn't want to make any unnecessary mistakes."

"You know the political situation in the city," he said. "Anarchy, riots, lawless mobs roaming the streets . . ." He waited for me to confirm that.

"The disorder is not so spontaneous as it may appear. The crowd is being manipulated for a purpose—the purpose being treason."

I got out one of my weeds and rolled it between my fingers.

"That's a pretty heavy word, Senator," I said. "You don't hear it much nowadays."

"No doubt Van Wouk spoke of the approaching elections, the dangers of political chaos, economic collapse, planetary disaster."

"He mentioned them."

"There's another thing which perhaps he failed to mention. Our planet has been invaded."

I lit up my cigarette, snorted the stink of it out of my nostrils.

"It must have slipped his mind. Who's doing the invading?"

"The world has·been under a single government for twenty years; obviously, there is no domestic enemy to launch an attack . . ."

"So what does that leave? The little green men from Andromeda?"

"Not men," he said gravely. "As for Andromeda—I don't know."

"Funny," I said. "I haven't noticed them around."

"You don't believe me."

"Why should I?" I put it to him flatly.

He laughed a little. "Why, indeed?" The faint smile faded. "But suppose I give you proof."

"Go ahead."

"As you might have expected, I don't have it here; nothing that would convince you."

I nodded, watching him. He didn't look wild-eyed; but lots of them don't.

"I realize that what I'm telling you seems to lend credence to Van Wouk's story," he said calmly. "I took that risk. It's important that I be utterly candid with you."

"Sure."

"Let me make myself perfectly clear. You came here as Van Wouk's agent. I'm asking you to forget him and the council; to give me your personal loyalty."

"I was hired to bodyguard you, Senator," I said. "I intend to do my job. But you're not making it any easier. You tell me things that seem to call for the boys with the butterfly nets; you know I don't believe you; and then you ask me to back your play and I don't even know what your play is."

"I also told you things that Van Wouk didn't know I

knew. The fact is, I maneuvered him, Florin." He looked strong, confident, sane, determined—except for a little hint of nerves around the eyes.

"I wanted you here, beside me," he said. "Van Wouk can think what he likes. I got you here, that's what counts. Score that one for me."

"All right, I'm here. Now what?"

"They've been in communication with the enemy— Van Wouk and his crowd. They intend to collaborate. They hope for special rewards under an alien regime; God knows what they've been promised. I intend to stop them."

"How?"

"I have a certain personal following, a small cadre of loyal men of ability. Van Wouk knows that; that's why he's determined on my death."

"What's he waiting for?"

"Raw murder would make a martyr of me. He prefers to discredit me first. The insanity story is the first step. With your help he hoped to drive me into actions that would both cause and justify my death."

"He sent me here to help you escape," I reminded him.

"Via a route leaked to me by his hireling. But I have resources of which he's unaware. That's how I learned of the invasion—and of the other escape route."

"Why didn't you leave sooner?"

"I waited for you."

"What makes me that important?"

"I know my chances alone, Florin. I need a man like you with me—a man who won't quail in the face of danger."

"Don't let them kid you, Senator," I said. "I go down two collar sizes just at the idea of a manicure."

He twitched a little smile into position and let it drop. "You shame me, Florin. But of course you're famous for your sardonic humor. Forgive me if I seem less than appreciative. But quite frankly—I'm afraid. I'm not like you—the man of steel. My flesh is vulnerable. I shrink from the thought of death—particularly death by violence."

"Don't build me up into something I'm not, Senator. I'm human, don't ever doubt it. I like living, in spite of its drawbacks. If I've stuck my neck out a few times it was because that was less uncomfortable than the other choices."

"Then why are you here?"

"Curiosity, maybe."

He gave me the shadow smile. "Don't you want to find out if I'm really as crazy as Van Wouk says? Aren't you interested in seeing what I'll offer you as proof that we've been invaded by nonhumans?"

"It's a point."

He looked me in the eye. "I want you with me as my ally, faithful unto death. That—or nothing."

"You'd get that—or nothing."

"I know."

"You're aware that you'll be in deadly danger from the moment we deviate from Van Wouk's prepared script," he said.

"The thought had occurred to me."

"Good," he said, curt again. "Let's get on with it." He went to a closet and got out a trench coat that showed signs of heavy wear and pulled it on. It took a little of the shine off the distinguished look, but not enough. While he was busy with that, I took a look in the open wall safe. There was a bundle of official-looking documents wrapped with purple ribbon, letters, a thick sheaf of what looked like money except that it was printed in purple ink and had a picture of a lion on it and the words *Legal Tender of the Lastrian Concord For All Debts Public and Private*. There was also a flat handgun of a type I'd never seen.

"What's the Lastrian Concord, Senator?" I said.

"A trade organization in which I hold shares," he said after a hesitation. "Their currency is almost valueless now. I keep it as a souvenir of my bad financial judgment."

He wasn't watching me; I slid the play gun into my side pocket; the Senator was at the window, running his fingers along the gray metal frame.

"It's a long way down," I said. "But I suppose you've got a rope ladder in your sock."

"Better than that, Florin." There was a soft *snick!* and the sash swung into the room like a gate. No blustery night air blew in; there was a featureless gray wall eighteen inches away.

"A repeater panel in the wall," he said. "The house has a number of features Van Wouk would be surprised to know about."

"What was the other route, Senator?" I said. "The one Van Wouk expected you to use?"

"It's an official emergency exit; a panel at the back of the closet leads down to the garages. A guard is supposed to be bribed to supply a car. This way is somewhat less luxurious but considerably more private."

He stepped in ahead of me, slid away out of sight to the left. As I was about to follow, a cricket chirped behind my ear.

"*Good work,*" a tiny voice whispered. "*Everything is proceeding nicely. Stay with him.*"

I took a last look around the room and followed the Senator into his secret passage.

We came out onto the grounds in the shelter of a giant kapok tree that had cost somebody a lot of money to transplant alive. The Senator led the way without any dramatic dashes through an ornamental garden to a row of imported poplars, along that to the fence. From somewhere inside his coat he produced a set of snippers and some jumper wires. He cut a hole for us and we went through and were in a cornfield under the stars. The Senator had turned to me and started to say something when the alarm went off.

There were no jangling bells, no sirens; just the floodlights blossoming all across the grounds. I grabbed the Senator's arms as he started to look back.

"Don't look at the lights," I said. "Or is this part of your plan?"

"Come on—this way!" He set off at a run toward the wooded rise beyond the field. There was plenty of light leaking through the poplars to cast long shadows that scrambled ahead of us. I felt as conspicuous as a cockroach in a cocktail glass, but if there was an alternative course of action I couldn't think of it right then. There was another fence to get through; on the other side we were in light woods that got denser as the ground got steeper. We pulled up for a breather a quarter of a mile above the house, which floated peacefully in its pooled light down below. There were no armed men swarming across the lawn, no engines gunning down the drive, no copters whiffling into the air, no PA systems blaring.

"It's too easy," I said.

"What do you mean?" The Senator was breathing hard, but no harder than I was. He was in shape, a point for our side.

"They didn't switch those floods on just to light our way—or did they?"

"There's a rather elaborate system of electronic surveillance devices," he said, and I saw he was grinning. "Some time ago I took the precaution of tampering with the master panel in a small way."

"You think of everything, Senator. What comes next?"

"Radial 180 passes a mile to the west. However . . ." He waved a hand toward the ridge above us. "Secondary 96 skirts the foothills, about seven miles from here. It's difficult country, but I know the route. We can be at the road in two hours, in time to catch a produce flat dead-heading for the coast."

"Why the coast?"

"I have a standing rendezvous arrangement with a man named Eridani. He has the contacts I need."

"For a man under house arrest, you do pretty well, Senator."

"I told you I have extraordinary methods of communication."

"So you did."

Down below, there was some activity now. A personnel carrier had cranked up and was taking on uniformed men.

A squad was on its way down the drive on foot. You could hear a few shouts, but nobody seemed very excited—at least not from fifteen hundred yards away.

"Van Wouk's plans covered every eventuality except this one," the Senator said. "By slipping out of the net at this point, we sidestep his entire apparatus."

"Not if we sit here too long talking about it."

"If you've caught your breath, let's get started."

Visibility wasn't too bad, once my eyes had adapted to the starlight. The Senator was a competent climber and seemed to know exactly where he was going. We topped the ridge and he pointed out a faint glow in the north that he said was Homeport, forty miles away. A copter went over, raking searchlights across the treetops half a mile away. IR gear might have found us at closer range; but there was an awful lot of virgin-forested hill country for us to be lost in.

The hike took ten minutes over the Senator's estimates, with no breaks. We came sliding down the angle of a steep cut onto a narrow pike that sliced through the rough country like a sabre wound. We moved on a few hundred yards north to a spot beside a gorge that offered better cover if we needed to get out of sight in a hurry. The Senator handed me a small silver flask and a square pill.

"Brandy," he said. "And a metabolic booster."

I tasted the brandy; it was the real stuff. "I get it," I said. "This is the deluxe prison break, American plan."

He laughed. "I've had plenty of time to prepare. It was obvious to me as much as three months ago that Van Wouk and the Council were up to something. I waited until I was sure."

"Are you sure you're sure? Maybe they know things you don't know they know."

"What are you getting at?"

"Maybe the route through the closet was a dummy. Maybe they're watching you right now."

"I could have decided to go south just as easily, to the capital."

"But you had reasons for coming this way. Maybe they know the reasons."

"Are you just talking at random, Florin? Or . . .?"

"If it was 'or,' I wouldn't be talking."

He laughed again, not a loud or merry laugh, but still a laugh. "Where does that line of reasoning end, Florin? Everything is something other than what it seems, or what it seems to seem. You have to draw the line somewhere. I prefer to believe I'm thinking my own thoughts, and that they're as good as or better than anything Van Wouk has planned."

"What happens after you meet your pal Eridani?"

"He has access to broadcast facilities. A surprise Trideo appearance by me, informing the public of the situation, will tie their hands."

"Or play into them."

"Meaning?"

"Suppose you dreamed these aliens?"

"But I didn't. I told you I have proof of their presence, Florin."

"If you can imagine aliens, you can imagine proof."

"If you doubt my sanity, why are you here?"

"I agreed to help you, Senator, not believe all your ideas."

"Indeed? And your idea of helping me might be to lead me docilely to Van Wouk."

"You sent for me, Senator; it wasn't my idea."

"But you agreed to ally yourself with me."

"That's right."

"Then don't attempt to interfere with my plans."

"I'm just making conversation, Senator. People do have illusions, you know. And they believe in them. What makes *you* immune?"

He started to snap off a sharp answer, but instead he shook his head and smiled. "I decline to tackle a paradox at this time of night." He broke off and cocked his head. I heard it too: turbines howling on a grade to the south, not far away.

"Here's our ride," I said. "Just as you predicted, Senator."

"It's common knowledge that this is a cargo artery; don't try to read anything mystical into it."

"I guess Van Wouk knows that, too."

"Hide in the ditch if you like. I'm flagging it."

"You hide: I'm the one with the bulletproof vest."

"What the hell," the Senator said abruptly, sounding a little out of character. "A man has to trust somebody." He strode into the center of the road and planted himself and waved the flat down as it came in view. We climbed on the back and settled down comfortably among some empty chicken crates.

The driver dropped us in the warehouse district a block from the waterfront, on a cracked sidewalk where a cold, gusty wind that smelled like dead fish and tarred hemp pushed grit and old newspapers ahead of it. Weak, morgue-colored light from a pole-lamp at the corner shone on storefronts with shaded windows like blinded eyes above them. There were a few people in sight, men in felt hats and women in cloches and bare legs and fur boots, bucking the wind. A boxy taxicab rolled past, splattering muddy water from the gutter.

"What is it, Florin?" the Senator said sharply.

"Nothing much," I said. "It doesn't look like what I expected."

"Were you expecting something in particular?"

"Don't count that one, Senator; it just slipped out. Where to now?"

"A place near here; there's a rendezvous arranged for every fourth hour until I arrive." He looked at a strap watch. "Less than half an hour now." We went past a closed tailor shop with dummies wearing double-breasted tuxes with dust on the shoulders, past a candy store with plates of fudge on paper doilies, a drugstore with bottles of colored water and a Dr. Pepper sign. I stopped him at the corner.

"Suppose we vary the route," I said, "just for the hell of it."

"Nonsense." He started through me but I didn't move.

"Humor me, Senator."

"Look here, Florin—your job is to carry out my orders, not to try to bully me!"

"Correction. I'm here to try to keep you alive. How I do that is my business."

He glared at me, then shrugged.

"Very well. It's two blocks west, one south."

We went along the dark street. All the other pedestrians seemed to be on the other side of the street, though I didn't see anyone cross to avoid us. A surprising number of women were tall and slim, and wore gray coats with squirrel collars. A Nile green open car with its side curtains buttoned up tight rolled slowly by. I picked a corner at random and turned in. A match flared halfway down the block. A green car was parked there, lights off, motor running, the off-side door hanging open. I saw that much in the flare of the match. The man who had struck it dropped it, stepped into the car. Its lights went on, dazzling at us from two nickel-plated bowls half the size of washtubs.

"Run for it!" the Senator blurted.

"Stand fast!" I said, and caught his arm, pushed him back into a doorway. The car gunned past, took the corner on two sidewalls. Its racketing died out along the dark street.

"Close," the Senator said in a strained voice. "Fast thinking, Florin."

"Uh-huh," I said. "Phony play. They wanted us to see them. Who were they, friends of yours?"

"What are you implying?"

"Not a thing, Senator. Just groping in the dark."

"Not nervous, are you, Florin?"

I gave him my best death-row grin. "Why should I be? You're the one they want to kill."

"Perhaps I exaggerated the dangers."

"Any idea why? The routine with the car, I mean."

"Coincidence," he said. "Stop reading deep significance into every incident, Florin."

He started past me and I stopped him. "Maybe I'd better go scout the area alone."

"For God's sake, Florin—you'll be seeing burglars under the bed next!"

"Sometimes they're there, Senator."

He made a disgusted sound. "I made a mistake in sending for you, Florin. You're not the man I was led to believe—" He broke off, listening to what he'd just said.

"Gets to you after a while, doesn't it, Senator?"

"What the devil does that mean?"

"I'm the man that took the job of guarding you, Senator. I take the job seriously—but you're not giving me much help."

He chewed his teeth and looked at me.

"Fire me and I'll walk away right now," I said. "But as long as I'm working for you we do it my way."

"You can't—" he started, but I waved that away.

"Name it, Senator."

"Damn it, man, can't you simply . . . go along?"

I looked at him.

"All right. We'll do it your way," he said between his teeth.

Something whispered behind my ear. The miniature voice said, *"Florin—there has been a slight hitch. You're to keep the subject away from the rendezvous for the present. Walk east; you'll receive further instructions shortly."*

"Well?" the Senator said.

"I changed my mind," I said. "Let's skip the meeting. You can make the next one in four hours."

"Damn it, man, every hour counts!"

"Only the ones while you're alive, Senator."

"All right, all right! What do you have in mind?"

"Suppose we walk east for a while."

He looked at me warily. "Florin—is there something you're not telling me?"

"I asked you first."

He snarled and pushed past me and headed east, and I followed. The blocks looked just like the ones we'd already walked along. A big green car with the top up cruised across an intersection half a block ahead. We kept going.

"*All right, Florin,*" the little voice whispered. "*Stop at the next corner and wait.*"

We came to the intersection and crossed. "You go ahead," I said. "I want to check something."

He gave me a disgusted look and strolled on fifty feet and stared into a dark window. I got out a cigarette and tamped the end and saw the green car round a corner two blocks down. I dropped the weed and faded back, sprinted toward the Senator.

"Now what?" he snarled, and put his back to the wall.

"In the alley—out of sight!" I snapped, and grabbed his arm.

"What for? What—"

"Hunch." I hustled him ahead, back into darkness and evil odors and things that crunched underfoot. I heard the purr of the big engine; it came closer, then stayed in one place and idled. A car door slammed. The car moved on, passed the alley mouth.

"Why, that's the same car . . ." the Senator whispered.

"You know the owner?"

"Of course not. What is this, Florin?"

"Somebody's playing games. I get a feeling I don't like the rules."

"Can you, for God's sake, speak plainly?"

"No plainer than I can think. Let's get out of here, Senator. That way." I pointed deeper into the alley. He grumbled but moved. We came out on a dark street that was wider but no more fragrant than the alley.

"Where are you leading me, Florin?" the Senator said in a voice that had gotten noticeably hoarser. "What are you getting me into?"

"I'm playing this one by ear," I said. "Let's find a quiet corner where we can talk—" I got that far with my reasonable proposal before the green car boomed out of a side street. It raked the curb, straightened out and roared down at us. I heard the Senator yell, heard glass tinkle, heard the *ba-ba-bam!* of a thirty caliber on full automatic, saw flame spurt and felt the sting of brick chips across my cheek. I was turning, grabbing the Senator and shoving him ahead of me, hearing the gun stutter again in the bellow of the big straight-eight that echoed and dwindled away and left us alone in a ringing silence bigger than a cathedral.

The Senator was leaning against the bricks, his back to me, folding slowly at the knees. I got to him and held him up and saw the big stain spreading on his side. Out in the street someone called cautiously. Feet clattered on pavement, coming our way. It was time to go. I got the Senator's arm over my shoulders; his feet fumbled at the bricks underfoot and some of his weight went off me. We did twenty drunken feet that way before I saw the door, set back in a deep recess on the left. It didn't look clean or inviting, but I lurched toward it and got the knob turned and we more or less fell into a dark little room with packing cases and scattered excelsior and odds and ends of wire and rope, barely visible in some dirty light leaking over the transom.

I settled the Senator on the floor and checked him and found two holes, low on his side, about six inches apart.

"How bad?" he whispered.

"Busted rib. The slug glanced off. You were lucky."

"You're hurt, too," he accused. I felt over my jaw, found some abraded skin that was bleeding a little.

"I take that back about your friends," I said. "Those were real bullets."

"They were trying to kill me!" He tried to sit up and I pressed him back.

"Don't sound so surprised. You told me that was the idea, remember?"

"Yes, but—" he stoppered it up. "They've gone out of their minds," he tried again, and let it go. "Florin, what are we going to do?"

"First, I'd better plug those holes." I peeled his shirt back and started to work.

"This chum you were supposed to meet: Eridani," I said. "Tell me about him."

"You were right. It was a trap. I can't go there now, I—"

"Hold it, Senator. I had my doubts about your story, but those slugs change things. This Eridani may be our out. How long have you known him?"

"Why—long enough, I suppose. A matter of years. I trusted him—"

"Any reason to tie him to the shooting?"

"Well . . . not specifically—but this whole thing has gone sour. I want to get clear of here, Florin, my life's not safe in this place; I—"

"Where will you go?"

"I don't know."

"Then maybe we'd better think about making that rendezvous."

"We can't go out there—into those streets!"

"We can't stay here."

"What the devil do you know about it? You're just—" He caught himself and sank back and glared at me.

"Sure; I'm the hired help. Why not let me work at what I was hired for? I'll check Eridani out alone. If it looks good, I'll bring him here—"

"No! I'm not staying alone!"

"It's the safest way."

He slumped. "I deserved that. I haven't borne up very well in the clutch, have I, Florin? Well, I told you violence wasn't my forte. But I'm all right now. I won't make a fool of myself again."

I finished my first-aid and wrapped a strip of shirt around him.

"Think you can walk?"

"Certainly." I helped him get to his feet. There was a faint *click!* behind my right ear and a voice said : "*All right, Florin; wait there for the next development.*"

The Senator was busy buttoning his coat, grunting with pain at the movement. I felt back of my ear and found the gadget and pried it loose and ground it under my heel. A door across the room opened into a grimy hall that led to a glass door that let us out into the street.

No green Buicks were in sight; nobody shot at us. We kept to the shadows like a couple of mice caught outside the family hole and headed for the waterfront.

It was a mean-looking dive on a street only a little less shabby than the one where we'd been shot up. Two steps led down into dim brown light and the odors of booze and cigarettes. We took a booth at the back and ordered beer from an ex-heavyweight with broken-down arches and a face that had been hammered flat. He put two bleary glasses in front of us and went back behind the bar to brood. I had used my handkerchief to wipe the gore off my face, and with the coat folded the other way the Senator's stains didn't show; if our host noticed anything unusual for the neighborhood he was thoughtful enough not to mention it.

"He's late," the Senator said nervously. He was sitting on the side facing the door. "I don't like this, Florin. We're sitting ducks. They could fire through the window—"

"They could have done that any time. They didn't; maybe later we'll figure out why."

He wasn't listening; he was looking toward the door. I turned and saw a slim, dark-haired girl wrapped to the eyes in a red fox collar come down the two steps and look around. Her glance may have hesitated for a moment at our booth; or maybe it was just wishful thinking. She had a face like you see in dreams, and even then only at a distance. She went across the room and disappeared through a door at the back.

"Nice," I said. "On our side?"

"Who?"

"Don't overplay your hand, Senator," I said. "Nobody misses one like that."

He frowned at me. "See here, Florin, I don't care for your tone."

"Could it be there's something you're not telling me, Senator?"

"I've told you everything," he snapped. "This farce has gone far enough." He started to stand and froze that way, staring toward the windows. I turned my head and through the glass saw a Nile green Buick ease to a stop at the curb. The nearside door opened and a man stepped out. Under the brim of his dark hat I recognized the gray man. He seemed to see me through the windows and halted in midstride.

"You know him?" I snapped. The Senator didn't answer. His face was a trifle wavery around the edges. A high, singing noise was coming from somewhere in the middle distance. I tried to get my feet under me to stand, but couldn't seem to find them. The Senator was leaning over me, shouting something, but I couldn't make out the words. They ran together into a booming sound like a fast freight going through a tunnel, with me hanging onto the side. Then my grip loosened and I fell off and the train hurtled away into the dark, making mournful sounds that trailed away into nothingness.

I was lying on my back on hot sand, and the sun was burning my face like a blast oven. Fire ants were crawling over me, taking a bite here and there, picking out a place to start lunch. I tried to move, but my arms and legs were tied down.

"You're a damned coward," somebody was saying.

"Damn you, I did all I could! It was all coming apart on me!"

The voices came from the sky. I tried to get my eyelids up to see who was talking, but they were tied down like the rest of me.

"It's your own fault, Bardell," another voice said. This one reminded me of somebody. Trait. Lenwell Trait, the name came from somewhere a long way off, a long time ago. It didn't sound like the name of anybody I'd know.

"My fault, hell! You were the masterminds, the ones who knew what you were doing! I went through hell, I tell you! You don't know what it's like!"

"You quit—ran out! You ought to be shot!"

"Shut up—all of you!" Big Nose talking. I didn't know his name, or where I'd met him, but I knew that voice. "Lloyd, reset everything for situation one. Bardell, get ready."

"Are you all crazy? I've had enough!"

"You're going back. You're a bungling incompetent, but you're all we have. No arguments. The time for that's long past."

"You can't do it! I've lost confidence! I don't believe in the technique anymore! It would be murder!"

"Suicide," Big Nose said. "Unless you buck up and meet it. We're committed now. We can't back out."

"I need help—at least give me that! Things aren't breaking the way you said!"

"What about it, Lloyd?"

"All right, all right. For God's sake, settle it! I have my hands full!"

There was more talk, but another sound was drowning it.

The rising wind was hot as a blowtorch across my skin. A buzz saw started up and sliced its way across the sky; it split and darkness poured in like Niagara, swept away the voices, the ants, the desert, and me . . .

I opened my eyes and the girl was sitting across from me, not wearing her fox skin now, looking at me with an anxious expression.

"Are you all right?" she said in a voice like doves cooing. Or like a spring breeze among the daffodils. Or like the gurgle of happy waters. Or maybe it was just a voice. Maybe I was slaphappy, coming out of it.

"Far from it," I said, using somebody else's voice by remote control. "I've got the damnedest urge to climb the chandelier and yodel the opening bars of *William Tell*. It's only my years of training that prevent me; that and my rheumatism. How long was I out?"

She frowned. "You mean . . . ?"

"That's right, kid. Out. Cold. Doped. You know: unconscious."

"You were just sitting here. You looked a little strange, so I . . ."

"They got him, huh?"

"Him? You mean your brother. He . . . just left."

"Which way? Did he go, that is. My drinking buddy, I mean. What makes you think he's my brother?"

"I . . . just assumed—"

"I don't suppose there's any point in asking where they took him, or why?"

"I don't know what you mean."

"This is where I'm supposed to work you over with my blackjack and get all your secrets. But frankly, honey, I'm not up to it."

I stood. That didn't feel at all good. I sat down again.

"You shouldn't exert yourself."

"What's it to you, doll?"

"Nothing—really. It's just . . ." She let it go.

"Another time, maybe." I stood again. This time it worked a little better; but my head still felt like bagged gravel.

"Please wait!" she said, and put a hand on my arm.

"Another time I'll linger," I said, "but duty calls. Or something calls."

"You're hurt and sick—"

"Sorry, kid, I'm on my way. Sorry about no tip, but I seem to have left my change in my other suit. By the way, did you ever hear of the Lastrian Concord?"

She didn't answer, just shook her head. When I looked back from the door she was still watching me with those big lovely eyes. I let the door close between us and was back out in the street. A light snow was falling. In the thin layer of slush on the pavement I could see footprints leading back the way the Senator and I had come. I followed them, weaving a little, but still on the job.

The trail retraced the route the Senator and I had taken when we made our daring escape from the assassins, or whatever it was we had escaped from, if we had escaped. It ended at the spot where we had unloaded from the cargo flat. The tailor shop was still closed, but the second dummy from the left seemed to have an eye on me.

"Be my guest, buddy," I said. "We're two of a kind." He didn't answer, which suited me OK.

I felt as weak as a newborn squirrel and just about as smart. My wrists and ankles hurt. I wanted to lie down on something soft and wait for something nice to happen to me, but instead I moved along to a dark doorway and got comfortable in it and waited. I didn't know what I was waiting for. I thought about the girl back in the bar. She was nice to think about. I wondered if she'd been part of the dope-dream. I had an urge to go back and check, but just then a man stepped out of the alley-mouth across the street. He was in a dark overcoat and hat, but I knew the face. It was the scruffy redhead who had called at my hotel with the gray man.

He looked both ways along the street, then turned and set off at a brisk walk. I let him get to the corner, then followed. When I reached it, he was nowhere in sight. I kept going, passed a dark entry just in time to see the revolving door glide to a stop. I pushed through, was in a small lobby floored with black and white tiles, the small, rectangular unglazed kind, set in a pattern that zigged and zagged—just like my thoughts. The stairs led up to a landing; I could hear feet up above. They seemed to be in a hurry. I went up after them.

Two flights higher, the climb ended in a dark corridor. A faint greenish light was coming under a panel door at the far end. My feet made no sound at all on the Nile green carpet. No sounds came from behind the door. I didn't knock, just turned the knob and walked in.

There was a nice rug, a filing cabinet, a chair, a desk. And behind the desk, dressed in a snappy gray pinstripe, a cobra smiled at me.

Well, maybe not a cobra. A lizard. Pale violet, shading to powder blue, white at the throat. Smooth-scaled, glistening, round-snouted, with lidless eyes and a lipless mouth. Something not human. Something that leaned back in the chair and gave a careless wave of what was almost a hand and said, "Well, Mr. Florin—you've surprised us all." His voice was as light and dry as old rose petals.

I groped the Browning out into view and waved it at him. He lit up a cigarette and blew smoke through two small, noseless nostrils.

"Are you part of the first nightmare?" I said. "Or is this a double feature?"

He chuckled; a nice, friendly, relaxed chuckle such as you seldom hear from a reptile. Maybe he was all right at that.

"You're a most amusing fellow, Florin," he said. "But what are you attempting to accomplish? What do you seek in these ghostly rooms, these haunted corridors, eh?"

"You left out the phantom-ridden streets," I said. "I give up; what am I looking for?"

"Let me give you a word of friendly advice, Florin. Let it go. Stop seeking, stop probing. Let life flow past you. Accept what comes. You're Florin, a man of deeds, not philosophies. Accept what is."

"One at a time or all at once?" I raised the gun and aimed it at the middle of the smile.

"Tell me things," I said. "Anything at all. If I don't like it, I'll shoot."

The reptilian smile floated in a soft haze of cigarette smoke. A buzzing sound was coming out of the woodwork. I tried to say something, but there was no air in my lungs, only thick pink fog. I tried to squeeze the trigger, but it was welded in place, and I strained harder, and the buzzing got louder and the mist thickened and whirled around the little red eyes that gleamed now like two fading sparks far away across the sea and then winked out.

The girl was sitting across from me, wearing a close-fitting dark blue dress that shimmered like polished fish scales. She was looking at me with an anxious expression, like a bird-watcher watching a problem bird.

"No good," I said. "No bird watcher ever had eyes like those." The sound of my own voice startled me.

"Are you . . . all right now?" she said. Her voice was smooth as honey, as soft as a morning cloud, as sweet as music. Anyway, it was a nice voice. "Your friend left," she said, and looked worried.

I looked around. I was at the table in the beer joint, the same place I'd been the last time I swam up out of a Mickey. The Senator was nowhere in sight. Neither was the gray man or the Nile green car.

"Don't get the wrong idea," I said. "I'm not one of those habitual drunks. What makes you think he's my friend?"

"I . . . I just assumed—"

"How long was I out?"

"I'm not sure; I mean—you were just sitting here; you looked a little strange, so . . ." Her voice trailed off.

I rubbed my temples; there was a light throbbing

behind them that could become a heavy throbbing with very little encouragement.

"Did you ever get the feeling you'd been through a scene before?" I said. "I can almost guess your next line. You're going to suggest that I sit tight until I get to feeling better."

"I . . . think you should. You don't look well."

"I appreciate your interest, Miss—but why would you care?"

"Why wouldn't I? I'm a human being."

"That's more than I can say for some of the folks I've been advised by lately. Say, you didn't see a fellow with a head like a garter snake? Only larger. His head, I mean."

"Please don't talk nonsense." She looked at me with an unreadable expression that I tried to read anyway.

"I knew you'd say that too. *Deja vu*, they call it. Or something. Have I come out of the smoke once, or twice? A question for the philosophers."

"I don't know what you're talking about," the girl said. "I thought you needed help. If I was wrong . . ." She started to get up and I caught her hand and pulled her back.

"Don't rush off. You're my sole link with whatever you're my sole link with, if that makes any sense—or even if it doesn't."

She pulled against my grip, but not very hard. I let go and she didn't move.

"Maybe the Senator slipped me something," I said. "Or maybe he didn't. Maybe the gray man shot me with a dope dart . . ."

"You've been shot?"

"At. They got the Senator, but it was just a graze. You wouldn't know who?"

She shook her head.

"Did you see the gray man? Or the green car?"

"No."

"But you saw the Senator. He was sitting with me when you came in. He pretended not to notice you. Why?"

"I have no idea."

"I'm his bodyguard," I said. "Or that's what they said. It turned out I was the finger. Dirty pool, don't you agree, Miss . . .?"

"Regis. You're not making sense."

"I kind of don't like that, Miss Regis. I think maybe the Senator's lost confidence after what happened. Can't say I blame him. So maybe he ditched me; or maybe they got him. Either way, I don't care for it."

"Who is the Senator?"

"*The* Senator. A very big man. But no names. Not for the present. That's what the gray man said. I wish I knew which side he was on. I wish I knew which side *I* was on— or if there are any sides. How many sides to a ring-around-the-rosy, Miss Regis?"

She shook her head, just watching me.

"You'll have to overlook any little eccentricities I seem to demonstrate," I said. "I've been having a few mild hallucinations. Hard to tell which are which. You, for example. Why are you sitting here listening to me? You ought to be in full flight by now, yelling for the boys with the strap-down cots."

"I don't believe you're dangerous," she said calmly.

"Do you know me?"

"I never saw you before."

"What brought you out in the chill night air, to a place like this—alone?"

"I really can't say. It was . . . an impulse."

I nodded. "Swell. That clears that up. Any other points you'd like to cover before I go?"

"Please don't go—wherever it is you mean to go."

"Why not—except for those big blue eyes?" I got to my feet; my legs felt twelve feet long and the diameter of soda straws. I leaned on the table as if intentionally.

"I've got stuff to do, baby," I said. "I've got questions that want answers and answers looking for the right questions. And time's a-wasting." I tottered away, and she didn't call after me. I was a little sorry about that, but I kept going.

Outside I looked for tracks in the snow, but there wasn't any snow. In a way that was reassuring; the snow was part of the dream. The street was still there; that was something. I turned right and headed the way I had gone the last time, or dreamed I had, or dreamed I'd dreamed I had, the time I met the fellow with the purple head. Meeting him had been a break. It helped me remember he wasn't really there. Whatever they'd fed me, it was potent stuff. I still felt woozy as a conventioneer discovering it's Tuesday morning in a strange town.

The streets were empty, even for the wee hours. No lights were on in the windows. No cars moved. Just the fitful wind and a feeling of mice scuttling behind the wainscoting. I made it back to the street where I'd made my debut in town a few hundred years—or maybe two hours—before. I turned the last corner and saw a man in a dark hat and

overcoat standing in front of the tailor shop, looking into
the window. I recognized him; it was Red, the rangy man
who had paid the call at my hotel in company with the
gray man. As prophecy, my dope-dream hadn't been too
bad so far.

Then the Senator walked out of the alley across the
way. I eased back out of sight and ran through the data.
That confused me, so I ran through it again, in the other
direction. That confused me still more.

"To hell with the data," I growled. "Let's get back to
essentials." I patted my gun and came around the corner
ready for action. They were gone.

I strolled on up to the place where Red had been
standing, but I'm not enough of a tracker to pick out the
spoor of a leather sole on concrete. I looked up and down
the street, saw nobody, heard nothing.

"All right, come on out," I called. "I know you're there."

Nobody answered, which was just as well. I went along
to the corner. Nobody there. The city looked as deserted
as Pompeii—and as full of ancient sin.

In the dream I had followed Red through a door
halfway down the block. Maybe that was a clue. In the
absence of any other, it would have to do. I went along to
the spot and found a big glass door with a large number 13
painted on it in swooping gold characters. It opened to a
push, and I stepped into a foyer with Nile green walls and
a spiral staircase and an odor like an abandoned library.
Listening revealed a lot of stately silence. I went up the
carpeted steps, came out on a landing with a gray door. I
eased it open and saw the scruffy man six feet away with
his back to me. He wasn't hiding; he was in the act of

unlocking the door; I had my gun in his left kidney before he had time to turn around.

"Don't ever think I won't squeeze a few rounds into your spine if it works out that way," I said in what I was using for a voice. It had a big, hollow ring to it, like a speech in an empty auditorium.

His eyes looked like mice caught outside their holes. His mouth sagged sideways like an overloaded pocket.

"Tell me things," I said. "Don't worry about getting it all in order. Just start. I'll tell you when to stop."

"You—can't be here," he said in a choked version of the high-pitched squeak.

"I know. Let's just pretend I am anyway. Where's the Senator?"

"You can forget the Senator now," he said, talking so fast his tongue couldn't keep up. "That's all over now."

"Been for a ride in a green Buick lately?" I said, and ground the gun in harder.

"I never meant to kill you; you'd have been phased back to Eta Level, I swear it!"

"That's a big load off my mind," I said. "Keep going."

"You have to believe me! When the operation's over, I can show you the tape—" He paused to gulp. "Look here; I can prove everything I'm saying. Just let me key the retriever, and—" He jammed the key in and turned it. I made a grab for him but all of a sudden the air was as thick as syrup and the same color, full of little whirly lights.

"You fool—you'll lose him!" somebody yelled. It was the Senator's voice but it was coming to me via satellite relay, backed by a massed chorus and a drum as big as the world, beating sixty beats a minute. I sucked in some of the dead air and grabbed for Red with a vague idea of holding on and going where he went; but he turned to smoke that spread out and washed up around me like surf, and I took a breath to yell and the water rose and covered me, and I sank down in a graceful spiral while the light faded from green through turquoise to indigo to black like the dark side of Pluto.

She was sitting across from me, dressed in a sissified white blouse and a powder blue jacket. Her hair was a soft brown, and so were her eyes. She was looking at me with an anxious expression, like a mother hen watching her first egg hatch.

"Wrong." My voice sounded blurry in my own ears. "A swan, maybe. But not a hen. And definitely not a mother." I reached across the table and caught her wrist. I was good at grabbing people's wrists. Holding on was another matter. She didn't struggle.

"I . . . thought perhaps you needed help," she said in a breathless whisper.

"The thought does you credit," I looked around the room. It was the same room it had been the last time I ran through the scene. The barman was still polishing the same glass; there was the same odor of fried onions and spilled wine, the same blackened beams, the same tarnished copper pots beside the fireplace. Or were they the same? Maybe not. The flames looked cheery and comforting, but if they gave any warmth I couldn't feel it from where I sat.

"The other man—your friend—went off and left you," the girl said. "You looked—"

"Sure—a little strange," I said. "Let's skip over the rest of the routine, honey. There's a deeper conversation that's been wanting us to have it."

"I don't know what you mean," she said in a small voice that still sounded like Gypsy guitars in the night.

"What's your name?" I said.

"Miss Regis. Curia Regis."

"And you already know mine, right?"

"Of course. I think perhaps you've made a mistake—"

"I had a wide choice of mistakes to make, and I made them all." I let go of her and rubbed my wrists, but it didn't help. I wanted to rub my ankles, but restrained the impulse. My chest hurt every time I breathed, but I breathed anyway.

"You can start by clearing up a point," I said. "Have we ever sat here before—at this table—in this room?"

"Of course not."

"Why are you here?"

"Because of your message—of course." Her eyes searched mine for something she didn't seem to find.

"Tell me about my message."

"In the newspaper. The Personals column."

"What did it say?"

"Just—*I need you*. And your name."

"And you came—just like that."

"If you don't need me, I'll go away."

"Sit tight. Order a sandwich. Count to a million by hundreds. If I'm not back by then, start without me." I got a grip on the edge of the table and wrestled my feet under me. They were steady enough, but the room had a tendency to rock.

"Here I go again," I said. "Third time's the charm."

When I looked back from the door, the table was empty.

"Florin," I told myself, "there's something you're doing wrong; or something you're not doing right."

I looked up and down the street. A light snow was falling. There were no people in sight, no footprints on the sidewalk, no tire tracks in the street. I had the world to myself.

"I got doped," I said. "I'm having French fits coming out of it. But how many tries do I have to make before the big one? How do I know when it's for real?"

"It's a learning process," I said. "You're unconscious, thinking about it. Each time you take a wrong turning in your logic you get sent back to square one. Your subconscious is trying to tell you something."

"How about now?" I asked, cagey. "Am I really standing here having a friendly conversation with myself like any normal guy, or—"

I got that far with the question when the whole world disappeared.

Now, it's always a shock to the nervous system when the power fails, even when it's only a bridge lamp that goes off. But this time the sky went out, too. It was total, impenetrable black in every direction. I put out a hand and felt the wall beside me; with my nose an inch from it, I could sense it, but not see it.

"New rules, Florin," I said aloud, just to be hearing something. "But the same game."

I felt over the wall behind me, found the door I had just

come out of. It was locked, frozen harder than a Nazi's
Swiss account.

"No going back," I counseled myself. "That leaves forward, if you can call it forward. Back to the spot where the
action is. You can do it by dead reckoning."

It wasn't much of an idea, but I didn't have a better
one.

It took me half an hour, shuffling along with one hand
on the wall and the other out in front, feeling the air. I
stepped down curbs and up again on the other side, avoided
falling over fireplugs, didn't get run over, all without a
seeing-eye dog. I was proud of myself. Good work, Florin.
If your enemies could see you now . . .

That gave me a creepy sensation along the back of my
neck. My being blind didn't mean anybody else was.
Maybe they were watching me, tracking me every foot of
the way, closing in for the kill.

I didn't know who I meant by "they." That made it
worse. I had started off working for the Inner Council but
had neglected to get the names. Then the Senator took
over, and for a while we had worked out pretty well
together, but then that went sour, too. There was a chance
that he had given me the Mickey himself, but in the
absence of proof he was still my client. If Van Wouk or
someone else of the same nature had grabbed him out
from under my slumbering nose it was up to me to get
him back, which meant I had to keep right on picking my
way, counting the paces and the blocks, back to where I
had last seen him and the scruffy man.

I was at the corner. I turned left and felt my way along
to the glass door with the big 13. There wasn't any door.

Maybe I'd counted wrong. Maybe somebody had come along and sealed it up just to confuse me. Maybe it hadn't been there in the first place.

I went on another few feet and stumbled into a revolving door; it revolved and palmed me into the blinding glare of a forty-watt bulb hanging on a kinked wire in a lobby that was either being built or torn down.

There was nothing pretty in sight, but it was nice to have my eyes back, even if all I was looking at was bare lath walls, a rough concrete floor, temporary wooden steps leading up.

"This time," I told myself, "you play it a little smoother. No blundering around with a gun in your fist; no pushing open strange doors and sticking your head in to see what they hit it with. Foxy all the way, that's the motto."

I went up. There was a landing covered with shavings and brick dust. A black fire door had the number 13 in heavy brass above it. With an ear pressed to it, I could make out the sound of voices. They seemed to be disagreeing about something. That suited me; I was in a mood to be disagreeable. I tried the knob; it turned, and I stepped through into a passage with a plastered wall on one side and obscure-glass cubicles on the other. The voices were coming from the third cubicle in line. I soft-footed along to it.

". . . what do you mean, lost him?" Big Nose was saying.

"I tell you, there's a factor of unpredictability involved! I'm getting interference!" This in a thin, high-pitched tone.

"Get him back—before irreparable damage is done!"

"I don't understand it. The recovery was made in time. . . ."

"You see?" a voice that was not quite that of the Senator said. "I'm telling you I can't take many more shocks like the last one."

"Never mind what you can take! You knew what you were signing up for!"

"Did I? Not even the Professor knows what's going on!"

"Don't call me 'Professor,' Bardell!"

"Gentlemen—let's not lose sight of the objective! Everything else is secondary."

There was a rather long silence. I breathed through my mouth and tried to read minds through the door. Either I couldn't read minds or there was nobody there. I eased the door open. The room was empty, looked as though it had been empty for a long time. In the closet were three bent coat hangers and some brown paper on the shelf. That and a few dead flies. A connecting door into the next office had been boarded up. I checked the boards; something clicked and the wall glided back and ocher light blazed through. I palmed my toy gun and stepped through into a wide avenue of colored tiles.

I squinted up at the sky. The strange yellow light was the sun. It was midafternoon of a pleasant summer day. Not a snowstorm. A drop of water ran down my chin. I put the back of my hand against my face; the skin was as cold as frozen fish.

"Fake money, fake Senator, fake weather," I said. "Or maybe this is the fake. Maybe I'm in a big room with a sky-blue ceiling and an imitation sun."

"*Could be,*" I agreed. "*The question remains—why?*"

"The Senator will know," I pointed out.

"*Sure—but will he talk?*"

"When I finish bouncing his phony head off this phony pavement he'll sing like three canaries," I stated with less confidence than I felt.

"You've got to catch him first."

"Nothing to it. He can't escape the eagle eye of Florin, the Master Sleuth—unless I happen to step on my shoelace and rupture my spleen."

"Do I detect a note of disillusionment? Not getting tired of your tricks, are you, Florin?"

"That's the trouble with tricks. They pall. God, how they pall."

"Try the park."

I was looking across the wide avenue at a stretch of downy-looking green grass set with tall, feathery trees. Beyond them tall, misty buildings loomed, gleaming white. A vehicle swung a corner and rolled toward me on high wheels. It was light, fragile-looking, like a buggy without a horse, painted a soft purple and decorated with curly corners and a complicated pattern in gold lines. A man and a woman sat in it, looking at each other while the buggy drove itself. They were both dressed in filmy white stuff with flecks of color here and there. The rubber tires made a soft whooshing sound against the tiles as it glided past.

"I knew Henry was planning a big surprise for '30, but I wasn't expecting this," I said, and realized I was not only talking aloud, I was waiting for an answer. Whatever it was the Senator had used to spike my beer had more side-effects than six months of hormone injections—perhaps including hallucinations involving purple carriages rolling down tile streets under a sun two sizes too big and three shades too yellow. It was time for me to curl up somewhere and sweat it out of my system. I headed for the biggest clump of flowering shrub in sight, rounded it, and almost collided with the Senator.

His head jerked. "You!" he said, not sounding pleased. "What are you doing *here!*"

"Sorry, I dozed off while you were talking," I said. "Rude of me. How's your busted rib feeling?"

"Florin—go back! Quickly! You have no business here! This is all wrong!"

"What is this place, Senator?"

He backed away. "I can't tell you. I can't even speak of it!"

"Sorry to be insistent," I said, and grabbed for him as he jumped back. He ducked aside and sprinted for it. I gave chase, using a pair of borrowed legs and towing a head the size of a blimp at the end of a hundred-foot cable.

It was a strange chase along the curving graveled path. We ran past fountains that threw tinkling jets of ink into green-crystal pools, past banked flowers like daubs of fluorescent paint, under the blue shadows of trees with bark like polished lacquer and foliage like antique lace. He ran hard, head down and legs pumping; I floated along behind, watching him get farther and farther away. Then he jumped a hedge, tripped, and was still rolling when I landed on him. He was a big boy and plenty strong, but he didn't know how to use it. A couple of solid hooks to the jaw took the shine off his eyes. I laid him out comfortably under what looked like a juniper except for the little crimson blossoms and worked on getting my wind back. After a while he blinked and sat up. He saw me and looked glum.

"You and I need to have a little talk," I said. "I'm two paradoxes and a miracle behind."

"You're a fool," he snarled. "You don't know what you're involving yourself in."

"But I'd like to," I said. "By the way, tell me again what the Lastrian Concord is."

He snorted. "I never heard of it."

"Too bad," I said. "I guess I imagined it. I saw this in the same place." I slid the flat-gun I had taken from his safe into sight. "Maybe I'm imagining it, too."

"What does this mean, Florin?" the Senator said in a tight voice. "Are you selling me out, then?"

It was my turn to grin the lazy grin. "Nuts," I said. "Who do you think you're kidding, Senator—or whoever you are."

He looked astounded. "Why should I want to deceive you?"

"It was laid on with a trowel," I said. "The callers in the night, the fancy reception room, the hints of dark deeds in the offing. And the details were nice: fake official forms, fake money—maybe even a fake gun." I bounced it on my palm.

"It's a two-mm. needler," he said, sounding angry or maybe scared. "Be careful with it!"

"Yeah, the details were good," I went on. "It's just the big things that fit like a rented tuxedo. I went along to find out why."

"I'm out of it," the Senator said. "I wash my hands of the whole affair."

"What about the invasion?"

He looked at me and frowned.

"No invasion, huh?" I said. "Too bad. I kind of liked the invasion. It had possibilities. What then?"

His jaw muscles worked. "Aw, hell," he said, and made a face. "My name's Bardell. I'm an actor. I was hired to impersonate the Senator."

"Why?"

"Ask the man who hired me," he said in a nasty tone, and felt of his jaw.

"Hurts, huh?" I said. "I did that. I owed you a couple anyway for the beer. It was worth one without the Mickey."

"You're quite a fellow, aren't you? That dose should have held you until . . ." He cut himself off. "Never mind. I can see we handled it wrong from the beginning."

"Tell me about the beginning." He started to get up and I stood over him and shook my head. "I never hit a man when he's down," I said. "Unless I have to. Talk it up, chum."

He looked at me and grinned. He laughed a short laugh. "Florin, the Man of Iron," he said. "Florin, the poor unsuspecting boob who lets himself be roped in with the old call to duty. They fixed you up with a costume and makeup and lines to say—plus a little gadget back of the ear to coach you through the rough spots. And what do you do? You kick a hole in it you could march a Shriners' band through."

"Looks like you've got all the good lines," I said.

"Don't misunderstand me, Florin," he said. "Hell, don't you get it yet?" He tapped the mastoid bulge behind his ear. "I've got the twin to it right here. I was roped in the same way you were."

"By who? Or 'whom'—if it means a lot to you."

"The Council."

"Keep going; you're doing fine."

"All right! They had plans; obviously they aren't working."

"Don't make me coax you, Bardell. I'm the guy who wants to be told things. Start tying it all together. I don't like all these loose ends."

"What I could tell you won't make you any happier."

"Try me."

He gave me a crafty look. "Let me ask you one instead, Florin: how did you get from your room—in a rather seedy hotel, as I recall—to Government House? For that matter, how did you get to the hotel?"

I thought back. I remembered the room. It was seedy, all right. I tried to recall the details of checking in, the face of the room clerk. Nothing. I must have let my poker face slip because Bardell grinned a savage grin.

"What about yesterday, Florin? How about your last case? Your old parents, the long happy days of your boyhood? Tell me about them."

"It must be the dope," I said, and my tongue felt thick.

"There seem to be a few small blank spots in the Florin total recall," the ex-Senator jeered.

"What's the name of your hometown, Florin?"

"Chicago," I said, pronouncing it like a word in a foreign language. The Senator looked puzzled. "Where's that?"

"Between New York and LA, unless you've moved it."

"Ellay? You mean . . . California? On Earth?"

"You guessed it," I said, and paused to moisten my lips with the dry sock I found where my tongue used to be.

"That explains a few things," he muttered. "Brace yourself, fellow. You're in for a shock."

"Go ahead," I said, "but remember my heart murmur."

"We're not on Earth. We're on Grayfell, the fourth planet of the Wolf 9 system, twenty-eight light years from Sol."

"It's a switch," I said, and my voice felt as hollow as a Christmas tree ornament. "We're not being invaded by an alien planet; we've invaded *them*."

"You don't have to take my word for it, Florin." A split lip blurred his voice a little; or something did. "Look around you. Do these look like Terran plants? Don't you notice the gravity is eighteen percent light, the air is oxygen-rich? Look at the sun; it's a diffuse yellow giant, four hundred million miles away."

"All right. My old mother, if I had an old mother, always told me to look the truth in the eye. You're not helping much. It was bad enough when I was chasing my tail back in Chi. Start making it all clear, Bardell. Somebody went to a lot of trouble, either to transport me to a place called Grayfell or to build a pretty convincing set. There'll be a reason for that. What is it?"

He looked at me the way a surgeon looks at a leg that has to come off.

"You don't know what you're doing. You're getting in out of your depth; matters aren't what they seem—"

"Don't tell me what they aren't, Bardell; tell me what they are."

"I can't do that." He had something in his hands, fiddling

with it; something with shiny knobs and a crystalline loop at the top that was hard to look at. "I've been patient with you, Florin," he said, but his voice was sliding away from me, talking faster and faster like a runaway Victrola.

My head was throbbing worse than ever; my vision wasn't all it could have been. I made a grab for the blurry face in front of me; but it slid back out of reach. I saw something glint in the sunlight, and heard a voice from over the hills saying, ". . . Sorry, Florin. . . ."

Then pink darkness exploded in my face and I was back on that freight, riding it over a cliff and down into an abyss filled with fading thunder.

"Mr. Florin," the feather-light voice was saying, "you're creating something of a problem for us all."

I opened my eyes and the chap with the snake's head smiled his lipless smile at me and puffed pink smoke from his noseless nostrils and glittered his lidless eyes. He was lounging in a deck chair, wearing an open jacket made of orange toweling, and a pair of yellow shorts, the color of which reminded me of something that I couldn't quite get a grip on.

"That's something," I said, and sat down in a camp chair. There was a table between us with a blue and white umbrella over it. There was a stretch of white sand behind the terrace that looked like the seashore except that there wasn't any sea. I tried not to look at his glistening silver-violet thighs, the ribby pale gray chest with tiny crimson flecks, the finger-thin toes in the wide-strapped sandals. He saw me not looking and made a soft clucking sound that seemed to be laughter.

"Forgive me," he said. "I find this curiosity of yours amazing. I suspect that in the moment of your dissolution, you'd crane your neck to discover the nature of the solvent."

"It's just a harmless eccentricity," I said, "like your taste in clothes."

"You pride yourself on your self-control," he said, not quite as genially as before. "But what if your equanimity is presented with anomalies too great to be assimilated? What then, eh?" He raised a hand and snapped his fingers. Fire billowed up around him; his smile rippled in the heat shimmer as gusts of flame whipped toward me. I sat tight, partly from paralysis and partly because I didn't believe it. He snapped his fingers again and green water was all around us, the sun dazzling on the surface ten feet above. A small fish came nosing between us, and he waved it away negligently and snapped his fingers again. Snow was falling. A thick layer of it covered the table, capped his head. His breath was a plume of ice crystals.

"Neat," I said. "Are you any good at card tricks?"

He waved the ice away and put his fingertips together.

"You're not impressed," he said matter-of-factly. "The manipulation of the Universe implies nothing to you?"

I faked a yawn. Then it wasn't a fake. "The Universe?" I said. "Or my eyeballs?"

"Umm. You're a surprising creature, Florin. What is it you want? What motivates you?"

"Who's asking?"

"You may call me Diss."

"That's not what I asked you."

"Just consider that . . . there are other interested parties

*than those you traditionally know. You act on a larger
stage than you hitherto suspected. You should therefore
conduct yourself with circumspection."*

I yawned again. "I'm tired," I said. "I'm behind on
sleep, on food, on love—on everything except mysterious
phonies who drop large hints that big affairs are in the offing and that my best bet is to play along and keep my nose
clean. Who are you, Diss? What are you? Do you really
look like Alexander the croc, or is that just my bilious out-
look?"

"I am a representative of certain powers active in the
Cosmos. My appearance is of no importance. The fact of
my existence is enough."

"Bardell said something about an invasion."

"A word reflecting a primitive view of reality."

"What are you invading? Earth—or Grayfell?"

I had the pleasure of seeing his head jerk.

"What do you know of Grayfell, Mr. Florin?"

"You know—in the Wolf 9 group, twenty-eight lights
from old Chicago." I smiled a big happy smile. He
frowned and reached almost casually for something on the
table. I started to get up fast, and a flashbulb as big as the
sky winked and folded down on blackness blacker than the
inside of a sealed paint can. I lunged across the table, and
my fingers brushed something as hot as a cook-stove, as
slippery as raw liver. I heard an excited hiss and grabbed
again and got a grip on something small and hard and
complicated that resisted and then came free. There was
an angry yell, a sense of words being shouted faster than I
could follow, a blinding explosion—

***

She was sitting across the table from me, wrapped in a threadbare old cloth coat with a ratty squirrel skin collar. Her eyes looked into mine with a searching expression.

"Don't tell me," I said, sounding groggy even to me. "I was sitting here with my eyes crossed, singing old sea chanteys to myself in colloquial Amharic; so you sat down to see if I was all right. Good girl. I'm not all right. I'm a long way from all right. I'm about as far from all right as you can get and still count your own marbles."

She started to say something but I cut her off: "Let's not run through the rest of the lines; let's skip ahead to where you tell me I'm in danger, and I go charging out into the night to get my head bent some more."

"I don't know what you mean."

"I mean it seems we sat and talked like this before. We looked at each other in the same way then—"

"That's an old popular song."

"It seems to be. Everything seems to be something. Usually what it isn't. What are you?" I reached across and took her hand. It was cool and smooth and didn't move when my fingers closed around it. I said, "Listen carefully, Currie. I know your name because you told it to me. Sitting right where you're sitting now . . ." I paused to take a look around the room. It was done in pine paneling with varnish that was black with age and lack of laundering. A sign on the wall invited me to drink Manru beer.

". . . or almost. You said you came in answer to my ad—"

"You mean your telephone call."

"OK, make it a phone call. Or a carrier pigeon. That's not important. At least I don't think it's important. Maybe I'm wrong. Who knows? Do you?"

"Florin—you're not making sense. You told me on the telephone that it was urgent."

"And you came running—in the middle of the night."

"Of course I did."

"Who are you, Miss Regis?"

She looked at me with eyes as big and tragic as the cave where Floyd Collins was trapped.

"Florin," she whispered. "Don't you remember me? I'm your wife."

I leered at her. "Oh, yeah? Last time we talked you said we'd never met."

"I knew you'd been working too hard. It was too much—for anyone—"

"Ever heard of a place called Grayfell?" I cut into her routine.

"Of course. Our summer place at Wolf Lake."

"Sure. Silly of me. Twenty-eight miles from—where?"

"Chicago."

"One other point: among our close-knit circle of friends, does there happen to be a fellow with a purple head?"

She almost smiled. "You mean poor old Sid?"

"That's Diss spelled backward. Only with one S. Better make a note of that. Maybe it's important."

"Poor Florin," she started, but I waved that away.

"Let's marshal our facts," I said. "Maybe we don't have any facts, but let's marshal them anyway. Fact number one, a couple of hours ago I woke out of a sound sleep and found two men in my room. They gave me a pitch that smelled plenty fishy, but I went along. They took me to a committee of VIP's who told me the Senator was subject to delusions; that they'd arrange to make his delusions real; and I was to enter into his fantasy with him. But I have a feeling the fantasy had already started. Big Nose was part of it. But I didn't know that then. That was a couple of hours ago.

"Since then, I've been asking myself just how much I know about their boss—the 'Senator.' That one comes up blank too. Senator who? I don't even know the man's name. That strikes me as odd. How does it strike you?"

"Florin—you're raving—"

"I'm just starting, baby. Wait till I really get going. Fact number two, the Senator may or may not be someone else of the same name, got me? Possibly an actor named Bardell. Does the name ring a bell?"

"You mean Lance Bardell, the Trideo star?"

"Trideo . . . now that's an interesting word. But let's skip it for now. As I was saying, this Senator fellow is kind of an inconsistent player. First it was a murder plot. Then we had alien invaders. Next, he was an actor, a kidnap victim, or maybe a planted spy—I can't quite remember which. But I went along, followed him to a tavern where he fed me something that put me out like two runners at third. When I woke up you were there."

She just looked at me with those big, wide, hurt eyes.

"I won't ask the old one about what a nice girl like you was doing in a place like this," I said. "Or maybe I will. What was a nice girl like you doing in a place like this?"

"Now you're mocking me. Why must you be cruel, Florin? I only want to help."

"Back to the facts. How far did I get? Fact number

three? That was where I hotfooted it on somebody's back-trail and found a missing door. Or didn't find it."

"Does that really matter now—?"

"You're not paying attention. First there was a door, then there wasn't. Doesn't that seem odd to you? Or am I confused?"

"You make a joke of everything."

"Baby, after considerable thought I've reached the conclusion that the only conceivable legitimate answer to the Universe as constituted is a peal of hysterical laughter. But I digress."

"This isn't a joke, Florin. It's deadly seriously."

"I remember once waking up in the middle of the night with the phone ringing. I groped around in the dark and picked it up and got it in position and all of a sudden I was asking myself a question: *Is this right? Do you really talk to an inanimate object?*"

"Florin, please stop—"

"But I was telling you about the door that wasn't there. I settled down to wait. My old associate, the gray man, came out of an alley and I followed him. He led me to a room with nobody in it, not even him."

"I don't understand—"

"Me, too, kid. But let me get back to my story. I want to see how it turns out. Where was I? Oh, yes—all alone with some bent coat hangers. So I prowled around until I found somebody to talk to. He turned out to be the fellow with a head like a garter snake."

"Florin—"

I held up a hand. "No interruptions, please. I'm learning plenty, just listening to me talk. For example, I just said he looked like a garter snake. The first time I saw him it was a cobra I thought of. Maybe I'm licking my neurosis. If I can work him down to a harmless angleworm maybe I can live with that. The funny thing is, he was like you in some ways."

She tried to smile. She was humoring me now. "Oh? In what way?"

"He advised me to stop asking questions and drift with the current. I promptly blacked out. And guess what? I was back here—with you—again."

"Go on."

"Aha—I'm getting your attention at last. That was the second time we met—but you don't remember."

"No—I don't remember."

"Sure. You warned me I was in trouble and I went out and ran around the block looking for it, and found enough to end up back here. It made me feel kind of like one of those rubber balls they tie to ping pong rackets."

"That was . . . our third meeting, then."

"Now you're catching on, girl. Stay with me. From here on it gets complicated. I still had a yen to see my old boss, the Senator. This time there was a trick door. I went through it and suddenly it was a summer afternoon in a place with eighteen percent light gravity, too much sun, and trees like lace underwear. The Senator was there. We were just beginning to get somewhere when he pulled a swifty and knocked me colder than a plate of Army eggs."

She waited, watching my face.

"That was when I saw Snake Head the second time. Diss, he said his name was. Wanted me to smarten up and play by the rules. Said he was a big shot—but he blew his cool when I mentioned Grayfell. He turned out the lights and I heard voices and passed out. . . ."

"And now—you're here."

"When I wake up you're always there to greet me. It's enough to make a man look forward to a tire-iron on the head. Except that I don't exactly wake up. First I'm *there*—then I'm here."

"You spoke of *déjà vu*—the already seen," she said in a brisk, case-worker tone. "There's a theory that it results from a momentary distraction; when your attention returns to your surroundings you have a sense of having been there before. And of course you have—a split second earlier."

"Nice theory. Of course it doesn't explain how I know your name. But I'm forgetting: you're my wife."

"Yes."

"Where did we meet?"

"Why, we met . . ." Her face became as still as a pond at dawn. The tip of her tongue came out and reassured itself that her upper lip was still there.

"I don't know," she said in a voice you could have printed on the head of a pin.

"Welcome to the group. Do I begin to interest you in my problem, Miss Regis?"

"But—why?" She grabbed a finger and started twisting it. "What does it mean?"

"Who says it means anything? Maybe it's all a game, played for someone else's amusement."

"No—I can't believe that; I won't!" She said this in a shocked gasp.

"But we can refuse to play."

"That's what you've been doing, isn't it, Florin? Has it helped you?"

I grunted. "There's a certain satisfaction in messing up their plans—if they're there and they have plans."

"Please, Florin—don't drop back into that brittle, cynical pose! It isn't like you—not really."

"How would you know?"

"Some things one simply knows."

"And some things one finds out. I've picked up a few items I don't think they intended me to know."

"Go on." Her eyes held on mine. They were a pellucid green with flecks of gold swimming in their depths.

"Maybe I wasn't supposed to see the purple money with 'Lastrian Concord' printed across it," I said. "Or maybe it was another plant. But then Red stuck his head up. I can't figure that. He ran when he saw me. After that I listened in on a conversation I'm pretty sure I wasn't intended to hear. Big voices, talking in the sky, arguing about things going wrong. Maybe they meant me. Or maybe I dreamed it. The Senator was there, and Big Nose. They talked about situation one. Not much help here."

"Go on, Florin."

"Then you stepped into the picture. I don't know why, but I have a feeling you're not part of Big Nose's plans."

"I'm not, Florin! Please believe me! I'm not part of anything—that I know of," she finished in a whisper.

"Then there's Grayfell," I said. "Magic gates into other worlds don't fit any world-picture of mine. Bardell was surprised to see me there. And when I squeezed him he told me things I don't think Big Nose wanted me to know.

Or maybe not. Maybe I'm being led every foot of the way. Maybe there are coils within coils, traps within traps—"

"Florin! Stop! You have to believe in something! You have to have a starting point! You mustn't begin to doubt yourself!"

"Yeah. *Cogito ergo sum.* I've always got that to fall back on. I wonder what a polyplex computer's first thought is when they shoot the juice to it?"

"Is that what they expect you to say, Florin? Is that the role they want you to act out?"

I shook my head. "How much of myself can I peel away and have anything left? If the itch I've got to get my hands on the Senator isn't my own, I'm no judge of compulsions."

"Florin—can't you just—forget the Senator? Forget all of it, come home with me?"

"Not now, baby," I said, and felt myself start to smile. "Probably not before, and definitely not now. Because they goofed."

She waited; she knew there was more. I opened the hand that I had been holding in a tight fist for the past quarter hour and looked at the gadget I was holding. It was small, intricate, with bulges and perforations and points of brilliance that scintillated in the dim light; a manufactured article, and manufactured by an industry that was a long way from human.

"I took it away from Snake Head," I said. "That means Snake Head is real—at least as real as you and me."

"What is it?"

"Evidence. I don't know what of. I want to show it to people and see what happens. I can hardly wait. I've got a feeling they won't like it, and that alone will be worth the price of admission."

"Where will you go?"

"Back where they don't want me to."

"Don't do it, Florin! Please!"

"Sorry. No turning back for the Man of Iron. Straight ahead into the brick wall, that's my style."

"Then I'm going with you."

"You always let me go before. What's different now?"

"I don't know anything about all that. Shall we go?"

"It's a switch," I said. "Maybe it's a good omen."

Outside, the chilly wind was blowing in the empty street. She hugged herself, a chore I'd have been glad to do for her.

"Florin—it's so bleak—so lonely. . . ."

"Not with you along, doll." I took her arm; I could feel her shivering as we started off.

The tailor shop was still there, and the candy store; but now there was a vacant lot between them, full of dry weed-stalks and rusty cans and broken bottles.

"Tsk," I said. "No attention to details." I led the way to the corner and along to where the revolving door had been. It was gone. In its place was a tattoo parlor with a display like a retired Buchenwald guard might have on his den wall. But no door. Not even a place where a door could have been. This started my head hurting again. On the third throb, a voice the size of a cricket rubbed its wing cases together inside my ear and said, *"All right, Florin. Wait there for the next development."*

"What is it?" the girl said.

"Nothing: just a twinge from my sciatica," I said, and felt back of my ear. No little pink chip seemed to be there. I checked the other side. OK. So now I was hearing voices without the aid of hardware. It wasn't an unheard-of-trick: lots of psychotics could do it.

We went along to an archway that opened on a musty arcade full of cobwebs and damp air. I tried the first door I came to and stepped into a room I'd seen before.

The thick rug was gone, the heavy drapes were missing, the plaster walls were cracked and blotched with age. Newspapers that looked as if someone had slept in them were scattered across the floor. The only furniture was the collapsing steel frame of what might have been a leather lounge. But the door to the safe, somewhat corroded but still intact, hung half open, just as it had the last time I'd been here.

"Do you know this place?" Miss Regis whispered.

"It's my old pal the ex-Senator's private hideaway. The only trouble is, it's sixty miles from here, in a big house with lots of lawn and fence and a full set of security men. Either that, or I had a ride on a cargo flat that drove in circles for three hours."

I looked in the safe; there was nothing there but some dust and a torn envelope with a purple postage stamp, addressed to *Occupant, Suite 13*. I checked the fake window, the one the Senator had opened like a door for our midnight escape; but if there was a latch there I couldn't find it.

"It seems the Senator moved out and took all his clues with him," I said. "A dirty trick, but maybe I know a dirtier one." I went to the closet and felt over the back wall.

"He told me the official escape route was here," I told the girl. "Maybe he was lying, but—" The chunk of wall I was pushing on pivoted sideways and cool air blew in from the darkness beyond.

"Aha," I said. "Predictability is the test of any theory; now all we need is a theory." I had the gun the Senator had called a 2-mm. needler in my hand. I poked it out ahead of me and stepped through into a narrow passage with another door at the end. It was locked, but a well-placed kick splintered wood and it bounced open. Outside was a standard-model dark alley with empty apple crates and battered galvanized garbage cans and clumps of weed between weathered bricks. A high board fence barred the way to the left.

"Well, well," I said. "It seems to me I've been here before, too. Last time there was some shooting, but I don't see any spent slugs lying around. And they've added a fence."

"This is all wrong," the girl said. "I have a good sense of direction; there can't be anything like this here. We should be in the middle of the building now, not outside!"

"I couldn't agree with you more, pet." I went toward the street where the car had rolled past the last time, spraying lead. This time everything was quiet; much too quiet. The street looked all right, except that instead of the buildings across the way, there was just a featureless gray. Not a fog, exactly; solider than that, but less tangible.

"Florin, I'm afraid," the girl said, sounding brave.

"Smart girl," I said. "Let's look around."

I picked a direction and started off. We turned a couple of corners. There was a sort of syrupy haze hanging over everything, blurring details. The sidewalk seemed to be running uphill now. We were in an alley, cluttered with the usual assortment of slopped-over garbage cans, defunct orange crates, dead cats, and drifted paper—for the first five yards. After that the bricks were clean, the way unimpeded. There was enough filtered light from the street to show me a high board fence that closed the space between buildings.

"It looks like the same fence," Miss Regis said.

"But the other side. s" I felt of the boards; they were just boards.

"It stinks," I said. "Topologically speaking."

"What does that mean?"

"There are relationships of surfaces that aren't modified by distortion of the surface. But we've seen two faces of the same plane—and we haven't turned enough corners. Somebody's getting careless; we're pressing them harder than they like. That makes me want to press harder."

"Why? Why not just go back—"

"Aren't *you* a little curious, Miss Regis? Aren't you a little tired of the man at the other end of the string, pulling whenever he feels like it? Wouldn't you like to squeeze back?"

"What are we going to do?"

"Funny," I said. "It could have been a brick wall or concrete—or armor plate. But it's just pine planks. It's almost an invitation to tear it down." I put my gun away and stooped to examine the bottom edges of the boards. There was room to get a hand under them. I heaved and the wood resisted and then splintered and broke away. I threw the pieces aside and stepped through into the conference room, looking just as I'd seen it last, fancy spiral chandelier and all.

"We're getting closer to home," I said. I went around the long table to the door I had entered the room by last time and pulled it open.

I was back in my hotel room, complete with blotched wallpaper, chipped enamel washbowl, broken roller shade, and sprung mattress. The door I had come through was the one that had had the bathroom behind it in an earlier incarnation.

"No wonder the boys came in so nice," I said. "I've been feeling kind of bad about not hearing the door. But it never opened."

"What is this place?" Miss Regis said, and came close to me.

"It's where it all started, and I do mean started. As the Senator pointed out, my life story begins here. Before this—nothing. No home, no past. Just a lot of unexamined preconceptions that are due for examination." I took a step toward the hall door and it burst open and the scruffy man came through it holding the biggest hogleg .44 I ever saw, aimed right between my eyes. The hole in the end looked wide enough to drive a small truck through, or maybe even a large one. No words were needed to tell me that the time for words wasn't now. I went sideways as the gun roared and exploded plaster from the wall behind the spot where I'd been standing. Red shouted something, and the girl cried out and I worked hard to get my feet under me and get turned around, but the floor seemed to be swinging up at me like the deck of a sinking liner. I held on and watched the ceiling swing past, then another wall;

nothing spectacular, just a nice easy procession. Red sailed by, and the girl, moving faster now, sliding by. I heard her call: "Florin—come back!"

It took a long time for the words to push through the gray fog where my brains used to be. *Come back*, she'd said. It was a thought, at that. I'd had the ride before, but maybe I didn't have to go again—not if I fought back. The world was spinning like bathwater getting ready for that last long dive down the drain, and somehow suddenly I knew that if I went with it, this time it was for real.

There was nothing to hold onto, but I held on anyway.

I felt pressure against one side of me. That would do for a floor. I swung it around under me and built walls and a roof and held them in place by sheer willpower, and the roaring faded and the world slowed to a stop and I opened my eyes and was lying on my back in the middle of the world's biggest parking lot.

A dead flat sugar-white expanse of concrete marked off by blue lines into fifty-foot squares ran all the way to the horizon. That was all there was. No buildings, no trees, no people. The sky was a pale fluorescent azure, without clouds, without an identifiable source of light.

Voices came out of the sky.

". . . *now! Follow emergency procedures, damn you!*" That in Big Nose's bell-shaped tones.

"*I'm trying . . . but—*" Lard Face speaking.

"*This is no time to blunder, you cretin!*"

"*I can't . . . it won't . . .*"

"*Here—get out of my way!*"

"*I tell you—I threw in the wipe circuit! Nothing happened. It's . . . He's . . .*"

"He what? Don't talk like a fool! He's got nothing to do with it! I control this experiment!"

Hysterical tittering. "Do you? Do you really? Are you sure? Are you sure we haven't been taken, had, gulled—"

"Damn you, kill the power! All the way back!"

"I did—or tried to. Nothing happened!"

"Close down, damn you!" Big Nose's voice rose to a scream. At the same time the pain in my wrists and ankles and the ache in my chest rose to a crescendo, like bands of fire cutting me into pieces; and suddenly thunder rolled and the sky cracked and fell, showering me with sharp-edged fragments that turned to smoke and blew away and I was lying strapped down on my back looking up at the rectangular grid of a glare-ceiling, in a small green-walled room, and the man I had known as Big Nose was bending over me.

"Well, I'll be damned," he said. "He's alive after all."

A man with gray hair and a matching face, dressed in a white smock, and a scruffy man in a scruffy coverall came over and looked at me. Somebody finally got around to unstrapping me, unclamping something from my head. I sat up and felt dizzy and they handed me a cup of stuff that tasted terrible but seemed to be the right prescription. The dizziness went away, leaving me with nothing worse than a queasy stomach, a mouth that a family of moles had nested in, a dull headache, and an ache in my wrists and my ankles that wasn't so dull. The gray man—Dr. Eridani was his name, I remembered, the way you remember things you haven't thought about for a long time—

smeared some salve over the raw spots. The rest of them were busy looking at the dials on a big console that filled up most of one wall, and muttering together.

"Where's the Senator?" I said. My thoughts seemed to be moving slowly, like heavy animals in deep mud.

Big Nose looked up from his work and frowned.

"He's just kidding," the scruffy man said. His name was Lenwell Trait, and he was a lab assistant. I didn't quite remember how I knew that, but I knew.

Big Nose—Van Wouk to his intimates—came over and looked at me without any visible affection.

"Look here, Bardell," he said, "I don't know what kind of ideas you're getting, but forget them: We have a legal agreement, signed and witnessed. You went into this with your eyes open, you'll get what's coming to you, not a penny more, and that's final!"

"*You're* giving him ideas," Eridani said quietly. Trait handed me a cup of coffee.

"Bardell's not getting any ideas," he said, and grinned a sly grin at me. "He knows better than that."

"Bardell's an actor," I said. My voice sounded weak and old.

"You're a stumblebum we picked out of a gutter and gave an opportunity to," Van Wouk growled. "Like all your kind, you now imagine you're in a position to exert pressure. Well, it won't work. Your health hasn't suffered, so don't start whining."

"Don't kid me, Doc," I said, firing from the hip. "What about the wipe circuits? How about Eta Level? Everything jake all down the line?"

That shut them up for a couple seconds.

"Where did you pick up those terms?" Lard Face asked me.

"A little lizard told me," I said, and suddenly felt too tired to bother with games. "Forget it; I was just ribbing you. You wouldn't have a drink handy?"

Trait went off and came back in a minute with a flask of rye. I took a couple ounces from the neck and things started to seem a little brighter.

"Something was said about payment," I said.

"One hundred dollars," Big Nose snapped. "Not bad for an hour or two of a rummy's time."

"I had a feeling it was longer," I said. "No damage, eh? How about amnesia?"

"Uh-uh," Trait said lazily. "You know better, Bardell."

"Get him out of here," Van Wouk said. "I'm sick of the sight of him. Here." He grabbed at his pocket and brought out a wallet and extracted some worn currency and pushed it at me. I counted the spots.

"A hundred is right," I said. "But that was the straight dope about the amnesia. I'm a little confused, gents. I remember you boys. . . ." I looked at them, remembering. "But I kind of don't remember our deal—"

"Get him out!" Van Wouk yelled.

"I'm going," I told Trait. He had hold of my arm, twisting it, moving me toward the door. "You don't have to get tough."

He walked me out into the corridor, green tile like the room, along it to steps that went up with light at the top.

"Just between pals," I said, "what happened to me in there?"

"Nothing, chum. A little scientific experiment, that's all."

"Then how come I don't remember it? Hell, I don't even know where I live. What town is this?"

"Chicago, chum. And you don't live no place. You just kind of get by."

Double doors that opened out onto concrete steps. There were lawn and trees that looked familiar in the dark.

"The Senator's Summer Retreat," I said. "Only no searchlights."

"You can't count on them politicos," Trait said. "Take my advice and don't squeeze it, Bardell. You got your century, even if maybe your marbles is scrambled a little, but hell, they wasn't in too good shape when you come in. I'd watch that off-brand Muscatel if I was you, chum."

"The Lastrian Concord," I said. "Diss. Miss Regis. None of that happened, huh?"

"You had like a nightmare. You damn near blew all the tubes in old Pickle-puss' pet Frankenstein. Go tank up and sleep it off and you'll be good as new."

We were down the steps now, and he turned me and pointed me toward the gate.

"By the way, what color do you call those tiles?" I said.

"Nile green. Why?"

"Just curious," I said, and did a half-turn and rammed the old stiff-finger jab to the breastbone and doubled him over like peeling a banana. I held him up and pried my hundred out of his left hand that I'd felt making the touch, and then checked his hip and got thirty more, just for carfare.

"So long, Red," I said. "I never cottoned to you much anyway." I left him there and beat it by a back route out the side gate.

✿ ✿ ✿

It was cold in town that winter. I headed for the water-front with the idea of making an early start on my bender. With a hundred and thirty to blow at $2.79 per fifth, that was a lot of Muscatel. I tried to work out just how much, and got to about fifteen gallons and happened to catch sight of myself in a window I was passing.

At least I guessed it was me. I hardly knew me. My eyes stared back from the dark glass like a pair of prisoners doing life in solitary. My face looked left out in the weather, worn out, caved in. There was gray stubble a quarter of an inch long on my jaw, wild grayish locks on my head. My Adam's apple bobbed like a yo-yo when I swallowed. I stuck my tongue out; it didn't look good either.

"You're in bad shape, old man," I told the stranger in the glass. "Maybe fifteen gallons of rotgut isn't what you need."

I stood there and stared at the reflection staring at me and waited for the little voice to pipe up and remind me how good the old heartwarmer was, how it slid down so nice and tongue-filling and hit bottom and burned its way out, taking the ache out of bones and the strain out of joints, bringing comfort to the body and ease to the mind.

But it didn't. Or if it did I didn't hear it. I was feeling my heart thump with a dull, sick thump, working too hard just to keep going. I listened to the wheeze and grunt of my lungs trying to suck in enough air, felt the tremors that wobbled my knees like base viol strings, the sour, drained feel of unhealthy muscles, the sag of dying skin, the sick weight of neglected organs.

"What's happened to me?" I asked the old man in the

glass. He didn't answer, just touched his withered lips with a gray tongue.

"You look as scared as I feel, Pop," I said. "By the way, do I know your name?"

Big Nose called you Bardell.

"Yeah. Bardell. I . . . used to be an actor." I tried the idea on for size. It fit like a second-hand coffin.

"They hauled me in off the street," I told myself. *"The white-coat boys, Van Wouk and the rest. They needed a guinea pig. I volunteered."*

"So they said. And before that—what?"

"I don't remember so good. Must be the Muscatel, old man. It's rotted your brain. My brain. Our brain."

"So—what are we going to do about it?"

I thought of booze and felt a stir of seasickness. *"No more booze,"* I said. *"Definitely no more booze. Maybe a doctor. But not like Eridani. Food, maybe. Sleep. How long since you slept in a bed, old man?"*

I couldn't remember that, either. I was good and scared now. It's a lonely feeling not to know who you are, where you are. I looked along the street. If I'd ever seen it before, I didn't know when. But I knew, without knowing how I knew, that the waterfront was *that* way; and a block of old frame houses with *Room to Let—Day, Week, Year* signs in the windows was *that* way.

"That's it," I said. My voice was as cracked and worn as a thrown-away work shoe. "A clean bed, a night's sleep. Tomorrow you'll feel better. You'll remember, then."

"Sure. Everything will be jake—mañana."

"Thanks, pal; you've been a big help." I waved to the

old man in the glass and he waved back as I turned and started off, not toward the waterfront.

The old woman didn't like my looks, for which I didn't blame her, but she liked my ten-dollar bills. She puffed her way up two flights and to the back, threw open the door of a bare, ugly high-ceilinged little room with a black floor showing around a bald rug, a brass single bed, a chiffonier with washstand. It was the kind of room that would be an icebox in winter and a steam bath in summer. Rusty springs squeaked with an ill-tempered sound as I sat down on the threadbare chenille. I said, "I'll take it."

"Bathtub at the end of the hall," my new landlady said. "You got to bathe off 'fore you go to laying in my beds."

For an extra buck she supplied a yellowish-white towel and a washcloth with a thin spot in the middle, as stiff as a currycomb, and an only slightly used bar of coral-colored soap that smelled like formaldehyde. The feel of eleven dollars in cash must have gone to her head, because she went along and started pipes clanking and spurting brownish water into the tub. She even wished me a good night, and handed me an old safety razor before she went away.

I soaked for a while, which felt good in spite of the rusty patch right where my *glutei maximi* rested. Afterward I raked at my whiskers and went on to trim a few of the drake's tails curling around my neck.

"Nice work, old timer," I told the face in the mirror. "You'll make a good-looking corpse yet."

Back in the room, I slid in between the sheets which felt like starched burlap and smelled like chlorine, curled myself around a couple of broken springs that were poking up through the cotton padding, and sailed off someplace where age and sickness and human frailty don't exist, where the skies are pink all day, and the soft voices of those we love tell us what great guys we are, forever and ever, amen.

I felt better in the morning, but not good. When I started to get dressed I noticed the goaty smell coming from my clothes. There were heavy feet in the hall just then, and I stuck my head out and entrusted my landlady with another ten-spot and the commission of buying me some new BVDs and socks. What she brought back weren't new, but they were clean and there was nine dollars change.

I turned down her offer of breakfast (seventy-five cents) and bought an apple at a fruit stand. There were plenty of sartorial emporia in the neighborhood specializing in mismatched pinstripes and shirts with darned elbows, all with the same dusty look, as if the owners had died and been buried in them. I selected a snazzy pinkish-tan double-breasted coat and a pair of greenish-black slacks which were thick and solid if not stylish, a couple of shirts, formerly white, a pair of cracked high-top shoes made for somebody's grandpa, and a snappy red and green tie that probably belonged to a regiment of Swiss Marines. The ensemble wasn't what anyone would call tasteful, but it was clean and warm, and mothballs smell better than goats any day.

After that I gave a lucky barber a crack at my locks. He trimmed me back to an early Johnny Weissmuller length, and said, "That's a switch. I seen black hair with gray roots, but never before visey-versey."

"It's my diet," I said. "I just went on distilled carrot juice and virgin duck eggs, boiled in pure spring water."

He made a note of that on the back of an envelope, threw in a free shave that hit the spots I'd missed the evening before, and offered me a chance in what he called a lottery.

"I'm doing you a favor," he said, getting confidential. "This here is the hottest game in town." He showed me a purple ticket to prove it. If fancy engraving was any indication, I was onto something. I paid my buck and tucked it away. As I left he was looking at me over the cash register, grinning a lipless grin and glittering his eyes in a way that reminded me of something I couldn't put a finger on.

I sat in the park after that and breathed fresh air and watched the people pass. None of them looked at me. I bought my dinner at a grocery store, making a point of including lettuce and carrots and other wholesome items. I ate in my room, without much appetite.

Two weeks went by that way, at the end of which I had drunk no booze, had gained five pounds, lost the stomachache, and was broke. I spent the last day looking for work, but there seemed to be a shortage of job opportunities for applicants of indefinite age and uncertain abilities. My landlady seemed uneager to extend any credit. We parted with expressions of mutual regret, and I went and sat in the park a little longer than was my custom, right through dinner time, as a matter of fact.

It got cold when the sun went down. The lights were still on in the Public Library across the way. The librarian gave me a sharp look but said nothing. I found a quiet corner and settled down to enjoy as much of the warmth as possible before closing time. There's something soothing about the quiet stacks, and the heavy old yellow oak chairs and the smell of dusty paper and bindings; even the whispers and the soft footsteps.

The footsteps stopped, and a chair scraped gently, being pulled out. Cloth rustled. I kept my eyes shut and tried to look like an old gent who'd come in to browse through the bound volumes of *Harper's* and just happened to doze off in mid-1931; but I could hear soft breathing, and feel eyes on me.

I opened mine and she was sitting across the table from me, looking young and tragic and a bit threadbare, and she said, "Are you all right?"

"Don't disappear, lady," I said. "Don't turn into smoke and vanish. Don't even get up and walk away. Just sit there and let me get my pulse back down into the low nineties."

She blushed a little and frowned.

"I . . . thought perhaps you were ill," she said, all prim and proper and ready to say all the magic words that made her a conforming member of the current establishment.

"Sure. What about the fellow I came in with? Isn't that the way the next line goes?"

"I haven't any idea what you mean. No one came in with you—not that I saw. And—"

"How long have you been watching me?"

This time she really blushed. "Why, the very idea—"

I reached across and took her hand. It was soft as the first breath of spring, as smooth as ancient brandy, as warm as mother love. My hand closing around it felt like a hawk's talon getting a grip on a baby chick. I let go, but she hadn't moved.

"Let's skip over all the ritual responses," I said. "Something pretty strange is happening; you know it and I know it, right?"

The blush went away and left her pale, her eyes clinging to mine as if maybe I knew the secret that would save a life.

"You . . . you *know*?" she whispered.

"Maybe not, Miss, but I've got a strong suspicion."

It was the wrong word; she tensed up and her lips got stiff and righteous.

"Well! It was merely a Christian impulse—"

"Balls," I said. "Pardon my crudeness, if it is crudeness. You sat down here, you spoke to me. Why?"

"I told you—"

"I know. Now tell me the real reason."

She looked at the end of my nose, my left ear, finally my eyes. "I . . . had a dream," she said.

"A bar," I said. "On the shabby side. A fat bartender. A booth, on the right of the door as you come in."

"My God," she said, like somebody who never takes the name of her deity in vain.

"Me too," I said. "What's your name?"

"Regis. Miss Regis." She stopped, as if she'd said too much.

"Go ahead, Miss Regis."

"In the dream I was someone who was needed," she said, not really talking to me now, but to someone inside herself maybe, someone who hadn't had a whole lot of attention in the past. "I was important—not in the sense of rank and titles, but because I'd been entrusted with something of importance. I had a duty to perform, a sense of . . . of honor to live up to."

I had sense enough not to say anything while she thought about it, remembering how it had been.

"The call came in the middle of the night, the secret message I'd been waiting for. I was ready. I knew there was great danger, but that was unimportant. I knew what to do. I got up, dressed, went to the appointed place. And . . . you were there." She looked at me then. "You were younger, bigger, stronger. But it was you. I'm certain of that."

"Go on."

"I had to warn you. There was danger—I don't know what sort of danger. You were going to face it, alone."

"You asked me not to go," I said. "But you knew I had to go away."

She nodded. "And . . . you went. I wanted to cry out, to run after you—but . . . instead, I woke up." She smiled uncertainly. "I tried to tell myself it was just a foolish dream. And yet—I knew it was important."

"So you came back."

"We walked through cold, empty streets. We entered a building. Nothing was as it seemed. We went through room after room, searching for . . . something. We came to a wall. You broke it down. We were in a big room with a strange, elaborate chandelier, like a place where kings and ambassadors might sign treaties. And the next room was a flophouse."

"Oh, I don't know," I said, "I've seen worse."

"Then a man burst in," she went on, ignoring me. "He

had a gun. He aimed it at you and . . . shot you down at my feet." The tragic look was back, a look to break a stone heart down into gravel.

"Not quite," I said. "I'm here. I'm alive. It didn't really happen. None of it. We dreamed it—together."

"But—how?"

"I was in an experiment. A human guinea pig. Big machines, hooked to my head. They made me dream, crazy stuff, all mixed up. Somehow, you got mixed into my dream. And the funny thing is—I don't think they know it."

"Who are they—the people you're talking about?"

I waved a hand. "At the university. The lab. Some big-domes, doctors, physicists. I don't know. The kind of guys who spend their time in little rooms full of radio tubes and dials, making marks on a clipboard."

"How did you happen to be taking part in their tests?"

I shook my head. "That's all a little vague. I think I was on the sauce pretty heavy, for a long time."

"Where's your family, your home? Won't they be worried about you?"

"Don't waste your sympathy, Miss Regis. I don't have any."

"Nonsense," she said, "no human being exists in a vacuum." But she let it go at that. "You mentioned a university." She tried a new tack. "What university was it?"

"How many you got in your town, lady?"

"Please don't talk like a hobo. You don't have to, you know."

"Apologies, Miss Regis. The one over that way." I

jerked a thumb over my shoulder. "Nice grounds, big trees. You must have noticed it, if you live here."

"I've lived here all my life. There's no university in this town."

"OK, so maybe it's a research lab; a government project."

"There's nothing like that. Not here, Mr. Florin."

"Three blocks from where we're sitting," I said. "Maybe four. Ten acres if it's an inch."

"Are you sure it wasn't part of the dream?"

"I've been living on their money for the last two weeks."

"Can you lead me there?"

"Why?"

She stared at me. "Because we can't just drop it, can we?"

"I guess it can't hurt to take a look," I said. "Maybe I can touch 'em for a new stake."

She followed me out into the night, trailed by the disapproving eyes of the elderly virgin at the front desk. It took us ten minutes to do the three blocks to where I had left the university grounds two weeks before. A block away I knew something was wrong with my calculations. The stores and gas stations and pawnshops along the way looked all right, but where the high red brick wall should have been there was an abandoned warehouse: an acre or so of warped siding and broken glass.

Miss Regis didn't say any of the things she could have. She came along quietly while I retraced the route. I found a familiar pawnshop with a dummy in the window wearing a dusty tux, the candy shop with the dusty fudge, the street where my ex-boardinghouse was. But when we got back to the university, it was still a warehouse.

"The neighborhood's still here," I said. "All that's missing is the college campus. Kind of big to mislay, but at my age a man tends to get careless."

"Are you sure you walked all the way from—wherever you were—to the rooming house? Maybe you took a cab, or—"

"Uh-uh. No cab, no bus, no trolley, not even a bicycle. Shanks' mare. I don't remember much, maybe, but what I remember I remember good. The way I felt I couldn't have walked over a quarter of a mile. Let's face it, Miss Regis. Somebody swiped the university and left this dump in its place, maybe for a reason. My trick is to figure the reason."

"Mr. Florin—it's late. You're tired. Perhaps it would be better if you rested now. Tomorrow we can meet after work, perhaps . . ." Her voice trailed off.

"Sure," I said. "Good idea, Miss Regis. Sorry to have wasted your time. You were right all along. No university, no scientists, no dream machine. But the hundred bucks was real. Let's leave it at that. Good night, and thanks for your company."

She stood there looking undecided. "Where will you go?"

"Who knows, Miss Regis? The world is a big place, especially when you aren't tied down by any arbitrary limitations. Grayfell, maybe. It's a nice place, with eighteen percent light gravity and plenty of O_2 and a big yellow sun, a couple hundred lights from here."

"Who told you about Grayfell?" she whispered.

"Bardell. He was an actor. Not a very good one. Funny thing, Big Nose thought I was him. Can you figure it?"

"Grayfell was our summer place," she said, sounding puzzled.

"Don't tell me: at the lake, twenty-eight miles from here."

"Where did you get that idea?"

"All right—you tell me."

"Grayfell is in Wisconsin—near Chicago."

"Stop me if I'm singing off-key—but isn't this Chicago?"

"Why—no. Of course not. It's Wolfton, Kansas."

"I knew there was something unfamiliar about the place."

"How could you have been here for weeks, as you said, without knowing that?"

"The question never arose. Of course, my social contacts were limited."

She looked at me and I could almost hear her thinking over all the things she might say. What she came up with was, "Where will you sleep tonight?"

"I feel like walking," I said. "A night of contemplation under the stars."

"Come home with me. I have room for you."

"Thanks, Miss Regis. You're a nice kid—too nice to get mixed up in my private war with the universe."

"What are you *really* going to do?" she whispered.

I tilted my head toward the warehouse. "Poke my nose in there."

She looked earnest and businesslike. "Yes, of course, we'll have to."

"Not you. Me."

"Both of us. After all . . ." she gave me a glimpse of a smile like an angel's sigh. "It's my dream too."

"I keep forgetting," I said. "Let's go."

The doors were locked, but I found a loose board and pried it free and we slid into big dark gloom and dust and cobwebs and the flutter of bats' wings, or of something that fluttered. Maybe it was my heart.

"There's nothing here," Miss Regis said. "It's just an old abandoned building."

"Correction: it's a place that looks like an old abandoned building. Maybe that's window dressing. Maybe if you scratch the dust you'll find shiny paint underneath."

She made a mark on the wall with her finger. Under the dust there was more dust.

"Proves nothing," I said. "For that matter nothing proves anything. If you can dream a thing you can dream it's real."

"You think you're dreaming now?"

"That's the question, isn't it, Miss Regis? How do you know when you're alive and awake?"

"Dreams aren't like this; they're vague and fuzzy around the edges. They're two-dimensional."

"I remember once thinking about dreams while I was walking up a hill in a college town in the fall. I could feel the dry leaves crunching under my shoes, and the pull of gravity at my legs; I could smell leaves burning some-where, and feel the bite of the nippy autumn air, and I thought: 'Dreams aren't like reality. Reality is *real*. All the senses are involved, everything is in color and dimension.'" I paused for effect. "Then I woke up."

She shivered. "Then you can never be sure. A dream within a dream within a dream. I'm dreaming you—or you're dreaming me. We can never know—really."

"Maybe there's a message in that for us. Maybe we should be looking for truths that are true awake or asleep. Permanent things."

"What things?"

"Loyalty," I said. "Courage. Like you. Here with me, now."

She said, "Don't be silly," but she sounded pleased. I could barely see her face in the gloom.

"What do we do now? Go back?" she said.

"Let's look around first. Who knows? Maybe it's a game of blindman's bluff and we're only an inch from winning." I felt my way forward across the littered floor, over scraps of board and paper and cardboard and tangles of baling wire. A rickety door was set in the far wall. It opened into a dark passage no neater than the big room.

"We should have brought a flashlight," Miss Regis said.

"Or a squad car full of cops," I said. "Look—or maybe you'd better not." But she was beside me, staring at what I was staring at. It was the Senator, lying on his back, with his head smashed like an egg. I felt the girl go rigid, and then relax and laugh, a shaky laugh, but a laugh for all that.

"You frightened me," she said, and went past me and looked down at the body sprawled on its back in its dusty tuxedo.

"It's only a dummy," she said.

I looked closer and saw the paint peeling from the wooden face.

"It looks . . ." Miss Regis gave me a troubled look. "It looks like you, Mr. Florin."

"Not me; the Senator," I said. "Maybe they're trying to tell me something."

"Who is the senator?"

"The man I was hired to protect. I did my usual swell job, as you can see."

"Was he . . . part of the experiment?"

"Or it was part of him. Who knows?" I stepped over the imitation corpse and went on along the passage. It seemed too long to fit inside the building. There were no doors or intersecting corridors for a hundred yards, but there was one at the end, with a line of light under it.

"Always another door," I said. The knob turned, the door opened on a room I had seen before. Behind me Miss Regis gasped. Dim moonlight shone through tall windows on damask walls, oriental carpets. I went across the deep pile to the long mahogany table and pulled out a chair. It felt heavy and smooth, the way a heavy, smooth chair ought to feel. The chandelier caught my eye. For some reason it was hard to look at. The lines of cut-crystal facets spiraled up and up and around in a pattern that wove and rewove itself endlessly.

"Mr. Florin—why would such a room as this be here— in this derelict building?"

"It's not."

"What do you mean?"

"Don't you remember your last visit?"

"Is it really the same room? Is all this really just a dream?"

"It wasn't a dream then and it isn't a dream now. I don't know what it is, but at some level it's *happening*."

Miss Regis had paused, her head tilted alertly.

"There's someone near," she whispered. "I can hear them talking."

I got up and soft-footed it over and put my ear to the door. There were two voices, both familiar, one high-pitched, one as resonant as a commercial for a funeral parlor.

". . . getting out now," the latter was saying. "I want no part of the responsibility. You've all lost whatever sense you had."

"You can't," Trait's voice said, sounding like a cop turning down a speeder's alibi. "We'll recover him, never fear. It's only a matter of time."

"What if he dies?"

"He won't. And if he should—we're covered. You've been given assurances on that point."

"I don't believe them."

"You're not going anywhere, Bardell."

"Get out of my way, Len."

"Put the bag down, Bardell."

"I'm warning you—"

Someone hit a cast-iron stove with a ball-peen hammer. Someone made a gargling sound. Someone dropped a hundred-pound bag of potatoes on the floor. I threw the door open and slammed through into my old original bedroom and almost collided with the Senator, standing over Trait's body with a smoking gun in his hand.

He looked at me and his mouth came open but no words came out. I lifted the gun from his hand and sniffed it, just to be doing something. It smelled like a gun.

"I never liked him either," I said. "Where are you off to?"

"I didn't mean to kill him," he said. "It was an accident."

"Don't sweat it, Senator. Maybe this one doesn't count."

I squatted beside Trait and went through his pockets. I didn't like doing it but I did it anyway. I could have saved myself the trouble. They were empty. I looked at his face, gray-green now, not pretty.

"Tell me about it," I said to the Senator—the ex-Senator—Bardell: whoever he was.

"I thought he had a gun. He's crazy enough to use it. I shot first."

"Skip on to who you are and who Trait is and what you were doing here, and where here is. And, oh yeah—what it's got to do with me."

He gave me a sharp glance with something that might have been hope in it.

"You don't remember?"

I cocked his gun and aimed it at his vest. "There seem to be a few blanks. Start filling them."

"I hardly know where to begin. What *do* you remember?"

"Tell me about the Lastrian Concord."

He shook his head and frowned. "Look here, I swear to you—"

"Skip it. What about Eridani?"

"Oh." He licked his lips and looked disappointed. "Very well. You know what I was up against there. It wasn't as though I had a great deal of choice—"

"What were you up against?"

"He threatened to wipe me. Otherwise, I'd never have—"

"Start further back."

"Well—Eridani approached me on the seventeenth. His story was that my services were needed in a professional capacity. I needed the work, frankly. Once I'd seen the situation, they couldn't afford to let me go—or so they said."

I turned to Miss Regis. "Has he said anything yet?"

She shook her head. "I think he's playing for time. Who is he?"

"An actor named Bardell."

"My God," Bardell said. "If you know that, you know—" He cut himself off. "How did you find out?"

"You told me."

"Never."

"In the park," I said, "on Grayfell."

His face fell apart like a dropped pie. "But you're not supposed—" he said in a strangled voice, and turned and lunged for the window. I put a round past him without slowing him; he hit the opening like a runaway egg truck and went through in a cloud of smashed mullion and glass splinters. I got there in time to hear his fading scream and the impact far, far below.

Miss Regis made a shocked sound. I felt over the metal frame, touched a spot that clicked. The whole window, dribbling glass chips, swung into the room like a gate. Behind it was a plain gray wall.

"If a phony man jumps out a phony window," I said, "is it suicide or just a harmless prank?"

"It's a nightmare," the girl said. "But I can't wake up." Her eyes were wide and frightened.

I wet my lips, which felt like blotting paper, and thought of two or three smart remarks, and said, "I've got a hunch this wasn't part of their plan. I don't know what the plan is, or who planned it, or why, but things aren't going just the way they were supposed to. That means they aren't as smart as they think they are—or that we're smarter. That gives us a kind of edge, maybe. Check?"

"We're going in circles," she said. "We're like blind people in a maze. We stumble on, deeper and deeper—"

"Sometimes when you're going in circles you're skirting the edge of something. If we get deep enough we'll break through, maybe."

"Into what?"

"Funny—I would have said '*out of what*'." I stuck my head inside the gray-walled passage, scarcely eighteen inches deep. It might have been the one the Senator and I had used for our fake escape from the fake Senatorial mansion, or its twin.

"Call it, Miss Regis," I said. "Shall we go on—or go back?"

"Back—to what?"

"Not losing faith in Wolfton, Kansas, are you?"

"Did I ever really live there?" she whispered. "A mousy little woman in a drab little town, working in an insurance office with varnished doors and creaky floors and wooden filing cabinets, typing up reports on an old open-frame LC Smith, going home at night to a dreary little room, dreaming impossible dreams—"

"And waking up and living them. I wish I could answer that, Miss Regis. Maybe the answer's in there." I nodded toward the dark and narrow way behind the dummy window.

"Are we probing into dark tunnels in a fantastic building?" she said. "Or are the tunnels in our minds?"

"Maybe our minds are the tunnels. Maybe we're thoughts in the minds of the gods, burrowing our way through the infinite solidity of the Universe. And maybe we're a couple of cuckoos chirping in the dark to cheer each other up. If so, we're doing a bad job of it. Come on, girl. Let's go exploring. We might stumble out the other end into the pink sunshine on the white sugar beach beside the popcorn sea." I stepped through and turned to give her a hand, but there was something in the way, something invisible and hard, like clean plate glass. She spoke, but no sound came through the barrier. I hit it with my shoulder and something splintered, maybe my shoulder, but I plowed on through the enveloping folds of darkness and stumbled out into noise and a blaze of light.

I was in a vast, high-ceilinged hall that went on and on into the misty distance. On one side was a formal garden beyond a high glass wall, on the other huge panels like airline arrivals boards covered with lines of luminous print that winked and changed as I looked at them. Down the center of the hall white plastic desks were ranked, and behind each desk was a man, or almost a man, in a white uniform and a pillbox cap with a chin strap, and soft brown hair covering every square inch of exposed skin except the pink palms of the long-fingered hands, and the face from eyebrows to receding chin. There were lines of men and women in assorted costumes queued up in front of each desk, and I was in one of the lines.

The customer in front of me—a dazzling female in a tiny jeweled sarong and a lot of smooth, golden suntan—picked up her papers and disappeared behind a white screen. That made me number one.

"Right; Florin, Florin . . . yes, here we are," the monkey man said in clipped Oxonian tones, and gave me a bright-eyed look that included a row of big square yellow teeth. "Welcome back. How did it go this trip?"

"Like Halloween in the bughouse," I said. "Don't bother telling me who you are, or what. I wouldn't believe a word of it. Just tell me what this is."

"Oh—oh, a nine-oh-two," he said, and poked a button and white walls sprang up on all four sides of us, making a cozy cubicle with just him and me inside.

"What did you do with the girl?" I said, and tried to watch all four walls at once.

"All right, Florin, just take it easy, lad. You're an IDMS operative just returning from an official mission into Locus C 992A4." He pursed his wide, thin monkey-lips at me, frowning. "Frankly, I'm surprised to encounter an amnesiacal fugue syndrome cropping up in a field agent of your experience. How far back have you blanked?"

I felt in my pocket for the Senator's gun. It wasn't there. Neither was the 2-mm. needler. I found a ball-point pen that I didn't remember owning. On impulse I pointed it at the ape-man behind the desk. He looked startled and one hand stole toward the row of buttons on his desktop. It stopped when I jabbed the pen at him.

"Talk it up, Slim," I said. "Don't bother with the rehearsed pitch. I want her and then I want out—all the way out."

"Be calm, Florin," he said steadily. "Nothing's to be gained by hasty action, no matter what you imagine the situation to be. Won't you take a seat so that we can get to the bottom of this?"

"I'm tired of the game," I said. "I've been flim-flammed, gulled, hookwinked, and had; no hard feelings, but I want the girl back. Now."

"I can't help you there, Florin. As you see, there's no girl here."

"On the count of three, I fire. One . . . two . . ." I paused to take a new breath, but someone had pumped all the air out of the room and substituted chalk dust. It hung as a white haze between me and the monkey-man. My fingers dropped the pen and my knees folded without any help from me and I was sitting on the edge of a chair like a nervous interviewee for a secretarial job, listening to him talk through a filter from his position on the other side of the desk, half a mile away across unexplored country.

"What's happening to you is a recognized hazard of the profession," he was telling me. "You've been well briefed on the symptoms, but of course if the fugue becomes well advanced before you notice something's amiss, you can of course slip too far; hence, no doubt, your auto-recaller returned you here to HQ. Let me assure you you're perfectly safe now, and in a very short time will again be in full command of your faculties—"

"Where's Miss Regis, damn you, Monkey-puss?" I snarled, but it came out sounding like a drunk trying to order his tenth martini.

"You were dispatched on assignment to observe an experimental machine detected in operation at the Locus," he went on calmly. "A primitive apparatus, but it was causing certain minor probability anomalies in the Net. Apparently you were caught up in the field of the device and overwhelmed. Naturally, this created a rather nasty stress system, ego-gestalt-wise; a confusing experience, I don't doubt. I want you now to make an effort to recognize that what you've been through was entirely subjective, with no real-world referential basis."

"Oh, yeah?" I managed to say well enough to cut into his rhetoric. "Then where'd I get the gun?"

"It's IDMS issue, of course."

"Wrong, chum. It's a ball-point pen. Where's the girl?"

"There is no girl."

"You're a liar, Hairy-face," I tried to get my legs under me and succeeded and lunged across the desk and hit sheet ice that shattered into a fiery cascade that tinkled down around me like a shower of cut gems that rose higher and higher, and I drew a breath to yell and smelled pipe smoke, the kind that's half orange peel and soaked in honey. I snorted it out of my nose and blinked and the air cleared and Big Nose was sitting across the desk from me, smiling comfortably.

"Now, now, lad, don't panic," he said soothingly. "You're a bit confused, coming out of the ether, nothing more."

I looked down at myself. I was wearing a long-sleeved sweater, corduroy knickers, argyle stockings and worn sneakers, and my shanks were thin, skinny adolescent teen-age shanks. I stood and he jerked the pipe out of his mouth and pointed the stem at me and said, "You behave, boy, or I'll report this entire matter to your mother!"

There was a window behind him. I ran around his desk and ducked under his grab and pulled the Venetian blind aside and was looking out at wide campus lawns and trees and walks under a yellow summer sun.

"I'll see you expelled from this institution!" Big Nose yelled.

"What did you do with her?" I yelled back, and threw myself at him with no higher ambition in life than to get my fingers into the soft fat under his chin, but he faded back before me and I clawed my way through a syrupy substance full of little bright lights and stumbled out into a room with curved walls covered with dials and winking lights, and a gray man in a form-fitting green uniform put out a hand and said, "Are you all right now, Captain?"

I looked past him. Lard Face sat before a round ground-glass screen, squinting at wiggly green lines; the bird man was next to him, tapping keys like a grocer adding up a week's supplies for a family of twelve. Trait looked over his shoulder and grinned a crooked grin and winked.

"We've just passed a field-inversion screen, Captain," the gray man was saying. "Possibly you're a bit disoriented for the moment; it sometimes has that effect . . .?"

"Where's Miss Regis?" I said, and pushed his hand away, noticing as I did that I had a fancy ring on my index finger, a complicated spiral of diamond chips. On impulse I made a fist, ring out, and pushed it at him.

"Ever see that before?" I said—and surprised myself. I'd never seen it before either—but my gesture suggested itself to me as a cagey thing to do.

The gray man's eyes bugged and he shied violently. "Put that thing away!" he gasped.

"Why should I, Eridani?"

All heads in sight jerked around when I called his name. Trait came out of his chair clawing for the gun at his hip; the gray man spun to face him just in time for a beam of green light to lance out from where Lard Face sat and bore a hole through his back. He went down coughing blood and smoke, and everyone was around me, all talking at once.

"How did you spot him, Captain?" the bird man said. "How did you know he was a spy?" Big Nose loomed up then, barking orders, clearing the mob.

"Come with me, Captain," he said. "As ship's medical officer I'm ordering you to your quarters."

I let him walk me past the door, and then turned and rammed the fist with the ring into his paunch.

"Bring her back, Van Wouk," I said.

"What . . .!" he coughed, half bent and looking up at me. "What . . .? Why . . .? Who . . .?"

"When, where, and how. Yeah," I admitted. "There are a lot of questions a guy could ask. The difference is you know some of the answers and I don't know any. Start supplying me."

He just kept gasping and looking at me as if I'd gone too far round the bend to catch sight of any longer.

But Trait stepped up jabbering fast: "Why did you strike him, Captain? We're all loyal! You know that! Can't you see what we're doing is for your benefit? Just tell us what you want—"

"What's my name?"

"Captain Florin of Security Ship 43; you've been temporarily incapacitated."

"Where am I?"

"On the command deck; the ship is nearing Grayfell in the Wolf System."

"What's this ring?" It had suddenly begun to burn my finger. In fact the glow of fire at my hand had already taken over top billing in my attention. I looked at it with care for the first time, while Trait's voice in explanation died to a buzzing in my ears. Somehow the ring was hard to look at. There were loops of what looked like miniature neon tubing, and curious twisted planes of polished metal, and rods and wires that seemed to go out of focus as I tried to trace their connections. At the center a glowing point pulsated like something alive; fire darted through the tubes and sparkled along the wires. I made a fierce gesture to pull it off my finger.

But my finger rippled and waved as if a sheet of iridescent water had come between my eyes and it. I stepped back and found the plate glass of the haberdashery stiff and unbroken at my back. Trait, Eridani, and the others still stood around me but the dust on their tuxedos showed they hadn't conversed or shaken hands or clapped each other on the back for a long long time. I turned and bumped a dummy I hadn't seen and it fell down.

I bent to look at the shattered head and found it was the Senator—again. I looked up, recognized the echoing dust-draped passage in the abandoned warehouse.

"Damn you, Florin," said a familiar voice. Bardell was getting up off the floor, rubbing his face.

"That slap in the puss wasn't in the script," he whined. "When I hired on for the good of the republic and a pair of cees they said nothing about a belaboring by the beneficiary of the project."

I grabbed him by the collar. "Cough it up. Who are you? What are you? What am I?"

"We'll give you all the information you require," said a voice behind me. I whirled and saw Lard Face and the full complement of henchmen alighting from the Nile green Buick, tommy guns at the ready. I wished for an instant of time I had the ring again—then didn't know why I wished it. I advanced to meet them. The bullets rattled around me like horizontal hail and I reached out with the idea I'd take somebody with me wherever I was going.

But I made the trip alone. The Buick shimmered and slid away. The street was gone. I turned and was standing in a desert and the lizard man was leaning against a rock ten feet away, dressed all in pink and smiling at me lazily.

"Well," he said. "At last. I was beginning to fear you'd never tread the maze to its conclusion."

I took a deep breath of hot, dry air that had a faint smell of eucalyptus, or of something that smelled like eucalyptus, and had a look around. Sand, a few pebbles, rocks, plenty of stone, all well-worn by time and the patient elements. No signs of life, not even a cactus.

"A swell place to visit," I said. "But I wouldn't want to die here."

"No need for any talk of dying," Diss said in his ashes-of-roses voice. "The only danger that existed was to your sanity, and it seems to me you've handled that quite nicely. In fact, you showed unexpected resourcefulness. I was quite surprised, actually."

"That relieves my mind a whole lot," I said. "What do you do now, stick a gold star in my book?"

"Now," he said briskly, "we can begin to deal." He twinkled his little red eyes expectantly at me.

"That's my cue to ask you what kind of deal," I said. "OK—what kind of deal?"

"There's only one kind of deal, wherever in the Universe one happens to be. There's something you need, and something I need. We exchange."

"Sounds simple. What do I need?"

"Information, of course."

"What's your end of it?"

He shifted position and waved a lean lilac-colored hand. "There's a service you can perform for me."

"Let's start with the information."

"Certainly. What first? The Senator?"

"He's not a Senator; he's an actor named Bardell."

"Bardell is Bardell," the lilac lizard stated. "The Senator . . . is the Senator."

"If that's a sample, I don't think we're going to get together."

"You," the lizard man said with the air of one enjoying himself, "are the victim of a plot."

"I knew it all along."

"Now, Florin, don't discount what I tell you in advance." He produced a long cigarette holder from under his pink vest, fitted a brown cigarette to it and tucked it in a corner of a mouth that was made for catching flies on the wing. He puffed and pale smoke filtered out his noseholes.

"That doesn't make you any easier to believe," I said. "If this pitch is supposed to convince me, you're going at it all wrong."

"Oh, I'm not interested in convincing you of anything in particular. I feel the facts will speak for themselves—"

"Where's Miss Regis?"

Diss frowned; even his cigarette holder drooped.

"Who?"

"The girl. A nice, quiet little lady, not like the rest of the inmates of this menagerie. She was trying to help me; I don't know why."

Diss was shaking his head. "No," he said judiciously. "Really, Florin, it's time you began to distinguish the actual players from the simulacra. There is no young lady involved."

I took a step toward him and he recoiled slightly.

"Dear me," he said, sounding amused, "surely it's not necessary for me to point out that I'm not susceptible to any hasty, violent impulses on your part." He curved the smile at me. "I'm not precisely an ally, Florin, but I mean you no harm—and as I've said, you can be of service to me. Wouldn't it be best if we simply explore matters in a rational way and seek an accommodation?"

"Go ahead," I said. "I'm too tired to argue."

"Ah, there's a clever chap. Now, the plot: A benign plot, you understand, but a plot nonetheless. A plot, to be brief, to restore you to sanity."

"Late reports from the front indicate it's not working. You may not believe this, but at this very moment I'm imagining I'm having a heart-to-heart with a fatherly salamander."

Diss opened his mouth and made some hissing sounds that I guessed were supposed to be laughter.

"It must be confusing for you at this point, I concede;

however, remember to apply the simple criterion: facts are facts, however revealed. And if my revelations illuminate the situation—why then, if I'm not real I'm as good as, eh?"

"I've also got a headache," I said. "You just got to where they were saving my sanity. How about mentioning who 'they' are, and why they're interested in unscrambling my wits, if I've got any."

"They . . . are the Research Council, a high-level governmental group—of which you were—or are—chairman."

"You must have the wrong pigeon, Diss. The only research I do is into who pulled the trigger or pushed the breadknife, as the case may be."

He waved that away. "A transparent rationalization. Your own common sense must tell you that it's necessary now to widen the scope of your self-concept. Would I waste my time interviewing an obscure private eye, with or without his wits about him?"

"I pass. Keep talking."

"You last project as Chairman was the development of a device for the study of dreams, an apparatus designed to search the subconscious for operative symbols, and concretize and externalize them, making the unconscious mental activities available for study. You insisted on being the first test subject. Unfortunately, due to fatigue and stress factors, you were unequal to the experience. Your mind embraced this new avenue of escape; you slipped away into a fantasy world of your own devising."

"I'm disappointed in me; I'd have thought I could devise something that was more fun than being chased, run away from, shot at, slugged, and generally scared to death."

"Indeed?" Diss chuckled, like a safety valve letting off a little extra pressure. "Know thyself, Florin. You're a scientist, a theoretician, not a doer of deeds. You welcomed the opportunity to shed responsibility in a simpler world of brute law, of kill or be killed. But your loyal henchmen, naturally enough, were far from content with this turn of events. It was necessary that they bring you back from your dream-world. You had escaped into the *persona* of a legendary character of Old Earth—Florin by name. Van Wouk countered this move by setting you a task—in your chosen guise, of course—and thereupon introducing difficulties into your path, with the object of rendering your refuge untenable. Matters proceeded as planned—to a point. You entered the fantasy, accepted the charge. Abruptly, things went awry. Unplanned elements cropped up, complicating affairs. Van Wouk attempted to abort the treatment, but found himself unable to do so. Matters had been taken out of his hands. He was no longer in control of the dream machine." He paused for the question. I asked it.

"*You* were now in charge, of course," he said. "Rather than acting as a passive receiver of the impulses fed to your brain, you seized on them and wove them into a new fabric, closer to your needs: specifically, the need to cling to your chosen role."

"Why don't I remember any of this? And what do you mean, 'Old Earth'?"

"You still don't remember, eh?" Diss said. "A portion of your mind has carefully blanked out the evidence of the

situation you found insupportable. By supplying the data
from another source, I am in effect outflanking your own
mental defenses. As for Old Earth—it's the name given to
a minor world thought by some to be the original home of
humanity."

"I guess this is where I say I thought humanity only had
one home."

"Oh, of course—Earth was the setting you chose for
yourself, as appropriate to your role as Florin, the Man of
Steel. But by now you must be ready to accept the thesis
that such a stage is a trifle too small to contain both you
and—myself." He gave the lipless smile.

"Not to mention Grayfell—and the monkey man."

Diss made his hissing laughter again. "Van Wouk was
growing desperate. He intended to pacify you by offering
you an alternate avenue of rational escape, an acceptable
alibi to seize on: that you were a secret agent, suffering
from a brainwashing during which you had gained certain
false impressions; but you carried his gambit on to a
reduction ad absurdum, discrediting it. He then attempted
to overawe you with authority, convince you you were
delirious, emerging from anesthetic—and again you twisted
his charade into absurdity. He tried again, closer to home,
thrusting you into the role of an authority figure broken by
overwork—and a third time you used his strength against
him, reaching out, in fact, to attack and nearly destroy
him. It was at that point that I felt it essential to step in—
both to save your sanity and to prevent a wider tragedy."

"I see; just a selfless individual, out to do a little good
in the big bad imaginary world."

"Not quite." He tipped the ashes from his cigarette.

"I mentioned that there was a service you could perform for me."

"I guess you'll tell me what it is, whether I coax you or not."

"The dream machine," he said, "is a most ingenious device; *too* ingenious, I fear. You're to be congratulated, my dear Florin, on your achievement. But it won't do, you know. It will have to be shut down—permanently."

I scratched my jaw, which I discovered hadn't been shaved for quite a while, which might have been a clue to something, but at the moment I didn't stop to chase it down.

"Picture the problems which would be created," Diss went on, "if a band of untutored aborigines on some remote ocean isle accidentally stumbled on a means of generating powerful radio waves. Some incidental by-product, perhaps, of an improved anti-devil charm. In all innocence they could well disrupt planetary communications, interfere with satellite operations, wreak havoc with Trideo, and open and close carport doors on the other side of the planet."

"It doesn't sound all bad. But I get the point."

"The dream machine, unhappily, has such side-effects. Unwittingly, when you and your Council set it in operation, you created repercussions in the probability fabric that extend half across the galaxy. This is, of course, an intolerable situation. Yet, galactic law closely restricts direct interventions. Candidly, my present activities in confronting you in a semicorporeal state border on the illegal. But I judged that the circumstances warranted a slight bending of regulations."

"What does semicorporeal mean?"

"Only that I'm not actually here—no more than you."

"Where are you?"

"In the transmission cubicle of my transport, on station some two light-years from Sol. While you, of course, are occupying the dream machine in your own laboratory."

"Why the exotic Saharan background?"

"Oh, you see a desert, do you? You're supplying it from your own fund of imagery, of course. I merely dialed a neutral setting."

I looked at the desert behind him; it looked as real as a desert ever looked. He gave me time for that idea to soak through.

"I'll now intervene in the operation of the machine," he said, "to bring you back to consciousness—and sanity. In return—you will destroy the machine, including all notes and diagrams. Agreed?"

"Suppose I don't?"

"Then it will inevitably be shut down by other means, less soothing to your planetary pride."

"Just like that, eh? What if I don't believe you?"

"That's of course your option."

"I'll still know how to rebuild it—if what you say is true."

"So you will. But if you should be so unwise as to attempt to do so—or to allow any other to do so—you'll find yourself back here—quite alone. So—what do you say?"

"No deal," I said.

"Oh, come now, Florin. Surely you place some value on life and sanity?"

"I don't like blind deals. Maybe this is all happening, and maybe it isn't. Maybe you can do what you say and maybe you can't. Maybe I'm a great inventor—and maybe I'm swinging from the chandelier by my tail. You'll have to show me."

Diss jammed his cigarette out angrily, shredded the weed into the wind, and tucked the holder away.

"Look here, Florin. I've been most patient with you, considerate. I could have taken violent steps at once; I refrained. Now you seek to blackmail me—"

"Put up or shut up, Diss."

"You're a stubborn man, Florin—most stubborn!" He folded his lean arms and drummed his fingers on his biceps. "If I return you to your normal base-line in full possession of your senses and you see that matters are as I described—will you *then* destroy the machine?"

"I'll make the decision when I get there."

"Bah! You're incorrigible! I don't know why I waste time with you! But I'm a benign being. I'll go along. But I warn you—"

"Don't. It would blight our beautiful friendship."

He made an impatient gesture and turned and I got a brief, ghostly impression of vertical panels and lines of light; Diss made quick motions with his hands, and the light faded, changed quality; the distant horizon rushed closer, blanked out the sky. There was an instant of total darkness, and a sound like a series of doors slamming, far away. Ideas, names, faces rushed into my mind like water filling a bucket.

Then the lights came up slowly.

I was lying on my back in a room thirty feet on a side,

ceiled with glare-panels, floored in patterned tiles, walled
with complex apparatus. Big Nose stood by a console that
winked and flared with emergency signals that bleeped
and shrilled in strident alarm. Beside him, the gray man in
a white smock bent over a smaller panel, jabbing at
switches. Bardell was stretched out on the next cot, snor-
ing.

I made a sound and Big Nose whirled and stared at me.
His mouth worked, but no words came out.

"You can unstrap me now, Doctor Van Wouk," I said.
"I'm no longer violent."

Half an hour had passed, as half hours are wont to do.
The lard-faced man—Dr. Wolff as he was known to his
intimates—had unsnapped the contacts, clucked over my
wrists and ankles where the straps had cut in, and
smeared some salve over the raw spots. The gray man—
Dr. Eridani—had hurried out and come back with hot
coffee laced with something that restored the glow to my
cheeks, if not to my pride. The others—Trait, Tomey,
Hyde, Jonas, et al. (the names were there, ready in my
memory, along with a lot of other things) gathered around
and took turns telling me how worried they'd been. The
only one who hung back and sulked was Bardell. Eridani
had administered a hypo that had brought him out of his
doze yelling; they had calmed him down, but he still
seemed to be nursing a grudge.

"My God, Jim," Van Wouk said to me, "we thought for
a while we'd lost you."

"Nevertheless I'm here," I said. "Give me a report, the
whole thing, from the beginning."

"Well . . ." He ran his fat fingers through his thinning hair. "As you know—"

"Assume I know nothing," I said. "My memory's been affected. I'm still hazy."

"Of course, Jim. Why, then, on completion of SAVE— the Symbolic Abstractor and Visual Elaborator, that is to say—you authorized an operational test, with yourself as subject. I objected, but—"

"Stick to the substantive, Doctor."

"Of course, sir. Ah, an operational test was initiated, with you as subject. You were placed under light hypnosis and the electrodes positioned. Calibration proceeded normally. The program was introduced, the integrator energized. Almost at once, power demand jumped tenfold. Feedback protection devices were activated without result. I tried various control and damping measures in an effort to regain control, to no avail. I reluctantly ordered an abort, and cut all power—but you remained in a deep coma, failing to respond to the recall signals. It was as though you were drawing power from some other source, fantastic though that seems.

"In desperation, I tried corrective reprogramming, to no avail. Then—out of a clear sky—you snapped out of it."

"Any idea why?"

"None. It was as though an external vector had been introduced. Neural potentials that had been running sky-high—at full emergency stimulus level—suddenly dropped back to rest state. The next moment—you were with us again."

I tipped my head toward Bardell, who was sitting

across the room, nursing a cup of coffee and looking resentful. "What does he do?"

"Why, that's Bardell. Temporary employee; he was used as an ancillary vector in the mock-ups during the test. A sort of, ah, bit player, you might say."

"All part of the dream machinery, eh?"

"The . . .? Oh, yes, a very appropriate nickname, Jim."

"How does it work?"

He stared at me. "You mean . . .?"

"Just pretend I've forgotten."

"Yes. Why, then, ah, it's simply a matter of first monitoring the dream mechanism, then stimulating the visual, olfactory, and auditory cortex in accordance with previously determined symbolic coding to create the desired, eh, hallucinatory experiences. The program mock-ups occupy the adjacent bay—"

"Show me."

"Why . . . certainly, Jim. Just this way." He walked across to a blank wall and pushed a button and a plain gray panel slid back on two walls of a shabby hotel room, complete with brass bed and broken windows.

He noticed me looking at the latter and chuckled insincerely. "You grew rather violent a time or two, Jim—"

"Have you always called me Jim?" I cut in.

"I—" He stopped and glittered his eyes at me; his jowls quivered a little. "I beg your pardon, Doctor," he said stiffly. "I suppose during these tense hours I've allowed protocol to lapse, somewhat."

"Just asking," I said. "Show me the rest."

He led the way through the conference room—not nearly so plush, in a good light—the street scenes—cardboard and plaster—the boardinghouse; all just shabby, hastily built sets, that wouldn't fool a blind man.

"All that was required," Van Wouk explained importantly, "was a triggering stimulus; you supplied the rest from your subconscious."

The series of sets ended at a heavy fire door, locked.

"Our premises end here," Van Wouk said. "Another agency has that space."

The route back led through the warehouse scene. I poked a toe at the broken dummy that looked like Bardell.

"What was this for?"

He seemed to notice it with surprise. "That? Oh, we hoped at first to make use of manikins; but we soon determined that human actors were necessary." He gave me a twitch of his jowls. "A human being is a rather complex device, not easy to simulate."

"How does all this get into the picture? If I was strapped down in the next room—"

"Oh, that was only at the end. After you, er, ran out of control. We began with you in an ambulatory state, under light narcosis."

"How long since this test began?"

Van Wouk looked at a big watch expensively strapped to his fat hairy wrist.

"Nearly eight hours," he said, and wagged his head in sympathy for himself. "A trying eight hours, Jim—ah, sir, that is."

"And now what, Doctor?"

"Now? Why, an analysis of the tapes, determination of just what it was that went wrong, corrective action, and then—new tests, I would assume."

"I'd have to authorize that, of course."

"Naturally, sir."

"What would you think of suspending testing?"

Van Wouk pulled at his lower lip; he cocked an eye at me. "That's for you to determine, of course, sir," he murmured, "if you're convinced there's danger—"

"Maybe we ought to smash the machine," I said.

"Hmmm. Perhaps you're right."

In the next room, voices were raised excitedly.

". . . I don't know what you're trying to pull now," Bardell was yelling, "but I won't stand for it! Unlock this door, damn you! I'm leaving here, right now!"

We went back in. Bardell was at the hall door, wrenching at the knob, his face pink from exertion. Eridani was fluttering around him; Trait was at the side door, rattling the knob. He looked up at Van Wouk.

"Some joker has locked this from the outside," he said. He went across to Bardell, shouldered the bigger man aside, twisted the knob, then stepped back and gave the door a kick at latch height. It looked as if it hurt his toe, if not the door.

"Here—what the devil are you doing, Trait!" Van Wouk went to the door and tried it, turned and looked at me with a disturbed expression.

"Do you know—" he started, then changed his tack. "Some error," he said. "Somehow, I suppose, the security system has become engaged."

"You won't get away with this," Bardell shouted. He grabbed up a metal chair and crashed it against the door; it bounced off, one leg bent. Van Wouk brushed past me into the room we had just come out of, hurried to the broken window and swung the frame out and recoiled.

"Is this your doing?" he said in a choked voice. I went across and looked at what he was looking at: solid concrete, filling the space where the passage had been.

"That's right," I said. "While you were watching Red kick the door I ordered up two yards of ready-mix and had it poured in here. Sorry, I forgot to scratch my initials in it."

He snarled and ducked around me, ran back into the green-tiled lab. Eridani and Trait and the others were in a huddle; Bardell was against the wall at the far side, watching everybody. I went to the door he had tried first and pounded on it; it gave back a solid *thunk!* that suggested an armored bunker.

"No phone in here?" I asked.

"No, nothing," Eridani said quickly. "Special isolation arrangements—"

"Got a pry bar?"

"Here—a locking bar from the filing cabinet." Trait hefted the four-foot length of one-inch steel as if he might be thinking about using it on my head; but he went to the door, jimmied the flat end in between door and jamb, and heaved. Wood splintered; the door popped wide.

Solid concrete filled the opening.

Trait staggered back as if he were the one who'd been hit with the bar. Bardell let out a yelp and scuttled sideways to a corner.

"You plan to kill me," he yelled. "I'm on to you now—but it won't work—" He broke off, his eyes fixed on me. "You," he said. "They'll get you, too; you're no safer than I am! Maybe together we can—"

Van Wouk whirled on him. "You damned fool! Don't appeal to 'him for help! We're all his victims! He's the one who's responsible for this! It's *his* doing!"

"Liar!" Bardell yelled, and swung back to me. "You're the one they were out to get! They tricked you into the dream machine! They intended to drive you insane—certifiably insane! It was the only way to eliminate you without killing you—"

Trait reached him then, slammed a hard-looking fist into his stomach, straightened him up with a left hook. It didn't knock him out, but it shut him up. He sagged against the wall, his mouth open.

"All right!" Van Wouk said, his voice a little high, a trifle shaky. He swallowed hard and lowered his head as if I were a brick wall and he was going to ram me.

"Call it off," he snapped. "Whatever it is you're up to—call it off!"

"Let's you and him make me," I said.

"I told you," Eridani said. "We were tampering with forces we couldn't control. I warned you he was taking over!"

"He's taking over nothing," Van Wouk snapped, and groped inside his coat and brought out a flat gun with a familiar look.

"Call it off, Florin," he snapped. "Or I'll kill you like a snake, I swear it!"

"I thought Florin was folklore," I said. "And your needler won't work; I jimmied it."

He gave a start and aimed the gun off-side. It went *bzzaap!* and something screamed past my knees as I went low and took him just under the belt-line and slammed

him back and down across the slick floor and into the wall.
His head hit pretty hard; he went limp and I scooped up
the gun and came up facing them before they had gotten
more than halfway to me.

"Fun's over," I said. "Back, all of you." I jerked a thumb
at the connecting door. "Through there."

Bardell advanced, blubbering.

"Listen to me, Florin, you're making a mistake, I was
on your side all along, I warned you, remember? I tried to
help, did all I could—"

"Shut up," Trait snapped, and he did. "Florin, somehow you've managed to take over the dream machine and
use it against us. I don't claim to know how; I'm just the
fellow who follows the wiring diagrams. But Eridani's
right: you're tinkering with forces that are too big for you.
All right, so you've walled us up in concrete. You've
showed what you can do. But you're caught too! The air
will start getting foul in a matter of minutes; in a couple of
hours, we'll be dead—all of us! So back down now, before
it goes too far, before it runs away with you! Get us out of
this and I swear we'll make an accommodation with you!
We were wrong—"

"Shut up, you damned fool!" Van Wouk yelled. "You'd
blabber your guts to *him*? We don't need him! Smash the
machine!"

I squeezed a careless burst at the door at his feet; he
leaped and yelped and a red patch appeared on his
shin.

"Next one's higher," I said.

"Rush him!" Van Wouk squealed, but he didn't move; I
raised my sights and was squeezing when he broke and

scuttled for it. Trait backed to the indicated door. Eridani, looking pale but calm, started to make a pitch but I chipped the door frame beside him and he faded back.

"Bardell, you know how to rig the dream machine?" I said.

"Y-yes, certainly, but—".

"I'm going back," I said. "You're going to help me." I went to the door the others had disappeared through, closed it and shot the heavy barrel bolt, came back and sat in a chair beside the control panel.

"Florin—are you sure?" Bardell was shaking. "I mean—wouldn't it be better if we did as they said? Disabled the infernal machine?"

"Listen carefully, Bardell," I said. "One wrong move and no more sweet you. Got it? Now start things moving."

He tottered to the board, flipped keys and punched buttons as if he knew what he was doing. A row of red lights went on.

"It's hot," he said, as if he hated saying it.

I picked up the gadget with the wires attached. There was a power pack that went into my pocket. The rest clipped to my collar just under my right ear, with a little pink chip in the ear itself.

"What program?" Bardell asked in a quivery voice.

"No program. Just fire me up and let me run free."

"It might kill you! What if you die—?"

"Then I made a mistake. Now, Bardell."

He nodded, and reached for a switch. Something jabbed inside my head. I felt dizzy, and wondered if maybe this time I'd made my last mistake. The ceiling went past, then a wall, then Bardell, looking sad and worried.

The floor drifted into view, another wall, then the ceiling again, nothing spectacular, just a nice gentle processing. Bardell's mouth was moving now, but I didn't hear any words. Then I speeded up and everything blurred and I shot off into space and burned up like a meteorite in the atmosphere, leaving a tiny ember that glowed red, then cooled and went out, slowly, lingeringly, reluctantly, amid a clamor of forgotten voices reminding me of blasted hopes and vain regrets that dwindled in their turn and faded into nothingness.

I opened my eyes and she was sitting across the table from me, dressed in a form-fitting gray outfit with bits of silver and scarlet braid on the shoulders. The table was smooth and white and not perfectly flat, like a slab of hard-carved ivory. The walls behind her were in many shades of russet and gold and tawny, textured like the bark of a Shaggy-man tree. There were sounds in the air that weren't music, but were soothing for all that. She looked at me with compassion and put a hand over mine and said, "Was it bad, Florin?"

"Bad enough, Miss Regis. Glad to see you looking so well. How did you get from there to here?"

She shook her head. "Oh, Florin—I'm afraid for you. Are you sure what you're doing is the right thing?"

"Miss Regis, I'm winging it. I wouldn't tell anyone else that. Funny thing, but I trust you. I don't know why. Who are you, anyway?"

She looked from one of my eyes to the other, as if I were hiding somewhere behind them. "You're not joking, are you? *You really don't know.*"

"I really don't. We've met before: in a beer joint, in a library. Now here. What is this place?"

"It's the Temple of Concord. We came here together, Florin, hoping to find peace and understanding. You've been under narco-meditation for many hours. Seeker Eridani let you come with me—but I sensed you weren't really yourself." Her hand held mine tighter. "Was it a mistake, Florin? Have they hurt you?"

"I'm fine, my dear," I said, and patted her hand. "Just a little mixed up. And every time I try to unmix myself, I step off another ledge in the dark. Sometimes it's Big Nose and his boys, sometimes Diss, the lilac lizard, and now and then it's you. I have a kind of line on Van Wouk, and Diss explained himself more or less plausibly, once you accept the impossible. But you don't fit in. You aren't part of the pattern. You aren't trying to sell me anything. Maybe that would tell me something if I just knew how to listen."

"We shouldn't have come here," she whispered. "Let's leave now, Florin. We won't go any further with it. It was a forlorn hope—"

"That's the best kind, Miss Regis."

"Can't you call me Curia?"

"I can't leave here now, Curia. I don't know why, but that's what the little bird called instinct tells me. What I have to do is break down a few doors, peek into a few dark places, intrude in some sanctuaries, unveil a couple of veiled mysteries. Where should I start?"

She got paler as I spoke. She shook her head and her grip on my hand was almost painful. "No, Florin! You can't! Don't even speak of it!"

"It has to be that way. Just point me in the right direction and stand back."

"Come with me—now. Please, Florin!"

"I can't. And I can't explain why. I could talk about dummies with bashed heads and Nile green Buicks and little voices back of the ear, but it would take too long, and wouldn't mean anything anyway. See, I'm learning? All I know is I've got to keep pushing. I don't really have any evidence, but somehow I sense I'm rocking something on its foundations. Maybe the next push will bring it down with a smash. Maybe I'll be caught in the wreckage, but that doesn't seem so important." I stood, feeling weak in the knees and with a faint, distant buzzing in my skull.

"I see I can't stop you," Miss Regis said. All the life had gone out of her voice. Her clutch on my hand loosened and I took it back. She stared ahead, not looking at me.

"Through there," she said, and lifted a hand to point at the big carved bronze door across the room. "Along the corridor to the black door at the end. It's the Inner Chamber. No one but the anointed can enter there." She still didn't look at me. She blinked and a tear ran down the curve of her cheek.

"So long, Miss Regis," I said. She didn't answer.

The door was big and black and lumpy with sculptured cherubs and devils and vindictive-looking old men with beards and haloes, plus a few sportive angels hovering about the crowd. I fingered the worn spot at one side and it swung back with a soft hiss on a room walled with green tiles. Van Wouk, Eridani, Trait and the rest were grouped around a chair beside the panel with all the dials. No lights were lit on the board now. The door behind them that led to the stage sets was open. Bardell lay on the floor, breathing through his mouth rather noisily. The dummy with the bashed head was seated in the chair.

I said, "Ahem," and they all turned around as if they were mounted on swivels.

"Mother of God," Wolff said, and made a magic sign in the air. Van Wouk made a sound that wasn't speech. Eridani flared his nostrils. Trait cursed and reached for his hip.

"Naughty, naughty," I said. "Try anything cute and I'll turn you into an ugly redhead with a bad complexion."

"This has got to stop, Florin," Van Wouk blustered, but weakly. "We can't go on this way any longer!"

I sidestepped and glanced at the door I had just come through. It was just an ordinary door, splintered around the lock, with a blank surface of ordinary concrete behind it.

"I agree," I said. "In fact, we can't go as far as we've gone, but you notice I didn't let that slow me down. Now, who wants to spill the beans? Eridani? Wolff?"

"The truth?" Van Wouk made a noise that might have been a laugh being strangled at birth. "Who knows what the truth is? Who knows anything? Do you, Florin? If so, you have the advantage over us, I assure you!"

"The machine must be disabled, put out of action once and for all," Eridani said in a cold voice. "I assume you see that now, Florin?"

"Not yet," I said. "What's the matter with Bardell?"

"He fell down and bumped his head," Trait said in a nasty tone.

"Wake him up so he can join the party."

"Forget him, he's unimportant, merely a hired flunky," Van Wouk spoke up. "We're the ones who're in a position to deal with you."

"Who taught him to operate the dream machine?"

"What? No one. He knows nothing about it."

Bardell groaned and rolled over. At my insistence, Eridani and Trait helped him up and walked him up and down the room until he threw them off and rubbed at his face and looked around at the company assembled.

"They tried to kill me," he said in a voice like broken bottles. "I told you they wanted to kill me, and—"

"Quiet, Bardell," I said. "I'm about to try an experiment. You can help."

"What do you mean?" Van Wouk blurted. "You, and this . . . this—"

"Yeah. I admit Bardell doesn't have a lot going for him; but you boys don't seem to like him. That makes him a pal. How about it, Bardell? Will you throw in with me; or ride it down in flames with Van Wouk and company?"

Bardell looked from them to me and back again. "Now, wait just a minute, Florin—"

"The waiting's over. Now we act. Are you in, or out?"

"What are you going to do?"

"Make up your mind."

He gnawed his lip; he twitched. He opened his mouth to speak, he hesitated.

Trait laughed. "You picked a poor stick to lean on, Florin," he said. "That's not a man, it's a bowl full of jelly."

"All right, I'll help you," Bardell said quite calmly, and walked over to stand beside me.

"Trait, will you never learn to keep your stupid mouth shut?" Eridani said in a tone stamped out of cold, rolled steel.

"Sure, be tricky," I said. "It adds to the game." I waved a hand. "Back against the wall, all of you." They obeyed, in spite of no guns in sight.

"Bardell, fire up the dream machine."

"But—you're not linked to it."

"Just get the circuits hot. I'll take it from there."

"I demand you tell us what you intend doing!" Van Wouk growled.

"Easy," I said. "Up to now I've just been along for the ride. Now I'm taking the wheel."

"Meaning?"

"Somebody along the line dropped hints that I was responsible for the certain anomalies. The old 'monsters-from-the-id' idea. According to that theory I've been the prime mover as well as the prime victim—unconsciously. I'm moving the action over to the conscious area. The next trick you see will be on purpose."

Eridani and Van Wouk made simultaneous inarticulate noises; Trait pushed away from the wall and stopped, poised. Bardell called, "Activated!"

"Don't do it, Florin!" Van Wouk barked. "Can't you see the terrible danger inherent—" He got that far before Eridani and Trait charged me, heads down, legs pumping. I stood where I was and pictured a knee-high brick wall across the room, between them and me.

And it was there.

Trait hit it in full stride, did a forward flip and slammed the deck on his back like a body falling off a roof. Eridani checked, skidded, hands out in front, his mouth in a tight little *moue* of anticipated pain; he smacked the bricks and tumbled over mewing like a stepped-on cat.

"For the love of God!" Van Wouk blurted and tried to crawl up the wall behind him. Eridani bleated like a sheep, mooed like a soprano cow, rolling around and clutching his shins. Bardell clucked like a chicken in the throes of an epileptic seizure. Trait just lay where he was, as inert as a dead horse.

"That'll be all from the menagerie for the present," I said, and pictured them not there anymore. They weren't.

"Now we're getting somewhere," I said, and imagined the side wall of the room out of existence.

It disappeared obediently, leaving a porous surface of concrete in its place.

"Go away, concrete," I wished; but it stayed put. I threw away the other three walls and the roof and the floor, furniture and all, exposing rough concrete on all six sides of me, glowing faintly with an eerie, violet glow.

I tried again, harder. Nothing.

"OK," I said aloud, and my words hit the blind walls and fell dead. "Let's try a little concentrated effort." I picked a spot on the wall and told myself it wasn't there. Maybe it got a little hazy; but it didn't go away. I narrowed my focus down to a spot the size of a dime. The violet glow dimmed there; nothing else. I tightened down to a pinpoint, threw everything I had at it—

Zigzag cracks ran across the concrete, radiating from the target. A large chunk fell, letting in gray light and curling tendrils of fog. The rest of the wall collapsed like damp pastry, almost soundlessly. I picked my way across the soft debris, into swirling mist. A light gleamed ahead, a fuzzy puffball in the gloom. As I came closer, it resolved itself into a streetlight, an old-fashioned carbide lamp in a wrought-iron cage on a tall cast-iron pole. I stopped under it and listened. Someone was coming. A moment later Diss, the mauve monster, strolled into view, dapper in black evening dress.

"Well, well," he said, somehow not sounding as casual as he might have. "And how did you get *here*?"

"I didn't," I said. "You're in your cubbyhole, two lights from Sol, and I'm driving matched nightmares down that ol' Street of Dreams, remember?"

He trotted out a light chuckle for my benefit and put it away again, almost unused. "You failed to fulfill our agreement," he said in a tone that suggested feelings that were hurt, but not fatally.

"Maybe it slipped my mind. I've learned a few tricks since then, Diss. Like this." I turned the lamppost into a tree and set the crown afire. The flames leaped up into the night, crackling merrily. Diss hardly twitched an eyebrow—or the place where an eyebrow would be if he had an eyebrow.

"What you're doing," he said over the roar of fire, "is dangerous. Far too dangerous to be tolerated. I've told you—"

"Uh-huh, you told me," I said. "Who are you, Diss? What team do you play on?"

The shadows danced on his face as the fire burned itself out. "That's a matter of no concern to you," he said in the sharp tone of one who wants to stop a line of argument before it gets started. "You're a petty creature, involved in great affairs. Out of compassion, I've offered you guidance; ignore it at your peril!"

"The next line is, you're giving me one more chance, right, Diss? What if I turn you down?"

"Don't be an utter fool, Florin! Go back to where you belong and destroy the apparatus that's precipitated you into your present difficulties."

"Why should I? Just for the sake of your little red eyes?"

"You owe me a debt, Florin! They thrust you into their machine as a guinea pig, a puppet, responsive to their wishes. How do you suppose it was that you threw off their control? By your own unaided efforts?" He smiled his contempt at the thought. "Do you have a lottery ticket in your pocket, dear fellow? No matter—I know you do. I planted it there, I believe the expression is. In actuality it's an extraordinarily complex printed circuit, keyed to your control rhythms. I gave it to you to help you regain your freedom of action so that I could deal with you as an equal. So you see, you owe me something, eh?"

"You'll have to spell it out better than that, Diss. I'm just a small-town boy, remember? Or so you've been telling me."

Diss made an exasperated gesture. "By sheer good luck you have it in your power to preserve your world's innocence, hopefully until a time in the far future when you'll be capable of a confrontation with the Galactic Power! Don't throw that chance away out of some misguided sense of pique, some atavistic simian curiosity—"

"You know too much about my little backwater world, Diss. That worries me. Lies always worry me, especially when there seems to be no good reason for them. What are you really after?"

"That's enough, Florin! I've been patient with you—far more patient than you deserve! You'll return now to your prime locus and carry out the destruction of the dream machine!"

"If it's all that important, why haven't you smashed it yourself, a long time ago?"

"Reasons of policy have restrained me; but now my patience runs thin—"

"Fooey. I don't believe you. You're bluffing, Diss."

"Bah, I'll waste no more time on you!" He started to turn away—and banged his nose on a stone wall I'd thrown up in his path.

"You fool! You unspeakable fool! Is this the reward I get for my restraint, for my desire to spare you suffering?"

"Right now I'm suffering most from curiosity. Tell me things, Diss. Start anywhere, I'm not particular anymore."

He scuttled off to the right; I planted another wall in front of him. He doubled back and I hemmed him in on the third side. He screeched in frustration—I thought.

"Get on with the exposé, Diss," I said, "before I yield to my yen to practice some more of my magic tricks."

"Magic! You use the word sardonically, but I assure you that there are forces in the Universe that would make turning princesses into pumpkins seem as routine as winking an eye!"

"Talk, Diss. If I don't like what I hear, I turn you into a mouse pulling a coach and go for a ride, got it? You can start now." I was still in charge, but somehow I had a feeling he wasn't as worried as he had been a few seconds before.

I tried to spot my blunder while he edged past me toward the open side of the space I had walled in.

"You're a child—an idiot child with a new toy," he shrilled at me. "I order you—I *command* you to cease this inane harassment at once—" He jumped for freedom and I slammed a fourth wall across to close us both in and he turned and grinned at me like a sculpture peering down from the top of Notre Dame and placed his thumb between his noseholes and waggled his fingers and disappeared just like the pumpkin coach, without even a puff of purple smoke to mark the spot where he'd been standing.

"Suckered," I told myself, and watched the light fade as the walls I'd trapped myself inside of moved closer. They were rough-poured concrete with the form-marks plain on them, still slightly green, but hard for all that. I had my back against one and was pushing at another with everything I had, but it wasn't enough, and they came together and squashed me flat, spreading me out as thin as the wax on a gum wrapper, as thin as the gold on a Gideon Bible, as thin as a politician's ethics. Somewhere along the line I lost consciousness.

. . . and came to strapped in a gimbaled chair suspended high before the face of a gigantic illuminated grid where patterns of light winked and flashed in sequences too fast for the eye to follow.

"Hold on, Florin," the Senator's voice called from somewhere above and to my right. I was groggy, but I managed to swivel my head far enough to see him, perched in a chair like mine, gripping the arms and leaning forward, his eyes on the big board.

"You held them," he called. "You've won us some time! Maybe there's still hope!"

I was as weak as yesterday's tea bag. He got me down and helped me to a cot and shot something cool into my arm and broke something pungent under my nose and after a while I felt better. I sat up and looked around. It was a big, empty room with smooth ivory walls, curved like the inside of an observatory, occupied by the lighted grid and banks of controls and not much else. Two round ports looked out on the black loneliness of deep space.

Bardell sat down on a stool he had brought over and said, "You held them off, Florin. I was going under; you took over the board just in time. That was as close as they've come. Next time . . ." He looked at me, level-eyed, firm-jawed. "Next time nothing will stop them."

I sat up.

"Where are Van Wouk and Trait and the rest of the cast?"

"You ordered them back, Florin. Don't you remember? There's just you and me now, manning the mind-grid."

"Your name's Bardell?" I asked him. He looked surprised.

"Yes—of course, Florin."

"I seem to have a slight touch of total amnesia. You'd better give me a little fill-in on where I am and what's going on."

Bardell looked disconcerted for a moment, then smoothed his face.

"A certain amount of disorientation is normal after a session on the grid," he said heartily. "You'll soon be yourself again." He gave me a tense smile. "You're at Grayfell Station, in retrograde orbit twenty-eight parsecs from Imperial Center. We're manning the grid against the Diss attack."

I looked across at the glistening curve of wall, imagined it blushing a deep pink. Nothing happened.

"What is it?" Bardell turned to look the way I was looking.

"Nothing. Just clearing away the fog. I dreamed I was having an argument with a lizard—"

"The Diss are reptilian in appearance, you know."

"I thought the name belonged to just one lilac lizard," I said. "He wanted me to wreck the dream machine—"

Bardell started to say something, broke off, looked at me a bit warily.

"Don't worry, I turned down the idea," I said. "I don't know why. Just to be contrary, maybe. He seemed a little too insistent."

Bardell gave a short sample of a laugh. "I should think so! If they'd managed to subvert you—Florin himself—it would have been the end."

"Tell me about this enemy you say we're fighting."

"We don't know where they come from; they appeared a few years ago out of nowhere, attacking the worlds of the Empire—vicious mind-attacks that turn a man into a shambling zombie, without meaning or direction. There are billions of the devils, unimpressive individually, but potent *en masse*. They possess a degree of group consciousness that enables them to combine their intellectual energies for brief periods. It's in that way that they hurl their attacks against us. We fight back by way of the grid—an artificial means of joining a multitude of minds in a single gestalt. Few human brains can stand the strain of controlling the weapon: yours, mine, Van Wouk's, and the others'. We make up the slim ranks of the Mind Corps, manning the Deep Space Grid Stations, fighting humanity's battles for her." He snorted, a tired, cynical ghost of a laugh. "For which we receive scant thanks—or even awareness. They don't know the war is going on, the vast mass of our fellowmen. They don't understand the kind of attack they're under. How can you explain a light symphony to a blind man? Oh, they accept the indications of the instruments; they can see for themselves some of the results of the Diss attack. But only intellectually. Emotionally they suspect us of being charlatans, self-styled heroes, fighting our lonely battles in our imaginations. Only a handful even bother to link up now when the call goes out. That's why we're losing, Florin. If the entire race would recognize the threat, join together to pour their mental energies into the grid system—we'd neutralize the Diss at a stroke!"

"Van Wouk and the rest," I said, "how did they feel about it?"

Bardell looked at me sharply. "I see it's coming back to you. They were losing heart. They'd had enough. They spoke of peace terms; you wouldn't hear of it. You called them traitors and sent them home."

"And how do you feel, Bardell?"

He hesitated before answering, like a man trying words on for size.

"I stood by you last time," he said. "Now—I can see it's hopeless. We don't have the strength, Florin; we don't have the backing of our own kind—and we can't do it alone." As he spoke he got more excited. "If we go on the grid again it means death. Worse than death: destruction of our minds! And for what? They'll overwhelm us, we know that; we'll be swept aside as if we weren't here, and the Diss will move into Human Space—whether we fight or not. If we recognize that fact now, face it—and evacuate the station before it's too late—we can still save our own sanity!"

"What about the rest of the population?"

"They aren't lifting a finger to help us," Bardell said flatly. "They go about their petty pursuits, business as usual. Our appeals don't touch them. They don't care. *They don't care, Florin!* And why should we?"

"How do you know we'll lose?"

"Wasn't this last assault proof enough for you?" He was on his feet, his eyes a little wild, his diction not quite so precise. "It was only a routine probe, tapping for a weak spot in the station line—but it almost broke through! You know what that means! Right now they're gathering their power for an all-out assault on our station—on you and me, Florin. Our minds can't stand against them. We're doomed! Unless . . ." He broke off and looked sideways at me.

"Go ahead, Bardell. Get it off your chest."

He drew a breath and let it out. "Unless we act swiftly. We don't know how long the present respite will last. We have to move before they do. They caught me short last time—" He broke off. "That is, before we had time to discuss the matter they were on us—but now—"

"I thought you volunteered to stay."

"I could have gone with the others. Obviously, I didn't."

"So you stayed—but not to fight, eh? You had other plans—but they hit before you were ready. Ready for what, Bardell?"

He tried a shaky laugh. "Well, you're recovering your old sharpness, I see, Florin. Yes, I had a reason for staying—and the reason wasn't suicide. With their Mind Corps credentials and priorities Van Wouk, Eridani, and the others can be well on their way toward the hinterlands by now. But what will that avail them, when the Diss advance—as they will—in five years or ten? They're fleeing in panic, Florin—but not me. Not us. We have an alternative."

"Spell it out."

"The grid." His eyes went to the high, wide, glittering construction that filled and dominated the white-walled room. "We can use the energies of the grid for something other than futile efforts to shield a mob of ingrates, Florin."

"Tell me about it."

"I've studied it," he said, talking fast now, spilling the beans. "I've experimented during extended lulls. The grid is a fantastic device, Florin, capable of things the designers never dreamed of! It can transmit matter—including men—instantaneously—across the Galaxy!"

"Wouldn't we feel a little lonely there?"

"Not just ourselves, Florin; whatever we choose goes with us. We can take our pick of the human-occupied worlds, transfer to it whatever we like—*whom*ever we like—and shift the entire planet into a stable orbit around a congenial sun a hundred thousand light years from the

Diss threat. It will be generations before they penetrate that far—and perhaps in that time we can ready a new and better defense against them."

"Aren't you afraid the population of the planet in question might resent being ripped untimely from the bosom of the Empire?"

Bardell grinned a fierce grin. "What does it matter what those sybarites think? Not that it has to be Grayfell, of course; naturally, you'll have a say in the matter." He gave me a smile to reassure me, but refrained from patting me on the head. "As for any potential hostile actions by the ingrates we've saved, it will be simple enough to arrange matters so that we'll be quite invulnerable from them. We'll have vast powers, Florin, unassailable powers."

"Why not take an unoccupied planet?"

"And live like savages? No, thank you. I've no taste for hewing down jungles and opening stasispacks. Nor do I wish to live in solitude. We want cities, parks, dining places, gracious avenues, cultivated gardens. We want people around us, Florin. There are so many services that only a human servant can provide."

"I see you've given this a lot of thought, Bardell. Are you sure the grid can handle it?"

"Certainly. We simply send the emergency signal via trans-L; when the still-active units have linked, one single, well-directed pulse—and it's done."

"How many still-active units are there?"

"Less than half a billion in the entire sector," he said with a curl of his well-chiseled lip. "Still, it's sufficient— for a single pulse."

"Why a single pulse?"

His smile was a bit grim this time. "First, because the instantaneous peak demand will drain the contributing units dry in a fractional hemiquaver of time—and secondly, the discharge energies will melt the grid to slag in a matter of moments."

"So all we have to do is reduce to idiocy half a billion people who still trust in us, and destroy the station they entrusted us with, and we're home free."

"Well—those are rather emotional terms—but essentially, yes."

"I can't help wondering, Bardell, why you're letting me in on the deal."

He spread his hands and smiled benignly. "Why not? After all, we're friends, associates; I've always respected you . . ." His smile widened, became self-indulgent. "Your talents, that is, if not always your judgment."

"Help me up," I said.

He jumped forward and put a hand under my elbow and I came up fast and drove a straight right-hand punch to his solar plexus with all the power in my body behind it. He made an ugly sound and jackknifed past me and hit on his face.

"My judgment is still off," I said. "I'm staying."

Just then the alarm went off. Even through his agony, Bardell heard it. He rolled to his side, still curled like a worm on a griddle, and gasped out: "Florin . . . quickly . . . it's our . . . last chance . . ." He was still talking as I turned back to the battle board to do what I could before the end.

The knowledge was all there, crowding into the forefront of my mind; all I had to do was let my body respond automatically: my hands going out to touch the coding keys, punching in the sequences that summoned up the power of the grid; then walking to the chair, seating myself, strapping in, tripping the action station sequence. The chair rose swiftly to its position at the focal point. I felt the first preliminary vibrations strike the grid and saw the lights flash across it in response, felt the energies pouring into my brain, filling it, felt my mind reaching out for contact, while around me the curving bone-white walls faded and dissolved. I had one last fleeting image of the tiny mote that was the station, alone in interstellar space— and myself, alone inside it. Then it was gone, lost in the immensity behind me. And out of the darkness ahead, Diss appeared. I saw him at a great distance, a gigantic figure striding toward me, dinosaurian, magnificent, irresistible, light glinting from his polished purple scale-armor, from his flashing violet eyes. He halted, towering against a backdrop of stars.

"Florin!" his voice boomed out, filling all space the way an organ fills a cathedral. "We meet again, then! I thought last time you'd had your fill of dueling."

I didn't answer him. I picked a spot on the pale curve of his exposed belly and thought a hole in it, or tried to. Diss didn't seem to notice.

"It's still not too late for an accommodation," he thundered. "I can, of course, wipe you out of existence, as Bardell so rightly warned you. But I have no vindictiveness toward you, no wish to injure you. Bardell lied when he painted me as a villain, determined to eat away the minds of your kind." He laughed, a gargantuan laugh.

"Why would I wish to commit any such atrocity? What would I gain from that?"

I narrowed down the scope of my target, concentrated everything I had at it. Diss raised a Herculean hand and scratched idly at the spot.

"I admire your spirit, of course—standing alone, defending your forlorn cause. You see, I am not without emotion. But I can't allow such sentimental considerations to stand in the way of my duty. I asked you once, on a gentlemanly basis, to destroy the dream machine. Well, you didn't do it. Instead you've persisting in your prying, turned up a few small facts—but to what end? Very well, the machine is not quite so innocent as I painted it; your role not quite so minor as that of a delegate representing a trivial planet in your Galactic Parliament. But is anything changed—except in scale? The Galactic Consensus is old, Florin—older than your infant race. It can no more tolerate your chaos-producing expansionism than a human body can tolerate cancer cells. As the body marshals its defenses to destroy the malignancy, so we marshal whatever force is needed to contain you. That's all we intend, Florin: to restrict you to your own sector of space, put an end to your disturbments. Surely you see the wisdom now of bowing to the inevitable?"

I didn't answer, concentrating on my attack. He fingered the spot absently and frowned.

"Withdraw from the grid, Florin. Use the method Bardell proposed to destroy the apparatus; I have no objection if you skip nimbly across the Galaxy with whatever loot you choose; I assure you, you'll be allowed to dwell in peaceful obscurity thereafter—" He broke off and put a hand over his belly. "Florin," he bellowed. "What are you—" He screeched suddenly and clawed at himself.

"Treacher! Under cover of parley, you attacked me—" He broke off to beat at the bright purple flames that were licking up around him, curling and blackening the bright scales. Suddenly he looked a lot smaller, as if my whole perspective on him had changed. He wasn't a giant across the plain now, just a man-sized reptile capering in front of me, squealing in fury more than pain, I thought.

"Whee," I said. "This is easy—and a lot more fun than having it done to me."

"Stop," he cried, in a tone that was half an octave higher than the one he'd been using. "I confess I've been misleading you! I'll tell you the truth now—but stop, before it's too late for all of us!"

I lowered the heat. "Start talking, Diss," I said.

"What I told you before was true, in the main," he yelped. "I merely distorted certain elements. I see now that was a mistake. My only intention was to avoid complicating matters, settle the affair as quickly and simply as possible. But I misjudged you." He gave me a wild-eyed reptilian look, while the smoke from the damped-down blaze curled about his narrow head. "You are not an easy being to manipulate, Florin.

"As I told you, you voluntarily entered the environment simulator—the dream machine—but not for the purpose of testing as I said. It was for treatment. You're an important human, Florin. They needed you, you see. You were hypnoed, your superficial memories suppressed, new conditioning taped into your brain—conditioning matching your imagined role. The intention was to manipulate your hallucinations in such a way as to render them an untenable escape, and thus to force you back to rationality."

"It sounds kind of familiar," I said. "Except it was the Senator who was off the rails."

Diss looked disconcerted. "But haven't you understood yet?" he said. "You are the Senator."

"It's really quite amusing," Diss said. "You escaped into the *persona* of the legendary Florin, whereupon Van Wouk arranged for you to be engaged—as Florin, the Man of Steel—as bodyguard to the Senator. He set you to guard yourself, thereby presenting you with an insoluble paradox."

"That sounds like a dirty trick. Why didn't it work?"

"With commendable ingenuity, your beleaguered imagination produced a Senator who was yourself, and who was yet not yourself. In due course, as the pressure to recognize yourself mounted, you explained him away by calling him an actor. This was, however, merely begging the question. It left unanswered the more threatening mystery of the identity of the real Senator—yourself. You became obsessed with the need to find and confront him. Van Wouk and his group, monitoring your fantasy, attempted, without success, to remove Bardell from the scene. In the end they presented you with his corpse—a measure of desperation. But you—or your subconscious— were equal to the challenge. You could not, of course, accept your own removal from the board. You transformed the dead impostor into a lifeless puppet, and went on to confront your bugaboo yet again—whereupon you promptly drove him to apparently destroy himself. But even then you were dissatisfied; you saw through the deception, and persevered—to the discomfiture of the Galactic Community."

"So you stepped in and gave me pieces of the story and sent me back to wreck the gizmo you call the dream machine."

"Which you failed to do. I hope that now you realize you can never rid yourself of yourself, Florin; your nemesis whom you pursue, and who pursues you—whom you've sworn to protect, but must attack—or is it the other way round?" He glittered his eyes at me, regaining his confidence.

"Try as you will, Florin, you're doomed forever to walk where you would have flown, to crawl where you would have run—dragging always the intolerable but inescapable burden of yourself."

"Very poetic," I said. "Why didn't you tell me I was the Senator to begin with? Why the story about an experiment?"

"I was unsure how you'd accept the news that you had been declared insane," he said, rather tartly. "Now, having seen your monumental ego in action, I'm not so inhibited."

"Just that, huh? You make it all so simple and sweet. And I don't remember any of it because part of the treatment was to blank out my memory, eh? And the joker in the deck was that we were playing with a loaded gun, and you're the nice policeman who came along to take it away. You know what, Diss? You're a nice fellow, and I like you, but I think you're lying."

"What, me lie? That's preposterous. Now, I mean.

Before, of course, when I hadn't yet fully assessed your capabilities—"

"Don't bother, Diss. You've developed what they used to call a credibility gap. As polite a way as they could think up for calling a man a damned liar. Why do you want the dream machine smashed?"

"I've already explained—"

"I know. And I didn't believe you. Try again."

"That's absurd! What I've told you is absolutely factual!"

"You don't like me playing around with this substitute reality we're making do with, do you, Diss?" I pictured us boxed in by walls. We were. I turned the walls into backdrops painted to represent the green-tiled lab. Then I made the pictures real. Diss hissed and backed against the big console, where every light in sight was lit up now. I could see the lettering on them: *Emergency Overload.* Somehow, the lizard man looked smaller in this context; a rather pathetic little lizard in an out-of-style stiff collar and string tie.

"What do you want, Florin?" he whispered. "*What do you want?*"

"I don't know," I said, and put a pale blue Persian carpet on the floor. It clashed with the walls. I changed it to pale green. Diss screeched and danced as if the floor had gotten hot under him.

"No more! *No more!*" he hissed.

"Ready to give up?" I said. "Before I change this dump into a Playboy club, complete with cold-blooded bunnies with armor-plated bosoms?"

"Y-you can't!" His voice had now developed a quaver to go with the soprano pitch.

"I'm getting reckless, Diss. I don't care if school keeps or not. I want to see something give at the seams." I took away the green tiles and put flowered wallpaper in their place. I added a window with a view across a landscape that, somewhat to my surprise, was a yellow desert, stretching farther than any desert had a right to stretch. I looked at Diss and he was dressed in a skin-tight, golden uniform, with sparkling insignias and silver braid and rainbow-colored medals and polished boots and sharp-looking spurs and he held a quirt in his right hand that he *whap!*ped against his armored shin in a gesture of impatience. Somehow the outfit made him look smaller than ever.

"Very well, Florin, since you leave me no choice, I now inform you that I am a Chief-Inspector of Galactic Security Forces and that you are under arrest." He yanked a large and elaborate handgun from the bejeweled holster at his lean hip and pointed it at me, left-handed.

"Will you come quietly?" he chirped, "or will I be forced to place you in ambulatory coma?"

"I've already been there," I said, and shot the gun out of his hand with a nickel-plated double-action .44 caliber revolver. He whipped a saber out of a sheath I hadn't noticed and aimed a vicious cut at my head. I got my cutlass up in time, and metal clanged on metal and Diss staggered back, whipped out a bamboo tube and propelled a curare-tipped dart in my direction. I ducked under it and he produced a flame-thrower and flame bellowed and spurted at me, licking harmlessly off my asbestos suit until I hosed it out, sputtering and smoking, with a big brass nozzle.

Diss was scarcely two feet high now; he lobbed a grenade at me, and I bounced it back off a garbage-can lid; the detonation knocked him back against the control panel. All the red lights went to green, and a strident alarm bell began to clang. Diss jumped up and on the chart-table, no longer wearing his natty gold threads. His hide was a dull purplish-gray. He chattered like an enraged squirrel and threw a thunderbolt that exploded harmlessly, with a crash like a falling cliff, filling the air with the reek of ozone and scorched plastic. A foot high now, Diss danced in fury, shook his fist, and launched a nuclear rocket. I watched it come across the room toward me, and leaned aside, gave it a nudge as it passed; it flipped end-for-end and streaked back toward its owner. He dove over the side—he was about six inches long now—and the whole room blew up in my face. Luckily, I was wearing my full-spectrum invulnerable armor, so no harm came to me. I waded through the ruins and out into yellow sunlight filled with boiling dust. The dust settled and a small pale-violet lizard coiled on a rock just before me uttered a supersonic hiss and spat a stream of venom at my eyes. That annoyed me. I raised my gigantic flyswatter to crush the grasshopper-sized lizard, and he uttered a piercing miniature shriek and ducked into a crack in the rock, and I jammed my crowbar in after him and levered and cracks opened all across the stone.

"Florin! I surrender! I yield utterly! Only stop now!" His eyes glittered like red sparks from the depths of the cleft. I laughed at him and jammed the pry-bar in deeper.

"Florin, I confess I tampered with the dream machine! Van Wouk and the others had nothing to do with it!

They're unwitting dupes, nothing more. When I came upon you in a vulnerable state—your mind open to me like a broached mollusk—I couldn't resist the temptation to meddle! I thought to frighten you, make you amenable to my wishes—but instead you seized on my own sources of energy and added them to your own. As a result, you've acquired powers I never dreamed of—fantastic powers! You'll rend the very fabric of the Cosmos if you go on!"

"Swell; it could stand a little rending." I heaved hard on the bar and felt something give, deep inside the rock, as if the planetary crust was readjusting along a fault line. I heard Diss screech.

"Florin—I've been a fool, an utter fool! I see now that all along you've been drawing on another source, one I never suspected! The woman—Miss Regis—she's linked to you by a bond of such power as could shift Galaxies in their courses!"

"Yeah, the kid likes me; that's what makes the world go round . . ." I levered again, and heard boulders rumble. Diss gave a shriek.

"Florin—what avails victory if you leave only ruins behind you?"

He was just a cricket chirping in a desert. I levered again and the whole gigantic boulder split with a noise like thunder and fell apart carrying the earth and the sky with it, exposing the velvet blackness of absolute nothingness.

"Nice," I called into the emptiness, "but a trifle stark for my taste. Let there be light!"

And there was light.

And I saw that it was good, and I divided the light from

the darkness. It still looked a little empty, so I added a firmament, and divided the waters under it from the waters above it. That gave me an ocean with a lot of wet clouds looking down on it.

"Kind of monotonous," I said. "Let the waters be gathered together off to the side and let's see a little dry land around here."

And it was so.

"Better," I said. "But still dead looking. Let there be life."

Slime spread across the water and elaborated into seaweed and clumps floated ashore and lodged there and put out new shoots and crawled up on the bare rocks and sunned itself; and the earth brought forth grass and herbs yielding seeds, and fruit trees and lawns and jungles and flower boxes and herbaceous borders and moss and celery and a lot of other green stuff.

"Too static," I announced. "Let's have some animals."

And the earth brought forth whales and cattle and fowl and creeping things, and they splashed and mooed and clucked and crept, livening things up a little, but not enough.

"The trouble is, it's too quiet," I pointed out to me. "Nothing's happening."

The earth trembled underfoot and the ground heaved and the top of a mountain blew off and lava belched out and set the forested slopes afire, and the black clouds of smoke and pumice came rolling down on me. I coughed and changed my mind and everything was peaceful again.

"What I meant was something pleasant," I said, "like a gorgeous sunset, with music."

The sky jerked and the sun sank in the south in a glory of purple and green and pink, while chords boomed down from an unseen source in the sky, or inside my head. After it had set I cranked it back up and set it again a few times. Something about it didn't seem quite right. Then I noticed it was the same each time. I varied it and ran through half a dozen more dusks before I acknowledged that there was still a certain sameness to the spectacle.

"It's hard work making up a new one each time," I conceded. "It gives me a headache. How about just the concert, without the light show?"

I played through what I could remember of the various symphonies, laments, concerti, ballads, madrigals, and singing commercials. After a while I ran out. I tried to make up one of my own, but nothing came. That was an area I would have to look into—later. Right now I wanted fun.

"Skiing," I specified. "Healthful exercise in the open air, the thrill of speed!" I was rushing down a slope, out of control, went head over insteps and broke both legs.

"Not like that," I complained, reassembling myself. "No falling down."

I whizzed down the slope, gripped in a sort of invisible padded frame that wrenched me this way and that, insulating me from all shocks.

"Talk about taking a bath in your BVDs," I cried, "I might as well be watching it on TV."

I tried surfing, riding the waves in like the rabbit at a dogtrack, locked to the rails. The surf was all around, but it had nothing to do with me.

"No good. You have to learn how—and that's hard

work. Skydiving, maybe?" I gripped the open door frame and stepped out. Wind screamed past me as I hung motionless, watching a pastel-toned tapestry a few feet below grow steadily larger. Suddenly it turned into trees and fields rushing up at me; I grabbed for the ring, yanked—

The jolt almost broke my back. I spun dizzily, swinging like the pendulum of a grandfather clock, and slammed into solid rock.

. . . I was being dragged by the chute. I managed to unbuckle the harness and crawl under a bush to recuperate.

"There's tricks to every trade," I reminded myself, "including being God. What's the point in doing something if I don't enjoy it?" That started me thinking about what I did enjoy.

"It's all yours, old man," I pointed out. "How about a million dollars to start with?"

The bills were neatly stacked, in bundles of $1,000, in tens, twenties, fifties, and hundreds. There were quite a lot of them.

"That's not quite it. What good is money per se? It's what you can buy with it. Like for example, a brand-new 1936 Auburn boat-tailed Speedster, with green leather upholstery."

It was there, parked on the drive. It smelled good. The doors had a nice slam. I cranked up, gunned it up to 50 along the road that I caused to appear in front of it. I went faster and faster: 90 . . . 110 . . . 200 . . . After a while I got tired of buffeting wind and dust in my eyes, and eliminated them. That left the roar and the jouncing.

"You're earthbound," I accused. So I added wings and a prop and was climbing steeply in my Gee Bee Sportster, the wind whipping back past my face bearing a heartening reek of castor oil and high octane. But quite suddenly the stubby racer whip-stalled and crashed in a ploughed field near Peoria. There wasn't enough left of me to pick up with a spoon. I got it together and was in a T-33, going straight up as smooth as silk. 30,000 feet . . . 40,000 feet . . . 50,000 feet. I leveled off and did snap rolls and loops and chandelles and started getting airsick. I sailed between heaped clouds, and got sicker. I came in low over the fence, holding her off for a perfect touchdown and barely made it before I urped.

The trouble is, chum, wherever you go, you're still stuck with yourself. How about a quieter pastime?

I produced a desert isle, furnished it with orchids and palm trees, a gentle breeze, white surf edging the blue lagoon. I built a house of red padauk wood and glass and rough stone high on the side of the central mountain, and set it about with tropical gardens and ponds and a waterfall, and strolled out on my patio to take my ease beside my pool with a tall drink ready to hand. The drink gave me an appetite. I summoned up a table groaning under roast fowl and cold melon and chocolate éclairs and white wine. I ate for a long time; when my appetite began to flag, I whipped it along with shrimp and roast beef and chef salad and fresh pineapple and rice with chicken and sweet-and-sour pork and cold beer. I felt urpy again.

I took a nap in my nine-foot square bed with silken sheets. After fourteen hours' sleep it wasn't comfortable anymore. I ate again, hot dogs and jelly doughnuts this time. It was very filling. I went for a dip in the lagoon. The water was cold and I cut my foot on the coral. Then I got a cramp, luckily in shallow water so that I didn't actually drown. Drowning, I decided, was one of the most unpleasant ways to go.

I limped back up and sat on the beach and thought about my 5,000-tape automatic music system, my 10,000-book library, my antique gun and coin collections, my closets full of hand-woven suits and hand-tooled shoes, my polo ponies, my yacht—

"Nuts," I said. "I get seasick, and don't know how to ride. And what can you do with old coins but look at them? And it'll take me forty years to get through the books. And—"

I suddenly felt tired. But I didn't want to sleep. Or eat. Or swim. Or anything.

"What good is it?" I wanted to know, "if you're alone? If there's nobody to show off to, or share it with, or impress, or have envy me? Or even play games with?" I addressed these poignant queries to the sky, but nobody answered, because I had neglected to put anybody up there for the purpose. I thought about doing it, but it seemed like too much effort.

"The trouble with this place is no people," I admitted glumly. "Let there be Man," I said, and created Him in my own image.

"It was Van Wouk's scheme," he said. "Once you'd decided to go ahead with the simulator project he said it was only justice that you should be the one to test it. I swear I didn't know he planned to drop you. I was just along for the ride, I was victimized as much as you—"

"My mistake," I said. "Go back where you came from." He disappeared without a backward glance.

"What I really want," I said, "is strangers. People I never saw before, people who won't start in telling me all the things I did wrong."

A small band of Neanderthals emerged from a copse, so intent on turning over logs looking for succulent grubs that they didn't see me at first. Then an old boy with grizzled hair all over him spotted me and barked like a dog and they all ran away.

"I had in mind something a bit more sophisticated," I carped. "Let's have a town, with streets and shops and places where a fellow can get in out of the rain."

The town was there, a straggle of mud-and-wattle huts, bleak under leaden skies. I ordered sunshine, and it broke through the clouds and I made a few improvements in the village, not many or important, just enough to make it homey, and it was Lower Manhattan on a bright afternoon. The Neanderthals were still there, shaved and wearing clothes, many of them driving cabs, others jostling me on the sidewalk. I went into a bar and took a table on the right side, facing the door, as if I were expecting someone. A fat waitress in a soiled dress two sizes too small came over and sneered at me and fetched her pencil down from behind an ear like a bagel.

I said, "Skip it," and waved the whole thing away and pictured a cozy little fire on the beach with people sitting around it cross-legged, toasting wieners and marshmallows.

"Ah, the simple life," I said, and moved up to join them and they looked up and a big fellow with a mat of black hair on his chest stood up and said, "Beat it, Jack. Private party."

"I just want to join the fun," I said. "Look, I brought my own weenie."

A girl screamed and Blackie came in fast throwing lefts and rights most of which I deftly intercepted with my chin. I went down on my back and got a mouthful of calloused foot before I whisked the little group out of existence. I spat sand and tried to appreciate the solitude and the quiet slap of the surf and the big moon hanging over the water and might have been making some headway when an insect sank his fangs into that spot under the shoulder blades, the one you can't reach. I eliminated animal life for the moment, and paused for thought.

"I've been going about it wrong. What I want is a spot I fit into; a spot where life is simpler and sweeter, and has a place for me. What better spot than my own past?"

I let my thoughts slide back down the trail to the memory of a little frame schoolhouse on a dirt road on a summer day, long ago. I was there, eight years old, wearing knickers and sneakers and a shirt and tie, sitting at a desk with an inkwell full of dried ink, and covered with carved initials, my hands folded, waiting for the bell to ring. It did, and I jumped up and ran outside into the glorious sunshine of youth and a kid three sizes bigger, with bristly red hair and little eyes like a pig grabbed me by the hair and scrubbed his knuckles rapidly back and forth across my scalp and threw me down and jumped on me, and I felt my nose start to bleed.

So I wrapped him in chains and dropped a seventeen-ton trip-hammer on him and was alone again.

"That was all wrong," I said. "That wasn't the idea at all. That wasn't facing real life, with all its joys and sorrows. That was a cop-out. To mean anything, the other guy has to have a chance; it has to be man to man, the free interplay of personality, that's what makes for the rich, full life."

I made myself six feet three and magnificently muscled, with crisp golden curls and a square jaw, and Pig Eyes came out of an alley with a length of pipe and smashed the side of my head in. I dressed myself in armor with a steel helmet and he came up behind me and slipped a dirk in through the chink where my gorget joined my *epauliere*. I threw the armor away and slipped into my black belt and went into a *neko-ashi-dashi* stance and ducked his slash and he shot me through the left eye.

I blanked it all out and was back on the beach, just me and the skeeters.

"That's enough acting on impulse," I told myself sternly. "Hand-to-hand combat isn't really your idea of fun; if you lose, it's unpleasant; and if you always win, why bother?"

I didn't have a good answer for that one. That encouraged me so I went on: "What you really want is companionship, not rivalry. Just the warmth of human society on a non-competitive basis."

At once, I was the center of a throng. They weren't doing anything much, just thronging. Warm, panting bodies, pressed close to me. I could smell them. That was perfectly normal, bodies do have smells. Someone stepped on my foot and said, "Excuse me." Somebody else stepped on my other foot and didn't say excuse me. A man fell down and died. Nobody paid any attention. I might not have either, except that the man was me. I cleared the stage and sat on the curb and watched the sad city sunlight shine down on the scrap paper blowing along the sidewalk. It was a dead, dirty city. On impulse, I cleaned it up, even to removing the grime from the building fronts.

That made it a dead, clean city.

"The ultimate in human companionship," I thought to myself, "is that of a desirable and affectionate female of nubile years and willing disposition."

Accordingly, I was in my penthouse apartment, the hi-fi turned low, the wine chilled, and she was reclining at ease on the commodious and cushion-scattered chaise lounge. She was tall, shapely, with abundant reddish-brown hair, smooth skin, large eyes, a small nose. I poured. She wrinkled her nose at the wine and yawned. She had nice teeth.

"Golly, haven't you got any groovy records?" she asked. Her voice was high, thin, and self-indulgent.

"What would you prefer?" I asked.

"I dunno. Something catchy." She yawned again and looked at the heavy emerald and diamond bracelet on her wrist.

"Come on, really," she said. "How much did it cost?"

"I got it free. I have a pal in the business. It's a demonstrator."

She took it off and threw it on the inch-thick rug. "I've got this terrible headache," she whined. "Call me a cab."

"That shows what you really think of the kind of girls who go with penthouses and hi-fi," I told myself, dismissing her with a wave of my hand. "What you really want is a home girl, sweet and innocent and unassuming."

I came up the steps of the little white cottage with the

candle in the window and she met me at the door with a plate of cookies. She chattered about her garden and her sewing and her cooking as we dined on corn bread and black-eyed peas with lumps of country ham in it. Afterward she washed and I dried. Then she tatted while I sat by the fire and oiled harness or something of the sort. After a while she said, "Well, good night," and left the room quietly. I waited five minutes and followed. She was just turning back the patchwork quilt; she was wearing a thick woolen nightgown, and her hair was in braids.

"Take it off," I said. She did. I looked at her. She looked like a woman.

"Uh, let's go to bed," I said. We did.

"Don't you have anything to say?" I wanted to know.

"What shall I say?"

"What's your name?"

"You didn't give me one."

"You're Charity. Where are you from, Charity?"

"You didn't say."

"You're from near Dotham. How old are you?"

"Forty-one minutes."

"Nonsense! You're at least, ah, twenty-three. You've lived a fully, happy life, and now you're here with me, the culmination of all your dreams."

"Yes."

"Is that all you have to say? Aren't you happy? Or sad? Don't you have any ideas of your own?"

"Of course. My name is Charity, and I'm twenty-three, and I'm here with you—"

"What would you do if I hit you? Suppose I set the house on fire? What if I said I was going to cut your throat?"

"Whatever you say."

I got a good grip on my head and suppressed a yell of fury.

"Wait a minute, Charity—this is all wrong. I didn't mean you to be an automaton, just mouthing what I put in your head. Be a real, live woman. React to me—"

She grabbed the covers up to her chin and screamed.

I sat in the kitchen alone and drank a glass of cold milk and sighed a lot.

"Let's think this thing through," I suggested. "You can make it any way you want it. But you're trying to do it too fast; you're taking too many shortcuts. The trick is to start slowly, build up the details, make it real."

So I thought up a small Midwestern city, with wide brick streets of roomy old frame houses under big trees with shady yards and gardens that weren't showplaces, just the comfortable kind where you can swing in a hammock and walk on the grass and pick the flowers without feeling like you're vandalizing a set piece.

I walked along the street, taking it all in, getting the feel of it. It was autumn, and someone was burning leaves somewhere. I climbed the hill, breathing the tangy evening air, being alive. The sound of a piano softly played floated down across the lawn of the big brick house at the top of the hill. Purity Atwater lived there. She was only seventeen, and the prettiest girl in town. I had an impulse to turn in right then, but I kept going.

"You're a stranger in town," I said. "You have to establish yourself, not just barge in. You have to meet her in the socially accepted way, impress her folks, buy her a soda, take her to the movies. Give her time. Make it real."

A room at the Y costs fifty cents. I slept well. The next morning I applied for work at only three places before I landed a job at two dollars a day at Siegal's Hardware and Feed. Mr. Siegal was favorably impressed with my frank, open countenance, polite and respectful manner, and apparent eagerness for hard work.

After three months, I was raised to $2.25 per day, and took over the bookkeeping. In my room at the boarding-house I kept a canary and a shelf of inspirational volumes. I attended divine service regularly, and contributed one dime per week to the collection plate. I took a night class in advanced accountancy, sent away for Charles Atlas' course, and allowed my muscles to grow no more than could be accounted for by dynamic tension.

In December I met Purity. I was shoveling snow from her father's walk when she emerged from the big house looking charming in furs. She gave me a smile. I treasured it for a week, and schemed to be present at a party attended by her. I dipped punch for the guests. She smiled at me again. She approved of my bronzed good looks, my curly hair, my engaging grin, my puppylike clumsiness. I asked her to the movies. She accepted. On the third date I held her hand briefly. On the tenth I kissed her cheek. Eighteen months later, while I was still kissing her cheek, she left town with the trumpeter from a jazz band I had taken her to hear.

Nothing daunted, I tried again. Hope Berman was the second prettiest girl in town. I wooed her via the same route, jumped ahead to kisses on the lips after only twenty-one dates, and was promptly called to an interview with Mr. Berman. He inquired as to my intentions. Her brothers,

large men all, also seemed interested. A position with
Berman and Sons, Clothiers, was hinted at. Hope giggled.
I fled.

Later in my room I criticized myself sternly. I was
ruined in Pottsville: word was all over town that I was a
trifler. I took my back wages, minus some vague deductions
and with a resentful speech from Mr. Siegal about ingrates
and grasshoppers, and traveled by train to St. Louis.
There I met and paid court to Faith, a winsome lass who
worked as a secretary in the office of a lawyer whose name
was painted on a second-story window on a side street a
few blocks from the more affluent business section. We
went to the movies, took long streetcar rides, visited
museums, had picnics. I noticed that she perspired mod-
erately in warm weather, had several expensive cavities,
was ignorant of many matters, and was a very ordinary lay.
And afterward she cried and chattered of marriage.

Omaha was a nicer town. I holed up at the Railroad
Men's Y there for a week and thought it through. It was
apparent I was still acting too hastily. I wasn't employing
my powers correctly. I had exchanged the loneliness of
God for the loneliness of Man, a pettier loneliness but no
less poignant. The trick was, I saw, to combine the highest
skills of each status, to live a human life, nudged here and
there in the desired direction.

Inspired, I repaired at once to the maternity ward of
the nearest hospital, and was born at 3:27 A.M. on a
Friday, a healthy, seven-pound boy whom my parents
named Melvin. I ate over four hundred pounds of Pablum
before my first taste of meat and potatoes. Afterward I had
a stomach-ache. In due course I learned to say bye-bye,

walk, and pull tablecloths off tables in order to hear the crash of crockery. I entered kindergarten, and played sand blocks in the band, sometimes doubling in a triangle, which was chrome-plated and had a red string. I mastered shoetying, pants-buttoning, and eventually rollerskating and falling off my bike. In Junior High I used my twenty cents lunch money for a mayonnaise sandwich, an RC Cola half of which I squirted at the ceiling and my classmates, and an O Henry. I read many dull books by Louisa May Alcott and G. A. Henty, and picked out Patience Froomwall as my intended.

She was a charming redhead with freckles. I took her to proms, picking her up in my first car, one of the early Fords, with a body handbuilt from planks. After graduation, I went away to college, maintaining our relationship via mail. In the summers we saw a lot of each other in a nonanatomical sense.

I received my degree in business administration, secured a post with the power company, married Patience, and fathered two nippers. They grew up, following much the same pattern I had, which occasioned some speculation on my part as to how much divine intervention had had to do with my remarkable success. Patience grew less and less like her name, gained weight, developed an interest in church work and gardens and a profound antipathy for everyone else doing church work and gardening.

I worked very hard at all this, never yielding to the temptation to take shortcuts, or to improve my lot by turning Patience into a movie starlet or converting our modest six-roomer into a palatial estate in Devon. The hardest part was sweating through a full sixty seconds of subjective time in every minute, sixty minutes every hour . . .

After fifty years of conscientious effort I ended up with a workbench in the garage.

At the local tavern, I drank four Scotches and pondered my dilemma. After five Scotches I became melancholy. After six I became defiant. After seven, angry. At this point the landlord was so injudicious as to suggest that I had had enough. I left in high dudgeon, pausing only long enough to throw a fire bomb through the front window. It made a lovely blaze. I went along the street firebombing the beauty parlor, the Christian Science Reading Room, the optometrist, the drugstore, the auto parts house, the Income Tax Prepared Here place.

"You're all phonies," I yelled. "All liars, cheats, fakes!"

The crowd which had gathered labored and brought forth a policeman, who shot me and three innocent bystanders. This annoyed me even in my exhilarated mood. I tarred and feathered the officious fellow, then proceeded to blow up the courthouse, the bank, the various churches, the supermarket, and the automobile agency. They burned splendidly.

I rejoiced to see the false temples going up in smoke, and toyed briefly with the idea of setting up my own religion, but at once found myself perplexed with questions of dogma, miracles, fund drives, canonicals, tax-free real estate, nunneries, and inquisitions, and shelved the idea.

All Omaha was blazing nicely now; I moved on other cities, eliminating the dross that had clogged our lives. Pausing to chat with a few survivors in the expectation of overhearing expressions of joy and relief at the lifting of the burden of civilization, and praise of the newfound freedom to rebuild a sensible world, I was dismayed to see they seemed more intent on tending their wounds, competing in the pursuit of small game, and looting TV sets and cash than in philosophy.

By now the glow of the Scotch was fading. I saw I had been hasty. I quickly re-established order, placing needful authority in the hands of outstanding Liberals. Since there was still a vociferous body of reactionaries creating unrest and interfering with the establishment of total social justice, it was necessary to designate certain personnel to keep order, dressing them in uniform garments, for ease of identification.

Alas, mild policies failed to convince the wreckers that the People meant business and were not to be robbed of the fruits of their hard-won victory over the bloodsuckers. Sterner measures were of necessity resorted to. Still the stubborn Fascists took advantage of their freedom to agitate, make inflammatory speeches, print disloyal books, and in other ways interfere with their comrades' fight for peace and plenty. Temporary controls were accordingly placed on treasonous talk, and exemplary executions were carried out. The burden of these duties proving onerous, the leaders found it necessary to retire to the more spacious estates surviving the holocaust, and to limit their diets to caviar, champagne, breast of chicken and other therapeutic items in order to keep up their strength for the battle against reaction. Malcontents naturally attributed the leaders' monopoly on limousines, palaces, custom tailoring and the company of trained nurses of appearance calculated to soothe the weary executive eye as evidence of decadence. Picture the fury and frustration when the State, refusing to tolerate sedition, hustled them off to remote areas where by performing useful labor under simple conditions, they received an opportunity to correct their thinking.

I called on the Prime Leader—affectionately known as the Dictator—and queried him as to his intentions, now that he had consolidated the economy, rooted out traitors, and established domestic tranquility.

"I'm thinking about taking over the adjacent continent," he confided.

"Are they bothering us?" I inquired.

"You bet. Every time I see a good-looking broad on their side of the line and realize she's out of reach . . ." He ground his teeth.

"Joking aside," I persisted. "Now that we have peace—"

"Next thing you know the mob will be getting restless," he said. "Wanting TV sets, cars, iceboxes—even refrigerators! Just because I and my boys have a few little amenities to help us over the intolerable burdens of leadership, they want to get into the act! What do those bums know about the problems we got? Did they ever have to mobilize along a frontier? Did they ever have to make up their minds: 'tanks or tractors'? Do they have to worry about the old international prestige? Not those bums! All they got to worry about is getting through enough groceries to stay alive long enough to have enough brats so there'll be somebody around to bury 'em—as if that was important."

I thought about it. I sighed. "I can't quite put my finger on it," I told the Dictator, "but somehow there's something lacking. It isn't exactly the Utopia I had in mind." I wiped him out and all his works and contemplated the desolation sadly. "Maybe the trouble was I let too many cooks into the broth," I reflected. "Next time I'll set the whole thing up, complete, just the way I like it—and then turn everybody loose in it."

It was a jolly thought. I did it. I turned the wilderness into a parkland, drained the bogs, planted flowers. I set up towns at wide intervals, each a jewel of design, with cozy dwellings and graceful trees and curving paths and fountains and reflecting pools and open-air theaters that fit into the landscape as if a part of it. I set up clean, well-lighted schools and swimming pools and dredged the rivers and stocked them with fish and provided abundant raw materials and a few discreet, well-concealed, nonpolluting factories to turn out the myriad simple, durable, miraculous devices that took all the drudgery out of my life, leaving humans free for the activities that only humans can perform, such as original research, art, massage, and prostitution, plus waiting on tables. Then I popped the population into the prepared setting and awaited the glad cries that would greet the realization that everything was perfect.

Somehow, there seemed to be a certain indifference right from the beginning. I asked a beautiful young couple strolling through a lovely park beside a placid lake if they weren't having a good time.

"I guess so," he said.

"There's nothing to do," she said.

"Think I'll take a nap," he said.

"You don't love me anymore," she said.

"Don't bug me," he said.

"I'll kill myself," she said.

"That'll be the day," he said, and yawned.

"You son of a bitch," she said.

I moved on. A child with golden curls a lot like mine was playing by the lake. It was drowning a kitten. It was just as well; it had already poked its eyes out. I resisted an impulse to tumble the tot in after the cat and approached an old gentleman with cherubic white locks who was standing on a stone bench, peering bemusedly at a large shrub. At close range I saw that he was peering *through* the shrub at two nubile maidens disporting themselves naked on the grass. He spun when he heard me coming.

"Scandalous," he quavered. "They've been doing that to each other for the better part of two hours, right out in public where a body can't help seeing them. Makes a body wonder if there aren't enough males to go around."

I had a moment of panic; had I overlooked that detail? But no, of course not. Male and female created I Them. It was something else that was wrong.

"I know," I cried. "I've been doing too much for Them; They're spoiled. What They need is a noble enterprise that They can tackle together, a brave crusade against the forces of evil, with the banners of Right floating over-head!"

We were arrayed in ranks, myself at the head, my loyal soldiery behind me. I rose in my stirrups and pointed to the walls of the embattled town ahead.

"There they are, lads," I cried. "The enemy—the killers, looters, rapists, vandals. Now's the time to get them! Forward once more into the breach, dear friends, for Harry, England and St. George!"

We charged, battered our way through the defenses; they surrendered; we rode triumphant into the city's streets. My lads leaped from their horses, began hacking at civilians, smashing windows and grabbing handfuls of costume jewelry, TV sets, and liquor. They raped all the females, sometimes killing them afterward and sometimes before. They set fire to what they couldn't eat, drink, or screw.

"God has won a glorious victory," my priests cried.

It annoyed me to have my name taken in vain; I caused a giant meteorite to crash down in the midst of the revelry. The survivors cited their survival as evidence of god's approval. I sent a plague of stinging flies, and half the people burned the other half at the stake to appease me. I sent a flood; they floated around, clinging to fragments of church pews, old TV chassis, and the swollen carcasses of dead cows, horses, and evangelists, yelling for help and making promises to me as to how they would behave if they only got out of this one.

I rescued a few and to my delight they set to work at once to save others, whom they immediately formed into platoons, congregations, labor unions, mobs, crowds, lobbies and political parties. Each group at once attacked another group, usually the one most similar to themselves. I gave a terrible yell and swept them all away under a tidal wave. The foaming of the waters around the ruins of temples, legislatures, court houses, clip joints, chemical factories, and the headquarters of large corporations amused me; I made bigger and better tidal waves, and washed away slums, eroded farmland, burned-off forest areas, silted-up river, and polluted seas. Adrenalin flooded my system; my lust to destroy was aroused. I pulverized the continents, shattered the crust, splashed around in the magma that boiled forth.

The moon caught my eye, riding aloof above my wrath. The bland smoothness of it annoyed me; I threw a handful of gravel at it, pocking the surface nicely. I grabbed the planet Oedipus and threw it at Saturn; it missed, but the close passage broke it up. Major chunks of rock went into orbit around Saturn and the dust formed rings; a few scraps were captured by Mars, and the rest trailed off around the sun.

I found that a satisfying spectacle, and turned to invite others to admire it, but of course there was no one there.

"This is the trouble with being god," I groaned. "I could set up a bunch of nincompoops to praise me, but what good is that? A fellow wants a response from an equal, dammit!"

Suddenly I was sick and tired of the whole thing. It should have been easy, when you have all the power there is, to make things the way you want them; but it wasn't. Part of the trouble was that I didn't really know what i wanted, and another part was that I didn't know how to achieve what I wanted when I did know what it was, and another part was that when I got what I thought I wanted it turned out not to be what I wanted. It was too hard, too complicated, being god. It was a lot easier just being a Man. There was a limit on a Man's abilities, but there was also a limit on His responsibilities.

"What i mean is," I told myself, "I'm only a Human

Being, no matter what kind of thunderbolts I can throw. I need a few hundred thousand years more evolution, and then maybe I can handle being god."

I stood—or floated, or drifted—in the midst of the Ylem that was all that was left of all my efforts, and remembered Van Wouk and Lard Face and their big plans for me. They weren't sinister anymore, only pathetic. I remembered Diss, the lizard man, and how frightened he had been just at the last. I thought of the Senator, his cowardice and his excuses, and suddenly he seemed merely human. And then I thought about me, and what a shabby figure I had cut, not just as god, but as a Man.

"You looked pretty good in there," I told Me, "up to a point. You're all right as a loser, but you're a lousy winner. Having it all your way is the real problem. Success is the challenge nobody's ever met. Because no matter how many you win, there's always a bigger and harder and more complicated problem ahead, and there always will be, and the secret isn't Victory Forever but to keep on doing the best you can one day at a time and remember you're a Man, not just god, and for you there aren't and never will be any easy answers, only questions, and no reasons, only causes, and no meaning, only intelligence, and no destination and no kindly magic smiling down from above, and no fires to goad you from below, only Yourself and the Universe and what You make out of the interface between the two equals."

And I rested from all my work which I had made.

I opened my eyes and she was sitting across the table from me.

"Are you all right?" she said. "You looked so strange, sitting here all alone, I thought perhaps you were sick."

"I feel like I've just made and destroyed the Universe," I said. "Or it's made and destroyed me. Or possibly both. Don't go away. There's one more detail I have to see to."

I got up and went across to the door and stepped through it into the Senator's study. He looked at me and gave me the smile that was as real as a billboard and as sincere.

"You've come," he said in a noble voice.

"I'm turning down the job," I said. "I just wanted you to know."

He looked dismayed. "You can't. I've counted on you."

"Not anymore," I said. "Come here; I want to show you something." I went over to the full-length mirror and he came reluctantly to stand beside me and I looked at the reflection: the square jaw, the well-tailored shoulders, the level gaze.

"What do you see?" I asked.

"A four-flusher," I answered. "All they ever asked you to do was live one little old life. And did you do it? No. You copped out—or tried to. But it didn't work. You're in, like it or not. So you'd better like it."

I turned to object, but I was alone in the room.

I went to the door and opened it. Councilor Van Wouk looked up from the long table under the spiral chandelier.

"See here, Bardell," he started, but I unfolded the newspaper in my hand to the Sunday funnies, and dropped it in front of him with the *Florin—the Man of Steel* strip on top.

"He almost went for it," I said. "But he changed his mind."

"Then—that means . . .?"

"It means forget the whole thing. It never happened."

"Well, in that case," Van Wouk said, and began to shrink. He dwindled down to the size of a monkey, a mouse, a *musca domestica*, and wasn't there anymore. Lard Face was gone too, and the Bird Man, and the rest.

In the corridor I ran into Trait and Eridani.

"You're fired," I told them. They tipped their hats and silently faded away.

"That leaves you," I said. "What are we going to do with you?"

The question seemed to echo along the gray-walled corridor, as if it hadn't been me that asked it. I tried to follow it to its source, but the walls turned to gray mist that swirled around me as palpable as gray draperies. Suddenly I was tired, too tired to stand. I sat down. My head was heavy. I held it tight in both hands and gave it a half-turn and lifted it off—

I was sitting behind my desk, holding the curious spiral artifact in my hands.

"Well," the Undersecretary for Science said. "Anything?"

"I thought for a moment you looked a bit odd," the Chief of Staff said stiffly, and almost let a smile mar the rigidity of his little round face.

"As I expected," my Science Adviser said, and curved the corners of his mouth down. It looked like a line drawn on a saucer of lard.

I got up and went over to the window and looked out at Pennsylvania Avenue and the cherry blossoms and the Washington Monument. I thought about turning it into a big cement doughnut, but nothing happened. It was a humid afternoon and the town looked hot and dirty and full of trouble, like I felt. I turned and looked at the men waiting expectantly, important men all, full of the affairs of the world and their roles therein.

"Let me get this straight," I said. "You people brought this gadget to me, claiming it was removed from the wreckage of an apparently alien space vessel which crash-landed and burned in Minnesota last night."

Half a dozen faces registered confirmation.

"You recovered the body of a small lizard-like animal, and this. No pilot was in evidence."

"I assure you, sir," the Director of the FBI said, "he won't get far—or *it* won't get far." He smiled grimly.

"Drop the search," I ordered. I put the spiral gadget on the desk. "Bury this thing at sea," I commanded.

"But—Mr. President—"

I silenced that with a look and glanced at the Chairman of the Joint Chiefs.

"Was there something you wanted to tell me, General Trait?"

He looked startled. "Why, as a matter of fact, sir . . ." He cleared his throat. "It's no doubt a hoax—but I've had a report of a radio transmission from space—not from any of our installations, I'm assured. It seems to originate from just beyond the orbit of Mars." He smiled a sickly smile.

"Go on," I said.

"The, er, caller represents himself as a native of a planet

he calls Grayfell. He states that we have, ah, passed preliminary inspection. He wants to open negotiations for a treaty of peace between the Lastrian Concord and Earth."

"Tell them we're willing," I said. "If they don't get too tricky."

There were other matters they wanted to present to me, each of vast importance, requiring my immediate attention. I waved it all away. They looked aghast when I stood and told them the cabinet meeting was over.

She was waiting for me in our apartment.

It was twilight. We were walking together in the park. We sat on a bench in the cool of evening and watched the pigeons on the grass.

"How do we know this isn't a dream?" she asked.

"Perhaps it is," I said. "Perhaps nothing in life is real. But it doesn't matter. We have to live it as if it were."

BOLO: The Future of War

What is a Bolo? The symbol of brute force, intransigent defiance, and adamantine will. But on a deeper level, the Bolo is the Lancelot of the future, the perfect knight, *sans peur et sans reproche*. With plated armor, a laser canon, an electronic brain, and wheels.

The Road to Damascus by John Ringo & Linda Evans
(HC) 0-7434-7187-3 • $25.00
(PB) 0-7434-9916-6 • $7.99

Bolo! by David Weber
(HC) 0-7434-9872-0 • $25.00
(PB) 1-4165-2062-7 • $7.99

Old Soldiers by David Weber
(HC) 1-4165-0898-8 • $26.00
(PB) 1-4165-2104-6 • $7.99

Bolo Brigade by William H. Keith, Jr.
(PB) 0-671-87781-X • $6.99

BOLOS COLLECTION, EDITED BY BILL FAWCETT:

Bolos: The Honor of the Regiment   0-671-72184-4 • $6.99
With stories by David Drake, Mercedes Lackey & Larry Dixon, Mike Resnick & Barry Malzberg, and others

Bolos II: The Unconquerable   0-671-87629-5 • $6.99
With stories by S.M. Stirling, William R. Forstchen, Christopher Stasheff, and others

Bolos V: The Old Guard   0-671-31957-4 • $6.99
With stories by J. Stephen York & Dean Smith, Wm. H. Keith, Jr., and others.

Available in bookstores everywhere.
Or order online at our secure, easy to use website:
www.baen.com

CLASSIC MASTERS OF SCIENCE FICTION BACK IN PRINT!

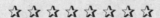

Philip José Farmer

Strange Relations   1-4165-0934-8 ★ $13.00 ★ Trade PB

Randall Garrett
edited by Eric Flint

Lord Darcy   0-7434-3548-6 ★ $18.00 ★ Trade PB

Murray Leinster
edited by Eric Flint

Planets of Adventure   0-7434-7162-8 ★ $7.99

Christopher Anvil
compiled and edited by Eric Flint

Interstellar Patrol   0-7434-8848-2 ★ $7.99

Interstellar Patrol II   0-7434-9892-5 ★ $26.00 ★ HC
    1-4165-2099-6 ★ $7.99 ★ PB

James Schmitz
compiled and edited by Eric Flint

Telzey Amberdon   0-671-57851-0 ★ $7.99